CRYSTAL JEANS has had two previous novels published by Welsh women's independent Honno Press. Her first, *The Vegetarian Tigers of Paradise*, was shortlisted for the Polari Prize and is currently in development for film. The second, *Light Switches are my Kryptonite*, won Wales Book of the Year in the English language. Crystal lives in Pontypridd with her partner and young children.

Praise for *The Inverts*:

'A glorious celebration of queer friendship and all kinds of love. Funny, outrageous, heartbreaking and so much fun'

Kate Davies, winner of the Polari Prize

'This delicious romp is the sort of thing Nancy Mitford might have written if she'd been gay . . . wonderfully blithe, witty and moving' *Daily Mail*

'Hilarious, fresh and sexy, with a tale that takes the reader from Egypt to Hollywood' *Irish Independent*

'Very funny and touching and quite filthy'

Louisa Young, author of *My Dear I Wanted To Tell You*

'I can't remember the last time I enjoyed a book so much. *The Inverts* is funny, filthy and phenomenally good – an exhilarating, extraordinary book, packed with dazzling dialogue, stiletto-sharp wit and a glorious serving of filth. It's like Sarah Waters and Alan Hollinghurst go to a party in *Downton Abbey* – and things get gloriously, hilariously, out of hand'

Matt Cain

'Filthy and hilarious, this is a gloriously naughty romp of a read that also has something serious to say about queer love. I didn't want it to end'

S.J. Watson

'Perfect for fans of *Tipping the Velvet* and *Gentleman Jack* . . . a delicious and diligent piece of fiction that will provide you with enough great comebacks to last a lifetime . . . This is a delightful book I wish to fling at my friends with affectionate abandon'

DIVA

'Bettina and Bart are not just larger-than-life – they are alive. By turns raucous and poignant, hilarious and shattering, this is a wonder of a story. A lifelong friendship, warts-and-all, where the sparkling moments and the sad are told in a voice as irresistible as the pair themselves. I LOVED it'

Jess Kidd

'An absolute *blinder* . . . so so funny and sexy. So excited now to read everything by Crystal Jeans'

Caroline O'Donoghue, author of *Scenes of a Graphic Nature*

ALSO BY CRYSTAL JEANS

The Vegetarian Tigers of Paradise
Light Switches are my Kryptonite

THE Inverts

CRYSTAL JEANS

THE BOROUGH PRESS

The Borough Press
An imprint of HarperCollins*Publishers* Ltd
1 London Bridge Street
London SE1 9GF

www.harpercollins.co.uk

HarperCollins*Publishers*
1st Floor, Watermarque Building, Ringsend Road,
Dublin 4, Ireland

This paperback edition 2022
1

First published by HarperCollins*Publishers* 2021

A catalogue record for this book is available from the British Library

ISBN: 978-0-00-836590-5

Set in Perpetua by Palimpsest Book Production Limited,
Falkirk, Stirlingshire

Printed and bound in the UK using
100% Renewable Electricity by CPI Group (UK) Ltd

MIX
Paper from
responsible sources
FSC C007454

This book is produced from independently certified FSC™ paper
to ensure responsible forest management.

For more information visit: www.harpercollins.co.uk/green

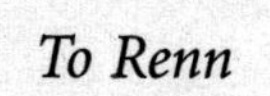

To Renn

Prologue

They were quiet for a while, sipping their drinks and smoking, Bart's leg draped over Bettina's. Two empty champagne bottles lay on top of the bedsheets, dripping out their dregs onto the purple silk and creating perfect dark circles.

'Wouldn't it be awful,' said Bart, eventually, 'if we ended up hating each other?'

'Oh, I would hate that,' said Bettina.

'You would hate the hate?'

'Yes, I'd abhor it. You're my absolute favourite person.'

'Same,' he said, smiling. 'I am my absolute favourite person.'

'Bart!' She nudged him with her elbow, causing his drink to slosh inside the glass. 'You pretend you're joking but you aren't really.'

'I *was* joking,' he said. 'Possibly.' He puffed on his cigarette with little smirk creases along the side of his mouth. 'In any case, I fucking adore you and if things ever soured between us I think a part of my soul would shrivel up. The scant ember of optimism in my heart would go out and I'd become an altogether bleaker human being.'

'Likewise,' said Bettina. 'I would become a crone, living in the shadows. A hag. I'd never be invited to parties.' She pulled a sad face and he laughed. 'We must promise to be kind to each other, always,' she continued. 'Kind and tolerant. And we mustn't be dreadful hypocrites about everything.'

'No,' agreed Bart. 'And we must always try to have fun. Because otherwise, what's the point?'

'Cheers to that.'

They clinked glasses and drank.

'Cheers to the queers,' said Bettina.

'Hurrah for the inverts!' said Bart.

They splurted out laughter.

'I love that we're funny,' said Bart. 'It's my favourite thing about us.'

'Me too,' said Bettina, stubbing out her cigarette. 'And I love that I'm the funnier one.' She turned onto her side, as did he, wiggling his behind into the dip of her crotch. He grabbed her arm and wrapped it around himself. 'You be the big spoon.'

Chapter 1

January 1990, Silverbeach Residential Home, Brighton

The snow was settling thick and deep, in a way it rarely did this close to the shore. Tabitha was not a good driver, had never been a good driver, and driving in snow gave her a sinus headache. But her son was drunk. Look at him, she kept saying to herself. He was side-slumped in the passenger seat, his face smearing the window. Just look at him. She pulled up onto Silverbeach Drive. The car ahead was parked at a 90-degree angle to the kerb and most of the snow on its bonnet had been scooped off. She lit a menthol cigarette and shook her son by the shoulders. 'Freddy. Freddy.'

'OK, OK, I'm awake.' He had a crease like a bracket around one eye from where his cheek had been pressed to the glass.

'Look,' she said, pointing through the windscreen. There was a news crew gathered outside the home – three men and a woman standing near a BBC van, all wrapped in winter coats and scarves with puffs of fog coming out of their mouths.

'Fucking vultures,' said Freddy.

'Well, of course they're *vultures*, darling. Will you comb your hair, please?'

He looked in the rear-view mirror and ran his fingers through his greying curly hair. He needed a haircut and a shave. Probably a wash. He'd been blessed with such lovely looks, his grandfather's looks, and now his stomach bulged out like a darts player's and his earholes were clogged with thick black hair and dead skin cells. Frankly, it was wasteful.

'Do eat some breath mints,' she said. 'You know they'll want to talk to us.'

Frowning, he helped himself to one of her cigarettes and tucked it in the corner of his mouth. 'How shocked they'll be that Bettina and Bartholomew Dawes spawned a bunch of pissheads. What a gobsmacking revelation.'

'Speak for yourself.' She went into the glove compartment and pulled out some Mint Imperials. 'Please,' she said, holding out the tin.

'After my fag,' he said, taking a handful. 'Can the heating go any higher?'

'No.' She watched as the front door of Silverbeach opened and a care worker stuck her head out. She said something to the reporters and closed the door. 'Probably telling them to bugger off,' said Tabitha. 'I don't know what they're hoping to achieve. I mean, are they honestly expecting my eighty-five-year-old mother to Zimmer her way out into the snow and confess to a murder that happened half a century ago? Preposterous. Freddy?'

'I'm listening.' He was fiddling with the heating knob.

'I told you it was on full. Why don't you ever—'

'OK. Just checking.' He rubbed his hands together, blowing on them. 'I personally would *love* to see Nana swan out here and confess to murder. In a Givenchy gown and her old fox fur, with a piss-bag strapped to her ankle.'

'Don't be mean.'

'With a cigarette holder longer than her arm. Remember that one with the diamonds going in little spirals? "I, Bettina Dawes, wife to the great thespian of yesteryear, Bartholomew Dawes, have a confession to make."' He tilted up his chin and smoke wafted from his nose in an oyster-white plume. '"The gun belonged to me! I murdered him. And goddammit, I'd do it again! Oh, bother, one seems to have shat oneself. Nurse!"' He hunched over laughing, spilling the mints onto the floor of the car.

'She's nothing like that, Freddy. And she's not incontinent. Hurry up and finish your cigarette.' She took her lipstick out of her purse and reapplied – her lips in their natural state had lost entirely all their colour. She was getting pouchy little flabs under her mouth, at the corners, and she hadn't enjoyed a jawline in twenty years. So bloody what? She was a sixty-one-year-old lawyer specialising in wills and probate. Nobody would expect her to look fantastic. Except . . . well, they might. Because look at her parents.

Freddy stubbed out his cigarette. 'Showtime.'

As they pushed open their doors and got out, the female reporter's head snapped around.

'Oh, look out,' said Freddy. 'She's got a whiff of carrion.'

'Don't you dare say anything rude,' said Tabitha. 'Take my arm, please.'

'What am I supposed to say to them when they ask questions?'

'No comment. Say you don't know anything. If they mention the gun, say you knew nothing about it.'

'I *don't* know anything about it. Nobody knows anything about it.'

'If they ask about your grandfather—'

'Which they undoubtedly will—'

'No comment. Just say no comment. Like in the films. And for God's sake, don't let them smell your breath.'

The snow under their shoes gave way in a flumpy-soft crunch. Tabitha almost lost her footing on a wedge of crystallised snow and Freddy held her up, barely, his feet skidding. The houses in this street were huge, with three levels and long, ploughed drives within beautiful landscaped gardens. Not too dissimilar to the sort of house she'd grown up in, actually. Possibly even a little inferior. The reporters watched their slow approach. She'd had dealings with reporters before, but never the predatory sort. Just magazine journalists wanting to ask the same tiresome questions about her parents. 'Retrospective,' was the word they often used. The last one had been trying to draw parallels between her mother and Zelda Fitzgerald, which was ridiculous and trite. Most asked about her father, who after all had been the more well-known of the two, and were often a smidge sycophantic, trying – quite transparently – to make her feel like an important person: but that was to be expected, and she didn't mind indulging them. Only it all felt a little pointless. Because everything had already been said. Until now.

They were roughly six car-lengths from the home. 'Do you think she did it?' said Freddy, quietly.

'Of course not.'

'She did hate him though.'

'So? You hate your wife and your boss. Do you plan to murder them?'

'I don't hate Theresa. I intensely dislike her.'

'I just can't imagine Mum doing such a thing. I've thought about it and thought about it and—'

'Maybe he took her gin away.'

'Oh, shut up, Freddy.'

'Prised it out of her vice-like alky grip.'

'Shhh.' Two car-lengths away now. The reporters were still watching, but not with much interest. There were a dozen or so public photographs of Tabitha with her parents, but most were ancient; Christmas family portrait shots of the Joan Crawford variety: oh, how her father had hated – positively *loathed* – posing for those! His sarcastic quips to the photographer: 'Look how fucking wholesome we are!' His whisky within reach on the bureau, just out of shot. The most recent picture of Tabitha with her mother, published in *Tatler* in 1958, showed them at the Royal Opera. Tabitha's face was partly obscured by her hair, deliberately so, and of course she looked so much younger, with her once-cherished jawline and a pair of lips unstripped of their rosy melanin. It was possible these reporters wouldn't even recognise her.

And they didn't.

'Morning,' said one of them, a young man – a child, practically – with his hair worn in bleached-blond curtains.

'Morning,' said Tabitha.

The female reporter was looking down at a clipboard, a steaming cup in her gloved hand.

A care worker let them in, glancing peevishly at the reporters before closing the door with admirable placidity. The home was warm, as it usually was, and this sudden change in temperature set off a tingle in Tabitha's toes.

'They've been here since six,' said the carer, whose name might have been Lindsey.

'Eager little beavers,' said Freddy, kicking the welcome mat to shake the snow off his shoes.

'The police were here earlier, too,' said the carer. 'For questioning.'

'Yes, we were informed by the manager,' said Tabitha.

'Cup of tea?' said the carer.

'Coffee,' said Freddy. 'Strong, three sugars.'

'Not for me, thanks,' said Tabitha. 'Can we see her?'

'Of course. She's in her room. Fancied some alone time – can't say I blame her. Give us a shout if there's an issue.'

'Can I have some biscuits with my coffee?' said Freddy.

A playful smile. 'I'll see what I can do, my love. Two tics.'

'She prefers men to women,' said Tabitha, beginning to climb the stairs. 'I can always tell. I hate women like that.'

'I love women like that.'

Her mother's room was on the second floor at the back of the house, with a view of the garden. She was often found in an armchair by the window, reading a large-print book through her pearl-handled magnifying glass, a plastic beaker full of sherry – sometimes gin – on her tray-table and a cigarette smouldering in an ashtray next to the whining, squealing hearing aids she refused to wear. The carers had tried to ration her alcohol once and she'd threatened to go on hunger strike (which was laughable), and the senior carer decided that since Mrs Dawes was still in full possession of her faculties, she was free to drink herself to death.

She was in her armchair now, looking out of the window.

Her book lay closed on the carpet, the magnifying glass placed on top. She looked like she always did – fat and sunken with one oedemic leg propped up on a footstool, but her silver hair immaculate and all her best jewellery on, a floral silk scarf tied around the neck that hung fat and super-soft like a post-pregnancy apron. An uneaten breakfast of poached eggs on toast was on her tray-table, pushed away. With warped fingers she held her beaker of sherry tight to her stomach, as if afraid someone was going to take it away. The room smelled of bananas going bad.

'Tabby, darling. I'm so glad you could make it. Freddy, oh! I didn't know you were coming. Come and have a drink! Tabby, where's your brother?'

'Still in the States. How are you feeling?'

'Bloody awful.' She pointed out of the window. 'The bastards keep sneaking round the back to try to get photos of me. They won't leave me alone.'

'Empty your bedpan over their heads,' said Freddy.

'What did he say?' said her mother.

'Nothing.'

Freddy leaned in closer. 'I said, empty your bedpan over their heads.'

She laughed. 'I should, shouldn't I? Only I don't have a bedpan, darling. I have my own en-suite lavatory. Sherry?'

'I shouldn't,' said Freddy, grinning. 'But I will.'

Tabitha made a point of looking at her watch – it wasn't even lunchtime yet, for God's sake – but Freddy didn't notice. He took the sherry from the cabinet and poured himself a glass. Hanging above the cabinet was an original Hannah Gluckstein of an androgynous woman in a beret. On the opposite wall was a Romaine Brooks watercolour – not a very good one – and underneath, a bookcase full of her mother's books.

'Top me up, there's a good boy,' said Bettina, holding out her beaker. She gave her daughter a defensive look. 'Well, it's either drink or cry. Don't judge me – I'll be dead soon.' She picked up her cigarette from the ashtray and took a puff, her jaw wobbling as she let the smoke out. 'They won't leave me alone, darling, honestly – it's awful. I feel like Quasimodo up in his bell tower. I think they've been throwing gravel at the window. Mind you, better the BBC than those fatheads at ITV. They've been here since early this morning, darling. In the snow. Honestly. It's either drink or cry. Drink or die.'

Tabitha sat down on her mother's bed and lit a menthol. 'You can hardly blame them, Mum. It's juicy stuff.'

'It's absolute horseshit. What would I be doing with a gun? Really? Your father would—'

A smattering of tiny stones hit the windowpane and her mother startled, spilling her sherry onto her crotch.

Chapter 2

September 1921, Wadley House, Brighton

It couldn't be – he wouldn't bloody dare. She opened her window and squinted out into the granular black night. He wouldn't dare though. He'd have to be blasted off his father's spirits, throwing stones and shouting his head off like that, with Heinous Henry just yards away, him with his nose like a beak, like a huge disgusting puffin's beak, rummaging around in everyone's business, plucking out grubs.

'Who's there?' It might even be one of the drunks from the munitions factory her father owned, someone recently fired. One of them had once shat into the bird bath and lopped all the rose heads from their stems.

'I would speak with you!'

It *was* him. Bart. Under the giant oak with his back to the trunk and his whole form in shadow.

'"Love grew apace, rocked by the anxious beating of this poor heart, which the cruel wanton boy took for a cradle!"'

He was doing Cyrano de Bergerac again. 'What are you *doing*?' she hissed. 'Go home!'

'Never in a trillion years!' Yes, drunk. His late father had left behind an impressive collection of liquors and spirits, the bottles carefully arranged, labels facing out, on top of two large bureaus in his dank and terrifying study. Some were imported from countries as far away as Japan and South Africa (and some dating back to the eighteenth century). Bart's mother Lucille had felt reluctant to part with them or drink them, so there they still stood, testament to Frederick Dawes's passion for accumulating rare and exotic fancies, the big joke being that he'd been teetotal; he might as well have been a cripple who collected running shoes or a whore who collected chastity belts. Bart was always taking a nip here and there of the less rare stuff. And he was annoying enough when sober.

'Go away,' she said again, glancing at the butler's dim window – the servants' quarters stuck out of the main house like the bottom of the letter L and Heinous Henry's room was across from her, diagonally so. He was most likely still downstairs, seeing to the accounts or bullying the cook, but you could never be sure. She imagined him – the awful creep – crouched below his windowpane, eyes greed-shiny in the gloom, ear cocked, hands down his trousers. And why imagine him with his hands in his trousers? What did that have to do with anything? Anyway, he was an awful, awful creep. 'Go away,' she repeated. 'I'm bored of you already. Genuinely.'

Bart stepped out from the dark, stopping under the high lantern. 'Come down to me or I'll wake up the whole fucking house, Bettina.'

Another glance at the butler's window. 'The house is still awake, you turnip – it's only ten. Go home.'

'I'm going to start singing. I'm going to sing. I really will – you *know* I will. I'll tell everyone that you tempted me with your flame-red tresses and your gorgeous wobbly boobies. You tart. I'm going to start singing.'

'Christ.' He was always trying to get her into trouble. He minimised the consequences because he had in his head that her parents were these easy-going, liberal-minded poodles, when in fact they were just playing a part and cared deeply what the old guard thought of them – even those they made fun of, such as the parson and his wife, who had 'such sticks up their backsides, they were basically God's lollipops', but heaven forbid that Venetia and Montgomery Wyn Thomas ever express a contrary opinion in their presence, atrocious frauds that they were.

'Go to our spot, I'll come and meet you. If I get caught I shall kick you where it hurts.'

He fell to his knees, hand on his heart. 'Oh, please don't make promises you cannot keep, my goddess.'

'I actually hate you.'

A small wood stood between Wadley House and the beach. Bettina loved this wood and as a child had considered it her own private playground, imagining faeries and wood-imps and will-o'-the-wisps behind every tree, and sometimes spying on the maids as they swam half naked in the waterlogged ditch they mistook for a lake. The moon was bright and the clouds sparse, allowing just enough illumination to see by. Bettina knew her way perfectly well, having made this journey thousands of times over her life and many of these in the dark (thanks to Bart), but still her slippers stumbled over rocks and into dips in the dry cracked mud – she hadn't dared bring a light of her own; there were too many eyes around here, twitching bright eyes like gold coins. She picked up a snapped-off branch and used it like a blind man's stick. Her robe was red. But it had no hood. And wolves did not exist in this part of England, not any more.

'Absurd,' she said to herself, in a whisper. 'Absolutely raving.'

Soon the wood faded, its trees growing sparser, its tangled undergrowth turning to pale, shorn grass. The sea lay ahead of her, its dark rolling mass swallowing the panorama. The moon was bright out here, in the open, without its pauper's beard of trees, causing a silvery gleam to coat the flat pebbles which preceded the sandy beach. She followed the thin boardwalk, seeing a small light up ahead, coming from under the pavilion. Her father had had it erected on Armistice Day, and for days afterwards it was kept lit through the night and was filled with drunk, exuberant people who tossed booze from their glasses as they danced uninhibited to live brass music or sat shivering in their winter coats and scarves with slippery smiles on their faces. One man had got so drunk that he went in the sea for a swim – this in the early hours of the morning – and got stunned by the freezing waters and was swept out with the current and drowned. Idiot. He'd been an unmarried schoolteacher, supposedly, from the boys' college. His death had been like a bucket of slop thrown over the party and the revellers went home finally and returned to their daily, sober miseries.

This was three years ago and still the pavilion stood, its steel rivets super-rusted by the salted air, the canvas awnings covered in gull shit, one half drooped and sulking. Bart was sitting on the ground inside with a paraffin lamp at his side, casting a defiant orb of light around him. In his lap was a bottle of rum, which was apt, since he looked as drunk as a sailor, his blond-tipped lashes bobbing under the weight of collapsing eyelids.

She'd played with Bart from a young age, since they were babies practically, and still they were monkey-nut close, writing daily letters to each other during term time and meeting by night in the holidays (her father, being a hypocrite and a tyrant, didn't approve of their spending time alone together). They had the same sense of humour, affecting a dry, ironic outlook, and they eschewed exclamation marks in their correspondence and looked down on earnest people. Sarcasm, contrary to popular belief, was the highest form of humour. Everyone else was wrong. Everyone else was stupid.

Bettina sat down opposite him, legs crossed, and fixed him with her most withering look (she practised these looks in the mirror). 'Bartholomew, you bastard,' she said, punching his shoulder. 'Dragging me out here at this hour.' She hit him again and he tried to bat her hand away. 'I could've been eaten by wolves, you awful nightmare.'

He smiled devilishly at her and offered the bottle of rum. 'Go on, don't let me drink alone.'

'I've got to pack for school tomorrow.'

He pushed the bottle in front of her face. 'Then let's celebrate the end of the holidays.'

'No, let's not.'

'Let's. Please. We haven't got long to have fun like this; we should take our opportunities. Soon you'll be a horrid debutante and you'll acquire a horrid husband and I'll never get to see you again, and it'll be fucking horrid.'

'You are relentless. I loathe this quality in you. I absolutely loathe it.'

The wind outside blew against the canvas flaps and they made a loud *thwap-thwap* sound. 'Drink, my goddess,' he said. 'Drink.'

She felt something cold and wet under her ankle – a ribbon of seaweed. She tossed it at him and took a sip of the rum. It was warm and disgusting. She didn't have a taste for alcohol, not really, except the creamy liqueurs her mother sometimes let her have at Christmas, and even these she would weaken with extra cream.

'Cigarette?' said Bart, taking two out of a silver case with a falcon engraved on the lid (it'd been his father's) and lighting both before she could answer.

'Thank you,' she said – she did in fact want one.

He snapped the case shut and leaned on one elbow, tilting his head back to blow out the smoke. 'I can't believe you were willing to leave without saying goodbye.'

'I was planning to say goodbye on the way to the station. I was going to wave my hanky out of the carriage window in a mournful fashion.'

'Bugger off. A proper goodbye, I meant.'

'So this is a proper goodbye? Drinking stolen booze under a mouldy canopy?'

'Indeed.' He squinted as though through a monocle. 'A jolly good send-off. The sea air in your lungs, what could be better, old chap?'

'My bed.'

He wiggled an eyebrow. 'We could do that.'

'Don't be disgusting.'

'Drink more,' he said.

'No. I've had enough.'

'Go on – drink more.'

She rolled her eyes and drank more. Bart could never take no for an answer. Better to get it over and done with. Once, when she was six and he seven, he'd persuaded her to eat a worm. He'd gone on about it for ages, dangling it in front of her face and coming up with a never-ending supply of reasons for why she should do such a thing, almost managing to package the idea attractively (only a very brave girl would eat a worm, only the very best, bravest, most boy-like girl would dare), and she finally accepted the challenge. The governess, Madame Choubert, a mean old toad with an entire forest of nose hair, caught her with the worm half in her mouth and slapped the back of her head to make her spit it out, slapped it hard, and all the while, Bart's hand was over his mouth to keep the hysterical laughter from exploding out, and the governess turned to look at him like a St Bernard spotting a squirrel, and she grabbed his ear and forced him to his feet and dragged him across the garden with her almighty buttocks swishing the train of her skirt and him wriggling in pain but still laughing, his earlobe stretched like warm toffee, and the next day he'd shown her the red tear under his ear. This was a typical memory.

'So Daddy Dearest wouldn't relent?' he said, taking the bottle from her.

'No. I'm going to take another crack at him tomorrow though.'

'Well. It *is* a damned good school. For a girls' school, I mean. Unless you'd prefer to learn etiquette at Lady Foster's Academy for Dead-Eyed Shrews.'

'Of course not,' she said. 'But what's the point?'

'Education is the point.'

'Yes, an education! Think of all the Aristotle I shall quote to impress my future husband's family. I shall order my scullery girl in only the best Latin. And Bart – I shall write my shopping lists in iambic pentameter. Give me the rum.'

Bart had picked up a cockle shell and was twisting the hot end of his cigarette against its serrated surface, twisting it into a point, ash and sparks flying off.

'Bart?'

'Hmm?'

'I said—'

'Are you going to miss me?' he said, a queer, thoughtful look in his eyes.

'Miss you? Well, I should think so, a little. In the same way that one misses a boil on one's nose after it's been lanced.'

'I'll miss you. Awfully.'

Bettina looked down at the sand. She dragged her finger through it, making a spiral. She and Bart were so seldom 'nice' to each other. She drank from the bottle, still avoiding his eyes.

'I always look forward to the holidays,' he said, 'because it means I'll get to see you. I always think of you, at school.' He laughed suddenly, and she glanced up, relieved. He was smiling. The lantern's flickering light cast shadows across his face, spreading his smile in a dark and clownish fashion. 'I love to make you squirm.'

'Those who take pleasure in the displeasure of others are generally regarded as evil,' she said. 'You know that, don't you?'

'I meant what I said though.' He took her hand and laced his thin, dry fingers through hers. 'I really did.'

She could feel her face tightening. She really should say something kind back to him, something real and true, a collection of words forming a stark, nude emotion, a collection of words like a brand-new baby. But she needn't have worried about it, about words, because suddenly Bart was plucking his cigarette out of his mouth, stabbing it in the sand and coming for her, his face for her face, his lips for hers, a look of brave focus in his grey-green eyes, like the look of someone who resolves, finally, to enter the burning building to rescue the child, and there was no time for Bettina to decide what she should do and what she wanted to do and what she might do, because his mouth was on hers and his body upon hers, and the weight of him was pushing her back to the sand, and as his soft lips wrestled against hers and his soggy tongue found entry, two distinct thoughts uttered, voice-like, in her mind:

I'm going to get sand in my hair.

And:

I might as well try this.

His breath came out of his nose as he kissed her, a warm zephyr from each nostril, in and out. His spit was a ghastly soup of liquor, smoke and onion. He rotated his hips, pressing his groin into hers. He put his hand on her breast. On it, just on it. He did not build up to this and he did not caress it or squeeze it. Just put his hand *on* it. And left it there, neither loose nor clamping. She blasted laughter into his mouth, wild shocked laughter, and he pulled his head away and looked down at her, gormlessly. She brought her arm over her face, pushing her nose into the fleshy crook of her elbow and laughed hard, her body shivering under him.

He rolled off and his arm reached out piston-like for the bottle of rum.

'I'm sorry,' she said. But the laughter was still bubbling wickedly. She wiped her eyes and stretched her cheeks down and tried to breathe. 'Genuinely, Bart, I'm sorry.' He was looking down at the sand with his face in shadow. 'Please don't be angry with me. Please don't, Bart. I didn't mean to laugh.'

He glanced up finally. Expressionless. He took out two cigarettes and lit them slowly, his hands shaking. He chuckled. Shook his head. Handed her a cigarette. 'You're going to think I'm being vengeful now, but I promise you I'm not,' he said. 'But this is the thing of it: I didn't—' He shook his head again. 'You'll think I'm being mean. You'll think I'm feeling rejected and want to hurt your feelings.'

She sat up straight. 'Well, you can't leave it unsaid now.'

'I promise you, my motives aren't petty.'

'Bloody well say it then.'

He nodded. 'Here's the thing. I didn't really *feel* anything, Betts. I thought I'd feel something. But I didn't. I mean – sorry to offend your delicate female sensibilities and all that, but not even *half* a cock-stand—'

'Bart!'

'I'm sorry. I thought you could handle the fact that I possess male genitalia. I'm just being honest. I felt nothing. Sweet fuck all. And look at you – you're Aphrodite. I wonder what could be the matter with me.'

She considered this, smoking her cigarette slowly. 'That's all right. I didn't feel anything either.'

'No?'

'No.'

'You're not just saying that because you feel slighted?'

'No! I mean, I suppose I *would* lie if I felt slighted, wouldn't I? To save face. But I'm one hundred per cent not lying. I felt nothing.'

'Save amusement?'

'Save amusement,' she agreed, nodding. 'And profound embarrassment.'

He gave her a look she knew well – he was about to say something rude, something that tested her. And he did: 'So in effect, you gave me the flop and I, in turn, turned your vagina to ice?'

'Bart!' She slapped the side of his head. 'Why do you always have to take everything too far?' She *hated* the v-word, and he knew it.

He was hunched over, laughing. And soon – she couldn't help it – she was laughing too, clutching her stomach and shaking, both their glowing cigarette ends dancing under the pavilion's dark arms.

'I've never admitted this to you,' she said, once the laughter was spent, 'on account of your overflowing vanity, but I *do* think you're handsome. Very handsome, actually. Bizarre, isn't it?'

'Maybe we're too close friends, do you think?' he said, lying down on his side, propped up with an elbow. 'Like siblings?'

She shrugged. Bart had once had a sister. Tabitha. Bettina could still remember her, just about – a fat, ringletted little thing, very sweet, always eating. One of her earliest memories, in fact, was of standing in the Dawes's stables, staring down at a dark-stained spot in the hay and noticing a scrap of bone with dried blood on it. From Tabitha's skull? She'd been about to prod it with her foot when the stable hand saw what she was looking at and quickly scooped her up in his arms and took her back to the house. 'Oh, the poor little thing just wants a sister again,' Venetia would say, whenever Monty caught Bart sneaking in through the servants' entrance to play with Bettina. 'Even so, it's a bit off, those two being so tight,' he'd say, or something like this. As if six-year-old girls and seven-year-old boys were in the habit of eloping. Idiot.

'That was the first time I've kissed a girl,' Bart said. 'Don't say anything unkind.'

'I wasn't going to.'

'I thought I should try it, you know?'

'I thought I should go along with it.'

'That's why I got so bonkers drunk. Because I was going to try it.'

She stubbed out her cigarette in the sand. 'Well. Perhaps it's a good thing you tried it. Because now we know. Now we don't have it hanging over us. Did you feel it hanging over us? Because I did.'

He nodded. 'I meant what I said about missing you and all that.' He reached out with grasping fingers and she took his hand. He brought his head down and kissed her knuckle. 'I suppose we're just not meant for each other, in that way. Perhaps I only long for blondes or brunettes. Or older women.'

'Or livestock,' said Bettina.

He laughed with his mouth wide open, all his teeth showing. He really was very handsome, even considering his eyebrows fighting to get to the centre of his face and the cluster of pimples on his forehead. He was probably right; they were too much like siblings. One day she'd be kissed by a man she did not know so intimately, one she hadn't known all her life, who hadn't made her eat worms. This strange unattached man from the future would grab her as Bart just had, kiss her as Bart just had, and she'd feel the quickness in her bosom like the women characters from a penny dreadful.

'One day we shall swoon for others,' she said, squeezing his hand.

He nodded, squeezing back.

'I think that would make a good poem,' she said. '"One day we shall swoon for others." Don't you think?'

He wrinkled up his face. 'God no. Do the world a favour and never write a poem as long as you live. Ugh.'

Chapter 3

She damn well hated him. Spread-eagled on the wicker lounger, his belly a hard dome beneath his ugly royal-blue swimsuit, his thick, arrogant fingers – yes, even his fingers were arrogant – tapping cigar ash into the sand. And his face, that look on his face – boredom spreading into something like – no, not disgust, not quite, because disgust was so taxing an emotion and she wasn't worth the energy required. 'I am not arguing with you any more,' said her father. 'You will do as I say.'

She pictured that cigar in his eye, the red tip sizzling through his retina. 'Yes, Daddy.'

He squinted up at her, his moustached lip pulled into a sneer. '"Daddy?" For heaven's sake, Bettina, are you five?'

She shrugged, her hands clasped behind her back, toes flexing into the warm sand. Her head itched against the band of her straw hat.

'I mean, don't be so trans*parent*, darling. You obviously

haven't been paying close enough attention to your mother.' He lay his head back down and laughed, shaking his head from side to side. 'Amateur.'

She stared down at his sun-bright body; his large bald thighs and shiny shins, the narrow pale feet with conjoined toes on the left side, the springy orange hair, the same as hers, spilling over his forehead. Placed next to the lounger was a tumbler of lemonade and a hardback book which, she guessed, was *awfully* clever. He was a fat old bastard. A fraud. God, she hated him.

She swung her leg back and kicked sand. And she turned and ran, gritting her teeth and wincing as if expecting his arm to somehow reach out to some ludicrous length and his hand to clasp around her ankle, she ran, heels sinking into the sand, knowing that he wouldn't follow – he had other ways – but all the same waiting, feeling that same ticklish dread that she'd felt, as a small girl, when exiting the small, dark outhouse at the end of her great-auntie's garden (hands reaching for ankles – she'd always been plagued by hands reaching for ankles); she ran until she reached the scalding boardwalk. Turned back to look. He was dusting the sand off his body and she could see, by the jerking of his head, that he was furious. Good.

Her mother was in the games room playing gin rummy with Bart's mother, Lucille. They were hunched over the poker table amidst a dense cumulus of smoke, their ankles crossed under their chairs, glasses of sherry at their elbows. Two cigarettes smouldered in the emerald-green ashtray in the centre of the table. Each woman stared at her respective hand with a shark-like focus, neither glancing up when Bettina sloped into the room. Lucille plucked a card from the deck, setting her bracelets to tinkling, and inspected it, her mouth a slick pink line, before scanning the fanned cards in her other hand. She was wearing a purple silk scarf tied around her head and her jewelled ears glinted with every tiny movement.

Bettina could hear the women breathing through their noses. She walked up to the billiards table and ran her palm along the soft felt. She saw her mother bring her sherry to her lips and heard the sound of glass knocking lightly against teeth followed by a dainty glug. She picked up a red ball, felt its weight and then tossed it back on the table where it clattered against another. Both women jerked their heads up.

'Betsy, darling,' said her mother, 'if you carry on like this I'll have to insist you start wearing a bell around your neck.'

'Moo,' said Lucille, laughing into her glass.

Bettina wasn't sure if she liked or disliked Lucille.

'Sorry,' she said to her mother. And then to Lucille: 'It's all that ballet she made me take. Turned me into quite the sneak.' She tiptoed clownishly to the table and peered at her mother's cards. 'Who's winning, then?'

Her mother eyed her with wary bemusement, bringing the cards to her chest. With her free hand she picked up her lipstick-smeared sherry glass and held it out for Bettina to take. 'Be a sweetie, eh?'

'Where's Gerty?' Gerty was her mother's maid. She was a mean-looking, roll-necked woman with the face of an exhausted turkey, but was in actual fact a very tender-hearted person deep down. Supposedly. Her mother was always mythologising the serving classes like this.

'I've given her the afternoon off. Her sister is dying, poor thing.' She shook the empty glass.

Bettina headed over to the bar. Her father had had it installed just before the start of the war and very much enjoyed hinting at its cost. A special kind of mahogany had been imported all the way from Bangor – the American Bangor, not the Welsh one – and he also very much enjoyed bringing this detail to the attention of whichever awful twit he was entertaining, running a lethargic hand along the wood. 'Not the Welsh one, of course – haha!' Large front teeth flashing underneath the giant foxbrush over his lip. 'Not the Welsh one,' she quietly mimicked, pouring the sherry into a fresh glass.

'Thanks, dear,' her mother said, eyes still burning into her card hand. She glanced up at Bettina. 'Do put some clothes on, won't you? You look like something the tide rejected. Are all your things packed for school yet?'

'Uh-huh.' Bettina curled her foot around the back of her sand-crumbed calf and watched them play. Lucille and Venetia had been best pals since early adulthood. They came from similar social backgrounds (wealthy but not stinking rich, as they saw it) and lived only one mile from each other. Since Lucille's husband had passed away five years ago, she was over most days. Only once had they properly quarrelled; Lucille had by all accounts been a 'know-it-all interferer' when it came to child-rearing, offering unsolicited advice at every turn. Venetia bore this with patience, since Lucille had not only suffered the loss of Tabitha, who had been kicked in the head by a shire horse, but also a stillbirth, and so her incessant commentary was of course motivated by loss. Venetia took her resentment and sat on it, like a letter she never wished to read. But one day, after Lucille had personally taken it upon herself to issue instructions to Bettina's piano tutor, Venetia snapped: 'If he wants her to do Chopin, she'll bloody well do Chopin! It's none of your business. I don't tell *you* how to raise your brat of a son.'

Lucille had covered her mouth with her hand and walked in a wordless daze to the front door. She stopped coming around and Venetia vented about her for weeks, usually over breakfast. 'She's spoiled, that's the thing of it, so just one cross word is enough to send her whimpering to lick her wounds like some pathetic mongrel.' Angry knife-hand slashing butter thickly over her pikelet. 'She should've tried growing up with three older sisters, then she'd know what it is to grow a thick hide.' A spoon rammed into the jam pot, striking the glass at the bottom; a peeved glance from Monty over his teacup. 'And I'm sorry, but he *is* a brat! Don't look at me like that, Betts – he is, for a fact, a brat. For. A. Fact. His name is even an anagram of brat.' She barked out a laugh. 'You can't argue with the alphabet, darling.'

But she missed Lucille and eventually turned up at her house with flowers and a bottle of her best claret, and Lucille had clearly missed her in return because she only made her grovel for two hours. 'I *know* you didn't mean that awful thing about Bart. After all, Bettina and my Barty are the same in nature, so to call him a brat' – a sly look over her wine glass – 'is to call your own daughter a brat.'

Lucille and Venetia mostly played gin rummy and cribbage. Lucille had a croquet lawn in her garden but they never used it because Venetia was a terrible shot and always ended up tossing her mallet into the flowerbeds and returning to her patio chair in a sulk. They ate cakes practically on the hour. On Sundays they chose to start drinking after lunch and got slowly sozzled on whatever drink suited their mood, smoking incessantly. Sometimes they gossiped about trivialities, such as the impossibility of finding a good butcher, or mean-spirited things – Sybil Palmer's eyes were too close together and she just had this look about her, like she'd do it with *anyone*, even the blessed gardener. Other times they discussed the suffrage movement or the 'situation in India' ('Bit of a pickle, I hear'), lolling back in their chairs, using unimaginative language and taking unoriginal viewpoints because they were close and comfortable friends who had no need to impress each other.

Once, after a whole afternoon of cribbage and fizz, they'd retired to the sitting room; Bettina had pressed her ear to the door and heard raucous, naked laughter, and one word had leapt out of the fragmented chatter – 'fuck' – and her ears heated up like steamed cockles. She caught a partial sentence, from Lucille: '. . . his hands squeezing my throat, just so, it was quite delicious'.

'You're loitering,' her mother said now. She took her eyes from her cards and looked up at Bettina. 'Let me get this right: you've talked to your father and didn't hear quite what you wanted to hear.'

'Correct,' said Bettina.

'And you think I can change his mind?'

'I know you can.'

Venetia put her cards down. 'Darling, I really can't. Not about this. Every year you do this, and every year he doesn't budge an inch.'

'Got his heels in the stirrups,' added Lucille, blasting thick smoke from the side of her mouth.

'He really does,' said her mother, her brows tilted in apology. 'This is something he feels awfully strongly about. And he *is* a benefactor. What would it look like if his own daughter dropped out?'

Bettina's body slumped and she rolled her head back. 'But they're all such horrible bitches!'

'Well, of course they are, darling. They're sixteen-year-old girls.'

'You're not being helpful.'

'I don't know what else to say.'

'Isn't there at least one nice one you can be friends with?' asked Lucille.

'No! Not one!' Actually, Bettina did have one 'nice' friend in school. But it was like finding one pearl in a field of sheep droppings. The pearl is lovely, but look – there's still all this sheep shit and one can't help but step in it.

'Perhaps the world is trying to tell you something,' said Lucille, raising an eyebrow.

'Oh, do be quiet, Lolly,' said Venetia, shooting her a cross look. She stood up and took Bettina by the arms – her hands were cold and digging. 'Look, lovey, it's only another two years and then you can come back home. Two years really isn't a terribly long time and you've already got through the worst of it. *My* father made me go to finishing school when I was your age, and what a dreadful bore *that* was.'

Lucille knocked back the last of her sherry. 'And just be thankful you're not a boy,' she said, dabbing the corner of her lips with her finger. 'From what I hear, it's all buggery, buggery, buggery—'

'Shut up, Lolly!'

'Please don't tell me to shut up, Neesh – I'm simply pointing out the positives.'

Bettina stared at the powder clinging to her mother's downy chin. The skin was soft, like an old woman's earlobe. She *should* be thankful she wasn't a boy, and she was reminded of this every bloody day, from the black armbanded women gusting into Our Lady of the Angels, the leftover mothers, wives, sisters

– in fact she'd passed by them just this morning on her way to St Mark's, watching through the cab screen with blank eyes but a swirling dark mischief in her stomach. And inside her own church it was all the same, just with nicer hats and better teeth.

She didn't even have to leave the house for a reminder of how *thankful* she should be: there, across the dining-room table, sat her older brother Jonathan every mealtime, struggling one-armed with his cutlery, face pale, proud and pinched as the broad beans or new potatoes rolled around on his plate or flew across the table. She should be *supremely* grateful. She should be kissing the trench-blackened feet of every young man in Great Britain, she should be worshipping their mangled stumps before skipping off to her prestigious, wonderful boarding school at the end of every holiday, because she was so privileged, so fortunate, skipping, skipping, white teeth shining, singing to the finches and marvelling over butterflies! Instead she mewled and scratched like a fat, spoiled housecat. She knew it. And she felt guilty about it. And guilt was a boring waste of time.

They really were such dreadful bitches, those girls.

Chapter 4

October 1922, Winchester College

Bart hung his head over the toilet, a thick white nausea in the foreground of his senses, and considered his options.

Actually, he didn't have any.

His diaphragm tensed with a jolt and more brown sick burst up and out, spattering the porcelain basin and leaving dots of coagulated matter like brown stars. It was the kippers, most likely. What a turd this 'fine institution' had turned out to be. The food wasn't fit for a cockroach – yesterday there'd been a fingernail clipping in his porridge. He felt a spasm in his bowel and quickly stumbled to his feet and yanked his trousers down, dropping to the toilet just in time. He groaned, fog blasting out of his mouth.

No – certainly he had no options.

In forty minutes he was supposed to enter the cricket field, leading his team against Repton. It was an especially important match. Last February a few Repton fellows had sneaked into the dormitory in the early hours, kidnapped their best batsman, taken him to the cricket field, stripped him entirely naked and shaved off his eyebrows. Bart and his teammates had found the poor boy the next morning, pale and shivering, his penis so shrunken by the cold (and possibly genetics) that it had burrowed up inside his pubic mound and resembled a vulva.

Bart's fag, Roger, entered the room with clean towels draped over his arm like a tiny waiter.

'I don't mean to be impertinent, sir, but it does appear that you mightn't be well enough to play today.' Spoken in such a stilted way that the little turd had probably rehearsed it.

Bart looked up with wretched eyes. 'Well observed, genius.' He wiped some drool from his chin and leaned back against the toilet. 'It's coming out of me like water, Rodge. I don't dare get off the pot.'

Roger nodded sympathetically. 'Is there anything I can do?'

Bart groaned again, his head rolling around on his shoulders. 'No. Just try not to irritate me. Oh fuck, here it comes.' He hunched over, elbows on his knees, hands covering his face as another cramp fist-squeezed his bowels and more liquid gushed out. 'Don't fucking look at me!' he cried, weakly, and then his face slackened and lost all its colour – the little that was left – and he quickly parted his thighs and aimed a stream of bile into the gap. Another groan, this one longer and lower, like the cry of a mare suffering a breech birth. He had sick all over his pubic hair. Roger averted his eyes – breathing through his mouth, he stared at the white wall over the washbasin, listening to the drip of the tap which acted as a percussive metronome for the melodic score of Bart's tortured moans.

October 1922, St Vincent's School for Girls

Bettina's only friend at school was Margueritte Finch, a French-born, Welsh-raised daughter of a nobleman father and prima-donna mother. Margueritte had framed photographs of her mother dating from the turn of the century, before marriage and child-rearing and all that fluff, and the woman was, thought Bettina, absolutely ravishing, with full, pouting lips and smoky black eyes. Though God knew what she looked like these days, after shooting out seven children. Margueritte often talked about her mother, usually disdainfully – 'Honestly, she can be so pretentious and dizzy; she walks about in the garden at midnight all dreamy-eyed like some kind of Titania, it makes me want to vomit' – but sometimes with reluctant praise, since she'd been a liberal mother who 'pretty much let me run free to do as I wished'. Bettina, having a similar sort of mother (and also a Welsh father), found she had a lot to talk about with Margueritte (or Margo, as she called her) and often their conversations would be a battle of one-upmanship to see who had the most lenient mother, and consequently, the wildest childhood stories.

Margo boasted that when she was fourteen she'd filched two bottles of her father's Bordeaux and gone off by herself camping in the woods, where she'd stayed for two days and one night, completely roughing it like a regular Huck Finn, and what's more, had shared the wine with a most sensual and dashing man – an Irish conscientious objector – hiding out in the woods, and what's more, she'd let him kiss her, but only kiss her, she wasn't a tart or anything – 'so get *that* idea out of your head', and by the way, he had the most uncommonly clear blue eyes and his stubble felt just exquisite, so perfectly manly, and what's more, she'd returned home after all this and her mother hadn't batted an eyelid, probably because she was too preoccupied with her own debauched affair with the local magistrate. 'So I got off scot-free and clean as a whistle, as they say.'

Bettina supposed that *parts* of this story might be true – perhaps Margo had indeed gone camping by herself, but only for a few hours, surely, and the business with the conscientious objector, well, perhaps she'd seen a man somewhere in the woods and had let her fancy run wild. But the fourteen-year-old daughter of a nobleman roughing it for two days and a night without attracting a search party – inconceivable. Nice try all the same.

In return Bettina told some embellished stories of her own. The night that Bart had kissed her, for example: she turned Bart into the gardener (Italian and tanned) and the pavilion into her mother's rose arbour. It was late in the afternoon and her mother had been *just* around the corner – quite literally, she was mere steps away, talking to the chauffeur – and as a result the kiss was rushed and hurried and he'd grabbed her in such a passion that she'd found bruises about her body later. Aware that this story, with the bronzed Italian gardener and rose arbour, was sounding like the silly romantic fiction it was, Bettina quickly added some grounding details in order to imitate realism – the gardener had onion breath (as Bart had had) and their teeth clashed quite awkwardly. 'I actually didn't enjoy it as much as I thought I might.' What was more realistic, after all, than dissolved dreams?

Margo leaned forward with flushed cheeks and huge eyes and whispered, 'Did he get a stiff-on?' And Bettina rolled her eyes as if Margo was the biggest simpleton ever to walk the

King's Isles and said, 'Of course he did!' She didn't know for sure what a 'stiff-on' was. She guessed it was related to a 'cock-stand'. But actually, she didn't entirely understand what that was either. She imagined the penis stiffening in a downwards direction like the third leg of a camera tripod. One day she was going to ask Bart all about it.

Margueritte was a pale, plump girl with black hair down to her hips, which she wore in a thick, perfect plait. She had the tiniest yet poutiest mouth, brown-black eyes framed by thick, innocent eyebrows and no cheekbones to speak of. No wrists either – her forearms were as chubby as a toddler's, swallowing any trace of bone, ending in tiny doll's hands. Bettina thought she looked like a fat, young Theda Bara – well, that wasn't entirely fair, to call her fat. She was soft and ample. To cuddle up to all that flesh would probably feel divine. Such thoughts as this came to her mind as objective, almost scientific conclusions. They were the thoughts she imagined a future father-in-law might have on behalf of his son, a sort of sizing-up. Bettina's gaze was often drawn to Margo's bosom, which was considerable, and again, she would imagine the future husband finding satisfaction with the pliant, squishy handfuls. Entirely objective.

They were sitting on Margo's bed, sharing a box of Turkish delight that her mother had sent to her, alongside a new set of stays, two pairs of stockings and a packet of Harrods stem-ginger biscuits. It was a four-bed room which Margo shared with Dionysus, a sinister-eyed daughter of bohemian parents who collected her toenail clippings in a heart-shaped locket and posted suffragette literature around school; Daphne, a shy, almost mute girl; and a tall, mousey girl who Bettina found so dull that she'd never bothered to learn her name. This four-bed set-up was the privilege of the upper-school girls; previously, they'd had to share a twenty-bed dorm. Many nights, Bettina had fallen asleep to the sounds of blanket-muffled sobs and desperate, whispered prayers; some of the girls had been spoiled senseless by kind governesses and indulgent mothers, and coming here to unsweetened lumpy porridge, slapped knuckles and exhausting monotony was a cruel awakening. This was a girls' school which prided itself on being just like a boys' school. But whereas a boy might benefit from this hardening-up, especially one keen on entering the Forces or a cut-throat trade, it was entirely wasted on a girl, thought Bettina, who would only go on to get married and have babies, so what was the bloody point?

'What makes you think marriage and procreation don't require some sort of hardening of spirit?' Venetia had said once, in reply to this argument. 'In fact, I think I'd rather a year in the trenches over twelve hours of childbirth.' Jonathan had dropped his spoon into his pudding bowl with a clatter and glared at his mother, before standing up and storming out of the room. 'I don't know what makes him think he has a monopoly on suffering,' said Venetia. 'After all, women die in childbirth all the time. You don't see us having tantrums about it at the dinner table.' Monty grinned at Bettina: 'There's that famous hardening of spirit!'

Bettina and Margo had the room to themselves; Daphne, Dionysus, Boring Nameless Girl and the rest of the upper school were playing hockey outside. Margo was excused from any physical activity on account of her chronic asthma and Bettina had complained of severe menstrual pains to get out of playing. Margo was lying on the bed, one cheek bulging with a large cube of Turkish delight – her customary way of consuming them was first to nibble off the pistachio slivers and then store the chunk, hamster-like, between teeth and cheek, letting it slowly dissolve. Bettina lay next to her, her head resting on Margo's shoulder. She could hear the yells and collisions of the hockey players outside.

'Do you think you'll marry Jasper?' she said. Jasper was Margo's sometime beau at home. He was twenty-one and stupid to the point of idiocy, apparently; but, being the son of a baron and set to inherit a humongous estate in Surrey, he was a tasty prospect. Also he was good-looking, which helped – said Margo – to distract from his puny intellect.

'I think I'd be foolish not to at least consider it,' she said. 'But I'm not counting on it. He might not want to wait for me. He might set his sights on someone else in the meantime.'

'Do you think he'll be a virgin on your hypothetical wedding night?'

Margo snorted. 'Don't be silly. Men are never virgins on their wedding night.'

'That's not at all fair.'

Bettina felt Margo shrug.

'I mean,' continued Bettina, 'the man gets to have all this experience so that when it comes to it, he can proceed with confidence. Whereas the woman hasn't a clue what she's doing and simply lies there like a . . . well, like a paralysed swan.'

'Speak for yourself.'

Bettina looked up. She could see Margo's jaw clenching as she sucked on the shrinking sweet. 'You mean you've done it?'

Margo angled her head to look down at her, frowning and two-chinned. 'Of course not. But I know some things.'

'What things?'

'Well. My father has a copy of the *Kama Sutra* that he thinks is well hidden. But is not. Ho hoho.'

'What's the *Kama Sutra*?'

'It's an ancient Indian sex book full of illustrations. Brown people twisting themselves into knots really. It's quite graphic. They're doing all sorts of outrageous things.'

'Like what?'

Margo sighed. 'I recall "the licking of the rose petals" and the "sucking of the mango fruit". Regarding the *oral tradition*.' She giggled, causing Bettina's head to wobble. 'I don't suppose my rose petals shall get any attention from a stuffy old bore like Jasper. He has no imagination. And from what I've been led to believe, a man gets that kind of pleasure from a tart and saves the most austere fundamentals for his wife.'

'But what *about* the wife?'

'The wife, if she has chosen a stupid enough husband, will take a lover and hopefully get away with it.'

Bettina laughed into the hollow of Margo's collarbone. 'You wouldn't!'

'I don't know. Who's to say how I'll feel about things in the future?'

A meaty splash from outside – the cook's assistant, tossing yesterday's vegetable water into the potted geraniums.

Margo ran her tongue along her gums to dislodge the last of the sweet, swallowing loudly. 'Can I tell you a secret?' she said. 'Only you've got to promise not to tell anyone.'

'I can keep a secret.'

'You'd better.'

'I *will*. Go on, tell me.'

'My great-aunt on my father's side, if rumours are to be believed, was a gigantic sapphic.'

Bettina hesitated. She didn't want to have to admit to yet another ignorance, after the *Kama Sutra* and the stuff about the rose petals and mangoes.

As if reading her mind, Margo said, 'It's quite all right, I didn't know what a sapphic was either, until someone told me. It's a woman who goes with other women. Comes from the poet Sappho, who was apparently inclined that way, though you'll notice that Miss Roundpenny missed that bit out in lesson.'

'Gosh. How awful.'

'Isn't it? Makes me feel quite sick to think about. My great-aunt supposedly refused to marry and she was obscenely beautiful and rich so there were *millions* of suitors drooling over her, a positive *parade* of stiff-ons, honestly. But she wouldn't have it. Drove her parents quite mad. She ended up a spinster, living in a large Tudor cottage with no servants. Can you imagine? And it's not as if she couldn't afford servants.'

'What a lonely existence,' said Bettina, brushing a few ticklish strands of Margo's hair away from her face.

'Oh, she wasn't lonely. She lived with another woman, a "friend". Her lover, of course. And get this: this "other woman" dressed as a man. Honestly. She wore breeches and kept her hair short. Hunted pheasants supposedly. Quite outrageous – I don't know *how* she escaped lynching, to be honest with you. They lived as man and wife in that cottage. One can only assume they shared a bed.'

'Not with any certainty.'

'Well, I haven't told you the whole of it yet.'

'Then do, tell me the whole of it, before I die of boredom.'

Margo gave Bettina a playful smack on the head. Bettina

flinched, her nose prodding Margo's pillowy breast. She was nowhere near bored.

'My great-uncle – the sapphic's brother – went to visit her one day, and since she had no butler or parlour-maid, he let himself in.'

'Oh dear, I don't like where this is going.'

Margo shook her head as if to say, 'Me neither,' and continued: 'So he lets himself in and looks around the house but finds no one. They must be out, he thinks, naturally enough. So he goes upstairs to the master bedroom, because the reason he'd called by was to collect his mother's wedding ring, which'd been left to the sister on her death, but since the sister had no need of it, being a gigantic pervert, it seemed reasonable that he should have it.'

'I'm almost too afraid to hear this.'

'Oh, grow up, Bettina. If you can hear about men dying in the trenches with their intestines coming out, then you can hear about a couple of women fucking each other.'

'Margueritte!'

Margo laughed with wicked delight, her whole body shuddering. She clearly took great enjoyment in shocking Bettina, just as Bart did. Bettina didn't mind the shock so much as the feeling of being made to feel like an innocent country child, a naive doe-eyed ingenue. It ran contrary to the image she was trying to cultivate.

'So is that what they were doing in there?' she asked.

'Well, it wouldn't be accurate to say they were doing *that*, because two women are physically incapable of *that*. But they *were* in sexual union, if you like.'

'I bloody well *don't* like! What were they doing exactly?'

'Exactly? Oh, I don't know. This story has been passed

around the family's men like an old dog-bone – who knows what's been added and embellished? The version I heard, or *over*heard, since I was indeed eavesdropping on my cousins' private conversation, the version I heard was that the two women were quite naked on the bed and one was gifting the other with – well, I believe I've already mentioned it. "The licking of the rose petals", as the *Kama Sutra* puts it.'

Bettina was silent for a while. 'Look, you're going to have to spell it out for me. I have no idea what the rose petals signify. Don't make fun of me.'

Margo pointed down at her crotch. 'The labia minora. Look in a mirror one day, why don't you? She was licking my great-aunt's—'

'Urgh! Yuck! Vile. Just vile. Oh, it makes me shudder.'

'I know,' said Margo. 'I don't even like to think of it.'

'How did the brother react?'

Margo laughed again. 'Apparently he said, "You sick mad wench, how will I ever unsee this?"'

'How will I ever unimagine it?' said Bettina. In her mind she saw a woman with short hair. An ugly woman – she'd have to be ugly. Yellow-toothed like some horrible matron. Would she have large breasts? How grotesque – a woman with short hair, dressed as a man, with a fat pair of breasts straining at the fabric of her waistcoat. Horrid.

The two girls lay quiet, their breathing loud in the spartan room, every small movement or sound amplified. Bettina, for some curious reason, was suddenly afraid to move, and her head now felt too heavy on Margo's shoulder, her breath too forceful against her collarbone. She closed her eyes and tried to control her breathing, to soften it. She listened to the sound outside of birds singing and girls running and grunting and wooden sticks hitting other wooden sticks. Their own silence started to feel too heavy, too conspicuous, like a drowsy fug in the air.

'Margo,' she whispered, and now that the silence had been broken, so had the paralysing spell.

'Hmm?'

'Can I tell *you* a secret?'

'Please do.'

'You've got to swear not to tell,' said Bettina, 'because otherwise I'll be in the absolute worst trouble.'

'Come off it,' said Margo. 'I've just let you in on my family's most guarded, ugly secret. Well, one of them.'

'The thing is, my friend Bart – you remember Bart, I've told you all about him. Last week he sent me a bottle of brandy and a case of cigarettes and I've got them hidden in the boiler room.'

Margo sat up with a jerk, dislodging Bettina's head. 'Bettina! You dark horse!'

'Well, Bart is the dark horse really. It was him who—'

'How did it get past The Barren One?'

The Barren One was Miss Cameron, the house mistress (so called because she was so averse to children that it was highly conceivable she ovulated sand). It was rumoured that she checked all packages the girls received. So as to avoid precisely this sort of thing. Probably not true, Bettina thought, but you never knew – some of the women here at St Vincent's were complete psychopaths.

She shook her head, bewildered. 'Maybe she was too busy sacrificing tiny infants to—'

Margo bounded off the bed with explosive excitement. 'Well, why are we wasting our time here, stuffing sweets and gossiping like a pair of ole fishwives?'

'You want to – now?'

'Does the Pope wear a hat?'

Bettina stared at Margo's face, trying to think of a witty comeback. But she could think of nothing, and besides, the opportunity had passed, so she got off the bed, took her friend's hand and together they left the room and began the exhilarating slow creep through the school's narrow passages.

The boiler room had a dark, heavy air, even when brightly lit. Black mould spread up the whitewashed walls, forming curious patterns, and the last time Bettina had been down here, to hide the drink and cigs, she'd sat on an old wonky piano stool, chin in hands and elbows on knees, trying to find shapes in the mould as one finds shapes in clouds (it was always dragons, continents and old men's faces).

When, at thirteen, she'd first started at St Vincent's (reluctantly, of course, and only because her father refused to submit to her year-long campaign of passive-aggressive resistance), the older students – all bitches – gleefully passed down the inevitable ghost stories, claiming that St Vincent's was well-known to be haunted, had in fact attracted spiritualists and macabre loners from all over the world on thrill-seeking and fact-gathering pilgrimages. The boiler room, they said, was the most malignant place in the whole building, the source of all the paranormal energy and telekinetic phenomena (Bettina had no idea what 'telekinetic' meant, and wasn't about to ask), and home to the Black Nun. The Black Nun had died in a fire in the boiler room some ninety years ago, back when the school was a sanatorium for the criminally insane (it never was, Monty told her later – it had been a great manor house belonging to a Norwegian whoremonger who frittered away his whole estate on opium, tarts and lavish orgies), and some nights, even now, her ghost could be seen gliding silently and footlessly along the corridors.

Only now did she understand the reason for this story. The necessity of it.

When she crept down to the boiler room that first time after receiving Bart's package there were countless traces of previous visitations – chocolate wrappers, pen ink, lipstick-kissed napkins, even a discarded pair of woollen knickers with dried blood on them. This was the place, she realised, where the older girls went to escape the oppressive prim cloud that hung over them; a place of cautious freedom. In one corner, concealed behind a dusty pile of broken musical instruments (on top of which a stringless, scratched harp was placed, leaning precariously) was an empty wine bottle – a dessert wine of the sort her parents served with plum pudding – and poked into the cracks of the wall's plaster next to the hot boiler tank were a few squashed cigarette ends.

She hid her own items with neurotic care. She also collected the cigarette stubs and various other leftovers and dropped them inside the tubed hollow of a rolled-up rug.

'Rather funky smelling in here,' said Margo, pulling a face like a fine lady wandering through a fish market.

'My most humble apologies,' said Bettina. 'Would you rather I set out a chaise longue for you in the headmaster's office, on which you can enjoy our contraband items?'

'Oh, shush,' said Margot, smiling. 'I am merely making a *comment.* I wasn't expecting the Ritz.'

There was a dented violin missing three strings in the pile of broken instruments. Bettina gently lifted it so as not to disturb the intricate structure, and there underneath was the bottle and cigarettes Bart had sent. She presented them to Margo with a self-conscious 'ta-da!' and Margo clapped her hands.

'My father has this,' she said, looking at the bottle. 'It's supposed to be good.'

'Have you ever tried it?' said Bettina.

'No. I've never had the inclination.'

'You mean you've never drunk?'

'Of course I have. Wine and port and so forth at dinner parties. In moderation, *bien entendu*. But never men's drink. I imagine it's ghastly.'

'It is.'

'Well, I don't care. Right now it seems like just the ticket.'

Bettina nodded, bringing a lit match towards the cigarette between her lips, aware that Margo was watching her with reserved awe. She inhaled, tilted her head and let out the smoke through her nostrils. 'Bart is always making me drink spirits. He delights in getting me drunk.'

'You'd better watch out for him then!'

'Oh, I do, he's a perfect scoundrel. Listen – don't you think we ought to be very careful? Suppose someone smells it on us at supper.'

'Oh, don't worry.' Margo opened the bottle and sniffed, pulling a face, before taking a sip and wincing. 'Acha vee!' She handed the bottle to Bettina, who took a huge swallow, fighting the urge to grimace. A man would never grimace. 'We'll have our little party,' said Margo, 'and then we'll immediately brush our teeth and take ourselves to bed with hot water bottles. We've already a great cover story after all – you've got the curse and I'm an asthmatic weakling.'

'And if I fall over I can always blame it on an iron deficiency.'

Margo took the bottle back. 'Exactly.' She pinched her nose with one hand and tilted the bottle into her mouth, draining an inch.

'Steady on, girl,' said Bettina, in a voice she didn't recognise.

'"Come into the garden, Maud, for the black bat, Night, has flown!"' Margo had one chubby leg up on the piano stool, her skirt hoiked up to reveal the stays of her stockings, like a bawdy cabaret performer. She was singing in a ridiculous man's tenor. '"Come into the garden, Maud, I am here at the gate alone."'

'Oh God, you're not going to sing the whole thing, are—'

Margo lifted a finger to shush her. '"And the woodbine spices are wafted abroad, and the musk of the roses blown."' She lifted the hem of her skirt and, flapping it, said, in a shrill cockney accent, 'How's the musk of *my* rose, dear?'

'Shhh!' said Bettina, before collapsing over in a fit of giggles.

Margo brought her leg off the stool and attempted to kick it away, but missed, lost her balance and fell onto her hands and knees. She looked up at Bettina, her back arched and her eyes pure carnival. Shrieking with laughter, Bettina rushed over and helped her up. Margo fell against her. She snatched the cigarette out of Bettina's mouth and, awkwardly tweezering it between her fingers, took a tiny puff. Her other hand lay just above Bettina's breasts, the hot palm pressing into the bony ridge of her chest. It was unnecessary, that hand, and it lingered.

'We're *such* good friends,' Margo said, smiling up at her.

'Of course we are.'

The hand crept higher, finding Bettina's red-flecked throat. The fingers gently squeezed.

'They're all such terrific wasps, the others, such vicious,

stinging wasps,' said Margo. She was looking at Bettina's mouth. 'But you're not. Well, only a smidge, and in the funniest way. I think you're wonderful actually.'

Bettina smiled foolishly, her eyes focused on Margo's hairline. 'I should think so.' Their bodies were pressed together. She could *not* meet her friend's eye, it was bizarre. And she was so terribly drunk – drunker than she'd ever been in her life. And that warm small hand squeezing her throat. Just so.

'We're *such* good friends,' Margo repeated, in a whisper now, bringing her mouth to Bettina's ear and softly, so, so softly, kissing the point where jawline meets ear, then a little lower – the neck. Higher – the chin, higher still – moving up with the soft kidskin lips bumping, brushing, rubbing, preceded by little hot breaths – up up up, slowly, clumsily, to her own lips, and beyond that, all reason left her.

Old Roundpenny. Halfway down the stairs. Frozen with one foot on the step below, hands curled in front of her, rodent-like. Such an expression; that of Jesus spying the money-lenders in the temple. Eyes made fantastically huge by her spectacles, and the horror therefore made fantastically huge within.

Margo had her back to the door, and for a long, tormented moment, Bettina's eyes were locked with Miss Roundpenny's while Margo's hand continued its slick see-sawing and her mouth continued its frenzied sucking.

'Get off, get off,' said Bettina, pushing Margo's mouth away from her nipple – dear God it was glossy with spit and sticking up like a peanut – and twisting her hips so as to dislodge her fingers. Margo looked down at Bettina, her mouth slack and her eyes still half glazed, and seeing her expression, turned her head to follow her gaze. A small gasp.

Bettina closed her eyes, wishing for unconsciousness. She didn't know at that moment what was worse – that they'd been caught, or that they had to stop.

You're a sick, mad wench, she told herself.

The brandy bottle and the half-smoked packet of cigarettes were placed neatly on the desk in front of Miss Cameron – The Barren One. She was sitting devil-straight with her hands folded on her lap. A mole the size of a sweetcorn kernel was stuck to her jawline and from it grew three curly hairs – a witch, an absolute witch. Her eyes were large and protuberant, the space between brow and eyelid deep and cavernous so that were she to have water tipped onto her face while in a horizontal position, a small moat would form around each eyeball.

Margo wept snottily in the chair next to Bettina. 'Please don't tell my father,' she was saying in a little girl's voice. 'Please – anything – but please don't tell my father. He'll kill me – literally, he'll kill me. Please don't tell my father.'

Miss Cameron picked up the thick leather-bound bible placed in front of her, walked around the desk and brought the book with a slam into the back of Margo's head. Her face hit the wood. She lifted her head, nose dribbling blood, and stared straight ahead, all emotion wiped away.

'Have you quite composed yourself?' said Miss Cameron.

'I have,' said Margo, swallowing and nodding calmly.

Miss Cameron placed the bible back in the centre of the desk, poking it until the edges were aligned with the sides of the desk, and re-took her seat.

'Bettina Wyn Thomas and Margueritte Morgan.' It was not a question, but both girls nodded.

She picked up her teacup delicately and sipped from it, her

eyes never leaving the girls. 'You understand the severity of your crimes?'

Bettina glanced sideways at Margo. 'Yes, Miss,' she said. 'Yes, Miss,' echoed Margo.

'What Miss Roundpenny had to witness . . .' She pursed her lips over her teeth. 'A hideous thing for anyone to look at, but especially someone as tender-hearted as Miss Roundpenny.'

Bettina's eyes bulged at this. Miss Roundpenny had once cut a girl's hair off for wearing rouge and she'd smiled while doing it.

'While I am *beyond* disgusted – nay, *horrified* – at this perverted tomfoolery, it is merely the cherry on the proverbial cake.' She glanced down at the items on the desk. 'Drinking on school grounds? Smoking? How could you be so *stupid*?'

Bettina looked down at her clasped hands. Her sinuses were aching with the beginnings of a headache.

'All I need do is report this incident to the headmaster and that's it – you're finished here. Goodbye, *bon voyage*.' Miss Cameron took another sip of her tea and returned it to its saucer, causing only the slightest clink. She stared at the girls down her pore-dotted nose, the nostrils like an extra pair of pious eyes. 'But I shan't be resorting to this measure today.'

Bettina let out a thin breath through dry lips. Again she side-glanced at Margo, who sat very still.

'Instead, I am giving you both a two-month suspension. Miss Wyn Thomas, you will pack your things and leave tonight. I have booked you a ticket for the last train and I will, of course, bill your father. Miss Morgan, you will leave tomorrow on the eight-fifteen train.' She snarled her lips into something resembling a grin. 'You appreciate why I am putting you on separate trains?'

Margo nodded. Blood was dripping from her chin onto her bosom – too terrified to make a move to wipe it away, most likely. She looked like she had a pistol trained on her.

Miss Cameron licked her lips with a small darting tongue-tip and picked up her teacup again. 'Bettina. Miss Roundpenny was looking for you for a reason.' A long whistling sip, the liquid forced through the gaps in her teeth. 'I received a telegram from your mother today. A friend of yours, a Master Bartholomew Dawes, has been taken ill with Spanish flu.'

Bettina made a small noise and gripped the desk edge, before quickly returning her hands to her lap.

'It is quite serious.' Was that a trace of pleasure in her tone? It was – it bloody was! *Witch.* 'He's been brought home and is supposedly near death.' She returned the cup to its saucer once more. Bettina stared at it, at the gleaming whiteness of the china. 'You have my sympathies. Now please, get out of my sight.'

Chapter 5

October 1922, Longworth House, Sussex

Bart opened his eyes. His face was pressed into the pillow and he could smell his rotten breath infused in the fabric of the slip. He'd been having the most depraved dream: he was on Brighton Pier at night and overhead turquoise Zeppelins drifted, benevolent as clouds, smiling almost, as if they had human personalities; and behind him, a man he couldn't see but who he knew to be Lord Kitchener was sliding cricket stumps up his arse, one at a time, one after the other, as if feeding blocks of timber into a wood-shaving machine, and then the stumps turned to sausages, a linked line of sausages. He laughed weakly through cracked lips. Kitchener, of all people. Really.

He felt a hand on his cheek and flinched. His mother. She loomed over him, smiling with glistening, tragic eyes.

'Mother?'

She nodded. Tears spilled down her cheeks, tracking a clean line through her face powder.

'Who let you . . . Mother? Am I—'

'You're home, darling.'

He screwed his face up. 'Rodge was just here. He was just here.'

She shook her head. 'You've been in delirium, darling. I thought you might die.' She stroked his cheek with the back of her fingers, her clusters of sharp jewels tickling. 'Dr Spielman said I should prepare myself.'

'Bloody hell – sorry, Mother. Jesus.'

'First your sisters, then your father, then you . . . I thought, well, I thought I shall be all on my own.' Her chin crumpled. 'I thought I was going to lose you.' A dignified sniff and a small, tight smile. 'But I haven't, have I?'

He sat up and looked around the room. The curtains were half open, allowing a block of fresh white sunlight in. He was in the day nursery, where he'd spent many boring hours as a baby and then a child. Outside, close by, he could hear the gorgeous snip-snip of the gardener pruning the hedges, and, further off, the singing of the canaries in his mother's prized aviary. A pale, red-haired nurse stood near the door, clutching her hands and smiling sentimentally. As if she gave a fart. Lucille placed a hand on his shoulder. 'Try not to exert yourself, Bartyboy. You're very weak.'

'I'm thirsty.' He aimed this at the nurse and she nodded and came over to the dresser, where a jug of water sat on a tray, next to some glasses.

'Who won the match?' he asked his mother.

'What match?'

'The cricket match.'

'Honestly, Bart! I thought my only child was dying and I was supposed to enquire after a cricket score?'

'Could you find out?' The nurse brought him a glass and held it for him as he drank.

'I don't see why not, if you promise to rest. Now, why don't we let Nurse Cooper here give you a wash and change and then we'll see about some broth.'

He nodded, glancing mistrustfully at the nurse. He'd never got on with nurses. They were, more often than not, condescending and domineering and they always poked and prodded too hard with bony, rough fingers. And if I wish to feel violated, he thought, all I need do is close my eyes and think of dear old Kitchener.

The next time he woke up, Bettina was sitting next to the bed.

'Afternoon, gorgeous,' she said, bending down to kiss his forehead. He held on to her in a clumsy hug, loose wisps of her hair sticking to his bottom lip. He hadn't realised how much he'd missed her.

'Your breath is like a brothel full of dead rats,' she said.

He opened his mouth wide and exhaled into her face.

'Damn you, Bart,' she said, struggling to get away, but laughing. She sat back down in her chair. 'You're all skin and bones.'

'I'll put it all back on in a flash, you watch.'

She looked around, her eyes lingering on the empty toy trunk and the small purple bookcase, also empty. 'You always hated this room.'

'Still do.'

'I used to love it. I always preferred your toys to mine.'

'I don't know why she brought me here,' he said. 'There are plenty of other rooms in this house I might've stayed in. I have a bedroom.'

Bettina shrugged. 'She thought her baby boy was dying. I imagine it made perfect sense to put you here.'

'I was never going to die of the flu. It's too boring.'

She glanced at the door. 'I can't stay long.'

'Why ever not?'

'I'm under house arrest. They're only letting me out to see you.'

He grinned. 'What have you done?'

'Oh, I can't really say.'

'Can't or won't?' He thumped the bed next to him. 'Come up here with me.'

Another nervy glance at the door. This should be good. Venetia and Monty were seldom strict with her – she must have done something truly atrocious. He thumped the bed again. 'Come on. Tell old Barty the trouble.'

She climbed onto the bed and they lay opposite each other, face to face, bodies slightly curled, like two mandarin segments.

'It's really quite embarrassing.' She fidgeted around and placed her pressed-together hands under her cheek, like a child at bedtime.

'I've been suspended from school.'

'Well, that's a result. You hate school.'

'Don't jest, Bart. It's really serious.'

'What did you do?'

She rolled onto her back. 'I'm afraid you'll think less of me.'

'Never.' He moved closer to her – her hair smelled of pears. 'You could murder someone in cold blood and I still wouldn't think less of you. Unless it was my mother. Please don't murder my mother.'

She did a hiccupping sort of laugh.

'Now bloody well tell me, won't you?'

She sighed, her eyes on the ceiling. 'You remember that gift you sent me?'

'Oh my dear God. You didn't get caught drinking it, did you? You fucking bungler.'

She turned her head so they were nose to nose. 'I did. But that's not even the worst of it. Well, it is according to the house mistress. It's grounds for expulsion according to *her*. But for me it's not the worst. I was planning not to tell you the whole story actually. It's just . . .' She shook her head.

'You're deliberately eking this out for dramatic effect,' he said.

'I am not! It's just a hard thing to say. Do you remember my talking to you about Margo?'

He nodded. She'd told him during the last summer holiday all about her new best friend and all their worldly conversations. He'd felt jealous. He'd had to stop himself making cutting remarks about this girl, not because he didn't want to be mean, but because Bettina was shrewd and would see the jealousy behind his words. He didn't like his jealousy to show itself. It was an especially ugly emotion.

'Well, we had your brandy in the boiler room and we got into very high spirits, and well . . . one thing led to another and we . . . do you know, I can't say it.'

'You danced the one-step? You juggled fire together?'

'Please do be serious, Bart. Have you ever had any desires that to you seem quite . . . abnormal?'

'Well, I once wanted to learn German.'

She jumped off the bed. 'Stop cracking jokes, Bart! You're always doing this! You always – every time.'

He laughed. 'I'm sorry, I can't help myself! Genuinely, I can't. Please, come back to bed.' He put on a repentant face.

'When you act like this, I feel I can't quite trust you. And if I can't trust you—'

'But you can! Honestly, you can. Look, I'm sorry. I'm a clown. I'm a stupid, childish clown. Come back to bed and tell me all about how you and Margo shared a passionate tryst in the romantic setting of your school boiler room.'

She stared at him. 'Your mother told you.'

He shook his head – his mother had told him nothing. But it'd been bloody obvious where all this was going. High spirits and abnormal urges. 'Really, it's not so shocking,' he said. 'Bunch of randy hormonal girls crammed teat-to-teat in a restrictive environment, I'd be shocked if it *didn't* happen. Now come here, come back to your Barty.' He patted the space next to him again.

Smiling, she got back into bed. 'And you don't think I'm a pervert?'

'Of course I do. Bravo, I say. Was she a better kisser than me?'

'Well, it was all very sloppy and excitable. You won't tell anyone?'

'Wouldn't dream of it.'

She huddled in closer, resting her temple against his stubbled jaw. 'I feel much better now, for having told you. But Mother and Father are frothing at the mouth about it. Father called me a silly little slut. His exact words.'

He hissed in air through his teeth. 'That's a tad uncalled for.'

A knock at the door. Bettina jumped off the bed just as it was flung open. It was Bart's mother.

'Bettina, darling, your father said to hurry things along.'

'Oh, tell him to keep his knickers on,' said Bart. 'I almost died, remember.'

Lucille slanted her head sardonically. 'I do remember, as it happens.' She brought her cigarette to her mouth with a graceful movement of the wrist and took a puff. 'I'm sorry, Bettina, but I must respect your father's wishes.' Smoke oozed out of her nose. 'I'm sure Bart is grateful for the visit, regardless of its brevity.'

Bettina nodded and thanked his mother. 'Well, goodbye then,' she said to Bart. 'I'm so relieved to see you well. The train journey over here was pure hell – I've never prayed so much in my life.' She stood awkwardly for a moment, probably not knowing whether she should hug him in front of his mother. She squeezed his arm and then left.

His mother stood there for some time, smoking and watching him. She was wearing a loose beige dress with a low waist, a gold-sequinned hairband and lots of gold bangles. He'd always thought his mother stylish and felt proud of her – well, as much as one can be proud of one's mother. She had big hips and a humongous arse – truly humongous – but she'd never let this stop her from embracing the newest styles, unlike his Auntie May, who unsuccessfully hid her wide arse under flouncy monstrosities leftover from the Victorian nightmare.

'The birdies have been tweeting,' his mother said finally, a twinkle in her eye, 'regarding your just-departed friend.'

'Don't the birdies have anything better to do?'

'No, they don't actually.'

'Save your breath – I already know it.'

'Do you now? If it was about someone else – Sir Percy's

daughter perhaps, or that plain girl you always like to make fun of—'

'Average Anastasia—'

'If it was about her or someone else, you'd be laughing your head off right now and we both know it.'

'It's true, I would. But it's not about them. It's about Bettina.'

'And lucky it was! Did *you* know her father is a benefactor to St Vincent's?'

'Of course.'

'A most generous benefactor, Neesh told me. He donated fifty pounds last year. And here's the hilarious thing – you are going to *love* this' – she leaned forward, the whites of her eyes glittering – 'it was *his* donation that paid for the new heating system in the very boiler room in which she was caught!' She held her hands out incredulously. 'The irony! Ha! She'd have been expelled otherwise, for the drinking. Bit of an idiotic thing to do.'

'I'll thank you to show some restraint, *Lucille*.'

His mother's mouth scythed into a grin. 'It *is* rather funny, though. I always thought her such a stuck-up sort.'

'Well, she's not. I'm very fond of her.'

'Don't get *too* fond of her.' A raised brow. 'If she does indeed prefer a stroll through the peach orchard to a jog through the banana grove.'

A laugh burst out of his chest. He couldn't help it. 'Away with you, witch!'

She tilted her head back and cackled, then left, a trail of loose-tendrilled smoke in her wake. His mother had this tendency to move through daily life as if she was being filmed, and this was another quality of hers that he grudgingly admired.

Chapter 6

Oh, the things they'd done! Pure carnality. Oh, and his *cock* . . . Bart brought a pillow down under the blankets and started to hump it, his breath quickening, when suddenly he remembered the letters. Hips slowed down, eyes opened. The pillow became a pillow again. 'Oh, shit and rot,' he whispered, rolling onto his back and staring ghoul-eyed at the ceiling.

Back at school he kept his personal correspondence and anything else of intimate value locked up in the battered but hardy tuck trunk he'd had since the age of eleven. Not to mention the contraband. There were two bottles of gin and a tin of tobacco. An illustration ripped out of a Berlin magazine depicting a sailor fellating another sailor, a pack of cards and a velvet drawstring pouch filled with poker chips.

He kept the trunk key in his trouser pocket at all times. And the last thing he could remember of his descent into sickness was sitting on the toilet with his trousers around his ankles as his entire insides steamed out . . . so, what became of those trousers? Did he manage to get them back on? Did Roger see to them? It's likely he got shit on them. Did they get sent to the cleaners?

He hadn't always been kind to them, the fags – especially Roger, whose very presence irritated him. He was always snotty and runny-eyed, scratching his neck eczema with his red, flaky claw-hands. His obsequiousness grated. Bart had given him a hiding a few times, and if he was being honest with himself, these hidings hadn't always been earned. If Roger got into that trunk, Bart's life was over. He wasn't being melodramatic. He would be in the same predicament as Bettina, only twenty times worse. Bettina had her father's protection, and anyway, she was just a silly girl play-acting – that's what everyone would think. Her future husband would smirk at such girlish nonsense. Just making do with what was available before the almighty cock came along with its dazzling finality! And likewise, if Bart had been caught messing around with the house tart, this too might be treated with some tolerance, because boys locked up with other boys will do their thing, whether it's in Eton or Oxford or fucking Swansea. But the letters, they spoke of love. Not brotherly love, not convenient love, not the awkward jism-handed love of a pair of confused schoolboys who would no doubt go on to marry and procreate in the proper way, but radical, crushing, self-aware love.

He'd met the boy while on a school trip to Paris in the spring of 1921 (he'd been seventeen). One supposedly went to Paris to look for romance, but Bart had already decided at a young age that he was going to marry Bettina because not only was she the funniest person he knew, she was also gorgeous and capable of reluctant kindness in the right circumstances. And she came from wealth, so there you go. He had been going to try to kiss her, in fact, and had almost done so on one occasion, but had bottled it when he'd caught the sarcastic curve of her mouth once in close enough range.

He went to Paris thinking of one thing – freedom. He'd twice been on school trips, once to Edinburgh to visit the castle and the other time to Caerleon to see the old Roman amphitheatre, and on both instances, he and his schoolmates had enjoyed a moderate loosening of the leash – a couple of hours here and there to explore places unwatched (the upper-school boys, far from keeping an eye on the younger boys as they were supposed to, had pissed off to find cigarettes and flirt with girls). It was the same in Paris. There were tours around the Louvre, visits to Notre-Dame cathedral and a showing of *Othello* at the Chaillot (with Mr Fletcher continuously nudging him throughout the performance to make sure he was paying attention; Bart was the most promising student of the school's drama cohort). On the fourth day, all boys were granted the afternoon to go off and explore by themselves, with explicit instruction to stick together and behave with the bearing and dignity of a Winchester boy. 'We will be checking your breath on your return, so don't do anything stupid,' added the headmaster.

The boys did not stick together. A band of six went off to the Folies-Bergère to see a burlesque show, a few others returned to the Louvre, some went to a picture house on one of the *grands boulevards* to see *The Mark of Zorro* and a brave bunch ventured into the Goutte d'Or district to look for a brothel (four out of seven would wind up contracting crabs and return to England in a blind panic, eventually procuring some ointment from a pharmacy in Weeke). Many others went off by themselves, some taking their fags along, but Bart had no intention of taking Roger with him. He told him to meet him 'back in this exact spot' in four hours. 'If you get into any trouble, I get into trouble, so bloody well watch yourself,' he said, before booting Roger's arse as he turned to run away.

Bart bought some cigarettes and found a café. He sat outside under the low hanging branches of a cypress tree and ordered a beer. A light breeze rustled the branches above him and the sun came out sporadically from behind slow-coasting white clouds. Heaven. He ordered more drink and a bowl of garlic mushrooms hoping it would conceal the alcohol on his breath. If the headmaster really wanted to check for immoral conduct, he'd be better off smelling all the boys' cocks, because it was women they were after more than anything else (except for those subhuman bores re-treading their steps in the Louvre), and even the boys at the cinema had only gone because they'd heard rumours of loose women giving out handies in the back seats. Bart laughed to himself, imagining his classmates standing in a long row with their cocks dangling out, the head going from boy to boy and sniffing them with the snooty air of a wine-taster inhaling a new vintage. 'Hmm, this has a fully rounded and robust bouquet and I'm getting spicy and syphilitic undertones of Parisian tart.'

'*Qu'est-ce qui est si drôle?*'

It was a boy at the next table. He looked around the same age as Bart and was dressed in a sailor's uniform – white middy blouse with a black and white striped undershirt and white beret. He had large brown eyes with the thickest, darkest lashes. A blocky, squarish nose, wide at the bridge. Deep dimples. Placed in front of him was a tiny coffee cup and a leather-bound notepad and pencil. He held a fatly rolled cigarette between thumb and forefinger.

'Nothing I care to share,' said Bart.

'That's a shame.' The boy made a mock-sulky face.

Bart turned away from him and fixed his eyes on the passing people. A very tall woman dressed in trousers marched haughtily past. Bart had never seen a woman in trousers before. A man in rumpled evening wear was thrown out of a restaurant door across the road. He jumped to his feet and screamed French obscenities before dusting himself off and looking around with a dignified air of hurt feelings. A group of black men in cheap brown suits were gathered around two other black men playing chess on a granite table, talking fast and gesticulating with jerky, sophisticated movements. Bart had only seen black people a handful of times before. It was all dizzying and marvellous.

'What do you think?' Sailor boy again. He was holding up his notepad. Bart squinted to see, but the sun was flashing off the white paper. He came over, handing the notepad to Bart. It was a pencilled profile sketch of Bart, hastily done with zippy little squiggles. It caught the pleasure in his observing eyes and the sardonic twitch of his mouth.

'A fair likeness,' said Bart. 'I expect you want me to give you money for it.'

'No, no,' he said, waving his hand and taking a seat at Bart's table. He ripped out the drawing and placed it in front of him. 'It is for you, a present.'

Bart looked at the boy with nude scrutiny. 'Then I suppose you're hoping to sell me something else.'

He affected a look of bewildered, shocked hurt. 'Such sharp words! I have no need for your money. Look . . .' He took out a thick band of notes from his pocket and waved them in Bart's face.

How many cocks did you have to suck for all that? Bart thought. No, he was being mean-spirited. It was a beautiful day. Why not just let it be beautiful? He offered the boy a vague apology. 'And thank you for the sketch, it's very good. Are you an artist?'

'Yes, I'm a street artist. Also I supply satire for some newspapers.' Up so close, Bart could smell the boy's sweat. Strong and spicy.

'Aren't you a sailor?'

The boy laughed. 'Never! It looks good though, *non*?'

'It looks very good.'

The boy plucked a pre-rolled cigarette out of his packet and lit it with quick hands. 'I have a special feeling about you,' he said, smiling brightly through a fog of grey smoke.

Bart drank his beer, trying to suppress the hooks of a smile. He was being duped in some way; he was an obvious tourist and the boy a shark, and yet . . . the boy's eyes were gentle, musical and emanating an earnestness that Bart would normally find embarrassing. He seemed at ease with himself, abnormally so. And those dimples. Bettina had a name for boys like him: musky cherubs. He couldn't remember how she'd come up with it, but it probably had something to do with working-class body odour.

A waitress came out to collect glasses and the boy got her attention, ordering two beers and two shots of peach schnapps. He turned back to Bart and said, 'Please, tell me about yourself,' and Bart said, 'Fantastic, my favourite topic,' and rubbed his hands together gleefully, and they both laughed, looking at each other while trying not to look at each other.

The walls were watermarked by damp with clusters of black mould in the corners, except for one wall, which was painted a shocking bright green, but only half-heartedly, with unfinished patches and the edges not yet done, as if he'd got bored of the project halfway through or run out of paint. There was a soot-blasted fire grate topped with blocks of wood and twists of newspaper, and in singeing distance, a small table and two wicker chairs. In one corner were piles of books, some mildewed along the edges. Empty wine bottles stuffed with candles dominated every surface, save for a space on the boy's work desk, which was kept relatively clear, the woodtop stained by a constellation of ink blots. Here were signs of the boy's artistic delusions – a box of pencils and pastels, jars filled with paintbrushes and muddy water. The bed was a mattress on top of box crates, and Bart was surprised to see it made, the blankets drawn tight around the mattress; but, ruining this, an overflowing ashtray lay on the pillow, and next to it was a tattered pamphlet of pornographic drawings. A smell of piss, eggs and tobacco smoke was in the air.

'You live very differently to this,' said the boy, watching Bart with an amused expression. 'You feel disgust, I can see this.'

Bart tried to smile. 'You're a perceptive chap.'

'Artists, by their very nature, are perceptive.' He smiled ironically, as if this observation was a well-known cliché (it was) and uncorked a bottle of wine, pouring two glasses. He handed one to Bart. 'I love my home. It is mine to do what I like with. I'm not ashamed. You should be ashamed.'

Bart laughed. 'Me, ashamed? You really don't know me. Let's not talk of shame. It's the most wasteful emotion, don't you find?'

The boy gave Bart a look that seemed to him deliberately

loaded. 'I do.' He drank his wine, keeping eye contact. 'You are very trusting.'

'I most certainly am not. That is the very opposite of what I am.'

The boy shook his head. 'You come into my room. Perhaps there are other men here, waiting for me to bring you in. Terrible men, criminals, vagrants, and they are waiting for you, like this' – he rubbed his hands together lasciviously – '*Non*? I showed you my money. It was a roll of money, yes? Perhaps it was a roll of scrap paper with notes on the outside.'

'I didn't think of that.'

The boy smiled again. 'Lucky for you, nor did I.'

'How did you make that money?' Bart asked.

'Let us not talk of money,' said the boy, in a gloriously snobby English accent, his nose tilted in the air. 'It is worse than shame, don't you find?'

'Good for you,' said Bart, laughing.

The boy put his glass of wine on the floor and took off his middy blouse. He pulled off his striped undershirt, lifting it over his head so that his stomach tightened, his ribs shimmered and his skinny biceps flexed. He didn't have an ounce of fat on him. His armpits sprouted the thickest, softest-looking hair, and as the boy caught the shirt collar on his chin and struggled to get free of the article, Bart stared hungrily at that hair.

Finally he was free of the shirt. Grinning bashfully (oh, those dimples) he tossed it on the chair and picked up his wine. He took Bart's hand and brought it to his crotch. Bart felt the soft bulge – a good handful – and squeezed it until it hardened, gazing at the boy's off-white teeth.

'You're very assuming,' Bart said.

'But I am correct in assuming.' His lips apart, a string of

pearl-white saliva between upper right fang and lower right fang.

Bart downed his drink and wrapped his arms around the boy's neck, the empty glass dribbling out its last drops onto his back.

His name was Étienne, or so he said. Bart thought this a beautiful name, the 't' like a tiny melting dagger of ice in a pool of clear water. They lay intertwined, hot and sticky, sometimes kissing, other times talking. Étienne read from a book of poetry (Rimbaud) in French and Bart listened with closed eyes, his hand on Étienne's chest, feeling the vibration as he spoke. He hated poetry. But coming from Étienne (Eh-tee-enn), it was tolerable. They smoked cigarette after cigarette, accidentally tapping the ash onto each other's bodies and then wiping it off with hushed apologies. They fell asleep, and though they moved around the bed in the stuffy night, they remained together, one arm draped over a shoulder, one leg thrust between the thighs of the other, a hand loosely cupping an ear.

Bart woke up first, and, staring at Étienne's sleep-crusted eyes and wine-purpled lips, he felt a capsule of despair. His saliva tasted like cheese and a sharp stinging pain streaked up his rectum. Étienne's genitals were plastered clammily to his thigh and a great stink of garlic sweat and stale farts rose out from their joined bodies.

But then Étienne opened his eyes and smiled.

They each washed over a bidet, using a bar of dry, shrivelled soap that had to be rubbed for ages to produce any lather, and Étienne boiled up some water for coffee over a gas camping stove. He cleared all the junk off his tiny table and they sat and drank their coffee and tore chunks of olive-dotted bread, eating it with spicy sausage and tiny, sweet tomatoes. It was simple but delicious and both ate like hogs, burping throughout. Downstairs someone was playing the piano freely and the notes tinkled out and rose through the ceiling. Bart's spine tingled.

'You like it here,' said Étienne. An observation more than a question – he was often doing this.

'Well, I won't pretend I'm enamoured by your living conditions, but it does have a certain quality that I enjoy.'

Étienne scattered tobacco into a paper, rolled it up, burped and stuffed it in the side of his mouth. 'You are a rich boy and this is a quaint novelty.'

'I wouldn't call it quaint.' Bart pointed at the last slice of meat. 'Are you having that?'

Étienne shook his head and lit his cigarette with a match. 'Do you have servants at home?'

Bart nodded, chewing. 'But not as many as we used to have. Things changed after the war.'

'Poor thing.'

'I know. It's heartbreaking.'

'How many servants?'

'Six.' Bart drained his coffee and lit his own cigarette. 'That's not that many, considering,' he said, leaning back in his chair. 'It's a big house. Not quite a country mansion or anything, but fairly big, and with a decent plot of land. When my father was alive we had a staff of twelve.'

'Are you dressed by staff?'

'Lord no. I dress myself. Wash myself . . .' He tried to think of something else he did for himself. No. That was about it. He'd shined his own shoes once – he'd been in a terrible rush and couldn't find the footman. 'I'd like to drive my own car one day. Once Mother's had the Rolls re-upholstered.'

'You are so brave. How many people live in your house?'

'Well, just my mother. During term time. But she entertains most evenings and always has guests staying over.'

'Are you a kind taskmaster?'

'No. I'm a mean bastard.' He rubbed his leg against Étienne's under the table. 'I could be a kind master to you, though.'

Étienne moved his leg away. 'Please, don't make these jokes.'

'Does my way of life offend you?'

'*Mais oui*! But I like to make love with you, so for now I am not thinking of it. In the same way that you are not thinking about all this.' He waved his hand to signify the room. 'It is a *compromis* . . . uh, what is it in English? Compromise? A temporary compromise. *Oui*? Born of cock-love and foolish romantic notions. That is what this is.'

Bart nodded, eyeing Étienne analytically through the thick smoke. 'We're very honest with each other. Do you know how rare that is?'

'It is life for me. Do you want more coffee?'

'No thanks.'

'Have you fucked other boys?'

'Not like this. I'm in public school. You must have heard about English public schools. I've never kissed anyone. Just some wrist action under the covers at lights-out. You?'

Étienne waved a dismissive hand. 'I have been with many men. One night only, you see? I like you though, rich boy. That is some more truth. You make me laugh. Do you like girls?'

'I think so. You?'

'*Non*. I am flaccid with girls. But breasts – I am fond of

breasts. The female form is beautiful. And the vulva, *c'est fascinant.* Some are pretty, some are ugly, but all are fascinating.'

'And what of cocks?'

'Also fascinating. And arousing.'

'I have a friend, a girl, who is very beautiful. Lovely red hair with a wave in it, like something from a Renoir, you know? Nice breasts, not too large or small. She's a dear, dear friend too, and always up for a laugh, I'm exceedingly fond of her.'

'Is she fond of you?'

'Yes. I think I might marry her, if she'll have me, and if our parents approve.'

'Have you kissed her?'

Bart laughed. 'God no. What a terrifying prospect. She'd slap me, I'm sure of it. No – she'd kick me. She's a kicker.'

Étienne gave him a pitying look full of conceited wisdom. It was irritating. 'Bart, do as I say: kiss her. Then you will know. *Parfois*, I have seen men or boys who are, how do I say – ugly? No, that's not kind. But certainly they were not *attractive* for me. And so I have kissed these imperfect specimens, to try it, and sometimes it has been magic and we have made love with much success. Also the opposite – I've kissed beautiful men and felt nothing. It is important, the kiss. It tells us many things.'

'I don't like hearing about you making love to other men.'

Étienne shrugged.

'Listen – you don't know what the time is, do you? I'm going to be in a world of trouble. I was supposed to be back at the lodging yesterday evening.'

Étienne tutted. 'Naughty boy. What will you say?'

'I shall say that I was accosted by a sailor boy with a beautiful big cock.'

Étienne laughed. All eyelashes and dimples and fangs and loose shoulders with the sun from the window hazing his skin. 'You flatter me. *C'est très grand, oui*, but also it is horrible. I have been *told* this. "What a hideous cock!" These words.'

'Whomever told you such a thing is clearly a jealous cad.'

'What will you say, truly?'

Bart picked a strand of tobacco from his tongue and wiped it on the rim of his coffee cup. 'I might say I was attacked. Mugged. That I lay unconscious in a Parisian alleyway all night, getting pissed on by sailors and whores.'

'I think you would enjoy that.'

Bart aimed his smoke in Étienne's face.

'No sign of any attack,' said Étienne, waving the smoke away.

'You could hit me. Bloody my lip.'

'I am a pacifist.'

'You weren't last night.'

'I have never struck a person, Bart. Only to defend my life.'

'But I'll be expelled. Honestly.' He pushed out his chair and stood up, looking around the room. 'Have you got a knife?'

'What will you do with a knife, silly boy?'

'Nothing too extreme. A knife, any sort of knife.'

Étienne gestured towards the kitchen knife on the table in front of him, the one they'd used to slice the sausage. 'Only this.'

'How do you shave?'

'I don't. My beard is slow to grow. My father was the same.'

'Then how do you sharpen your pencils?'

'With the sausage knife.'

Bart looked incredulously at the knife on the table. 'Really? You walk the streets of Paris dressed as a sailor and you mean to tell me you don't carry any sort of weapon?'

Étienne laced his hands under his chin and smiled sweetly. 'My charm is my weapon.'

'Oh for God's sake.' Bart picked up the knife, wiped its blade with the bottom of his shirt and went to the small cracked mirror by the bidet. 'If this gets infected I'll give you hell.' He twisted his head to the side, parted his hair, took a breath, then pressed the knife-point to his scalp at a point over his ear. 'Christ!' He dropped the knife and clutched his head. 'Jesus fucking Christ!'

'You silly boy!' said Étienne, laughing.

Bart looked in the mirror, turning his head to the side. The cut was an inch long and shallow. Blood – not enough to fill a thimble – trickled down his face. 'It's not enough.'

'It *is* enough,' said Étienne. He came over and examined the cut. 'It's getting on your collar.'

'That's the idea. It needs to look messy. Lots of blood, more blood, if I'm to carry this off.'

'"Carry this *awf*,"' mimicked Étienne. '*Écoute*, don't mutilate yourself any further.'

'It's not convincing.'

Étienne sighed. 'The things we do.' He picked up the knife from the floor, and before Bart could stop him, sliced the blade across his palm, wincing with little flashes of teeth. He opened his hand: a fat red line, the blood already swelling and threatening to wobble out. He clenched his fist and held it over Bart's ear and the blood dripped out, joining Bart's own blood and spattering his starched white shirt. 'I would never do this for anyone else,' he said.

So full of shit. They barely knew each other. *I would never do this for anyone else*. Laughable.

Still, Bart grabbed him and kissed him fiercely, surprised to feel a pressure building up in his sinuses, as if he might cry.

*

'Bring me the salt, please,' said Bart. Since meeting Étienne he'd starting tacking a 'please' on to the end of his demands. It wasn't like he had to – the servants were paid in money, not manners. But, well, why not? It was only a word. And a very easy word – just the one syllable.

Dottie handed him the salt-shaker and he sprinkled some over his poached eggs – the first solid food he'd braved since his illness. He was wearing a dressing gown and his mother wanted to say something about it, he could tell. He forked some eggwhite into his mouth and smiled at his mother. She was done up like some sort of Egyptian peacock, all feathers and silk cloth in an explosion of clashing colours. She'd recently hosted a ball for struggling artists and clearly their grubby bohemian ideas were rubbing off on her.

'Nice?' she said.

He nodded. 'Listen, Mother,' he said, his fork held aloft, 'you don't happen to know if the trousers I was wearing when I got sick were brought back with me?'

'They were not,' she said, stirring sugar into her tea. 'You came back in your nightclothes.'

He looked down at the quivering milk-sheened yolks.

'Why do you ask?'

He shook his head, mouth drawn down at the sides. 'No reason.'

Smiling, she rolled her eyes. 'I have your key. It was put in an envelope for you. All right?'

'Key? Oh. Oh. That's not what – thank you.'

'It's none of my business,' she said. 'You're a young man.' She sipped her tea, grimacing, and added more sugar. 'Though I hope you're not so reckless as to have anything in your possessions that might get you into trouble.'

'Of course not.'

'I am not a benefactor to your school.'

'I know.'

She chewed on a piece of toast. 'Dottie? Be a dear and tell Arthur to get the car ready, would you?' She turned her attention back to Bart. 'I'm meeting Augustus John for coffee. He wants to sell me his paintings.'

'Is that why you're . . .?' He gestured at her outfit.

'Yes.' She smiled self-consciously, like an adolescent girl. 'I thought it'd be fun.'

'Be careful with him.'

'I'm not daft, Bart.' She finished her tea and got out from the table, gesturing with an aggressive wave of her hand not to get up. Another girlish smile. 'Nothing wrong with a little flirt though.'

'Oh for God's sake, Mother.'

'I'm teasing, of course.' She kissed his head on the way out, her jewellery jingle-jangling. 'Eat your eggy-weggies!'

Chapter 7

The sun was a lemon sherbet, bright yellow and hard, and beneath it bloated clouds lounged on their endless blue bed like bored courtesans.

*

Having recently read T. S. Eliot's line in 'Prufrock' about the evening sky resembling a patient etherized upon a table, Bettina had sworn to better it, or at least come up with something equally inventive. She must, she thought, remember to make a note of 'bored courtesans'. But the lemon sherbet sun could be improved upon.

She was sitting with her mother under the giant oak tree in the garden, a frail white canopy over their heads to catch the falling golden leaves. Of course, they weren't really golden – they were brown. But Mother was in one of her whimsical moods; she was reading Tennyson, sometimes interrupting

Bettina's thoughts to recite a particularly 'marvellous passage'. Bettina didn't care for Tennyson, or any of the other Romantics. She liked Edna St. Vincent Millay and Hilda Doolittle and, of course, Eliot. Anything from the previous century was tedious.

A sun like a fierce, pale lord? In keeping with the bordello theme?

She was knitting in a pair of white fingerless gloves to keep out the cold, which was creeping into her bones despite the mildness of the autumn day. She loathed knitting – it was a kind of penance, this awful clattering of needles and the inane jolliness of these poetic utterings.

They were served tea and scones for elevenses, Venetia whingeing under her breath about the 'measly dollop' of clotted cream. Henry pretended not to hear. He often pretended not to hear. As a matter of fact, he heard everything – without a doubt he'd heard about a certain incident in a certain boiler room and he'd made sure Bettina knew that he knew in the most subtle ways possible – little lingering looks, a stiffening of his shoulders as he passed by her in the house.

Heinous Henry had been working for the family for close to twenty years. He had a squashed-looking head as if he'd come into this world through a particularly tight birth canal and never recovered. He ran the house and managed the wine cellar, and he did it with perfect diligence, never putting a foot out of line. Bettina hated his guts. He was always agreeable, nodding and smarming around with his flubbery lips pursed into a dog's anus of a smile, but the poison leached out of him like sap from a diseased tree, only no one else could see it. *Wanted* to see it.

The maid came out to inform Henry and milady that they

were needed in the drawing room. Henry gave Bettina a look before he left – a malicious flash of the eyes, too brief to rebuke, like a gnat at the corner of your vision, here then gone, zip zap – and Venetia sulked off after him with many hushed exclamations, leaving Bettina alone. She tossed her knitting on the table and leaned surreptitiously to the side to let out some gas she'd been holding in all morning.

'Bettina!'

A voice from above. She cried out in surprise, the cry blessedly covering up the crackerjack emission. Leaving the shelter of the canopy, she looked up into the tree. One of the larger branches shook, causing a rustling avalanche of loose brown – not golden – leaves to fall. It was Bart, arms and legs wrapped around the branch, dangling slothlike. He wriggled along to the trunk, brought his legs down, and, finding footholds within its gnarled dips, jumped, catlike, to the grass. He picked his hat off the ground and smoothed his waistcoat down. It was marked with bits of tree muck.

'Oh, bugger,' he murmured, trying to scrape away a sticky streak with his fingernail. 'Mother's going to knock my block off.'

'What in the name of God were you doing in my tree, Bartholomew?'

Bart looked up as if just noticing his friend's existence. He strode up to her and hugged her tight.

'How long were you there?' she said.

'Long enough to wish Tennyson had never been born.'

'How did you get *up* there?'

'I was spirited up there by the very capable hands of the Archangel Gabriel.'

'Bart. Don't irritate me.'

'Wouldn't *dream* of it, darling.' He took her arm and pulled her to the other side of the tree so that they were shielded from the house and its many windows. 'I saw Heinous Henry bringing out the tables and chairs earlier, while taking my morning constitutional. So I crept up the tree and waited. Awfully uncomfortable, and at one point I lit a ciggie and almost set fire to the leaves.'

'That would have been brilliant,' she said, laughing. 'You, setting the tree on fire and then dropping to my mother's feet like a charcoaled goat. When are you returning to school?'

'Tomorrow. I got the all-clear yesterday. Goat? I'm nothing like a goat.'

'It's awful that they won't let me see you.' She kicked the head off a dandelion. 'I don't understand what this isolation is supposed to achieve.'

'It's punishment. That's all. You're just not used to it because you're spoiled.'

'So are you!'

'Of course.'

'Reverend Pigface was giving a sermon about deviance and immorality last Sunday, the usual tosh, but it felt like it was aimed at *me*. Mother made me sit in the front row, she is *such* a hypocrite, really. I felt like I should be wearing the scarlet letter. I feel sick to the stomach about it all if you must know.'

'Meet me on the beach tonight. We can talk about it.'

'God no. I'm on such a tight leash. Mother keeps checking on me in my room. Did I mention she's a hypocrite? *Awful* woman.'

Bart sucked on his bottom lip and peered around the tree, checking for snoopers. 'It's just I wanted to talk to you about something.'

'Can't you say it now?'

'No. It's not the right time. It can wait. It's stupid, anyway. Will I see you at Christmas?'

'I should think so. They can't keep me locked away forever.'

'No. They can't.' He put his hands in his waistcoat pockets. Smiled at her. 'Well. Be a good girl, won't you?'

'I've no choice in the matter.'

'And you'll write to me?'

'I always do.'

'Your dress is beautiful, by the way. Sets off your eyes.'

'I know. Thank you.'

He took his hands out of his pockets, grabbed her hand, accidentally skimming her skin with the corner of his fingernail and apologising with a shrill laugh, kissed it just above the knuckle, and jogged off with his shirt tail poking out from his trousers, like a bridegroom who has just woken up, still drunk, to find himself late for his wedding.

She read by lamplight, knees drawn up under the covers, a bowl of powder-pink bonbons on her bedside table. *The Sheik* by E. M. Hull – not as salacious as promised, but then she was only thirty pages in. She'd swapped the book jacket with an Edith Wharton one. Her mother approved of Edith Wharton, of course.

She reached for her bonbons. Her arm froze mid-stretch as a floorboard groaned outside her door.

'This is getting ridiculous,' she hissed, snatching the covers away and getting off the bed. She yanked the door open. It wasn't her mother. It was Henry. Just standing there in the dark, his legs slightly parted. She couldn't clearly see his face.

'Why are you skulking around outside my bedroom door at this hour?' she said.

'Skulking?' he said.

'Yes, skulking.' She crossed her arms over her breasts – her nightdress was a flimsy summer one; most of her clothes were still at St Vincent's.

'I was merely passing,' he said, and the way he said it, she knew he was smiling.

She reached outside the door and groped along the wall until she found the light switch. '"Until the Lord come,"' she said, flicking the switch, '"who both will bring to light the hidden things of darkness . . ."' She trailed off. The way he was looking at her – eyes lowered, showing only a peep of iris, chin tilted down. She couldn't quite code that look – it seemed a lazy sort of repugnance but also something else, something like . . . no, she couldn't articulate it.

'Go away,' she said.

'Of course,' he said.

And just as he turned to go, she noticed it – the crotch of his black trousers pouched out – *poked* out.

Something like hunger.

He strode off down the corridor and she slammed the door shut. 'Disgusting, disgusting, disgusting,' she said, glaring at the door as if it was the disgusting thing. And she remembered the rest of that Bible quote – it was from Corinthians, wasn't it? Or Isaiah? 'Judge nothing before the time, until the Lord come, who both will bring to light the hidden things of darkness, and will make manifest the counsels of the hearts.' Quite.

Chapter 8

February 1924, The Old Vic, London

The man sitting – no, slouching – in the seat opposite her was called Harold Cromwell and he was, for heaven's sake, the biggest dullard she'd ever had the misfortune to converse with. He was a filthy rich publisher specialising in maritime fiction and non-fiction, although the majority of his fortune was amassed through his dead wife, who'd contracted malaria while visiting West Africa. Maritime fiction! What was she supposed to do with that? Her father had introduced him to her at a formal dinner in Brighton last week and they'd chatted politely. That should have been that, but then she had to go and tell him about her friend Bart's debut on the London stage and, spotting an opportunity with his greedy little blueberry eyes, he'd asked if she'd like to go with him to the opening night, and she was too taken aback to think up a fast fib.

'I'm sorry, what were you saying?' she said, reaching for her champagne.

'I was saying, your friend seems to be having a jolly good bash at old Mercutio. A natural if ever I saw one.'

'Oh, yes,' she said, sipping her drink. It was the interval. Bart *was* doing well and she felt supremely proud. He captured Mercutio's cocky posturing perfectly, no surprise there, and his oration was clear and musical.

'His first night, too! I wonder, how long has he been at it? Acting, I mean.'

'Not very long, actually.'

'One would think otherwise.'

'True. One of his schoolteachers spotted the talent. In all the years I've known him he's never confessed to having any interest in the theatrical arts at *all*. He was an absolute triumph at the audition, you know.' She kept back the part about the director being a friend of Lucille's. It possibly bore no significance.

Harold fiddled with his cigar case, eyes down. 'And how long have you known him, may I ask?'

Ah, thought Bettina, and so now we come to it. 'Since we were babies really.'

'And is he settled yet? With a spouse, I mean?'

'No. So far he has thwarted all of his mother's match-making attempts.'

Harold nodded for too long. 'Right. Right. Bit of a serious business, finding the right person.'

Bettina looked at him coolly, fingers laced around the delicate stem of the flute. 'It is. One must be very choosy.'

'Right. Right. You're not wrong there. Well, shall we make our way back to our seats?'

'Do you mind if I nip to the ladies' first?'

'I don't mind at all.' He jumped up to pull her seat out. He had very weak shoulders, she thought. Like the sloping roof of a derelict barn. No – there really wasn't any need for this cattiness. He was just a sad old widower. A sad, rich old widower after a young trophy wife to flaunt to his— oh, shut up, Bettina. She picked up her purse and walked away. 'Do you mind awfully if I nip to the lavatory to slit my wrists?' she said to herself. 'Do you mind *terribly* if I nip to the lavatory to bash my skull repeatedly against the porcelain?'

The ladies' was floor-to-ceiling marble and in the centre was a grand water fountain made of coral-pink stone. A black-haired woman stood at the far end, applying lipstick in the mirror. She wore a glittering, white sleeveless gown with a turquoise sash and matching turquoise gloves and her limbs were chubby and pale. Small doll hands. Large bosom. Bettina stopped and stared, and noticing, perhaps, the sudden halting of footsteps, the woman looked over at her.

'Margo?'

The lipstick was slowly lowered and returned to the beaded evening bag open on the counter. Lips were smacked and blotted with tissue. 'Oh,' said Margo. So prim, that 'oh', so nonchalant and prim, as if her cook had just told her that the parsnips had gone bad. 'Hello, Bettina.' Her peat-black eyes cool – no: cold. What a fine display, thought Bettina, what a superb performance. Well, I'm not going to stand for it. She marched up to her old friend and grabbed her around the upper arms. '*Please* drop the frosty cow routine. You were my only friend in that rotten school and I've missed you terribly.'

Margo gaped up at her, irises jittering as she processed this. And then quite suddenly, she laughed, her jaw clanging open and her eyebrows tilting in that helpless way, and she took Bettina in her arms and held her tight, the laughter still bubbling up. I will not, thought Bettina, take pleasure in this embrace. But the way she was laughing, her whole body shaking, and all of this pressed tight against her.

Margo pulled away, wiping a tear with a gloved finger. 'I forgot how bold you are. Oh dear.' She shook her head, smiling. 'I'm so glad you just said that, because if you hadn't, I would have carried on with it and we would have bid goodbye in polite, curt voices and that would have set the tone forever.'

'I would've hated you. Honestly.'

Margo had been pulled out of St Vincent's by her father after the boiler-room disgrace and Bettina hadn't seen her since. She'd constantly wondered how she was faring, and missed her horribly during term time, forcing herself to befriend a stout American girl called Isobel who criticised absolutely everything and everyone she came into contact with and had nothing good to say about England at all (if English food was so disagreeable to her then why did she fill her face with it at any given opportunity?). She imagined Margo locked in a room at the top of her house, like Mr Rochester's mad wife, and sometimes thought, meanly, Well, where's your liberal mother now? According to Lucille, who somehow knew everyone's business, Margo's father had been on the verge of sending her to a sanatorium. Bettina's parents, though incensed about the drinking and the smearing of her reputation (*their* reputation), were a little more level-headed about *the other stuff*, since 'everyone knows this type of thing happens in boarding schools, so no need to whip the silly mares over it' (her father's words). But Margo's family had that sapphic great-aunt locked up in the attic of their history.

'I have so much to tell you,' said Margo in a frantic whisper, 'only my auntie is waiting outside for me – she's my chaperone, can you believe it?'

'Oh, I don't need a chaperone,' said Bettina, 'because the man I'm with might as well be a eunuch and has been expressly instructed to allow me only one glass of fizz.'

Margo rolled her eyes. 'Isn't it dreadful, all because of . . . anyway, it's dreadful. Bart is bloody brilliant, by the way, and so dishy – why didn't you tell me he was dishy? Oh! An idea is forming! I'm to dine at Galliano's after the show, why don't you drop the eunuch and join me? I'll just tell Auntie Vera you're a different Bettina. Someone from church or something.'

'I can't just drop the eunuch.'

'Give him the slip! Go on, it'll be a riot.'

Bettina leaned against the sink in a way she hoped looked casually elegant. 'I suppose I could just bring him. Your auntie might fancy a bit.'

Margo laughed into her hands, her arms squishing her breasts together so that they resembled two netballs poking out of a sack. 'I forgot how funny you are!' Her face creased with affected fondness, to patronising effect, and she grabbed Bettina's shoulders, holding her at arm's length. 'I'm so glad I didn't snub you like I was intending to, you're so very dear to me, despite everything.'

Bettina nodded. The space between their bodies felt charged. She wanted to grab her and kiss her, and the urge was so strong she began to blink wildly.

Margo peeled her long velvet glove from her left arm. 'If you come tonight I can tell you all about this,' she said, showing off the huge diamond on her plump doll's finger.

Bettina's mouth stretched into a ghastly parody of a smile, her cheeks like dead flesh with an electric current running through it. 'Crikey, that's a dazzler.'

Bart tossed the flowers on the floor. He looked at them, nostrils flaring, jaw flexing. Carnations and roses. He picked them back up and thrashed them against the dressing-room table, lopping their heads off. Scraps of orange and scarlet petals flew around like confetti, fucking confetti – oh, the poetry of it! He thrashed and thrashed until his fist held only stems, then he sat down, grinding the heels of his hands into his eyes so that everything became a throbbing, womb-like miasma behind the lids.

A knock at the door.

He snapped his head up and stared into the mirror. 'What?'

'A visitor,' came the muted reply.

'Who?' His face as he spat the word – petulant and swollen-eyed. A brat who does not want to eat his liver. It was going to be Keith, hoping to start something. One last grope for the road before he fucked off to his silly, deluded fiancée – well, she was in for a surprise; if he mustered even *half* a cock-stand for her on the wedding night, it would be an actual miracle. The man could put on a good show with his manly back-slaps but behind dressing-room doors he turned into a shameless cocksucker, and oh God, he was *so* good at sucking cock, and so handsome it was all Bart could do to stop himself turning into a puddle at the sight of him thrusting his sword at Tybalt with his round little arse flexing beneath the tights, and honestly, it wasn't the getting-married part that Bart had a problem with – no, it was being strung along with googly love-eyes and passionate promises. It was all so *unnecessary.*

If the man had simply said outright, 'Listen, I'm getting married soon but how about a bit of no-strings fun during rehearsals?' then things wouldn't have escalated and Bart wouldn't now be left feeling betrayed and foolish, breaking his heart over a . . . over a . . . there was just no *need* for it.

He could shove his guilty flowers up his rectum.

'Sir?' came the voice again.

'*What?*'

'Sir, you have a visitor. A Miss Wyn Thomas, sir.'

'Let her in, let her in.'

In she came, looking around the room with polite expectation, wearing a cream fur cape over an emerald gown, her hair fashioned into a crimped bob – looking gorgeous, in other words. She was exactly who he needed right now – no one else would do.

'What did those poor flowers ever do to you?' she said, seeing the mess.

'I didn't deserve them! I was awful!'

Bettina rolled her eyes. 'Oh for God's sake, you silly neurotic boy, you were simply marvellous! You had three ovations.' She shook her head. 'I shan't waste my breath; I know what you're like. And by the way, it was me who sent them. You're welcome.'

'You? Oh, I'm so sorry, darling. It's just I fluffed my line!'

'Tosh! If you did, then nobody noticed. I didn't notice.'

'Horseshit.' He had indeed fluffed it. Because of that stupid cocksucker, giving him enigmatic looks from across the stage.

'Stop over-analysing everything.' She sat in his seat. 'Well, aren't you going to give me a cigarette?'

He took his cigarette box out of his pocket and gave her one, lighting it. 'Truly, I was good?'

'Truly.'

'I'll find out in the newspapers anyway, so you might as well tell me.'

Another eye-roll. 'This is getting boring. Guess who I saw in the ladies' earlier?'

He shrugged.

'Margo. She thought you were brilliant too, by the way, et cetera et cetera. She's getting married, Bart. I feel just wretched.' She saw the champagne sticking out of the ice bucket. 'Can I have some please?'

'Of course.' He took the bottle and prised the cork out slowly. How bizarre that Bettina was going through the exact same hell as him. It would be comforting to be able to share his pain with her – that's what pals did. Perhaps he should? Right now. Well, why not? He poured the drink into two flutes and they each turned to creamy pearl foam. No, he couldn't. She'd be disgusted. He felt very strongly that she'd be disgusted, even with her own proclivities. The churning deeps of her mind would forever be a hoard for suppressed images of cocks sliding into arseholes. It all came back to cocks in arseholes in the end. No one could ever stretch themselves to imagine that love might factor into it. Cocks and arseholes – the stars of the show! 'Why do you feel wretched?' he said.

'Don't feign innocence. Ugh, I hate it. And I hate *her*. It's probably that Jasper shitbag she used to talk about. She wants me to meet her at Galliano's but I shan't be going now.'

He was waiting for the foam to settle before topping up. 'How was your dinner date? What was his name? Harold something?'

She flipped back her head and let out a small scream. 'Argh, I hate it, Bart. He's just like the others. He's outside now, in the foyer, waiting for me. He was talking to the valet about steamship propellers when I left him. Can you imagine? God. My father must be snickering to himself about it. Why can't I have dinner with just one tasty man?'

He passed her a full glass and took a sip from his own. 'I think you'd rather a tasty woman.'

'Shut up, Bart. I won't be defined by just one regretful incident.'

'Regretful? I do seem to recall you saying that you enjoyed it.'

'Did I say that?'

He nodded.

'I hate it when people remember what I've said.'

'I think you should go to this dinner. Size up the rival.'

She shook her head and looked darkly into her glass. 'I don't want to see her ever again.' She lapsed into thoughtful silence, her shoulders sagging and her fingers fidgeting with the stem. Then she abruptly downed the rest of her drink and stood up. 'I'd better get back to my Prince Charming before he sends the valet to sleep.' She grabbed his face, one hand on each cheek, and pulled it down to plant a kiss on his forehead. 'You really were brilliant out there. You have a shining career ahead of you, if you wish to continue this petty rebellion against your mother.'

She still had hold of his face. He could see lipstick on her teeth. 'Oh, she can't complain too much,' he said. 'It's not as though I'm juggling fish in an East End music hall. "O O O, I'm Shakespe*hearian*, darling. So elegant, so intelligent."' He placed his hands over her hands, closing his eyes like a petted cat. He *so* wanted to tell her everything. His heart was smashed to pieces.

She left and he poured himself another glass. Her scent

stayed in the room, a lovely jasmine fragrance that he knew she sprayed liberally on her cleavage.

Another knock at the door.

'What is it?'

'It's me.' Keith.

Bart opened the door, drink in hand.

Keith smiled nervously. 'Can I come in?'

'No. Go home to your fiancée if you want your dick sucked.' And he slammed the door shut.

The next night, he knew something was wrong as soon as he entered the darkened auditorium. Actors and actresses were milling about half dressed in front of the stage when normally they'd be in their dressing rooms by now, putting on make-up, whining about the director, or – as in the case of old Spencer Hughes, who played the friar – shovelling stimulants up their noses. Tybalt was smoking a cigarette, his codpiece hanging half fastened and the buttons of his blouse undone. Agatha Chalmers, who played Lady Capulet, was sitting on the edge of the stage with her legs dangling childishly and her head jerking around like that of a nervous ostrich. She was dressed in a velvet cobalt-blue dress, the corset loose, and had a dowdy grey winter coat draped over her shoulders. Bart tapped her on the ankle to get her attention. 'What's going on, love?'

She leaned down in a conspiratorial manner, her eyes darting left and right, and said, 'Keith's been arrested.'

'Arrested? What in the world for?'

'You'll never guess,' she said, eyes boggling out of her head.

From this angle he could see up her nose – two red caves. 'I have no intention of guessing. Spit it out, will you.'

She pulled a haughty, offended look. 'I see, the good sir does not appreciate a build-up. Well, fair enough. Only, I am an actress with a flair for dramatic tension.'

You bloody well are not, you silly asinine whore, he thought. 'Agatha. Please.'

'As you like it. He was arrested last night for – actually, I can't remember the precise terminology for the offence, but it was the same thing that did for Oscar Wilde.'

Bart felt the skin on his face tightening. 'Gross indecency.'

'That's the one,' she said, nodding with prim lips. She leaned closer and cupped a hand to the side of her mouth. 'Sodomy,' she whispered. 'Up the bum and all that.' He could see flecks of green caught in her big yellow mule teeth. 'He was caught in the bushes of Hyde Park. Only two days till his wedding day, too. I just can't *imagine* what that poor girl is going through, though let's be honest – anyone can see the man's not a regular sort, so perhaps she should take better care choosing husbands in the future.' Agatha leaned back, satisfied with herself, took a tin of humbugs out of her coat pocket and popped one into her mouth. 'An hour till curtains and we've got *Romeo and Juliet* without a Romeo and the understudy is throwing up his lunch in the men's lav. So it's safe to say we're buggered.' A pause. 'Though not as much as Keith, I dare say.' And she cackled – you could never call it a laugh, it was certainly a cackle – her caruncled old turkey throat shivering and her mouth flung open with the humbug perched moistly on her tongue.

'Bloody choke,' he whispered, walking away.

Chapter 9

September 1924, London

She'd been staying with her cousin Petunia almost two months now in a huge Georgian house near Twickenham which overlooked the Thames. Petunia as a child had been an absolute brat – an under-table pincher, a petty blackmailer, a pot-stirrer, always ready to run to the parents with a twisted version of facts which placed her as the victim. She was thick-waisted and over freckled with thick, springy red hair that drew (unflattering) comparisons to Queen Elizabeth.

As an adult she was much changed. She now possessed the most full, sensual, plum-skinned mouth which served as her centrepiece and encouraged one to forgive any other imperfections – her freckles hadn't gone anywhere and her hair was the same frizzy mess, impervious to even the most brutal of treatments and therefore hidden always under a silk scarf or a cloche hat. She had enormous breasts, one noticeably far bigger than the other, a pot belly and shapely legs. Her eyes were a lovely green, her voice husky; she sounded like a fifty-year-old woman who'd chain-smoked since adolescence. She made everyone call her Tuna, as she was, in her own words, 'more fish than flower'. She didn't seem to mind how long Bettina stayed for, enjoying a busy house and putting on lavish meals almost every night for artists, intellectuals and other such 'free-thinkers'. Her husband Max was abroad most of the time and she was, by her own admission, terrified of being alone.

Jonathan came to visit on some weekends, staying in the guest room two doors down from Bettina. Her brother liked to go to museums and cricket matches but disliked clubs and pubs, and in the evening stayed in playing cards or snooker with whichever of Tuna's guests horrified him least. Only one night had Bettina succeeded in dragging him out to a club, and he'd refused to dance with her, predictably, remaining seated at a table and watching the band with a look on his face as if he were on the verge of throwing up. She called him a bore and danced with various men, drinking cocktails between songs, and it wasn't until she was properly drunk that she was jolted by an epiphany: Jonathan didn't like loud noises in confined spaces because Jonathan had fought in the trenches. How ridiculously obvious! What a thoughtless, self-involved boob she was – really, what a child. 'Let's go,' she said to him, taking his hand (clammy, of course) and leading him out of the club. They went home, raided Tuna's larder and stayed up till five in the morning, playing tiddlywinks and eating French cheese.

It wasn't as if she could ask Bart to go dancing either, because

Bart was being a perfect misery lately, often choosing to stay in and drink by himself. Ever since that actor friend of his got busted for that grubby business in the park. Which was interesting – tick-tock went her thoughts, tick-tock, tick-tock, what's up, Mr Dawes? And she remembered something her father had once said – back when Bart was nearing adolescence, this was. Venetia and Monty had been arguing about whether to let Bart and Bettina go on an Easter egg hunt alone together – there'd been a big hoo-ha about it, with Monty being dead against it, Venetia trying to change his mind and Lucille oblivious to the fact that a battle was even taking place. Bettina had listened to the argument through their bedroom door (as she often did) and heard her father say, 'Mind you, I'll admit this much: there's as much chance of that boy taking a fancy to Betsy as there is of me mounting a house cat, mark my words.' Tick-tock, tick-tock.

The pale mauve moon was just visible from a slit in the carriage curtains and a hanging lantern slowly swayed, its orb of light swelling and shrinking, swelling and shrinking, and the darkness surrounding it like a gently squeezing hand. And then there was the lovely clip-clop of the horses. Bettina felt serene and snug, the alcohol a light heat in her belly and veins – this one had broken the one-drink rule, topping her up after every mouthful practically. And *this* one was gorgeous.

'Can I have one?' she asked, as he took out his Turkish cigarette case.

'Of course.' His thigh pressed against hers.

His name was Francis Fitzgerald. He had wavy black hair slick with pomade, the parting down the side so straight and white it was like a perfect scar, and a long beautiful nose.

Isobel, her American friend from St Vincent's, had introduced them at a garden party in Buckinghamshire and Bettina had looked at him and felt immediately floored by his good looks – giddily and blushingly floored. She asked him if he'd ever considered crossing the Atlantic and trying his luck in Hollywood and he'd laughed and said, 'You've no idea how many people have said that exact thing to me.' And she'd understood that it was a question he was bored by, but not coming from *her*. 'I have no acting talent, not like your friend, Mr Dawes.' She tilted her head back and said, with a playful smile, 'I'm sure you have other talents.' She was not one given to flirting, in fact she found it vomit-inducing, but she couldn't have this marvellous specimen dismissing her as an attached woman. Bart was someone she need only dangle in front of the eunuchs and crustaceans.

'Why a carriage?' she asked him now. 'Are you trying to invoke a romantic atmosphere in order to seduce me?'

He laughed. 'I have two answers to that question: the one I tell most women, and the truth. Which would you rather?'

'Both.'

'All right. It's because I believe both in embracing modernity *and* preserving the past. Motorcars are our future, yes, as well as electric lights and telephones in every house and the vote for all women. But why completely dismiss the methods of the past?'

'Is that the truthful answer?'

'No, that's what I say in order to impress women.'

Bettina wasn't sure about the way Francis showed his inner workings. It was designed to flatter her ego – it was saying, You, and only you, are beyond the superficial frivolity of most other females.

'And what is the truth?' she said.

'I'm scared of motorcars.'

She laughed. 'Really?'

'Yes, really. Have you ever seen a crash? They crumple like tinfoil and the poor blighter stuck inside gets smashed to bits. I saw a chap once go flying through the windscreen. He was almost decapitated. His head was hanging on by a thread.'

'Oh my word.'

He placed a hand on her forearm. 'I'm sorry, dear. Was that too much?'

She nudged him with her elbow. 'I am not made out of flowers.'

'No, I dare say you're made out of thorns!'

She elbowed him again and he clasped a hand over his ribs as if mortally wounded.

'Don't be silly,' she said.

'You *make* me silly.' He took her hand and lifted it to his lips, looking silkily at her. His pale blue irises just around the pupils were flecked with tiny splinters of brown – but no one would ever say that. They would say gold.

This was it. He was going to make his move. Her legs were locked shut, the bony nubs of her ankles digging into each other. Staring at his just-open mouth, she relaxed her shoulders and then her legs, leaving a small, shivery gap between the knees. He took the cigarette out of her hand and tossed it out of his window – a flurry of amber sparks streaked the rushing black. This was it. He leaned in and let his lips stop just short of hers, his breath mingling with her breath. He kissed her, very softly. She kissed back, reaching up to stroke the back of his neck, which after all was the done thing. She took his tongue in her mouth and curled her fingers through his hair. The done thing. She imagined how they must look together – marvellous. He licked the soft wet flesh of her lower lip and she let out a little moan, and immediately distrusted the sincerity of it. He trailed a fingertip down her throat and chest and traced a spiral around the cloth-muted bump of her nipple. Another moan, a handful of his oily hair, an arching of her back. This is something I've read in a book, she thought, or seen in a picture. I'm playing a part. The weight of his body pushed her down on the seat and he was over her, on her, slipping a hand under her dress and trying to fumble his fingers inside her underwear. The carriage went over a bump and he grabbed her to stop her slipping off the seat. He was breathing hard and she was also breathing hard, and for the life of her, she didn't know how much of this panting was real and how much performed, and she guessed maybe it was a forty/sixty split – but then, if she was capable of roughing out percentages while his fingers were dabbing at the moistness down there, then it could hardly be that real, more like twenty/eighty, and admittedly, there was that moistness, she was wet and tingling, but if it had been Margo's hand down there, she would not be thinking of numbers and ratios, she would not be thinking at all.

He fidgeted a finger inside her and she gasped, in shock this time, not pleasure or performed pleasure in some silly estimated ratio, in genuine shock, because things had gone quite far enough. She pushed him away and he fell to the carriage floor with a heavy thud.

'Jesus Christ!' he yelled.

She sat up straight and shuffled to the very end of the seat, her shoulder pushed up against the door. She put her left breast back into her dress and smoothed down her hair. Clamped her legs together.

He climbed back onto the seat and stared furiously at her.

'Well, what the *hell* did you expect?' she said.

'You can't *do* that to a man,' he said.

'I bloody well can!' She let out a long breath, blinking rapidly. 'Do you think I'm a whore, Francis?'

He moved his mouth but no words came out.

'I'll ask again: do you think I'm a whore?'

'Of course not, I—'

'Seriously, Francis, did you think you were going to take my virginity in the back of a bloody carriage? Seriously?'

'You were leading me on!'

'I let you kiss me. I did not sign a contract offering you my virginity. Do you think I'm a bloody idiot, to let you do that to me?'

'You might have put a stop to it sooner.'

'You might not have started it! Really, I feel quite irritated by you right now, Francis. You top up my drinks and flatter me because I'm *so* bloody different to all the other girls, *so* bloody interesting, but actually, your motives were very singular, very ruthless.'

He shifted around on his seat and ran a hand through his hair, wiping the grease onto his trouser leg. 'I'm sorry. You're right. It's just, I thought you were the kind of girl who might like to, you know, have a bit of – I don't know, I mean . . . you like to drink and smoke and I—'

She let out a harsh bark of a laugh. 'So a woman who smokes automatically opens her legs to men? What an idiotic correlation. My mother smokes, why don't you test that theory out on her? Go on. Drive down to Brighton in your whimsical hansom and fuck my mother in a cloud of her tobacco smoke.'

He raised his hands in surrender. 'I'm sorry, really, I'm sorry.

My judgement was poor this evening. I haven't behaved like a gentleman.'

She scrutinised his face. It was pale and wretched and vulnerable. A child caught at the sugar bowl. She crossed a leg over a knee and leaned back. 'Well, I haven't exactly behaved like a lady, either. Let's have a cigarette and forget the whole thing. A cigarette, by the way, is merely a paper tube filled with tobacco and not a symbolic guarantee of sexual intercourse. You'd do well to remember that, hotstuff.'

Francis laughed and she laughed and the tension flew out of the window. He passed her a cigarette. 'You're awfully fun, Bettina. I feel like I've wasted you tonight. Treated you like a conquest when I should have been treating you as – well, as a serious prospect. I do hope we can still be friends.'

'Of course.' She reached out and patted his hand. She wasn't angry with him. In fact, she was probably being a hypocrite about the whole thing. 'I'd like you to drop me off at the Chelsea. I want to visit a friend.'

He nodded, cigarette wobbling in his mouth, and then leaned over to instruct his driver. His buttocks were divine. But then, so were sunsets and thunderstorms and Debussy's nocturnes.

'Little cleft in his chin?' said Bart, pointing to his own chin.

'Yes.'

'I know of him. Been to a few of the same parties. Tragically good-looking, you're not wrong there.'

Bettina opened the window (the room was smelly). The stars and moon were concealed by fog. London was horrible, actually. Down below, a hatless woman covered in sores was sitting on a bench, loudly sobbing and kissing what looked like a photograph. There – horrible. She blew smoke out of the window, watching the breeze snatch it away. 'Quite charming too, Barty. He knew exactly what he was doing.'

'Oh, I don't doubt it.' Bart came over and handed her a drink. He was unshaven and sleepy-eyed. He kept yawning and his tongue was crusted yellow. 'Well done you for thwarting his advances.'

'Well, it wasn't that difficult. My heart wasn't in it.'

'No?'

She shook her head, sipping at her drink. 'I won't lie, my body responded. Somewhat. I mean, I think I could have gone through with it and it wouldn't have been *entirely* disgusting.'

Bart went over to the gramophone and set the needle over the record already in place – his current favourite, 'Crazy Blues' by Mamie Smith. He was forever playing it – a cry for help probably. 'The thing is,' she continued, 'there was something missing. Know what I mean? No frisson, no passion. I felt . . . clinical.' Clinical yet wet, she wanted to say.

Bart sat in his armchair, draping a long pyjama'd leg over the other, and held his drink with both hands. 'You don't need me to tell you why, do you?'

A melancholy, dead-eyed shrug. 'He was so handsome.'

'And yet . . .?'

'And yet.' She sat on the floor by his feet, resting her head against his thigh and closing her eyes. Half-listening to the woman sing about her horrible life and horrible man. He ran his hands through her hair, his fingers grazing her scalp. 'How are you feeling, my lovely boy?' she said.

He sighed. 'A bit down, actually.'

'Oh? I had no idea. You've been such a joy.' She got up and climbed into his slippery lap (his pyjamas were silk). 'You can tell me anything, you know,' she said, running her finger along the small scar just over his right ear.

'I can't.'

'I tell you everything.'

'Nobody tells anybody *everything*.'

'Oh, shut up. I tell you as much as I'll ever tell anyone.'

He stared at her. His eyes were glassy and the skin around his nose was tightening and wrinkling, as if he was suppressing tears. 'You don't have to tell me anything,' she said, gently. 'But I bet that if you do, I'll be the most understanding person *ever*, literally ever, in the whole wide world. And I'll bet you something else . . .'

'What?'

'I bet I already know what's wrong. It doesn't take a genius.'

'Bet you anything you don't.'

She rolled her eyes. How boring. 'Will he tell me, will he not tell me, when will he bloody tell me?' She grabbed his face and twisted it so that he couldn't look away. 'You like men.'

He stared at her, his eyes fierce, his cheeks squished between her hands. She wanted to laugh – those fierce eyes coupled with the puffed cheeks and his lips like a sausagey figure eight. But this was a serious moment. What if he grew angry and denied everything? Perhaps she'd got it wrong after all; perhaps she was trying to make him the same as her so that she'd feel less . . . yucky; perhaps, these last couple of months, she'd built up this convenient, neat narrative, romantic in its way, with the two friends fantastically mirroring each other's persuasions, two best friends, the same all along, the same since childhood, when in actual fact, Bart was simply in love with a married woman or anxious about finances or dissatisfied with his career. How disgustingly alone she would feel.

'Marry me,' he said.

She let go of his cheeks. 'What?'

'Marry me.'

'Jesus, Bart. What are you trying to prove?'

He sat up straighter and again stared into her face, but this time with urgency. 'Nothing. You're right – I like men. I do, I fucking well do! And you like women. Let's get married. We love each other, don't we?'

She climbed off his lap, dazed, and headed straight for the drinks table. She poured wine into a fresh glass and downed it. Bart had followed her over and was standing next to her. 'Think about it,' he said. 'Take as long as you like.'

'You're genuinely serious?' she said, lighting a cigarette with shaking hands.

'Oh, I'm deadly serious! I think this might be the best idea I've ever had. Think about it, Betts: we live together, as friends. Perhaps we have children,' he waved a hand, 'some way or other, I don't know. We have people over for dinner, we behave like we always do, we have parties, we have fun, we go for long walks and have lovely darling picnics. If you meet a girl you like, I look away, if I meet a boy I like, you look away. No judgement, no shame, no secrets.'

'Us, have children? Are you joking?'

'Pretend I didn't say that bit. But the rest . . . can't you see?' He went over to the gramophone and put a new record on, a lively jazz number. He was smiling and tapping his slippered foot. 'Don't you see how lucky we are? Two good friends with the exact same – with the same problem and the means to help each other out? Don't you see how – look, just . . . it's almost as if . . . it's almost as if . . . no, I won't bring God into this. But it does whiff of fate. Something like that.' He looked at her with his hands spread out. 'Look. Imagine this: you marry a man. You have to sleep with him most nights. Maybe he's gorgeous like Francis and you tolerate it. By the way, I'm exceedingly attracted to Francis. I can say that now.' He laughed, almost manically. 'Oh my God, I'm so fucking relieved! You're married to this man, Betts, and let's say you grow fond of him. Like – he's like a Labrador who follows you around all the time. But after a year of this? Two years, ten years? You pretend to have a headache some nights, but you can't have a headache that lasts forty years. Are you seeing this? Do you want this?'

'Of course not! But it might not go that way! Some people are just very picky. And there was . . . I might just be very picky.' *And there was that wetness* – that's what she'd been about to say.

He gave her a look of mildly disgusted impatience, the sort her father excelled at. 'Horseshit. It's horseshit. I *know* you. Marry me, Bettina. Don't you see how perfect this is? We always said we'd get married, as children, don't you remember?' He was pacing now, his cigarette going from mouth to hip, mouth to hip, little blasts of smoke jettisoning from the side of his mouth. 'You've always considered yourself a rebel, Betts, always sneered at the common arrangements, the stale institutions and all that, and now, well, here's your chance to show you're not all talk, like your parents.' He was packaging this for her in a way he knew would entice, just like that time he'd made her eat the worm – only the bravest, boldest girl would dare eat a worm. Only the rarest trailblazer would sham-marry her queer best friend. 'And I'll tell you something else, Betts: I would mean my vows. Honest to God, I would. Well, except the fidelity bit.'

She looked at the glowing tip of her cigarette thoughtfully. 'This Keith fellow. Were you and he intimate?'

He nodded, his jaw clenching.

'And did you – I mean, have you—'

'Of course I have.'

'You don't even know what I'm going to ask you.'

'You're going to ask if me and Keith ever—'

'No, I wasn't. I was going to ask if you've ever done what he's done. Hyde Park at midnight and all that.'

'Oh. Well. Why do you ask?'

She gave him a withering look. 'Really, you have to ask? You want me to be your wife and you have to ask? Clearly you haven't thought this whole thing through.'

'I never judged you over the Margo business.' He sucked too hard on his cigarette and coughed out smoke, his eyes watering. 'Now, see, this is why I didn't want to tell you in the first place!'

'This isn't about judgement, you big nit. Just put yourself in my shoes for a moment. Yes – now it's *your* turn to imagine hypothetical situations. I'm your wife, everything's all tickety-boo, and then one night I get arrested for, I don't know' – she rolled her eyes – 'canoodling with some strange woman in a shrubbery at Hyde Park or Hampstead Heath – don't *laugh*, Bart, I know it's absurd. But listen – the next morning it's splashed all over the papers and not only is my reputation ruined forever, so is yours.'

Bart was still laughing, a hand over his mouth. 'A shrubbery?'

'If you want me to take this seriously, then so must you.' It *was* funny. Though why it should be funny that women do this, and not men, she had no idea.

'You might not believe me,' he said, 'but I haven't *ever* done anything like that. Nor will I.' He didn't quite look at her as he said this – a flickering glance. 'I'm in the theatre, I've no shortage of opportunities. Fairies practically falling from the rafters!'

The fast song finished and was followed by a slow waltzy number.

'You'd have to be extremely careful,' she said.

'It sounds as though you're considering this.'

She shrugged. 'It's a very pragmatic idea. I'm just not convinced yet that it's necessary. I haven't given up on myself. I'd like you to give me another year.'

'Really? You'll marry me in a year?'

'Maybe. If.'

'If?'

'Yes, *if*. Surely you can wait another year for your inheritance.'

'Oh, piss off,' he said, smiling. 'If I was that keen to come into my inheritance I would've married the first inbred society whore my mother nudged my way.' He held out his arms and ushered her over. 'Why do that when I already have the prettiest inbred society whore right here?'

She fell into his arms, laughing. 'I *knew* you were going to make that joke.'

They held each other and swayed to the music. 'Did you love Keith?' she said.

'No. No. Infatuated, I think.'

'His Romeo was wonderful.'

'It was all right.'

She felt his arm move about and heard the 'puh' sound of him sucking on his cigarette and then smelled the smoke drifting around her head, and still they moved together, slowly, and she imagined how it would be to be joined to this man forever. What would their life look like? Him in a smoking jacket entertaining other men after dinner, she playing cards with her friends, the tinkling of ice cubes in glasses and creaking leather seats and the monotonous droll chatter, their bedrooms separate but close – is that how it would work?

Anyway, it wouldn't come to that.

Chapter 10

September 1925, Longworth House, Brighton

'Oh God, oh God, oh God.'

'Stop fidgeting, will you?' said Lucille, her long nails grazing his Adam's apple as she scrabbled with the tie. 'I can't do it if you don't keep still.'

He grimaced. Her perfume was a warcry of rosehip and citrus. 'I'm dying of nerves, Mother.' They were in the drawing room. Lucille's domestic staff were at the church, along with everyone else, dismissed early not for their sake, but hers; in the next hour, he would belong to another woman and she clearly wanted to savour the dwindling moments of possession. She'd been fussing with the tie for the last five minutes, determined to get it 'ship-shape'.

'Nerves are a good sign.' She tugged at the fabric. 'You know, your father always insisted I do this for him. He'd let the valet do it first – now what was his name? For the love of God, will you keep still? Anyway, your father'd let him do it first, then he'd come to me and say it wasn't done properly, which was never true, and I'd undo it and start over. I think it had something to do with intimacy. You know he was very guarded and cool with people.'

Cold, Bart thought. Freezing cold.

'So, me fiddling around near his throat – well, it's the most vulnerable spot on a person, the throat. Next to the guts.'

'He wanted you to mother him,' said Bart.

Lucille rolled her eyes. 'There, done.' She pulled away from him, smiling. 'A very fine figure you cut, I must say.' Her mouth started to crumple and she jerked her head, sniffing. 'I'll hold it in. Save it for the vows.' She took her cigarettes from her purse and lit one. 'You know, I might be a little jealous of you. You're getting to spend the rest of your life with someone you actually like. You can laugh with each other. Your father didn't have much of a sense of humour.'

'He didn't have one at all,' said Bart. He couldn't remember his father ever laughing, which was shocking, if you stopped to think about it. How could someone never laugh and still call themselves a human being? Even lawyers laughed. His father had been missing something very vital – a soul, perhaps. But the funny thing was, the man had felt a great kindness towards animals and even refused to eat meat. Hunting he looked down upon with an indignant, hot-eared fury. He had over ten dogs and he fussed over them incessantly. When they died he wrapped them in blankets and carried them through to the garden and personally buried them, rain, shine, day, night, his face blanched and grim, his eyes belonging to a medieval martyr. Haunted – that's how he looked. Bart had a very vivid memory of watching his father through his bedroom window dig a grave late at night, plunging the shovel in the earth and digging it out in a perfect metronomic rhythm, pausing sometimes to wipe the sweat from his forehead with a black – yes, black – handkerchief while his mother stood by holding a lantern, clearly bored witless; shuffling from one leg to the other to keep warm and glancing up at Bart in the window every so often. Father gently dropped the blanketed lump into the hole, stood stiffly for a minute, silently mouthing a prayer, and then shovelled the earth back in. He didn't cry but he exhibited the characteristics of great suffering. Bart and his mother hated those fucking dogs.

Lucille stubbed out her cigarette in the ashtray. 'I'm going to tell you something now that will make you horribly uncomfortable.'

'Oh God.'

'Shush. Your father isn't around to impart any advice, so it falls to me. Son, if you want to have a successful marriage you must remember something that very few men do: pleasure is a two-way street.' She held her hands up. 'That is all I will say.'

'Thanks for that,' he said. 'I don't suppose you've thought to provide any diagrams depicting particular techniques?'

'Cut the sass.'

'I hear everyone's raving about the clitoris these days. Might you have a photograph you can—'

'Oh shut up, you horrible child,' she said, boxing his shoulder. 'I'd better re-join the other clucking hens. See you at the church.' Another kiss, a lingering hug, another wet-eyed smile, and she wafted out.

He slouched into an armchair, closing his eyes. The window was open and he could hear the birds in his mother's aviary twittering and singing. She'd had the aviary installed just after his father died – before that it'd been a conservatory and before that, a stable; a horrible, blood-soaked stable where his little sister had met her end. It was a large hexagonal structure, painted white, with a little domed roof. It sat near the edge of the croquet lawn, which had once been a huge kennel for all those stinking hounds his father favoured. Everything had changed after he died – the house quickly brightened and lightened, the raincloud having scudded on. All his stuffed owls and badgers and wall-mounted stag heads (those awful glass eyes following you around!) were donated to a gentlemen's club in Portslade, along with all the dark, ancient portraits of self-satisfied men in white wigs, and soon sixteen pretty, chirruping birds arrived to fill the new aviary – canaries, lovebirds, finches, lorikeets. '*I* choose life,' Lucille had told him.

Bart took out and re-read the letter he'd received this morning. '*Mon petit fleur du mal*,' it began. It was an encouraging letter – Étienne approved of the marriage, telling him of wealthy 'acquaintances' (never friends – he was only 'acquainted' with the rich) who'd done a similar thing in order to protect their reputations or come into their inheritances or both. 'For some it has been a disaster because they are strangers, very desperate and hurried. But for others it has yielded harmonious results. It will go well with you, I think, because you are, as you say, like *frère et soeur*, but you must try not to be an arsehole or she will divorce you.' He ended the letter with his usual affirmations of love and told him to please come and say hello during his visit (Bart and Bettina were headed to Paris for the first stage of their honeymoon) but not at the expense of his time with his new wife, 'because you will only ever have one honeymoon, but you will always have me.' But, he added, 'if you do decide to come and see me, this is what will be waiting for you:' and overleaf Étienne had sketched an intricate life-size portrait of his erect penis.

The last time Bart visited Paris had been three months ago. It'd been the usual order of business – frantic lovemaking, constant bickering and too much drinking. It was June and hot enough inside the garret to curdle milk within hours of buying it. They went about naked, Étienne sat on the chair sketching Bart as he prepared a simple dinner – he was trying this new technique of focusing on the light reflected off the body, neglecting all else ('We are made of light, everything is light') and the finished paintings were multi-layered blobs of white and silver oil paint exploding out of a shape that might be human. They went out only once, to a restaurant, and halfway through the meal, Bart offered to book a night in the Hôtel Plaza Athénée and Étienne was insulted. 'Well excuse me,' said Bart, 'for wanting to sleep in a bed that isn't crusted with a thousand layers of jism.' Étienne slammed his glass on the table and stormed off. Bart apologised later in bed, crawling down to kiss the old stains on the sheets, saying, 'I think this is my favourite patch, because it has earthy undercurrents of garlic,' and all was forgiven.

A knock at the door and a voice: 'Are you decent?' It was Jonathan, Bettina's brother.

Bart stuffed the letter back in his pocket. 'Yes.'

Jonathan came in, looking pale and squiffy and more nervous even than Bart himself. But this was his natural state. He wore his suit well, sharp-shouldered and slender as he was. His thick auburn hair was swept back and he'd shaved off his beard and moustache for the occasion. His throat above the tie was shave-grazed and pink, and this, coupled with the blush-red of his jug-handle ears, provided the only colour to his otherwise pallid demeanour. His prosthetic arm lay next to his body as stiff as a pastry roller, a cream kidskin glove covering the false hand.

Bart had once had a crush on Jonathan. A subconscious sort of crush that he never dared express, even within the secret-safe regions of his own skull. Hero worship, he convinced himself, though Jonathan hadn't been heroic, was in fact socially awkward and had digestive problems which led to uncontrollable cabbagey flatulence. But he was more kind than most boys his age, once even standing up for Bart against the bullying little cunts they played rugby with, and he had the most rippled, perfect body and powerful, bulging thighs. He was a good swimmer (before the war, obviously) and always at the beach. When no one else was around, he'd take his bathing suit off and swim naked. He had a humongous pair of ginger balls and an impressive fat willy, even at the age of fourteen. Bart had had his first erection watching him backstroke through the waves, his sun-bright cock bobbing around in the creamy sea spray.

Jonathan had returned from the war a shivering lettuce of a man, and it was heartbreaking, because he was also a man who insisted on maintaining a cliff-high dignity, hiding his anxiety as it bubbled up lava-like, and affecting a high-chinned, pinch-lipped, bolt-jawed poise. Watching him overcome his jitters was like watching a three-legged ant successfully carry a leaf up an incline – you couldn't help but root for him. Bettina, in her less self-absorbed moments, worried about him and tried to talk to him, to coax out all his traumas as if they were fleas picked off a dog, easily squashed, but Jonathan was not one to talk about his feelings. Lately, he'd taken to drinking, and though he never allowed himself to get visibly inebriated, he was constantly taking nips from a silver hip flask he kept in his coat pocket. Not that Bart was in a position to judge.

'Spot of whisky, old chum, old boy?' said Bart now.

Jonathan nodded thankfully. Bart poured a drink and passed it to him, before realising that he was holding it out towards Jonathan's prosthetic hand. He let out a shrill giggle and passed it to the other hand, sloshing some of the drink. 'Bottoms up,' he said, and they tapped glasses and drank. They stood there a while in aching silence, their eyes on their drinks.

'So,' said Bart, finally. 'Ever plan on walking up the aisle yourself one day?'

'Well, I'm not exactly a hot prospect at the moment.'

'You're rich, aren't you?'

Jonathan ignored this, furrowing his brow so subtly you could almost miss it.

'I shall have a word in Bettina's ear and ask her to aim the bouquet your way.'

A small, tight smile. 'The motor will be here soon.' He drained his glass. 'Thanks for the drink. And – um. Well. Thank you for asking me to be your best man. It was kind of you.'

Bart opened his mouth to protest – what do you mean, kind? It has nothing to do with kindness, you're a stand-up chap, blah blah blah. What was the point? It was obvious to everyone involved that the only reason he'd asked Jonathan to be his best man was because it would make Bettina happy. Bart patted his arm, thankfully the correct one.

'Look after my sister, won't you?' said Jonathan. 'She's not as tough as she makes out.'

'Oh, I know that. And I will.'

The sound of a car pulling up outside the house and then an insanely loud, jubilant honk of the horn.

Both men turned to look at the whisky decanter, and noticing this, their shared desire, they laughed. They had something in common, after all.

'Stop the car!'

Bart flung his door open and pushed his head out of it as the car was still moving, his vomit streaking backwards and splattering the flank. Jonathan, in the seat next to him, gripped his shoulder to stop him falling out. As the car lurched to a stop, a pendulum of bile hanging off Bart's lip violently wobbled and then stretched, landing on the gravel path. He pulled his head back inside and let out a long, wavering groan. Jonathan's hand still gripped his shoulder.

'Perhaps you've drunk too much?' he said.

Bart shook his head. 'Nerves.'

Jonathan offered him a cigarette and he took it with trembling hands. Wedding jitters, him? Really?

Bettina hadn't needed a year to make up her mind after all. She agreed to the marriage after confessing to making a terrible mistake with Francis; she'd gone all the way with him, desperate to prove that it would be an agreeable act after all, but of course it wasn't.

'It was horrible,' she told him afterwards, her eyes puffy and mascara-streaked. 'I just lay there like a . . . like a bloody *turkey* – don't you *dare* laugh – and I felt absolutely nothing, except for pain – of *course* it hurt, I expected it to *hurt*, but in that pain-pleasure way that women are always whispering about. And he was just there, looming over me with this awful vapid expression. Don't *laugh*!' Her brows were knitted but there was that spark of mirth in her eyes that never really went away; even in the midst of genuine pain – and it was genuine – Bettina was still trying to be funny. 'Well, it's my own fucking fault, isn't it?'

'Enough of this nonsense,' he told her, squeezing her cod of a hand, 'before you get yourself in real trouble. Marry me.'

She frowned thoughtfully, picking dry skin off her lip. 'Get on your knees and do it properly. I'm serious.'

'All right,' he said, getting down on his knees.

'I know marriage is a farce and all that,' she said, 'but I fear that if we're too frivolous about it, it'll be a bad omen.'

'Right you are,' he said, pulling off his father's Eton ring and holding it out to her. 'Will you marry me?'

'Will you get a proper ring?'

'Naturally. I'll go and buy one tomorrow.'

'Can I choose it?'

'Yes. Yes, you can choose it.'

She nodded, brow still tense. 'All right. Let's get married.'

Bart drove to Wadley the very next day and asked Montgomery for his daughter's hand in marriage, telling the man in a proud voice that he had loved her since childhood and had been waiting only for his stage career to take off before proposing so that he'd be in a secure, solid financial position, as befitting a suitor.

'Stage career?' Monty sneered. 'Hobby, you mean.'

Bart opened his mouth, about to inform the git that his income was more than adequate, actually, as well as his prospects, seeing as he'd recently been scouted by a henchman of Universal Studios and might soon be acting in a Hollywood movie alongside none other than Mary Pickford (none of this true). Monty fortunately didn't give him the chance to speak:

'I don't understand why you'd wait for your "career" to take off when you're set to inherit your father's estate upon marrying.'

Bart didn't even bother asking the man how he knew this detail because of *course* he knew, with his mother constantly dishing out family business to Venetia and Venetia inevitably passing it all on, the pair of them like scuzzy old hags sat open-legged among the sea spray, ripping the spines out of haddocks, gossip gossip, whisper whisper. 'I wished to make my own money first,' he told Monty, struggling to keep his tone calm, 'to prove to myself that I could. I thought you'd appreciate that, being a self-made man.'

Monty smiled with apparent good nature. 'Oh, but I do. I just wonder if Bettina knows about the provisions of your inheritance.'

Bart looked down at his tea, wishing it were whisky. Monty was a shrewd man. Of *course* Bart was thinking of his inheritance, he'd be a fool not to, but it wasn't his sole motive and what's more, he'd never treated it like some dirty secret. 'Yes, she knows.' Through gritted teeth. 'She's my closest friend, I tell her everything.'

'Friend?' said Monty. 'That's a queer way to refer to the woman you wish to marry.' Monty tilted his head slightly and looked at him – *through* him. It was the same way he'd always looked at him; a funny look – yes, a *queer* look – consisting of thoughtful intrigue and cynical amusement. When the little fairy realises what he is I shall be the first to throw him a party, haha.

Bart met his eye unwaveringly. 'It's true, though; she is my closest friend. And I happen to be in love with her. I'm a very lucky man. Or I will be if I gain your permission. Do I gain your permission, sir?'

Monty's mouth collapsed into a slippery grin, his moustache seeming to come alive like a small forest-floor-dwelling animal. 'You do, Bart. I think it a most agreeable match, actually, with its own peculiar conveniences.' Another glimmer of some hidden knowledge in his eyes. Such a gloating, omniscient shit – how did Bettina put up with him? Then his face pouched up in thought. 'I just wonder whether you can . . .' He trailed off and was silent for a while, his face still scrunched up with all his droll ponderousness, and then he waved the thought away. 'Anyway, you have my consent.'

Bart stood up and shook Monty's hand, making sure to squeeze hard, like a man, a real man. 'I'd better go and impart the good news to Venny,' said Monty, his eyebrows going up on 'good' like apostrophes, and that was that.

Bettina still had her doubts. She came to his place (he was renting a flat in Bedford Square now) and paced around, the ever-present cigarette trailing urgent wisps of smoke, seeking reassurance that they were doing the right thing. But then. Aha. But then – Bettina met a woman called Gertrude at one of Cousin Tuna's big dinners, and a stinker of a crush was born. Bettina met Gertrude regularly for lunch or shopping – just friends, Gertrude being a notorious cock-hungry tart. But nursing this crush prompted her to reflect on her predilection. 'I've never felt about a man the way I feel about Trude,' she told Bart. 'And in my heart of hearts, I know I never will.'

Took her long enough.

Jonathan touched his arm and he opened his eyes. 'I've got something for nerves, if you like,' he said, glancing out of the window at the chauffeur, who was still wiping sick off the car. 'Willy!' he called, and the chauffeur's head popped into view.

'Sir?'

'I wish to talk to the groom in private. If you'll be so good as to go over there and have a cigarette.' Willy touched his cap and walked off towards a grassy clearing full of crumbling sheep turds. Jonathan went in his pocket and brought out a small vial filled with white powder. He held it out between thumb and finger and looked at Bart inquisitively. 'You know what this is?'

'I believe I do,' said Bart.

'Well?'

'I wouldn't normally but it does seem that my situation calls for a little something.'

'Hold out your hand.'

Bart held out his hand, palm up.

'The other way.'

Jonathan prised the vial's tiny cork out with his teeth and tapped some out onto the back of Bart's hand. 'Have you done this before?' The cork was still between his teeth and the words came out garbled. *Ha you done is ahore*?

'No.' Bart pressed a finger to one nostril and snorted up the powder with the other. It shot up like hot sand.

'Don't tell Bettina,' said Jonathan, tipping some out onto his knee and then bending his head down while simultaneously bringing his knee to his face and snorting it up. He blinked, sniffing, and then licked his finger and wiped away the chalky residue from his black trousers.

Bart climbed out of the car and stretched his arms out, loosening the muscles in his neck and shoulders. Beautiful day. Really beautiful day. Good omen. He sniffed a few times and then crouched down to look in the car's side mirror. He ran a finger over his moustache; a perfectly trim pencil moustache, newly grown, that Bettina would no doubt want to laugh at as she walked down the aisle towards him.

Imagine there really was a God?

He frowned into the mirror – a stern, paternal glare. 'For perverting the holy sanctity of marriage,' he told himself, 'thou shalt burn forever in the fiery pits of hell.'

He widened his eyes. The stuff was dripping down the back of his throat like bitter phlegm. He licked his finger and smoothed down his eyebrows. He had very pleasing eyebrows. And eyebrows mattered. He stuck out his tongue and went cross-eyed. 'I choose hell,' he said. And laughed.

Jonathan fumbled the ring out of his pocket, dropped it, picked it up, dropped it again. It skittered across the stone tiles, coming to rest by Bettina's pearl-white slipper. He bent down to pick it up, sniffing and bird-like, and bashed his head into Bettina's knee, causing her to cry out and stumble backwards into their father's arms. Jonathan gasped out an apology, sweat beading his nose, ears practically throbbing, and retrieved the ring. Bettina gave him a tight-lipped smile and the priest looked on with tranquil bloodshot eyes. Bart curled his lips in to suppress a laugh. How memorable this would be! Only dull people were satisfied with perfection.

Bart took the ring from the poor wretch and turned to face Bettina. Her lips were painted a vibrant, shocking red and she had a red rose clipped just below the neckline of her dress.

'With this ring I thee wed . . .'

As he echoed the priest's words in his clear, trained voice, Bettina stared up into his face, her gaze zipping from his eyes to his moustache and back again. She was dying to laugh too, he could tell.

Bart peeled the silk glove from her left hand, upsetting the coil of pearls which clattered around her wrist, and, with an air of great ceremony, he slipped the ring on her now-nude finger.

'I now pronounce you man and wife,' said the priest.

A great roar of cheering and applause. Bettina, dazed and grinning, wrapped an arm around his neck and pressed her cheek to his. 'Your finest performance yet,' she whispered.

Chapter 11

September 1925, English Channel

Bettina was not a good water traveller and she did not like travelling with others. Bart, knowing this, went off to sit at the bar, sometimes coming back to check she was all right, and always preceding his queries with an incredulous, 'Hello, wifey.' 'Hello, hubby,' she croaked back, her cheek against the cabin window. She just wanted to fall on a bed and close her eyes. And think of Trude. She could barely think of anything else.

Trude was a blonde, bobbed wild thing, married but practically estranged from her ancient husband (he was fifty-eight and she thirty years his junior). She had one of those bodies seemingly designed to drive men crazy – large jiggling breasts, plump hips and a behind that looked like it was stuffed with pillows. *Vogue* was going potty over skinny waifs with boys' hips, all the better to drape flimsy dresses over, and that was all well and good, but in the real world, thought Bettina, it still took a big arse and breasts to send men over the edge. And some women, clearly.

She'd be sitting opposite Trude in a tea shop and find herself tuning out, a slippery montage of sexually explicit scenarios shooting like ticker tape across her mind – legs spread apart, positively *ripped* apart like a land mass split by earthquake, hands kneading soft buttock fat, tongues . . . tongues . . . 'Betts?' Trude would say. 'Bettina, darling, are you listening?' and her eyes would unglaze and she'd blink guiltily at her new friend, knowing that when she next went to the toilet she'd find a wet viscosity, a drool – vile.

'Are you sure you don't have narcolepsy, darling?'

'I wasn't sleeping.'

'What *were* you doing? Am I that boring that you must start day-dreaming whenever I open my mouth?'

There were times when Trude almost seemed to flirt with Bettina. Once they'd gone to an art exhibition in Mayfair and ambled arm in arm, swapping deadpan observations ('When one says "quintessentially English", what one invariably means is "bloody boring"'), and at one point, Trude gazed up at Bettina's lips as she was talking and there was a hunger to it – yes, a definite hunger, she couldn't be imagining it – and Trude visibly collected herself and said, 'I bet Constable's got a whopper on him.'

'Would you like a drink or something, my dearest, darlingest wifeypoos?' Bart. Leaning against the doorframe, eyes glassy with boozy bonhomie.

'Anything I put in my body is coming back up again,' she said.

'You'll feel better as soon as we're on land. I'll take you to Bras de Grenouilles for a slap-up meal.'

'I don't want to think of food right now.'

'Oh, but it'll be delicious,' he said. 'We'll have prawns and quails' eggs and oysters and more prawns – just imagine those pink, twitching, juicy prawns –and how could I forget about the snails? Slimy, succulent snails!' He kissed the tips of his fingers. '*Magnifique*!'

'You bastard.'

'Correction, my love – I am your bastard *husband*.' He blew her a kiss and strutted off. How long would it take before she began to hate him? Hopefully never – he was, after all, her favourite person. But hate was so easy.

At the hotel they had a bedroom each with a connecting door, a huge sitting room and a gothic-styled bathroom with a tub the size of a dining table. The light fixtures were dripping with fat crystals and all the soft furnishings and haberdashery were an opulent, silky gold. The beds were coated in red petals in a way that appeared random but which was probably artfully contrived – Bettina imagined the concierge deliberating over the placement of a particular petal, moving it around and standing at various angles with a finger at his pursed lips until he was satisfied.

She came into the sitting room to find Bart lying sultry-eyed on the chaise longue in one of her evening dresses, one hairy leg cocked up, cigarette held daintily. 'If you're after a woman, look no further,' he purred.

She laughed, her hands on her knees, then held up a finger as if to say, 'Wait a minute,' and ran to his room. She stripped her clothes off and started to put on his, fumbling pink-faced and giggling with the buttons (so many buttons) and stopping every few seconds to fan herself with her hand. She looked in the mirror and grinned. Winked. She stuffed a ball of socks down the crotch of the underpants, then another, and moulded them into position. She walked in a wide-legged saunter to her husband, who, of course, burst into loud, reckless cackling, beating the cushion of the chaise longue.

'What's a lovely lady like you doing in a place like this?' she asked, grabbing her sock-bulge and squeezing it. Bart was turning purple with laughter. She climbed on top of him, thrusting her hips up and down.

'Stop – stop. I'm going to piss myself. Please – I can't.'

She climbed off, slapping his behind. 'Tease.'

Bettina knew all about Étienne. Bart sometimes read out bits of his letters, the especially romantic lines ('My love for you is a crime for which I have been arrested,' he once wrote, 'and I pace this aching jail, a madman with bleeding feet.') He talked about the man's beauty ('You could eat your pudding out of his dimples') and his integrity, his ability to think for himself, which Bart valued above most other things. He lived a bohemian lifestyle but he wasn't a bohemian – and thank God, said Bart, because bohemians were superficial idiots. And they honked, the lot of them.

Bettina liked hearing about Étienne and was dying to meet him. 'Oh, you'd hate him,' Bart said. 'He doesn't enjoy the moneyed class one bit and only tolerates me because he loves me. And I him.'

Bettina had felt a pang of jealousy at that. Which was silly.

'In fact,' Bart continued, 'the only time he relaxes his views about inherent power struggles is when he's got a cock in his mouth.'

'Bart! Don't be vulgar.' They were lying in Bart's bed now, in their nightclothes, rose petals stuck to their skin. A bottle of champagne lay empty on the floor. 'I really wouldn't mind if you wanted to go and see Étienne now,' she said. Only half-meaning it.

'Stop saying that, would you? This is our wedding night.'

'But it's not a real wedding night.'

'Oh, stop it.' He picked a rose petal off his neck and started nibbling it. 'Anyway, he might come over on Tuesday. I asked if he wanted to have a meal at a restaurant. Meet the wifey and all that. But he loathes restaurants unless they're the humblest of shitholes, so I invited him here for a room-service supper. You must promise not to be all high and mighty around him. He's an urchin.'

'I won't be. I'll be open-minded.' She smiled. 'At the very least I'll pretend to be.'

'I'll be awfully upset if there's friction between you.'

'Bart! I am actually less of a snob than you.'

'On the surface.'

'Will you shut up, please? You're insulting me.'

'Sorry. Sorry. It's just I'm nervous about you meeting. You're my two favourite people and I want you to get on.'

'I'm sure we will. I'm sure I'll love him.'

And what if she didn't? Well, it was very easy to be around people you didn't like; society had prepared her well for such a likelihood. You just smiled a lot then feigned a headache and went to bed with a good book. Imagine she ended up with Trude – oh, she knew there was no chance in hell, but just imagine – and Bart displayed signs of not liking the woman. Would she care? Or would she be too busy indulging her pleasures? 'Good night, husband,' she said, kissing the side of

Bart's head and turning out the night lamp. And she drifted off to sleep, her belly hot and her heart dipping and soaring, owl-like, as she anticipated these same pleasures.

'Oh, but I've *tried* to appreciate it,' said Bettina, 'really I have.' They were talking about modern art, specifically the paintings of Picasso and Man Ray. 'Only, I feel like I'm missing something. As if someone has told me a joke and the punchline has gone right over my head. I feel the same about Virginia Woolf, actually. That's the first time I've ever admitted that to anyone, so keep it to yourself.'

Étienne took a sip of his wine – a very dainty sip, thought Bettina, as if he was trying to prove something. 'You are perhaps thinking too much about it. I will take you to an exhibition tomorrow. You must see the work with your own eyes.'

He had entered the hotel room wearing a brown tweed suit – ugly but a good fit – and grasping his cap in both hands, seemingly ill at ease but with a defiant look in his eyes (and very nice eyes they were). He started to relax after his first glass of wine. His left ear was pierced and he wore a maroon cravat around his neck. He was eloquent and – this was strange – both guarded and open at the same time. The guard, she assumed, only came up around people with money. People like her.

'Am I invited?' said Bart.

Étienne pouted, as if considering. 'If you promise to behave.'

'Oh, I like him!' said Bettina, clapping her hands.

'Don't you two gang up on me.'

Étienne squeezed Bart's thigh – quite high up. Bettina stared at his hand, quickly averting her gaze when Étienne looked at her. 'Many interesting people will attend. Women like you.'

'What, you mean the place will be rammed full of gorgeous, refined redheads with marvellous intellects?' She yanked her head back and laughed into the ceiling. She didn't normally laugh at her own jokes quite so flagrantly, but she was quite drunk.

'Lesbians,' said Étienne, smiling (he did indeed have lovely dimples). 'There will be lesbians.'

'Steady on,' said Bettina.

'She still isn't entirely convinced that the word is a good fit for her,' said Bart.

'But why?' said Étienne. 'It's a beautiful word.' He closed his eyes and said, 'Lesbian. Lezzzzbian,' swishing his wine glass around on the tail end of the word.

'It *is* a lovely word, starved of its context,' said Bettina. 'But so is "syphilis". You know, when I imagine an actual lesbian, all I see is a woman who hates men and dresses abysmally.'

'That is true of some,' said Étienne. 'But many are like yourself. You will see. Romaine Brooks will be there. And Djuna Barnes.' He placed his hands over his chest. 'Nice boobies.'

Bettina burst out laughing, spilling her drink on her stomach. Funny *and* gorgeous. She wondered what he would look like with no clothes on. Him and Bart with no clothes on. No. Better not to think of things like that. What the hell was she doing thinking of things like that?

They called up for room service and sat down together to eat, Bart and Bettina opting for cassoulet, Étienne wolfing down half a chicken and a bowl of potatoes in a herb-butter sauce. He had no table manners and his dainty sipping had made way for purple-lipped glugging. Bettina caught Bart glancing at her, challenging her to say something. Well, she damn well wouldn't.

They pushed their plates away and lit their cigarettes. Étienne talked about the Left Bank, the best bookshops and cafés. He lifted his legs onto Bart's lap and told them about the time he'd attended one of Gertrude Stein's salons and been kicked out for bringing alcohol ('She is a genius but she takes herself too seriously, I think'). He gave them a lecture on how language is used to perpetuate class oppression ('The wealthy "fuck" or "make love" but poor people "rut", and what is the difference, truly?'), Bettina nodding her head perhaps a little too eagerly and saying, 'Quite right, quite right.' He suggested authentic bistros they could visit in Naples and risqué clubs in Florence (for the second and third stages of their honeymoon), Bart watching him with love and pride in his eyes. He'd rolled up Étienne's trouser leg and was stroking his shin, up and down, up and down, his thumb skimming the soft dark hair.

'I need to piss,' said Étienne, after their fifth bottle of wine.

'Don't be a brute,' said Bart.

'Oh, but I am a brute! I am your bit of rough, no? Your obvious rebellion. That is what I am to you. Fuck you, dead father! That is what you say when you fuck me. *Non* – that is what you say when we are *rutting*.'

'Oh dear,' murmured Bettina, putting a hand over her eyes.

'Oh, look, we're embarrassing the wife,' said Bart. 'Sorry, wife.'

'Sorry, wife,' said Étienne.

'We must remember that she is still a lady,' said Bart to Étienne.

'Don't paint me as a prude.' She was not a prude. Nor a snob. But there was such a thing as over-sharing.

'She saw my cock earlier, you know,' Bart said.

'Lucky girl,' said Étienne.

'Oh my God,' said Bettina. 'Will you both please shut up?' She had indeed seen his 'cock' earlier – he'd come out of his bathroom wearing only a shirt and it had hung out, slapping his thigh as he walked. 'I'm going to bed.' She stood up. 'It's been lovely meeting you.'

Étienne came at her and hugged her tight. 'I like you, wifey, we will be good friends.' His words hot and boozy on her neck.

Bettina smiled unnaturally. 'Yes, yes, I'm sure we shall be.'

'For the love of God!' Bettina's eyes shimmered mercury-like in the dark. Next door a headboard was going thud-thud-thud against a wall. She sat up, pushing out an acidic red wine burp. She wasn't going to picture what they were doing. She wasn't going to picture what they were doing. How disgusting. She lay back down and pulled the covers over her face. Ghastly. We really are a degenerative breed, she thought. But especially them. She needed to urinate. She really oughtn't to have done it. Married him. And now she was doomed to this – perverts next door, slamming each other into the headboard, *rutting*, hands all over each other's . . . Horrid. She couldn't believe she'd seen Bart's cock. Never in a million years had she ever imagined . . . And why on *earth* was she calling it a cock? What was happening to her? It was Bart, it was. Filling her mind with smut. She really needed to urinate. Oh God.

She pulled the covers down and climbed out of bed, and maybe her subconscious was driving her with nasty little pitchforks, because she climbed out on the right side, the adjoining door side. Fidgeting her feet into her slippers, she tiptoed across the carpet, and there were those pitchforks again, poking at her hip, because suddenly she was veering off towards the adjoining door and pressing her ear to the lacquered wood, and why would she do a thing like that?

Thud, thud, thud.

'Whore. You whore.'

A slap. 'Oof.' Another slap. 'Ugh. Harder.'

Thudthudthudthudthud.

'Heavens.' Bettina walked in a hot daze to the bathroom and sat on the toilet. Her urine came out scalding. She wiped herself. Wiped again. Flushed. Washed her hands and walked out. Passed the mirror, did not look at it.

Chapter 12

May 1926, Davenport House, London

He spread out two lines on the poker table. Fuck them all. Fuck bloody Bettina with her moody eye-rolling face and boring sulks, and especially fuck Étienne, who was so judgemental and such a snob, which was indeed possible, a poor person being a snob, and in fact, they were the worst for it.

'You first, good sir,' he said to Jonathan.

Jonathan leaned over the table, his waxy red hair flopping forward and hanging over his face, and sniffed up the powder. Good old Jonathan, a man undergoing a nervous breakdown with such dignity, such class, his head held high as his spirits splatted to the floor like a disembowelment. Why couldn't Bettina be more like her brother?

It was her birthday and he'd treated her to a surprise party. He'd spent a bomb, ordering the best French caterers, extra serving staff and an all-black jazz band fronted by a fat woman dressed up as a man, complete with a gold tux. He'd done all this for her and yet she'd spent half the night whingeing about her wisdom teeth and flirting with a man. A man! So he'd grabbed her by the arm and pulled her out into the garden.

'You're making me look like a fucking cuckold,' he said.

'I am not flirting with him,' she said, lighting a cigarette.

'You were pressing your leg up against his leg. I saw and so did everyone else.'

She looked at him steadily then did a slow, drunken blink. 'Fine. I was flirting. But it's not as though I want to *do* anything with him. I know, I'm pathetic.'

Bart sighed. Trude was playing her like a violin, it was true. But she wasn't considering *him* in all this. He wanted to shake the silly child by the shoulders! It mattered what other people thought, it mattered a great deal. And he told her so.

'I can't make head nor tail of you,' she said. 'One minute you're the great iconoclast – Bartholomew Dawes, free-thinker extraordinaire! And the next you're fretting over what people think of you. You can't have it both ways! Choose!'

'*You* stop acting like such a spoiled, selfish little bitch!' he yelled, some spit spraying her face.

'Touched a nerve, have I?' she said.

He grabbed her by the shoulders. 'The world doesn't revolve around you.'

She jerked her body, dislodging his grip. 'Today it does,' she said, turning and walking away.

And of course she'd gone straight to Étienne and got him on her side.

'Quite the party,' said Jonathan, sniffing. His eyes were bruised and hollow with sleep deprivation and Bart could see a tiny muscle spasming at his temple. 'The singer was jolly marvellous. Fancy that, dressing as a man! How did you acquire her?'

Bart licked his finger and dabbed the powdered remnants, rubbing them into his gums. 'Good stuff. Yummy. What was that?'

'The singer. Where did you find her?'

'France. She was doing some clubs in Paris. Étienne knew of her, he arranged things. They go crazy for that sort of thing there. Originally from Harlem, I think.'

'I hear it's rather wild over there?'

'What, Paris or Harlem?'

'Well . . . both, come to think of it.'

Bart nodded.

'Bit much for me, I must confess,' said Jonathan. 'But then, things are very different now.'

'Much better too,' said Bart.

'Seems like a queer sort of present for your wife's birthday,' said Jonathan, thoughtfully, his brandy glass poised an inch from his lips. 'But then Bettina does go in for unusual things. Always liked to think of herself as a rebel.' He took a slow swallow. Sniffed. Then he smiled. 'You know, I just remembered something.' The smile grew – it was a lovely, lazy smile. 'How strange, I haven't thought of it in years.' He took a cigar from his breast pocket and bit off the end, spitting it into his hand and then idly fiddling with it between thumb and forefinger. 'One Christmas, when we were very young,

Bettina's governess – Madame Choveaux, I think her name was, something like that, horrible rotten old French hag, she was . . .'

'I remember her,' said Bart. 'Madame Choubert.'

'Do you? Of course you do. Anyway, she'd had Bettina rehearsing "O Holy Night" *en français*. Wanted her to perform it for the family on Christmas Eve.'

Jonathan lit his cigar and leaned back against the bar, tapping his foot as if to music, though the room was silent. 'It came to the time of the performance and Bettina was dressed as . . . well, frankly, I don't know what the hell she was dressed as. She had on knickerbockers, bizarrely, and long woollen socks up to the knees. And she had this screaming argument with the governess just before coming out – we could all hear it from the drawing room. My father was most embarrassed – he had some shareholders over. Anyway. Madame Choveaux – Choubert, sorry – comes into the room, furious, and takes my mother to the side and tells her that Bettina is insisting on wearing one sock up and the other down. Just to be contrary. And Mother said . . . now what did she say?'

Bart waited, smiling. Jonathan did not usually tell stories or offer commentaries.

'Oh, I remember. She said, "Tell her from me that if she continues to embarrass her father like this, then all of her presents shall be sent to the orphanage." I was hanging on my mother's hem like a monkey so I remember it well. I remember thinking how jolly well cruel that would be, to have one's presents sent to the snots at the orphanage. I know most older brothers would wish it so, for their little sisters to be deprived of their stupid dollies and frocks, but of course, I was – and forgive me my conceit – a very kind older brother, and I loved her exceedingly. Well, my father came over at this point, demanding to know what all the fuss was about, and so Mother told him. And he laughed. He said to old Choubert, he said, "Oh, let her do what she wants with her socks! She can't sing for toffee so it's going to be a butcher's job whichever way you try to package it."'

They laughed. Jonathan's teeth jutted out and his eyes half-closed. He looked like a little boy again.

'Your father is funny, I'll give him that,' said Bart.

'Oh yes. But mean with it. I haven't told you the best part.'

'Oh?'

'Well, after all that fuss, when the governess went in to tell Bettina she could do what she liked with her socks, she apparently fixed the woman with the most belligerent face and pulled *both* her socks up.'

'She didn't.'

'She jolly well did. You see what I mean? She just likes to be contrary. Mind you, you're the same.'

'How was her performance in the end?'

'In the words of my father, "Like an asthmatic puppy being clubbed to death."'

They roared out more laughter. Bart wrapped an arm around Jonathan's shoulder and they turned, laughing into each other's faces, their noses bumping. The laughter trailed off into a hoarse hee-hawing. Bart could see, through half-closed eyes, Jonathan's great orange beard quivering.

'My, you're in a bright mood tonight,' Bart said, wiping his eyes. 'It's good to see, really it is. Heartening.'

Jonathan patted his breast pocket with the vial in it. 'This is top-notch stuff.'

'Why don't we just stay here all night and finish the lot off? To hell with the party.'

'Oh, no,' said Jonathan, with a frown. 'Not on her birthday.' He took the vial out of his pocket and stuffed it into Bart's. 'You have this. I don't think I require any more.'

'You're sure?'

Jonathan nodded, sipping his brandy. 'Have you argued?'

'Indeed we have.'

'Look. Forgive my forwardness, but I've noticed my sister getting a little chummy with that French pal of yours. I *know* it's innocent, but I'd hate for the frog to get the wrong end of the stick.'

'Oh, it's completely innocent—'

'I *know* it is, heavens I know it is. Listen, Bart.' And here he turned to Bart and looked him imploringly in the eyes. 'You are taking care of her, aren't you?'

'Of course I am!'

'And relations are good?' He raised his one hand up. 'No details, please.'

'Yes, relations are fabulous.'

'Only, you've been married a fair while and she's yet to, you know . . .'

'That keen to be an uncle, are you?'

Jonathan's lips went tight and colourless from between his ginger bristles. 'Of course,' he murmured. He turned his head away and puffed on his cigar. A long moment of silence. Struggling with some torturous melancholic thought or other – Jonathan was always getting like this. Finally he turned back, visibly brighter, and slapped Bart on the arm. 'Anyway, it's none of my business. Come on, let's re-enter society. I wish to dance with my sister.'

'Pull one of her stockings down, I dare you.'

He looked at Bart with exaggerated disapproval. 'Don't be rude, brother.'

Bart laughed. Brother. He liked that. He'd always wanted a brother.

His prosthetic hand was digging into her lower back but she would not – absolutely *would* not – acknowledge the discomfort. He held her hand and they swayed – the band was playing a slow song, a lovers' song, the woman singer oozing out sugary words with eyes closed and head tilted back. Jonathan smiled awkwardly (did he ever smile any other way?), his bright pink lips twitching from out of his godawful beard. He had a contented air about him, an earthy sort of serenity. It reminded her of how he used to be, before the war; it wasn't like he'd been *born* a jittering wreck.

'You dance very well,' she said.

'I do not.'

'Oh, shut up. Do you have one positive opinion about yourself?'

He thought about it, sniffing. 'I have attractive feet.'

'That's it? That's all you can come up with?'

'Yes.'

She laughed. 'You're such a – right, I'm going to list your positive attributes right now.'

'Please don't,' he said.

'You're kind, honourable, brave—'

'Please stop,' he said. 'I'm quite serious.' And he was – she could see it in his eyes.

'Self-loathing is very boring,' she said.

'That's more like it. I'm boring.'

She kicked his shin and he let out a yelp.

'How have you not outgrown kicking?' he said, laughing. 'Always kicking me, you were. You kicking me, Tuna pinching me—'

'Oh, she was a one for pinching.'

'Here – do you remember that time you kicked me in the privates because I told Father on you for – now, what had you done?'

'I used profane language. I said, "Bugger me, it's cold." Don't pull that face!'

'What face?'

'It's only a word, Jonathan.'

'Yes, but you were seven.'

'It was Bart's fault. He told me to say it.'

The song ended. Couples extracted themselves from each other, glancing around with bleary embarrassment as if surprised to find they were not the only people in the room. The singer announced an intermission. Jonathan was still holding onto her, his prosthetic hand now poking her in the kidney.

'I might go soon,' he said.

She opened her mouth to protest. Closed it – it was enough that he'd danced with her. More than enough. 'Thank you for finally dancing with me, brother.'

'It was a pleasure.' He sniffed, his chin tilted up, and smiled at her – it was a bittersweet smile. 'I want you to be happy. Are you happy?'

'I am.'

He nodded. 'That's what matters. Being happy. That's the whole point.' He sniffed again, twice.

'Blow your nose, would you?'

He let her go and pulled a hanky from his breast pocket. Gave her cheek a kiss and abruptly walked away, the hanky clamped over his nose.

The band was still playing, minus their transvestite singer and lead trumpet player. The partygoers were dancing like lunatics, drunk and stumbling with big grins on their faces. Tuna was whooping and spinning round and round with the very same twerp Bettina had been flirting with earlier, she a whirling blur of peacock feathers and red sequins and he a sweaty, gurning nonsense.

He couldn't see Bettina. She was probably upstairs having a histrionic crying fit over Trude. Good.

No. He wasn't being fair. He wasn't. They'd argued, that was all. They'd get over it. 'Never go to bed on an argument,' his mother had told him. Not that she'd ever followed her own advice – she and his father would often go weeks without speaking to each other, turning every mealtime into an excruciating ordeal – averted glances, cutlery wielded with stiff wrists, jumpy footmen and maids, all this playing out to a soundtrack of soup-sipping and his father's adenoidal mouth-breathing.

He dodged past the dancers and made it out into the dining room, where people were helping themselves to food from the huge table and waiters in white jackets looked on with exasperation. Hashish smoke hung thick in the air. He saw Bettina and Étienne huddled together on the floor in the corner of the room. Bettina's lipstick was smeared across her cheek and her untapped cigarette ash was an inch long and ready to drop at any second. Étienne was wearing her tiara. They looked up and saw him and their faces clouded thunderously. Bart stopped mid-step. Étienne shook his head ever so slightly. A warning.

Bart swiped at a bowl of potato salad; it hurtled to the floor and smashed, off-white gloop splattering the parquet. Everyone turned to look, their cheeks bulging with food, *his* food that *he'd* paid for, well piss on them, piss on the lot of them.

He made his way to the back garden, passing Jonathan on the way and saying, 'She's in the dining room with her frog prince' in a tone so acidic that Jonathan's eyes shuddered. He stepped outside into the blessed cool darkness. It was a long, thin garden with various trees (the names of which he had no interest in finding out) lining a strip down the middle. He walked, his hands stuffed into his trouser pockets, the thudding, brassy sound of the band gradually fading. He was jealous, that was the thing. But how petty and misguided. The alternative – Bettina and Étienne hating each other – would be much worse. A small wood surrounded the garden in a horseshoe – the remains of a much larger forest, long since cut down and replaced with grand houses and ornate gardens. Bettina had fallen in love with this house on the strength of this poxy smear of woodland; it reminded her of the woods between their houses and the beach back in Brighton. He would've preferred somewhere in Chelsea or Knightsbridge. But what Bettina wanted, Bettina got.

He was surprised to find the bench at the end of the garden peopled; the transvestite singer and the lead trumpeter were sitting together, smoking; the woman with her wide legs spread, like a man, and the trumpeter like a woman, primly, one long, skinny leg crossed over the other. He was pale as driftwood, with a narrow pale head and a pencil moustache.

'What are you doing out here?' he asked, standing over them.

The woman lifted her cigarette. 'We're on break.'

'I'm not paying you to sit out here and smoke.'

They cast languid side glances at each other, and then, sighing, they stood up, she smoothing down her gold tux, he arching his back to get the crackles out of his joints.

'No, wait.' Bart took his hands out of his pockets and lifted them in apology. 'You've every right to a break, you've both performed terrifically. I've argued with my wife and I'm in a rancid mood. Please, sit back down. I'm sorry.'

They sat back down.

'Your wife, that the birthday girl?' said the woman, taking off her top hat and scratching her scalp – her hair was tethered tightly to her head in tiny plaits.

Bart nodded. 'The one and only. Mind if I sit with you?'

A shrug. 'It's your bench.'

He sat and took out his cigarettes. The man lit a match for him, his hands steady and strong-looking (Bart's own hands were buzzing like engines), the nails immaculate but the fingers nicotine-stained. He leaned back, looking up into a sky disappointingly starless.

'Nice place you got here,' said the man. His voice was musical, light and possibly a little educated (it was hard to tell with Americans). And fruity. The man was of course a fruit – Bart would bet his life on it.

'Thank you. It brings me much happiness and I am deeply fulfilled. That was sarcasm. Do you Yanks understand sarcasm?'

Blank-eyed, the man shook his head. 'Our culture is dumb and inferior to yours, mister. All we know is apple pie.' He grinned with all his teeth showing. He had high cheekbones and a nose that looked like it'd been broken a couple of times. Accompanying the thin moustache was a tuft of hair growing just under his bottom lip. 'Do you have apple pie over here?'

'We do. We eat it with fresh cream, it's delicious.' He drew out that last word – deelishhusss. 'Do you like our food? English food, I mean?'

'Not particularly,' said the man. 'French cuisine's my favourite.'

'May I ask what you were doing in France?'

He turned to face Bart, his eyes gleaming. 'She' – he stabbed a thumb in the direction of the woman – 'brought us to France. And I'll tell you why.'

'George,' said the woman, a warning in her tone. 'I *know* you ain't gonna say what I think you're gonna say.'

George smiled naughtily. 'She came to Paris—'

'You're gonna get yourself fired, fool—'

'*She* came to Paris with the sole intention of eating Josephine Baker's pussy.'

The whites of her eyes popped. 'George!' She clouted him around the head. He shrank away from her, leaning into Bart and laughing. 'That is ten shades of inappropriate!' she said. 'I am sorry, sir. He's got a problem with his mouth.' She hit him again. 'That ain't no way to speak to your employer, fool.' Back to Bart. 'I'm real sorry.' George was still cowering from her, his body shaking with wicked giggles – Bart could smell the pomade in his hair.

'It's fine,' he said, flapping a hand. 'I mean, who *wouldn't* want to eat Josephine Baker's pussy? One gets the added bonus of a free banana for dessert.'

She laughed, her neck vibrating, and he joined in, pleased with himself. Because she'd been expecting him to behave in a certain way. And look at him. Just look at him.

'Did you achieve your objective?'

'No. We friends.' She gave George a withering look. 'That *ain't* the reason I went to France. I only said that as a joke. A J-O-K-E. Paris is a good place to be right now.'

'Better than Harlem?' asked Bart.

'They both got their charms.' She opened her coat and rummaged in her inside pocket, bringing out a paper napkin. Inside were three medallions of herb-dotted pork piled on top of each other.

'Oh, come now,' said Bart. 'You don't need to be eating out of a napkin out here. Go inside and sit at a table.'

'Naw, I'm good, thanks,' said the woman. 'I don't like too many people watching me eat.' She started to nibble on the meat, daintily. 'So why'd you argue with your wife?'

Bart sighed. 'Because she's a child.'

She nodded. 'Been there. Usually with men though. Men be the most childish children of all. This is *nice.* I don't like English food. But this is tasty.'

'Well, it's French actually,' said Bart.

George lit a fresh cigarette and breathed out the smoke with a tilted chin and just-parted lips – he knew he was being watched.

'So,' said Bart to George. 'Do you have a man friend at the moment?'

The woman's brow arched and the pork paused just short of her lips.

'I have lots of friends who are men,' said George, coolly.

Bart crossed one leg over the other and leaned back. Rakishly. He felt very rakish all of a sudden. 'Let's not bounce this ball back and forth. Do you have a fella?'

'I do not,' said George.

'Good,' said Bart.

The woman stood up abruptly, her knees cracking. 'I think

I'll go back inside, leave you both to it.' She bowed, doffing her top hat to Bart. 'Evening.' Her eyes zipped to George's, wordlessly communicating something to him – a warning perhaps, or an encouragement; she had a good poker face, it was hard to tell – and then she was walking pigeon-toed back to the house, eating as she went.

'So,' said Bart.

'So,' said George.

They laughed with awkwardness, a lovely fizzing awkwardness.

'You play the trumpet.'

'I do.'

'What else?'

'I write poetry. You?'

'I'm an actor, *darling*.'

George grinned. 'Of *course* you're an actor. Ever been in a moving picture?'

Bart shook his head. 'The stage.'

A great cracking sound went off somewhere in the near-distance – a firework, possibly – and both turned to look. The sky was clear. Bart glanced at the strained cord in George's neck – he had a thing about necks. Necks, armpits and the dip in the back just above the buttocks.

He took Jonathan's vial out of his pocket. 'Want some?'

George held up his hand. 'Hell no. That shit'll put you in the ground.'

'It's not opium, if that's what you're thinking.'

George shrugged. 'Even so. Same applies.'

'Mind if I partake?'

'It's a free country. Supposedly.'

Bart tapped some powder onto the back of his hand and

snorted it up, George watching with a show of nonchalance crossing over into boredom. He put the vial back in his pocket. Glanced back up at the house. 'Just to be clear so as to avoid any embarrassment,' he said to George, 'I am about to suck you off. Yes?'

George did a taken-aback laugh, his hand flying involuntarily to the side of his face. 'Uh . . . wow. *Wow.*' He composed himself, leaning back and looking down at Bart through his lashes, a nervous smirk twisting his mouth. 'Like I said, it's a free country.'

'We're actually a pair of hypocrites if you stop to think about it,' said Bettina, passing Étienne the jazz joint (as he kept calling it).

'*Non.* No. I don't think so.'

They were lying on Bettina's bed, the door closed to all the chaos outside.

'Bart, he takes these nasty powders, these stimulations – stimu . . . I don't know the English for it,' continued Étienne. 'They magnify anger and fear. Which are the same things, I think. They bring out his negative qualities. But this' – he lifted the joint, upsetting its creamy trail of smoke – 'this is not like that. And it is medicine for your teeth.'

Her wisdom teeth were coming through – earlier, it had felt like every molar in the back of her mouth was screaming; an awful, tinfoil screaming. 'It's worked, too,' she said.

Footsteps going past the door, outside. They froze, their ears cocked. The footsteps faded. Someone looking for the bathroom, perhaps. Or snooping. Or looking for a spare room to smooch in. Snooping. Smooching. Such silly words.

Bettina let her head tilt back and sighed. 'I feel bad.'

'Don't feel bad. Why?'

'He put this party on for me. And here I am, hiding from him.'

Étienne exhaled smoke from his nose, his facial muscles taut. 'He must learn that he cannot get away with this behaviour. Or it will get worse. I know men like this. They always have indulgent mothers. "You are a special little king," these mothers say, "and you can do whatever you want." And so the little king does whatever he wants. And you know what I am going to say next?'

'The rich ones are the worst?'

'*Très bien*!'

'You're turning me into a Bolshevik.' She twisted around onto her back and started picking a spot on her chin. Bart hadn't even been that awful tonight – she had indeed been flirting publicly with a man, and that was indeed inconsiderate of her. But his grabbing her roughly and shouting into her face, well, she couldn't forgive that. Because last month, at a similar kind of party, Bart had slapped her. She couldn't even remember why; they'd both been so very drunk. But she could remember the slap, the clean, perfect smack; the jolting, mortifying shock of it; and his snarling, proud face, just like her father's.

She'd slapped him back, repeatedly, crazed, her hands flying out at his face and head. And in an ideal world, that would be the end of it – he erred and she punished. But he'd hit her first, and he was a man. She hated him viciously for it. A whole week of leaving rooms when he entered them and taking all her meals in the garden, and he was repentant of course, full of hand-wringing self-loathing. He slipped a letter under her door admitting his recent narcotic use. 'It wasn't *me*, Betts. I would never do something like that, not the *real* me.' How boring. How predictable.

But she'd forgiven him, or at least tried to, because he promised to stop using the cocaine. And then this afternoon, he'd come practically skipping out of the bathroom, sniffing like a bloodhound, his eyes sprung open and a frenetic energy about him.

Étienne passed back the joint with a lazy arm. She propped herself up on her pillow and had a small puff. Her mouth was horribly dry. She tapped Étienne's shoulder. 'Look at this.' She tucked her lips in, upper and lower, and they remained stuck there, showing all her teeth and gums.

He dropped his head back onto the bed, laughing. 'That is gruesome! Oh, why would you—'

She tapped his shoulder again. 'Etts. Look.' He raised his head, eyes pink and puffy. She stuck out her tongue and wiggled it.

'Stop it!'He shook his head weakly, his body racked with painful laughter. 'You make yourself ugly. Why?'

She smirked and unstuck her lips. 'I need a drink. My mouth is so dry. Shall we return to the fray?'

He shook his head. 'I don't want to see him.'

'Well, nor do I, frankly. Or bloody Trude. But we can't stay up here all night. God, my mouth is so dry.' She smacked his shoulder. 'Hey. Let's sneak down to the buffet and collect all the grub we can carry as well as a lovely big bottle of ice-cold bubbly. And bring them back up here.'

He opened his eyes. 'Now you have mentioned food.'

He pushed himself to an upright position with huge effort. 'Let's go.'

*

The band had stopped playing, except for one man, a bald honky-tonk player with a lumpy nose and a sheen of sweat on his conker of a head. He was hunched over the piano playing slow mournful tunes with slow mournful hands, his eyes closed. Couples danced crotch to crotch and hands were creeping towards buttocks. Bettina noticed what looked like vomit in the potted money tree. Dear God.

They passed the games room and Bettina's heart sped up. Bart was probably in there sniffing and fidgeting and thinking himself a small god. Étienne poked his head in, then clamped a hand to his mouth to hold in laughter. He pulled her to the doorway. The black drag king was playing strip poker with Cousin Tuna and several of Bart's stage chums from the *Pygmalion* show. Tuna was in a salmon-pink petticoat, one stocking on, one off, her frizzy red hair like a burning bush. The drag king was in only a pair of trousers, and her great fatheaded breasts hung to the tabletop, the purplish nipples grazing the surface. She looked up at Bettina. 'Wanna join us, birthday girl?'

'I want food,' said Bettina dumbly, and carried on down the hall. Étienne was hanging on her arm, laughing. 'They were *enormous*,' she said.

'They were beautiful! I would like to do this to them.' He buried his face in Bettina's cleavage and jiggled his face back and forth.

'You're off your head!' she said, pushing him away. He stumbled backwards and tripped, landing on his back, legs kicking the air like an unfortunate beetle. He curled up into a ball – now a woodlouse – and giggled uncontrollably.

Trude appeared in the hall. Her lipstick was smeared around her maw and a false eyelash stuck to her cheek. 'It's the birthday girl!' she said, spreading her arms wide and sashaying over with slinking hips and wobbling arm flesh. She clung onto Bettina's neck and breathed hot ethanol fumes into her face. 'Darling! What a perfect riot! What sheer debauch'ry! You scandalous little slag, I *love* it. Love, love, *love* it.' Her skin was hot. Bettina placed a hand on her waist, spreading her fingers and squeezing. 'Thanks for coming,' she said. Coming. Thanks for coming. She smiled down into the woman's car wreck of a face. Coming. Trude, coming. Teeth bared, thighs spread wide—

'Let's go,' said Étienne, touching her elbow. And then, in a whisper: 'Don't get sucked in.'

'Whadde say?' slurred Trude.

'Nothing,' said Bettina. 'Thanks for coming.' And she gripped Trude by the face and kissed her hard, forcing her tongue into her mouth. She pulled away and Trude was staring up at her, mouth slack and eyes glazed.

'*Bettina.* Oh my—'

'Good night and thanks for *coming*.' She grabbed Trude by the shoulders, spun her around, slapped her rear and shoved her lurching down the hall. 'That'll show her,' she said to Étienne, taking his arm and turning in the opposite direction. 'The awful tease.'

'*Bien joué*,' he said.

'I can't believe I just did that.'

'I think she liked it.'

'Oh, she did. But it won't come to anything. She likes to keep people dangling. She's very insecure, you know.'

'It's very sad. You deserve a good fuck.'

'I do! I'm in the prime of my life and it's my birthday, Etts. My birthday! How depressing.'

'You know what is almost as good as having sex?' he said,

wrapping an arm around her. 'Eating cake. Let's go and eat cake. And if you ask me nicely, I will rub your feet.'

The valet, Darlton, rushed through the door, almost crashing into them, his eyes huge with panic. Bettina disentangled herself from Étienne.

'Where's Mister Dawes?' said Darlton.

'*I* don't know. What do you want him for?'

'There's been an incident, Mrs Dawes.' He straightened his shoulders and breathed deeply. His face was the hue of rice pudding. 'Something terrible has happened.'

'What? What's happened?'

'I need to find Mister Dawes.'

'Tell me!'

'Someone's shot themselves in the wood. A man. Someone from this party.'

'What? Who?'

He shook his head. 'I don't know, Mrs Dawes. I need to find—'

She pushed past him, slamming open the door. The pianist had stopped playing and now sat on the stool with wide-open legs and a slumped back, a cigarette pinched between thumb and forefinger. A group of men she didn't recognise were murmuring together with solemn faces. One of them had blood up his white shirt. 'Who was it?' she asked the blood-streaked man, a feeling like muddy centipedes in her stomach.

'Do you know where your husband is?'

'Goddammit!' she yelled. 'I'm the woman of this house, not some – some hysterical silly girl! You can bloody well talk to *me*.'

'Tell her,' said Étienne.

'And who are you?'

'Never mind who he is. *I'm* here and this is my house and I demand an explanation. Who was it?'

The blood was a sickening bright red against the starched white of the shirt. Quite a sickening bright red.

The man looked up, relieved, because suddenly Bart was there, rushing in with wide eyes, his shirt tails hanging out of his trousers – yes, the husband was here, the big man. What a joke.

'Who was it?' he asked the bloody man. 'I heard a bang earlier. I thought it was a firework. Was it a gunshot? Who was it?'

The bloody man glanced at Bettina.

'Oh for God's sake!' she shouted. 'I'm not going to swoon to the floor!'

'I'm sorry,' he said. It was loaded, that sorry. He took Bart by the arm and led him away from the group.

Bettina stared at Étienne, her hands spread in a gesture of furious bewilderment. 'I can't *believe* this.' She started to cry – how humiliating! *I'm the woman of this house, not some hysterical silly girl* – and look at her: behaving exactly like a hysterical silly girl. The men looked down at the floor. She watched the bloody man whispering to Bart through a blur of tears. She turned around and looked at the partygoers, still in their clusters. 'You can all go now!' she yelled. 'Party's over.'

'They might need to be questioned by the police,' said one of the men.

She stared at his moustache. It was trim and blond with one solitary ginger hair growing long and wiry just at the edge of his lip. How had he neglected to notice it? How on earth could a sane person not notice it? She wanted to hit him. Her stomach was crawling. Centipedes and beetles and soil-crumbed worms.

'Bettina, darling.' It was Bart. Touching her arm gently, his voice soft. She couldn't take her eyes away from that stupid ginger hair. 'Sweetheart, come with me.' He was pulling on her arm. She closed her eyes and let herself be led. Bart wrapped his arm around her waist. He was shivering.

They walked up the stairs together, arm in arm.

'It was Jonathan, wasn't it?' she said.

Chapter 13

June 1926, St Mark's Church, Sussex

One mustn't *show* the burden, of course. One must keep a stiff upper lip, what? Shoulder your load, button your lip, show the fillies how it's done, what? Fucking stupid farce. Imagine it the other way round – Jonathan carrying *his* coffin. There'd be the issue of the arm. He'd only be able to carry on the one side. Would he bring it up with the chaplain first? 'Apologies, Father, but I need to go on the right side.' An awkward glancing around, a defiant crunch of the brow – *don't pity me.*

Bart fucking well hated funerals. He could remember Tabitha's – though he seldom let himself. The day had passed like radio static. He'd been in shock and his mind had played awful tricks on him – he'd known she was dead but he kept wondering where his little sister had got to. Like his mind was split in two. Mostly he remembered the weeks afterwards – the household sinking into an awful pit, a sort of sucking pit, where nothing grew properly any more, not even the potted plants, and the air seemed to taste of salt and wood dust. The servants ghosted around with puckered little mouths and darting eyes, his mother and father visibly aged and shrank, their hands moving cutlery around with a sort of desperate precision as they sat for their meals, their nightclothes seeming like shrouds as they stood together in dim hallways at unusual times of the night.

St Mark's had granted the Wyn Thomas family a special dispensation, allowing Jonathan to be buried in consecrated ground. Because it was the war that'd killed him really. That's what the pastor said. What he didn't mention was Monty's generous contributions to the church. Bart knew of two boys who'd killed themselves after the war, and both were buried in the shadow-tangled wasteland at the rectum end of the graveyard. Both were poor.

The day was bright and blue-skied, the grass dewy. Slippery. He concentrated on his feet as he walked, he concentrated on his burden. Bettina was walking behind with her mother and father. She had a lock of Jonathan's hair in her fist. She hadn't let go of it all morning. Magpies hopped around on the grass. Two for joy. Bart wondered what it was about the war that made men want to die afterwards. The killing of other men? That would do it, wouldn't it? The shattered nerves? Maybe they'd raped or been raped? Étienne had friends, queer friends, who'd fought in the war. One had seen his lover's face blown off by a grenade. Bart imagined cowering in a trench, cold and shivering with swollen feet and lice in his hair. Étienne beside him, covered in soot and mud and unshaven, but smiling with dimples, a halo of sunlight surrounding his head – no, that was hammy;

take away the halo. He stands up to go and ask another fellow for a match and suddenly there's a whistling overhead and half of Étienne's face explodes. Brains splashing, blood ribboning, chunks of skull spitting out like shrapnel. His lover flopping to the floor by his feet with only half a head. One dimple.

You have this. I don't think I require any more.

He didn't *think* he required any more? Of course he didn't – he was about to shoot his fucking brains out!

The selfish cunt. The selfish, serene-seeming, deceptive cunt. Why that night, at her party? Her birthday party? The selfish birthday-ruining cunt. She'd never be able to celebrate her birthday ever again. He was a grief-ruiner too, leaving his family to deal with the shameful stink of suicide.

Imagine he just stepped away from the coffin now, side-stepped away, allowing his corner to tip, to fall to the ground, spilling Jonathan's body onto the grass, everyone screaming. Imagine that.

Another two magpies. Joy again.

The first funeral she'd ever attended was her grandmother's, though she couldn't remember it. Rather, she remembered the bit *before* the funeral, the waiting bit – the men sitting in the drawing room with wide-open legs, hung-down heads and glasses of amber-coloured booze clenched between both hands, a grim-grey silence hanging over everything like a thickly cobwebbed chandelier. She'd never seen men sit like that before, not gentlemen at any rate. Now, whenever Bettina thought of funerals, her mind would conjure up an image of grey men sitting with extra-long, wide-open spiderlegs, like an illustration from a macabre children's book. It was funny, the way things came together in the mind.

They were at the reception supper now, trying to eat. Venetia smoked openly, inviting ambiguous glances. Lucille, in solidarity perhaps, took out her own cigarettes, and the pair of them puffed away in unison, their eyes extra-wrinkled and glassy. One surviving child left each. Snap. Venetia sat straight-backed and stiff-jawed, staring vapidly into the middle-distance for the most part (she'd been given sedatives). Monty pushed away his soup early on in the meal and stood up, apologising in a perplexed tone, before going off to the garden to stand, hands in pockets, under the giant oak – which had once held a swing, a child's swing, that he'd pushed, higher, higher, higher, a pendulous blur of red hair, higher, higher.

Bettina had always known who his favourite was.

But there you go.

Bart, seated next to her, looked tired and angry. He was refusing alcohol and drank bitter lemon with his meal. Why was he even so cut up? He'd only ever made fun of Jonathan behind his back, pulling his arm through his sleeve to let it hang limply and affecting a jittery, high-chinned air, sometimes to the point of frothing at the mouth and invariably ending with a long, drawn-out fart. Right now, he had his elbows on the table, all decorum vanished, and was pulling his cheeks down with his hands, exhausted. She could see the slimy pink flesh beneath his eyeballs.

'Do you know what my last words to him were?' she said, pushing her unfinished food away.

He shook his head.

'I said, "Blow your nose, would you?" Because he kept sniffing. And that's . . . that's . . .' No. She wouldn't cry. Not in front of everyone.

She felt his hand find hers under the table. 'We have each

other,' he said, in a quiet voice. 'You have me and I have you. We need to remember that, because it's thinking that you've got no one that leads to – you know. We have each other.'

She nodded, going in her pocket for her hanky. 'Now I'm the one sniffing!'

'Look,' he said, pointing out of the conservatory window. Monty was still out in the garden, standing under the tree, with this look on his face like he'd tasted something horrible, and Venetia had joined him. He'd taken his dress jacket off and loosened his tie, something he never did in public. The sun started setting behind them – a small blood orange, squeezing its juice all over the clouds. The ends of Monty's curly hair acquired a fluorescent glow and their shadows grew out elongated and skinny from their feet. Venetia said something and he did a little nod, that horrible taste still pinching his mouth. He allowed her to fix his tie. She pressed a hand to his cheek and held it there and he closed his eyes, and they stood like that for at least two minutes, her velvet-gloved hand pressed to his face, neither of them moving, the sun sinking behind the grasping black hands of distant trees.

'So when are you intending to start a family?'

Bettina rolled her eyes. 'Mother, now is not the time.'

'Now is exactly the time, darling,' said Venetia. She held a glass of white wine – her third in the space of an hour. A little colour had returned to her cheeks. 'You are twenty-three for God's sake.'

'I meant now is not the time to talk of this.'

Venetia puffed out air and sloshed her wine around in the glass. 'I repeat – now is *exactly* the time. Our family is diminishing, dear. Don't you *want* children?'

'Of course.'

'Well? Isn't Bart up to the task?'

'Mother!'

'Don't "Mother" me. It's at times like these that we must learn to open our mouths and say what we mean. Silence is lethal. I've learned that much.' She gripped Bettina's wrist. 'You are my last remaining child, darling. I want grandchildren.' She stared glassy-eyed at Bettina, blinking once like the shutter of a camera. 'Does that make me selfish? Well, of course it does. And I don't care.' Her chin twisted and wrinkled into a monkey-nut shell and her hand fluttered at her face. She glugged from her glass and lit a fresh cigarette. 'Does he pull out, darling? Is that it? Like the Catholics? Before he—'

'No!'

'Then maybe you're not doing it enough.'

'I am!' Tuna and her sisters glanced over nosily.

'The fact of the matter is,' said Bettina, in a low, measured voice, 'I haven't yet *wanted* to catch. I've not felt ready.'

'You modern girls. Too much drinking, too much dancing.' She waved a hand. 'Oh, I'm happy that you're having *fun*, darling. I wish I'd had the chance to have fun at your age. But you don't want to wait *too* long. Best have them young, when you've more bang in your cannon.'

'Do you think Jonathan would've had children? If he'd never . . .'

'Oh, I'm certain he would have. Eventually. He had prospects, you know.'

'Did he? He never told me that. He carried on like he was a social pariah. An undesirable.'

Venetia shook her head. 'He wasn't right in the head, darling.

His lens was smudged. Bunty's daughter was after him, you know.'

'Catherine Kingsley? Really?'

'Oh, yes.'

'But she's absolutely gorgeous! She's – all the men say so at any rate.'

'Well, why not?' said Venetia. 'Jonathan was a handsome young man.' She frowned. 'This business of speaking of him in the past tense, it feels so unnatural! Was. Was. Bloody hell.' She covered her eyes with one hand and her shoulders started shuddering. The wine glass dropped from her fingers, soaking the carpet but not breaking. Bettina wrapped an arm around her shoulders. Lucille came over and took the seat on her other side, draping her arm around the opposite shoulder so that hers and Bettina's crossed over like the carved links of a Celtic spoon.

She found Bart sitting alone in the library. It was lit by electric lamps under green glass shades, although her father, stubborn as always, still used his candles when reading at his desk. The walnut floor was freshly waxed. Bettina abhorred the smell of floor wax – it reminded her of church. Bart was sitting with a slumped back but very straight, pressed-together legs, his bitter lemon resting on his knee. What was it about grief that made men want to sit differently?

She lit two cigarettes, passing one to him. 'Jonathan liked to come in here,' she said. 'He had a special fondness for the Brontë sisters.'

'I don't want to talk about Jonathan any more.'

'You're angry with him.'

'Aren't you?'

'No. I just feel very, very sad. Empty.'

Bart leaned back, relaxing his legs. 'I'm just far more comfortable with anger.'

'Hmm. You remember learning about humourism? The four humours?'

Bart nodded. 'You're going to say that I would be diagnosed as being a choleric and you'd be a melancholic.'

'That *is* what I was going to say, actually.'

'It's all horseshit.'

'Of course it is.' She plucked a slice of lemon from Bart's glass and chewed it. Grimaced. Placed the rind on the armrest. 'If this was a party at our house, someone would be lying under that table over there with their knickers around their ankles.'

'This isn't a party.'

'I know. I'm just saying.'

His cigarette trembled between his fingers. 'I don't want any more of those parties.'

'Me neither.' She kissed his forehead, her thumb automatically swiping away the lipstick mark. His eyes were spilling tears, turning his grey-green irises to quivering puddles. Bart had always been fairly comfortable crying in front of her. It was at odds with his character.

'I was just starting to get fond of the bastard,' he said.

'You liked to play cards with him,' she said. 'I always wondered what your conversations were like.'

'Pretty one-sided for the most part.'

'I can imagine.' She lit another two cigarettes. 'Bart? Can I tell you something?'

'Of course.' He wiped his eyes, blinking, and pulled a hanky from his pocket to blow his nose.

'I think I want children.'

He stared at her, the hanky over his nose.

'Bart? What do you think?'

He balled up the hanky and looked at it with a curious frown. 'I've been sitting here this whole time thinking the exact same thing. Isn't that the—'

'Really?'

'Really. Well, that and unsolicited flashing images of your brother's corpse. Death and life, death and life, blah blah.'

'It is rather predictable, isn't it?'

He shrugged. 'It's not always a bad thing to do predictable things. Nothing makes death easier to bear than new life. It's why everyone started fucking like rabbits after the war.'

'I don't know how we'll carry it off though,' she said. 'Physically, I mean.'

'That's partly what I was thinking about actually, just before you came in.' He started picking the skin off his lower lip. 'Suppose we tried it in the dark? The pitch dark? Minimal contact? Imagine having to face each other when the lights come on after. Can you imagine?'

'Maybe it would be funny,' she said. 'Maybe we could make it funny.'

He grinned. 'I could dress like a clown.'

'I could honk your nose.' She reached out and squeezed an imaginary nose. 'Barp.' And they fell to sudden laughter – it was loud and ferocious and it filled the huge room with echoes. They leaned into each other, gasping. 'I could – I could put clown's noses on my – ha! I don't want to say it – oh sod it: nipples! I'd have clown's noses on my nipples and you'd . . .' She whipped her head back, shrieking, all her teeth showing. 'You'd – ha! Oh dear, oh dear. You'd . . .' She reached out again and enacted the imaginary squeezing with both hands. 'Beep beep.'

'I'm glad someone's having a jolly time.' Lucille. In the doorway. With a cigarette and a tumbler of booze. 'I hope you don't behave like this at my funeral.' She tossed back her drink and eyed them with a look that Bettina could only describe as rancid.

'Sorry,' muttered Bart, fanning his face with his hanky. 'We didn't mean any disrespect.'

Lucille nodded. 'Of course you didn't. Of course you didn't.' Her words slurred. She came into the room, almost stumbling on the edge of the rug. She looked down at the floor, her legs firmly planted as if she were in a boat, riding a storm, and waved a finger at the slippery rug. 'Stay,' she said to it.

'Oh, Christ,' whispered Bart.

'Go and help her,' whispered Bettina.

He shook his head. 'She won't let me.'

'What are you two collaborating about?' *Clabuhratin.* Lucille lurched over to the sofa and dumped herself between Bart and Bettina, her wide behind pushing the two apart. 'Thick as thieves, you two. Always were. Tweedledum and Tweedledee. Such good friends, *such* good friends.' She swung her head in Bettina's direction. 'When are you going to give my son a child?'

Bettina glanced at Bart. He shook his head: not yet.

Lucille took a long drag of her cigarette, her eyes gunky crescents; mascara and eyeshadow had gathered in the corners, liquid black seeping into the tributary network of wrinkles. Her usually light-green irises were dull as hay. 'Are you withholding, dear?' she said, her head nodding. 'Would you like me to order you some whores? They could stand at the end of your bed and wiggle their udders to get you in the mood, then maybe you'll open your legs for my son.'

Bettina's mouth snapped open.

'Mother!' said Bart. 'You shut your mouth!'

That awful head swung around in the opposite direction – it was like some mossy gorgon-like figurehead, lurching as the ship got battered by a sea storm. 'No! You shut *your* mouth!' She hit Bart around the head, bracelets jangling, sparks flying out of her cigarette. 'How dare you tell me to – I'm your *mother*!' Her head flopped back to Bettina. 'You'd like that, wouldn't you? Bunch of women, bunch of whores, pulling down their knickers for you. I know girls like you – I'm not stupid, I've heard stories about you. I *know* girls like you.' She was jabbing her cigarette at Bettina's face, the lit end coming close enough to warm her skin. 'Tell you what, pudding' – and here she affected a simpering, kindly tone – 'I'll get that she-man who runs the public house in Hove; I'll go and fetch her and maybe she can get you warmed up for my Barty. Great big bull-dagger with man's muscles and a clit like a blessed *bell*! You'd *like* that, wouldn't you?'

She glared at Bettina, her head dipping and rising – a gentle tide now for the gorgon mast. Bettina's hand was balled up into a pearl-knuckled fist. She held Lucille's gaze and said, arctic-cool, 'I think I *would* like that, Lucille. Very much. What a kind mother-in-law you are, to go to such lengths for me.'

Lucille's frown twitched as she processed this. Bettina focused on the sloppy black crud in the corner of her mother-in-law's left eye. Bart was perched on the edge of the sofa, his hand clamped to his mouth, eyes screwed shut. And then Lucille's face collapsed and a great huff came out of her chest and she was crying, really crying. Bart plucked the cigarette out of her hand, tossed it in the ashtray and wrapped his arms around her, saying, 'There, there,' and giving Bettina traumatised glances from over her jittering head.

She pulled a hanky out from between her cleavage and blew her nose. 'I'm sorry,' she said. 'I'm so sorry.' Sniffing, she turned to Bettina and grasped her wrist. 'I *do* like you, Bettina. I haven't always shown it, but I've always liked you, in my way. And there's nothing wrong with it!' She smiled in a way that was both sweet and gruesome and shook Bettina's wrist, her jewellery tinkling like a bell in a shop doorway. 'Nothing wrong with it.' She grabbed Bart's wrist too and held them both, like Jesus reassuring his apostles. 'Nothing wrong with it,' she said again, to Bart this time, still smiling that crooked, bittersweet smile. 'You think I haven't lived?' She looked back and forth between the two of them. 'You think *I* haven't tried it?'

'Dear God,' said Bart, under his breath.

'I just want you to be *happy*,' continued Lucille. 'And I want you to have babies, lots of babies. There are methods, dear. I *know*. There are ways around it. The man puts his spendings into a receptacle and the lady inserts it with a syringe. Even the royals have done it this way. Even the royals.' She burped quietly. 'Pardon me. And if it's good enough for the royals . . . you see?' She looked at Bettina with gushing, motherly love and stroked her cheek. 'I'm so sorry for my evil words.' There was a smear of mucus on her cheek. 'Do you forgive me?'

Her true meaning, of course, being, 'Will you tell your mother?' And Bettina would not. She forced a smile and patted the woman on the back. 'Perhaps you ought to lie down?'

Lucille nodded gratefully. Bettina pulled her shoes off (a hole in the foot of her stocking, a white toe poking out like a mushroom) and Bart fetched Monty's smoking jacket from the rack on the wall, draping it over her. 'Poor, poor Jonathan,' said Lucille, closing her eyes. 'Poor, sweet, sensitive boy.'

'A sick bowl, perhaps?' Bettina whispered to Bart.

Bart shook his head. 'She'll just pass out. I doubt she'll remember any of this.'

'I wish I didn't have to.'

Bart shook his head, blowing out air from his cheeks.

Lucille curled her knees tighter to her chest and wriggled her head into the armrest. Eyes still closed, she raised a finger in the air. 'Even the royals . . . I mean, it's just a means to an end, it doesn't matter, doesn't matter, there's nothing wrong with it, my lovely boy.' Her mouth sagged open and almost immediately her breathing slowed and deepened.

Bettina looked at Bart. 'Well.'

He shook his head slowly, darkly. 'I'm so sorry.'

'I'll laugh about it tomorrow. I almost want to laugh about it now. Just a bit shocked still.'

'She was *horrible* to you. I'm so, so sorry, Betts.'

She waved her hand. 'I can take it. I suppose. Anyway, she's the one who's come off the worst. I wonder who she tried it with? Not my mother, I hope.'

Bart grabbed his hair with both hands. 'Nooo. Please don't ever mention that again. Oh my God. I'm fucking mortified. I need a drink.' He held out his hand and she took it. 'You had her though. You shut her up. What a good sport you were!' He squeezed her hand. 'You absolutely had her.'

Chapter 14

July 1927, Davenport House, London

Her legs were up in the air, stockingless, and her skirt sunk down to her waist. Her shins were covered in soft blonde hair and her toenails needed cutting. One of them (on her big toe) was ingrown and the flesh around it looked pink and tender. He could see the scar on the bony ridge of her foot from when they'd been playing out in his mother's garden as children and she'd put a garden fork through it. Her scream! At first he'd laughed, thinking she was messing about. And then all the blood. He'd vomited – it had bubbled up yellow and milky, spilling onto his pullover.

'How long have I got to stay like this?' she asked, planting her feet against the wall and padding them so they made soft slapping sounds.

'Longer the better, I suppose,' he said.

'What do you think about when you – you know,' she said.

He looked at her blankly.

'*You* know. When you're producing the stuff.'

'Ah. I think of your toenails.'

She reached out to slap him, just missing. 'Seriously, Meow, what do you think about?'

Meow – his new nickname.

Sobriety had undeniably turned him into a sourpuss. He moped around all day, glugging back-to-back cups of strong tea and trying to occupy his mind with books (he was on D. H. Lawrence at the moment and it was rotten rubbish). The nights were the hardest. Bettina and Étienne continued to drink, and why shouldn't they? He'd sit with a script on his lap, moodily watching them larking around at the piano, singing songs with the lyrics dirtied up – he so used to enjoy a brandy while going over new scripts, the ritual of it, the crisp paper in his hands, the fire crackling, the brandy warming his belly. When Bettina troubled herself to speak to him he gave caustic replies. 'Me*ow*,' Bettina said one time. She giggled to herself. 'You know, I think I shall start to call you Bartholo*meow*. Meow for short.' Bart fixed her with a filthy look. Returned to his script. Bastards. Fucking nitwits and bastards.

'I don't *think* about anything,' he said now. 'I have a few pictures that I like to look at.' He had a whole book – wellworn, of course – full of photographs of various men sodomising each other. He kept it inside the locked wooden box alongside all his letters and drawings from Étienne.

'Oooh. Nudey piccies? Can you show them to me?'

'Never in a million years.'

'Do they depict buggery?'

'Mind your own business.'

'Does it hurt? Buggery?'

'Mind your own business.'

'It must get awfully messy. Have you ever had an accident? You know—'

'Why do you assume that I'm the bugge*ree*?'

Étienne came into the room barefoot, wearing Bettina's red satin dressing gown. '*Pourquoi*?' he said, gesturing at her legs.

'Keeps the little swimmers in the pool,' she said. Then: 'Etts? Are you the buggerer or the buggeree?'

'Don't tell her,' said Bart.

Étienne smiled at him, dimples like speech marks. 'Buggerer.'

'Lies!' said Bart.

'We're going to have to behave ourselves once the little one comes along,' said Bettina, reaching for her cigarettes on the bedside table, her legs swaying heavily in the air. 'No more cursing, no more naughty talk. You two will have to keep your hands to yourselves.'

'That's if he even sticks around,' said Bart.

Étienne was in the midst of an existential crisis. That's what he called it anyway. He didn't understand what his place could be within the forthcoming family. 'Who am I to this child? Why is the French artist tagging along always with this young couple? What does this French artist have to do with booties and cribs?' And of course, he missed his garret. He missed Paris. His whoring too, probably. He had his own studio here, in the unused conservatory, but found it too sterile. 'Stop being such a cliché,' Bart would say to him. 'If you're truly an artist it doesn't matter where you go to create art. You are in love with a romantic fallacy.'

'I am in love with you, that is the problem,' he'd shoot back.

Étienne stayed in one of the guest bedrooms two doors down from Bart's and Bettina's quarters (they had their own bedrooms, connected by a door). Bart and Étienne were constantly in and out of each other's beds. Some nights, usually after smoking hashish, Étienne grew paranoid, cocking his head at imagined footsteps outside the door. He was convinced that Humphrey the butler was spying on them. 'He thinks that we are living together as a *ménage à trois*, he is trying to catch us out.' He talked of installing trip wires outside his door. He hated all this sneaking around. He hated the way Humphrey looked at him. He hated Humphrey. He hated himself for hating Humphrey – he'd of course entered Bart's household bloated with ideals: he would befriend the servants and show them many kindnesses and treat them as equals, blah blah blah, but what the little twerp didn't anticipate was that the servants didn't want to be his friend. 'They are people who want my money,' Bart told him, 'and I am a person who wants their service. It's a simple transaction. We could all die tomorrow, me, you and Betts, and they wouldn't shed a single tear.'

'Ettie's not going anywhere,' said Bettina, now. 'Who else is going to teach little junior about class oppression?'

'Exactly,' said Bart. 'Who else is going to install an inescapable sense of guilt in our bundle of joy?'

'Very well, very well,' said Étienne, tired-smiling. 'Uncle Ettie will stay.'

And then, quite suddenly, he was gone. Gone. A letter on his pillow: 'I am sorry. My love for you is unchanged but I cannot do this and I must return to Paris. Tell Bettina I am sorry.' Bart drove his car to the station, hoping to catch him, to talk him out of it. Étienne was not at the station. Nobody was at the station. Bart cried with his chin on the steering wheel. He cried until his whole body ached. He cried himself raw.

He drove back home, took a bottle of whisky from the drinks cabinet, went upstairs to his bed, pulled the covers over his head and drank the whole bottle from under his blanketed fort. He came to ten hours later. He'd wet the bed and vomited on the pillow. It was caught up in the hair behind his ear. He stripped and put on a pair of pyjama bottoms. He could hear Bettina next door, listening to a Mistinguett record. He shoved the door open, snatched the gramophone needle away with a screech, ripped the record out and snapped it over his knee. 'No French music in this house ever again!'

Bettina was on the bed, reading a novel. She looked at him, unfazed. 'You're going to replace that record,' she said.

He dropped the pieces on the floor and sank into the armchair with his head in his hands.

'What is it?' she said. 'Have you and Etts been rowing again?'

He shook his head.

'Well? What's the matter?'

'He's left me.'

'What? No. Of course he hasn't.'

A nod.

'Really? For sure?'

Another nod.

'Oh, sweetheart.' She wrapped him up in her arms. 'What did he do a silly thing like that for?' He felt her fingers touch his sick-dampened hair and dart away. But she didn't let go of him, and that was a great kindness.

He slept in her bed that night (and for many nights after). The next morning he accompanied her to the doctor for a check-up as she hadn't started her monthlies on schedule, was a whole week late, in fact – which might mean nothing, she explained, because it'd happened before; women's reproductive organs were wilful and peculiar. He sat on the other side of the white curtain, staring unseeing at a framed painting of a fruit bowl, his stomach gurgling with hunger. He heard Bettina gasp – a lubricated finger rudely poking and sliding. He imagined the doctor pulling out a bunch of flowers with a flourish. Ta-da! The fruit bowl blurred, its red apples and green grapes blobbing and smearing. Nothing would be funny ever again.

The doctor came out from behind the curtain to wash his hands. He sat at his desk, scribbling something onto his notepad. Bettina emerged and he signalled for her to sit with a swish of his pen.

'Well,' said the doctor, looking up finally. 'It looks like congratulations are in order. You're expecting.'

Bettina clutched his hand.

'What wonderful news,' said Bart, knowing that it was indeed wonderful news, in an objective sort of way.

Nothing would be truly wonderful ever again.

The man was neither ugly nor attractive. On a scale of one to ten, with one being hideous and ten being gorgeous, he was a solid five. Not that it mattered – his head might as well be a potato on a stick. He was wearing a peaked cap atop a dandruff-dotted mop of curly brown hair. Tweed waistcoat over a white shirt, the sleeves rolled up. His age – somewhere between thirty and forty. Not that it mattered. He smelled strongly of pipe tobacco and pastry. His hands were clean.

Bart pushed him against the tree and started grappling with his trouser buttons. A long, thin cock bounced out, impossibly smooth, almost virginal-looking, like it'd never been touched, like it'd only just been created, there, in the man's underpants, seconds ago, by a misguided angel.

Bart dropped to his knees, his shin knocking a gnarled tree root, and took the thing in his mouth. It tasted of mushrooms. The man grabbed his hair, bunching it up in his hands, tugging it. Étienne used to do that. He grabbed the man's hips and pushed his head forward, relaxing his throat. His eyes started watering – the world became a blur. The man made a sound like a bull ready to charge.

And then.

And then.

Voices. Dry leaves crackling, twigs snapping. A torchlight skimming the ground nearby.

'Run,' said the man.

Bart groped for his hat and lurched away with a spool of saliva hanging off his chin.

A man's yell: 'Oi! Stop right there!'

But Bart was already running. His shoes landed in earthy dips hidden by a dry leaf carpet, his toes knocked against jutting roots and stones, his shins ripped through snares of low-lying bramble, yet miraculously he was still running, his hat clutched in one hand, the other stretched out ahead to ward off branches. He dodged the thin black trees that rose up suddenly from out of the fuzzy darkness, smacking his elbow or shoulder on them before bouncing away, still miraculously running, roaring bloody drunk, the air cold-burning his throat, mouth fixed in a grimace. The sound of his feet crashing through the undergrowth was the loudest thing in the world. He felt like an animal, a skunk or an otter, a wild, dumb thing.

He came out of the trees and saw the wooden sign with opening and closing times on it (a lavender handkerchief wrapped around the post). Beyond this – the gate. He ran for it, not daring to glance behind, a nerve-tickle between his shoulder blades. He reached the gate and threw his hat over. He could hear feet pounding turf close behind. Oh fuck oh fuck oh fuck. He launched himself up the gate using the bars as footholds, his body no longer his body, his thoughts flying bat-like out of his skull, and as he swung his leg over the top, he finally dared to look at the approaching man.

The man. Not a copper or a park warden. Mushroom Cock.

As he dropped down the outer side of the gate the man started climbing, slowly, confidently, and was soon dropping down beside him, one hand on his cap to keep it on. Bart started jogging towards his car. The man followed.

'It's all right, I knocked him out,' said the man in a northern accent, running to keep up with him. 'Look.' He held out his hand. His knuckle was grazed and bloody. A tiny scrap of skin was sticking up.

'Who was he?'

'The parky.'

Bart stuffed his hands in his pockets and sped up.

'Close call though, weren't it?'

Bart nodded curtly. He glanced around; the street was empty. He reached his car and opened the door.

The man grabbed his arm. 'Give us a lift home, eh?'

Bart ripped his arm away and got in the car, slamming the door. The man thumped the window with his palm. Bart started the engine and drove away, glancing at the rear-view mirror – the man was in the road, shouting and waving his cap around. Lunatic. Fucking lunatic. He drove in a frenzy, going around corners too fast and almost crashing into a hedgerow. He didn't have his lights on. He'd forgotten to put his lights on. He parked up in a lay-by, closed his eyes and waited until his breathing was back to normal.

I'm an arse, he thought, driving away. He drove past St James's Theatre, seeing the large *Major Barbara* poster with his face all over it. He pointed at it. 'You, sir, are an arse.'

Humphrey came rushing to meet him in the hall. He had shoe polish on his hands. 'Good evening, sir. It's quite late.' Humphrey had watery eyes, perpetually so, which glistened like raw egg whites. Bart and Bettina called him The Crying Butler behind his back and concocted stories about his life which accounted for such emotional fragility, the latest of which was that he was a virgin with a romantic history of unrequited love and brutal rejections, and all he wanted was someone to hold him.

'Are you my father now?'

'No, sir, I was merely making an observation.'

'Please don't.' Bart headed up the stairs. He paused halfway up and looked around to find Humphrey still there, an imposing, neat figure in the large hall, those wet wobbly eyes turned up to him. 'Humphrey?'

'Sir?'

'I want you to do something for me.'

'Sir?'

'I want you to start calling me Arse. That is my new name from now on. Arse.'

'Certainly not,' said Humphrey.

'That was an order.'

'There is nothing in my contract that stipulates that I must lower myself to such base terms. You're drunk. *Sir*.'

Bart waved his hand. 'Fine. You're fired.'

He tripped up the last step and landed with the whisky bottle between his body and the carpet runner.

Bettina was in her bed, reading a novel by lamplight.

'Your arse of a husband is home,' he said, bowing deeply.

She lowered her book. 'Where have you been?'

'I've been taking the night air, darling.' He shrugged off his coat and flopped onto the bed bellyfirst. 'Don't mind me. I'll be asleep shortly.'

She pulled his shoes off. 'Roll over,' she said, pushing at his waist. He rolled onto his back. She undid his belt and his buttons and pulled down his trousers. 'There's mud on the knees.'

'I was praying. In the garden.'

'Oh?' She pulled his socks off and started unbuttoning his shirt. 'What were you praying for?'

'For a fixed heart.'

'Oh, Bart.' She climbed onto the bed next to him and struggled with his shirt sleeves, rolling him this way and that. 'I don't think God listens to the prayers of drunks.'

Bart lifted his arm as she pulled his shirt. 'Or homosexuals.'

He was down to his underpants and vest. She made him move up the bed till his head was on a pillow. 'Turn onto your side. I'm going to get you a sick bowl.' She pulled the bottle out of his hand. 'This is going in the bin. Don't you dare get another.'

He called her just as she was nearly out of the door.

'What?'

He raised his head off the pillow and tried to focus on her face. 'While you're down there, tell Humphrey he's not really fired, will you? Tell him I'm sorry.'

'What have you done, Meow?'

He dropped his head back onto the pillow. 'Nothing. Nothing. Was just being a bit of an arse.'

Chapter 15

December 1927, Davenport House, London

Could she do better? The dress was divine – a luxurious silk that brought to mind creamy coffee pouring into a cup, and it had tiny opal charms embroidered along the neckline. One could always do better. She poked her fringe into place then bent forward, checking her cleavage in the mirror. Her breasts sagged and separated like large milk puddings. Maybe tonight called for something *less* lovely. She didn't need to go rubbing things in her poor cousin's face.

Tuna'd had a miscarriage recently, her third in a row, and had apparently taken to staying at home, bringing her five o'clock vermouth forward to half past four, then four, then half past three. She'd put on three stone. All of this gossip, of course; Bettina hadn't visited Cousin Tuna in over seven months.

But Tuna didn't have a monopoly on misery! Bettina had

suffered the most evil morning sickness in the early months, unable to keep anything down until mid-afternoon. She frequently felt dizzy with anaemia, endured sciatic nerve pain along her buttocks and needed to urinate every five minutes. Her feet and hands were bloating at such a rate that she fancied she could almost see them swelling in real time, like a beached whale carcass slowly filling up with gas.

The dress clung to her stomach. God no. Here, Tuna, would you look at this new life growing inside me! God no. Poor thing. She took out a magenta dress, picking off a speck of lint. Perhaps – and she was big enough to acknowledge this – perhaps, deep down, she'd been avoiding Tuna all this time. As if Tuna might taint her in some way. As if miscarriage was catching.

What a ghastly thought.

The magenta dress was fine. Fine. She checked her nostrils in the mirror and went downstairs to find Doris the cook at the kitchen table, fixing a clock with her sleeves rolled up and a small screw bit between her teeth. She asked her to do up her dress buttons and Doris gave her a peevish look, thinking, undoubtedly, that she wasn't a bloody lady's maid. Still, she did up the buttons, saying, 'Lovely fabric on this,' in her wheezy Scotch drawl.

They only had a live-in cook now, with the gardener coming in twice a week and a girl doubling as maid and housekeeper coming in every day until seven at night, noon on Sundays. Bart was unwilling to sell the Brighton house, not wanting to displace his mother. Bettina imagined Lucille as a huge, cracked tortoise, her scaly hide like peeling whitewash, slowly creeping from room to room, leaving her droppings under dust-sheeted furniture.

'My mother is too spoiled to tolerate a decline in her living standards,' Bart told her, 'and I am, as you know, a proud, unabashed mummy's boy.'

So they had to 'tighten their belts'. Bart's stage salary was glorified pocket money, he claimed, and the 'fortune' left to him by his father, while generous, would not last long if he insisted on employing butlers and valets, all of which he could do without frankly, because he wasn't a 'damn child or a cripple' and anyway, 'how can a nation call itself great when its elite cannot do basic things for themselves?'

Bettina remembered Étienne saying similar things.

'Can you imagine,' he said, 'if we were to lose everything? Every penny? And suddenly having to do everything, entirely everything for ourselves? Cooking our own food, cleaning our own home. Have you ever imagined that?'

Bettina nodded; she had. Of course she had. It was telling that he was thinking about loss. And of course there was the great unspoken thing: Bart and Bettina were idiots with their money and had squandered hundreds of pounds on wild parties and luxurious holidays abroad. After their wedding they'd been like children handed a hammer and a piggy bank and left unsupervised.

Bart was currently rehearsing for the part of Peter in Chekhov's *The Cherry Orchard.* He hated Chekhov, finding his plays 'dull enough to induce coma', but Bettina positively nagged him to take the part, thinking that any role was preferable to his constant moping around the house. 'You might even meet someone,' she came close to saying.

Bart did not want to meet anyone. Bart was terrified of love, if this was what its loss – there's that word again – could do to a person.

Jennings the butler opened the door and a cloud of incense smoke enveloped his shoulders, lending him a fantastical vampiric air. 'Please, come in, Mrs Dawes, you are very welcome,' he said, his tone kindling dry. Jennings had been on Tuna's staff ever since her marriage – he'd previously butlered for her husband Max's family. His hairline started in wispy jags three quarters of the way along his head, leaving a waxy, mole-dotted pate; his eyelids drooped like melted cheese and his forehead, in Bart's charming words, was as creased as an old spunk rag.

The front hall was the size of a ballroom (Max's family had in fact used it for this purpose throughout the previous century, hosting extravagant dances which were attended, apparently, by members of the royal family) and it was flanked by a staircase the width of a rugby goalpost. A crowd of people in bizarre costumes were chattering and dancing in this ex-ballroom now, under a heavy cumulus of cigarette smoke and incense.

'Oh, I didn't know it was fancy dress,' said Bettina.

Jennings let out a smirk. 'It isn't. Please, come in from the cold.' Bettina looked again: men in Russian Cossack costume, gypsy tweeds, floral waistcoats; women in Arabian harem-style fabrics, some in gothic funeral attire. He was having her on. 'I feel quite under-dressed,' she told him.

'You are dressed tastefully,' he said. 'May I take your coat?'

She shrugged off her coat for him and saw Tuna, in a scarlet dress with a humongous bustle and a ridiculous pair of painted-on eyebrows, crying and running barefoot across the hall. A skinny, sickly-looking man wearing dark-green eyeshadow followed her. He was bald and nude from the waist up and he wore only a green Highlander's kilt. He had the frame of a young boy and his ribcage stuck out. Tuna bundled up the train of her skirt and bounded up the stairs, still weeping. She stopped halfway up, turned back and shrieked, 'Don't you dare follow me, Bone!' before continuing up the steps. The party-goers stopped what they were doing to look. And then quickly resumed their dancing and chatting.

'What on earth sort of party is this?' she said to Jennings.

He shrugged. 'Mrs Garside has acquired some new friends. And some new ideas.' He ran his hands along the fur coat draping his arm. 'If she's not careful, she'll soon have to acquire some new staff.'

'Should I go up to her?'

'If you like.' He glanced down at her stomach. 'Congratulations by the way. I am of course thrilled for you and your husband.'

Thrilled? He looked like he'd just been diagnosed with cancer of the prostate.

She headed for the staircase, protecting her bump from errant elbows and hearing snippets of droll conversation: 'He never would have said that if he knew who you were—', '—spiritual frisson, you know, though I shouldn't think—', '—quite suicidal, honestly, so I said to her—', '—and I fucking hate hydrangeas—'

Max Garside was home roughly fifty days of the year. Tuna was by now used to doing without her husband and no longer pined for him, deciding instead to take a pro-active approach to her loneliness by sleeping with other men – usually artists and poets. She seemed to have a new favourite every month. So prolific was she in her philandering that it was entirely possible her miscarried babies had not been Max's at all.

Then again, Max probably had a woman in every port. Bettina imagined him arriving at some crumbling, lice-infested Ukrainian cottage with a stack of presents under his arm, breezing through the doorway and saying, 'Daddy's home!' to a clutch of dusky, barefoot brats (were Ukrainians dusky?), before sweeping up a big-hipped, scraggle-haired peasant in his arms and kissing a mouth marinated in garlic.

Bettina knocked on Tuna's bedroom door.

'Fuck off!'

'It's Bettina.'

A moment's silence then a sudden stampede, a flung-open door and Tuna's tear-blotched face. 'Oh, Betts, I'm so glad to see you!' Tuna yanked her into the room and crushed her in a strong hug. 'Have a little drinky-poos with me, will you?'

Bettina nodded, looking around the room. It had been entirely transformed, the wallpaper stripped and the walls painted an obscene bright orange. The tasteful paintings of pastoral scenes had been replaced by cubist doodles, zodiac charts and God knows what. Where the ottoman had once stood there was now an antique Punch and Judy theatre, the puppets drooping over the tiny stage like boneless trolls. The Welsh dresser had been painted red, its shelves filled with odd curios: eyeless dolls, rabbits' feet, a collection of crystals, vases filled with dead flowers and – wasn't that a monkey paw? The room stank like a church; on the dressing table a quartz ashtray held a tablet of smoking charcoal on which was placed a pinch of Frankincense.

Tuna went to her bar, her train dragging over the junk on the floor, and poured drinks. She had indeed put on weight. But she looked fantastic.

'Oh, I almost forgot,' she said, handing Bettina a drink. 'Congratulations! You did receive the flowers, I hope? And the rocking horse?' She got down on her knees and pressed her ear to Bettina's belly. She smiled, looking up at her. 'A girl. Mark my words. I've a gift for this.'

'Are you all right now?'

'Oh, I'm fine. Just a lovers' tiff.'

'That bald chap?'

'His name is Bone.'

'You're joking.'

Tuna took out a silver cigarette case – it was a Russian design inlaid with three small rubies – and lit a cigarette. 'Don't judge me, Bettina. The man is a genius. And I'll tell you something else: he's got a nine-incher. And I never exaggerate in these matters.'

'Him? Surely not.'

Tuna nodded matter-of-factly, squeezing out smoke through a gap in her teeth.

'Well,' said Bettina. 'I suppose I'm happy for you.'

'Don't be. He's also a sadist. I'm giving him the old heave-ho tonight. Here, sit down with me.' She swiped a pile of clothes off her sofa.

'I'm very sorry about the baby,' said Bettina, sitting down.

'It's fine, I'm fine. It was only a few weeks along – practically a blood clot. Don't look at me like that; I don't want any sympathy. I just want to have fun.'

'All the same . . .'

'It mightn't even be me with the problem. What about Max? Did you ever think of that? Might be something wrong with his little tadpoles.'

'Max?'

She must have sensed the incredulity in Bettina's tone because both sets of eyebrows went up. 'Yes, Max. Who else?'

'Oh, come on. You go through beaus almost as fast as you go through maids.'

Tuna laughed with delight, her chin doubling. 'Silly girl! I don't let them put it in *there*! Only Max has that dubious honour.'

Bettina sipped her drink. 'Oh.'

'We're having some poetry in the garden later. I tried to get Siegfried Sassoon down for a reading but it's impossible to nail the bugger down.'

'Is it a fancy-dress party? Jennings told me it wasn't but I think he was being snarky.'

Tuna swatted the air. 'Jennings can kiss my tits. You know what? We never really stop being young. We are forever those dreamy-eyed children, wanting to play, to pretend, to imagine other realities. But it gets knocked out of us, doesn't it? By old miseries like Jennings.'

Bettina wasn't paying full attention; she was looking down at her dress. 'I am the most boring person here.'

'Only aesthetically speaking, darling. Here, do you want to borrow something of mine?'

Down the stairs they went, arm in arm, stepping in unison (it had been agreed that they would step in unison). Tuna had changed her outfit and was now wearing a yellow smock made entirely out of bright canary feathers. She had dried turkey feet hanging from her ears, the claws painted with yellow nail polish. She was very proud of this touch. Bettina had transformed herself into Theda Bara's Salome, a rough approximation thereof at any rate, with a huge, heavy head-dress, white flowing gown and severe vampy eyeliner. Her own finishing touch: a false moustache.

Tuna took Jennings to one side and asked him to get rid of Bone and all his effects – she wanted him gone within the hour. 'Don't look at me like that,' she said, holding up a finger to his face. 'I hate it when you look at me like that.'

He raised a wry eyebrow. 'I don't know what you could possibly mean.'

'You may *judge* me,' said Tuna, 'but I *pay* you. Get rid of him. Don't let him take the portrait in the green room.'

'Which one?'

She leaned in and whispered into his ear.

'Ah,' he said. 'That one.'

'It was a gift,' said Tuna. 'He'll try and say it wasn't, but it was. It's mine.'

'Very well.'

'I do appreciate everything you do for me, Jen-Jens.'

His lips tightened and pursed as if he were trying out a smile for the first time. 'I'm sure, Mrs Garside,' he said, leaving.

'He's not fooling anyone,' said Tuna, snapping her fingers at the drinks' waiter. 'He absolutely adores me.' She took a drink and sipped it. 'I do hope Bone doesn't make a fuss. He's always threatening to kill himself.'

'Then let him.'

Tuna stared at Bettina, shocked. 'Me*ow*, darling. Bad kitty.'

'All I mean is, he's not your problem any more.' She waved her hand around the crowded room. 'Look at all these other problems you can choose from.'

'Give me five minutes to breathe, will you? I think I could do with a break from men, to be honest. He was so *mean* to me, Betts. Always trying to pick at me, to pick me to the bone. Ha! Bone! He called me a tourist, can you believe that? Here, let me light that for you.' She snapped open her lighter and hovered it under Bettina's cigarette. 'I mean, it's true that I've dipped my toe into a new way of life recently—'

'Dipped your toe? You've dived right in.'

'Well, yes. I know how it looks. But this is what I said to him: I said, for a start, even if I *am* a tourist, it is not for the sake of fashion, it's not so superficial as that – it's not like buying a pair of jodhpurs because jodhpurs happen to be in vogue, it's because I have an adventurous spirit, I aim to explore and celebrate all forms of culture, to feast at the table of life. And what could be more quintessentially bohemian than the possession of such— Are you listening to me, darling? I also said to him, "Well, I'd rather be a tourist than a bore!" And I poked him like this.' She jabbed a finger into Bettina's chest. '"*I'm* fucking interesting! And I'm funny! And those two qualities trump yours, you neurotic cry-baby!" Sorry, darling, did I poke you too hard there?'

'Oh, no, it's fine.' She gave her cousin a dazed smile. There was a woman across the room who she'd first thought a man, a very slender man, in a man's suit and bowler hat. But there was the suggestion of hips, of breasts. Her hair was short and black, or seemingly short; it was probably scooped up into a bun and hidden under her hat.

'Honestly, I think you really lucked out with Bart,' continued Tuna. 'He's such a riot. He doesn't care what anyone thinks, it's so very refreshing—'

Was the woman *looking* at her?

'—but then, I thought I'd lucked out with Max, and look at our situation. Him nipping back once in a blue moon to try to impregnate me—'

Winking?

'—and me just waiting in this huge house, neglected and bored and getting fat, like some tragic Dickensian figure. What was her name? Mrs Haber – you know, whenever I try to remember her name, I always think "Haberdashery"! Was she even fat? Something about a wedding dress, that's all I remember. Didn't she set herself on fire? Perhaps I should set myself on fire. Bettina, are you *actually* ignoring me?'

'Huh?'

'Perhaps I *should* set myself on fire if it meant I'd get your attention. That man you're staring at is actually a woman, by the way. In a man's suit.'

'I wasn't—'

'You wouldn't be the first gal fooled.' Tuna looked at the woman from under her white-blonde lashes, her head dipping slyly – setting the turkey's feet to waggling – and gave her an icy little wave. The woman started to stroll over, hands in her pockets. 'Her name is Jean, she's a complete pervert,' said Tuna. 'Be careful – she eats straight girls for breakfast.'

The woman – Jean – arrived. 'Petunia.' She poked Tuna's earrings with a gloved forefinger. 'Are those bird's feet?'

'They are indeed.'

'Fantastic. How are you not an artist?'

Tuna drew her lips into a lemon-sucking smile. 'You know very well that I am.'

Jean turned to Bettina and extended her hand. 'Janine Freeman, but everyone calls me Jean.'

Bettina took her hand, squeezed. 'Bettina Wyn Thomas. Sorry – Bettina Dawes.' And – how awful – she let out a shrill yelping laugh belonging to a baby seal. 'What a thing to forget!'

'If I was married to a man I'd want to forget it too,' said Jean.

'Oh for God's sake,' said Tuna, rolling her eyes. 'So it begins.'

She plunged her hand down her dress and plucked a pack of cards from her cleavage. 'I'm off to do tarot readings.' She leaned into Bettina, held out her hand and said, in a crone's whisper, 'Crosss my palm with seelver,' then stumbled off, dragging her leg.

Bettina let out another panicked laugh. It was like hundreds of pigeons suddenly flying off from Trafalgar Square – a vast empty silence left in its wake.

'Isn't she terrifically funny?' she said. 'Isn't she just – she's my cousin, you know.'

Jean took out a slim silver flask from her breast pocket. 'She did a tarot reading for me once and it was quite eye-opening.' Her eyes were so black that the pupil was indistinguishable from the iris, the skin around them bruised by lack of sleep or anaemia or some other deficiency. Her skin was flawless but very pale, almost unpleasantly so. She had a big nose, slightly hooked, and a full mouth that tucked in at the corners. She looked very sure of herself.

'So what do you do?' said Bettina.

'I have a bookshop in Piccadilly.'

'Oh? Which one?'

'The Cave of Virtue.'

Bettina smiled politely and emitted a quiet 'Oh'. She had nothing to say about a shop she'd never heard of. She had nothing to say at all.

'And you?' said Jean.

Bettina took a drag of her cigarette, turning and tilting her head to blow the smoke away. What answer could she give? What had she to recommend herself, besides money? 'Well.' Jean waited, amused. 'I suppose I don't do anything that *you* might consider valuable. I'm a wife and I run a household. I happen to be growing a human being inside me at the moment.' She looked at Jean with defiance – a child's defiance.

Jean frowned. 'Why do you think I wouldn't find value in these things?'

'I don't know.' Bettina felt her face go hot. 'Because you're a working woman? And I don't *do* anything? I don't know.' She took a big swallow of her drink. What an idiot she was being. What a weird baby.

'What do you *like* to do? By way of pleasure.'

'I like to . . .' What *did* she like to do? Really? She forced her eyes to meet Jean's. 'I'm going to be honest with you, Miss . . . Freeman, was it? I enjoy drinking, eating and sitting around saying marvellously witty things. I like spending my husband's money and dancing. That's about it. No, wait – I like to read books, lots of books. Does that redeem me somewhat?'

Jean laughed, clapping her hands. 'Bravo!'

Bettina grinned stupidly.

'What kind of books do you read?'

'Well, let me see.' Bettina affected a look of ponderment. Maybe she should profess a love for the poetry of Sappho? No. Too obvious. But why not be obvious? God, this was all so excruciating. She drained her drink.

'Sappho.'

There. Done. She squeezed her empty glass between both hands. As if she were wringing the neck of some unfortunate bird.

'You're not one of those foul degenerates, are you?' said Jean, her lips pulled back into a sneer.

Bettina gaped up at her. Fool. She was a fool. 'Of course not, I don't—'

'I'm joking!' said Jean.

'Oh my God,' said Bettina, her voice wire-thin. 'What a horrible thing to do.'

'You're upset? I've upset you? Oh, come on, it was a joke.' Jean took hold of her wrist and pulled her in. 'Look, I'm sorry.' She smelled like rosewater, alcohol and something mildly unpleasant – bad breath, possibly. Yes – bad breath.

'I wanted the ground to swallow me up.'

'I said I was sorry.'

Bettina blew out air, her eyes on Jean's necktie. 'I think I need to sit down.'

'You're not going to faint, are you?'

'No! Take me somewhere quiet.'

'As you wish.' Jean offered her arm and Bettina took it, warily, slipping her hand through the gap as if it housed a coiled snake.

Chapter 16

Bettina used to come to this room to practise new dances with Bart; it was large, uncarpeted and situated above the kitchen, ensuring no one below would be disturbed by the staccato thudding. They learned the Charleston here, and the Black Bottom, both of them pink-faced and sweating through their clothes. Now it was crammed with books, the floor littered with teacups, half-melted candles and discarded clothes. It smelled strongly of men – sour ale, cologne and the fungus stink of unwashed genitals.

'Not too cold?' said Jean. 'Good. Take off your clothes.'

Bettina laughed. 'What?'

Jean took off her bowler hat and tossed it onto the bed. Her hair was short, the front bits hanging sleekly down almost to the jaw like straps of oiled leather, the back and sides climbing jerkily shorter. Looking at Bettina with a bored, irritated expression, she loosened her tie. 'Take off your clothes.' She pulled out the dressing-table chair, sat on it, leaned back. Crossed her legs the man's way, an ankle resting on a knee.

'No preamble?' said Bettina, giggling.

'Take off your clothes.'

Bettina looked down at herself. 'But I'm pregnant.'

Jean waved an impatient hand. 'Take. Off. Your. Clothes.' She took out a box of cigarettes and lit one, her dark eyes never leaving Bettina.

Christ. Bettina shifted her weight from one leg to the other. She had in all earnest just wanted to go somewhere quiet to sit down. Have a bit of a flirt, maybe. Her feet were aching. She wasn't drunk enough. This was all a bit much. She could just go – leave. She pulled off the headdress and groped for her dress fastener, eyes on the silver tulle curtains, her skin tingling. A kiss. That was how it was supposed to go. Not this. The dress started to drop and she held it in place with her hands.

Jean nodded.

She let it fall to the floor. Looked down at her large, blue-veined breasts, the skin goose-prickled, her taut, round stomach. A human life growing inside. Absurd.

'And the rest,' said Jean, her features grotesquely twisting and blending behind the thick cigarette smoke.

Bettina lifted one foot onto the bed and undid one garter, followed by the other. There was nothing about the striptease in this. Absolutely nothing. Her hands were shaking. She felt like a berk. Really, there was nothing to stop her leaving. She could put a stop to this with one word. Oh, she badly wanted a cigarette! She pinched the elastic of her knickers. God. She hated being a redhead. It was so vulgar, that nest of orange frizz. Why would anyone want anything to do with that?

'Can't I keep them on?'

Jean glared at her, blinking slowly.

She pulled down her knickers. Kicked them away, far away. Stood, arms covering her breasts, in the middle of the room. The squeal of a saxophone came from downstairs.

A great plume of smoke. 'And the rest.'

She looked down at her body. 'What do you mean, the rest? I'm quite naked.' She put her hands on her waist. Then quickly crossed them over her breasts again. 'Shall I take my skin off, too?'

Smiling (only just), Jean touched her upper lip. Tapped it.

The moustache. Oh, for goodness' sake. She actually wanted to cry. This was awful. She ripped the moustache away and dropped it, watching it swoop to the floor like a baby bird's feather. 'Satisfied?'

'Not even close. Sit on the edge of the bed.'

'I'm starting to feel cold now, couldn't—'

'Sit on the edge of the bed.'

She sat on the edge of the bed.

Jean stood up, cigarette pinched between her lips. She undid her dress jacket, folding it in half and draping it over the arm of the chair, and then took off her cufflinks and pulled up her sleeves. She did all of this very slowly and fastidiously, the fag still pinched in the crook of her mouth. She undid her tie and took her shoes off, followed by her socks. She stood up straight, took one last puff of smoke and threw the butt on the ground. 'Open your legs.'

Bettina stared at her thighs. They looked like squeezed slabs of luncheon meat.

Jean clapped her hands right in front of Bettina's face. 'Open!'

Her thighs snapped open.

'As wide as they'll go.'

Bettina spread them to capacity.

'You're a belligerent little bitch, aren't you?'

'How dare you?' said Bettina. How dare she?

'Shut up.'

Jean hunched over Bettina, placing her hands on her thighs, just above the knees. She was going to kiss her. Well, she wouldn't kiss back. 'Bitch'? How *dare* she?

But she didn't kiss her – instead she abruptly pushed her back onto the bed with a firm shove to the breastbone. The shock of it caused a dribble of urine to come out. Jean grabbed her around the backs of the legs, yanked her closer to the edge of the mattress. And got down onto her knees.

Jean dressed slowly, an obnoxious self-satisfaction griming her face, and sat in the chair to light a cigarette. She'd hopped out of bed like the damn thing was on fire. No cuddles, no kisses. Well, of course not.

Bettina needed to use the toilet. There was an en suite just to the right of where Jean was sitting, but she remembered that the door didn't close properly.

'What's your favourite Sappho poem then?' said Jean.

So they were back to this. 'I wouldn't say I had a particular favourite.'

'Right, right,' said Jean, tapping her chin.

'You think I haven't read any?' In actual fact, she had – Étienne had once bought her a copy of Sappho's collected fragments. 'Well, I don't care what you think.'

'Yes, you do,' said Jean.

Bettina climbed out of bed and retrieved her clothes from

the floor. 'You're very smug, aren't you? Insufferably smug.' She pulled on her knickers, glaring at Jean. 'Ultimately, you're not very nice.'

'Nice? Who wants to be nice?'

'I do. Most people do.'

Jean uncrossed her legs and leaned back, legs spread wide. 'Want to know something?'

'What?' said Bettina.

'Me and Petunia, we had a thing going once.'

Bettina's fingers froze in the process of clipping stocking to garter belt. 'That's a lie.'

'It's a fact.'

'Tuna likes men.'

'She liked me plenty enough.'

'Tuna and you? That's – dear God.'

'You're upset?' said Jean, smiling.

Bettina laughed. 'You *wish* I was upset, you bloody sadist.' She sat heavily on Jean's lap. 'Upset? This is the juiciest, most delicious gossip I've tasted all year.' She went to pluck the cigarettes from Jean's breast pocket and Jean slapped at her hand.

'Ask first,' said Jean, wriggling around under the weight of her. 'And stop rolling your goddamn eyes – it's like you're twelve years old.'

'Please may I have a cigarette?'

'You may.'

'Dish the dirt then,' said Bettina, 'before I die of boredom.'

'It's quite simple. She came into my shop looking for books on the occult. She flirted with me, which is no great oddity – married women are always flirting with me because I'm an obvious target to which they can affix their desperate need for attention.' Jean was stroking Bettina's nude bump, fingers trailing so lightly they felt like silk handkerchiefs. 'So she invited me over for a tarot reading, and afterwards we fucked.'

'Just the once?'

'A few times. I put a stop to it once I realised she was getting attached. She bought me a silk-lined cloak for Valentine's Day. I wouldn't accept it. She dropped the cloak into a vat of wall-paper paste. It was a very fine cloak. This was a year ago, but naturally we're pretending to be friends now to show what good sports we are. Thus my invitation to the party.'

'I'm flabbergasted,' said Bettina, 'absolutely flabbergasted. All this time and I could have confided in her about—'

'No, no, no – don't ever confide in her about anything. She's got a big mouth.'

'I'll have you know she's very dear to me.'

'Still got a big mouth.'

Bettina looked down at the hand on her stomach. Around and around, counter-clockwise, feather-light. Her fingers were long, her nails neat and clean. 'When you were with Tuna, was it like how it was with us?'

'That's between me and Petunia.'

'Are you like that with everyone?'

'Why d'you ask?'

'I don't know. I don't want to come away from this feeling so cheap. And used.'

'Maybe I want you to feel cheap and used.'

'Oh, give it a rest, will you? I hope you realise what a cliché you are. At least kiss me or something.'

Jean considered this with the benign reluctance of a father giving in to his daughter's request for more shoes. Then she kissed her. *Nicely.*

*

It was snowing, a light diagonal flurry that coated the hedges, bushes and the morose limestone figures rising out of Tuna's Grecian fountain, but not the ground, not settling, so there was a resultant lack of any silly romanticism. It was most *definitely* unromantic. The plump flakes swirling busily under the warm yellow glow of the porch light and the specks landing on Jean's bowler hat and shoulders – nothing romantic here. Romance had come to this house tonight to die.

'Well, cheerio,' said Bettina, as they made their way down the porch steps.

'Thanks for an *interesting* evening.'

Jean touched the brim of her hat. 'Same.'

They stood, glancing at each other with a kind of awkward expectation. Jean looked like she was about to say something. A snowflake landed on her cheek and she brushed it away. Bettina saw her car driving up the path, its headlights illuminating the lopsided snowflurry.

'"On soft beds you satisfied your passion, and there was no dance, no holy place."' Bettina smiled. 'See? I do read Sappho.' And she knocked Jean's bowler hat off her head and ran towards the car, laughing gleefully, snowflakes catching on her tongue. She heard Jean yelling after her: 'You're a child!' and yelled back, 'Then you fucked a child!' and, still laughing, she reached the car and waited as the driver got out and rushed around to open the door for her. She climbed in, turning finally to look at Jean. She was angrily dusting her hat down. Good.

The car started, setting off down the long gravel path. Jean was going to come for her after this. She was going to casually enquire after her address from Tuna and she was going to pursue her. Because she'd challenged her. Piqued her interest.

Bettina knew how people worked. People were easy to figure out. And, well, when she came around sniffing, Bettina was going to slam the door in her face – no, she would say something first. She was going to say—

She pressed her hand to her stomach. A kick! The baby was kicking – a flutter, a mischievous rat-a-tat! And she was here, alone, in the back of a chilly car, experiencing this for the first time, without Bart. Another flutter. A foot, an elbow, a hand? Did it have fingernails yet?

Well. It was really in there. Irrefutably.

'Pleased to meet you, little one,' she whispered, feeling like she might cry.

The car braked suddenly and she was flung forward, her hands coming up just in time to protect her face from the seat in front.

'Sorry, Mrs Dawes – he came out of nowhere.'

There, staggering around in the middle of the path, was Bone, his nose bloodied – snowflakes were caught up in the blood, like mould on jam. He was struggling to keep hold of a large framed picture; an oil painting in vivid streaks of clashing colour of a portly red-haired woman with exaggerated, disproportionately sized breasts – completely naked, she was, her legs spread ludicrously wide, almost to the point of doing the splits, a hot-pink slash up the middle. She was smiling. But not like she meant it.

Chapter 17

A letter inside a lavender envelope. It was addressed to 'Lady Dawes', which was obnoxious to start with. The letter – more a note – was written in a thick, swooping hand (also obnoxious) and it read: 'I want another look at that wicked red cunt. J.'

Bettina immediately fed it to the fire. She wasn't going to indulge this rotten woman. There was the nursery to decorate. Yes, yes – all these other things to think about. A nanny to find, which would most likely be a headache, and baby names to consider.

All these other things to think about.

Cunt.

Awful, awful woman.

She went upstairs to take a bath, and with Bart's loud voice booming through the walls as he rehearsed his lines, she slipped into the hot water, submerging her whole body, except for the bump which stuck out like a small island, and immediately, with no preamble, without even *pretending* she was in this bathtub for the sake of cleanliness, she *immediately* started to touch herself

(cunt)

and didn't stop until she reached a loud, splashing climax. She closed her eyes and sighed. The worst kind of lies were the ones you told to yourself.

Dear Yank

Come to my house at 7.30 sharp this Thursday night.

B.

P.S. Never utter that foul obscenity in my presence ever again, nor write it in any further correspondence.

She watched her staff leave then began grooming herself while knocking back gin and tonic, at one point accidentally snipping her labia with the scissors and having to stem the bleeding with Bart's face flannel.

Jean arrived precisely on time. She took a leisurely tour of the house, hands in pockets, murmuring appreciatively at certain architectural touches. Bettina followed her around like a calf trailing its mother. Jean was wearing a man's shirt and blazer tailored specially to fit her female shape, the waist tapered in – all this over a woman's skirt. Men's black brogues. On her head was a black boater with a purple sash, and complementing this, a startling bright purple flower in the lapel of her jacket.

'No one's home,' said Bettina, 'nor will be for hours. I gave my staff tickets to see my husband's new play.'

'Oh, you sweetheart,' said Jean.

They were in the dining room. Jean dropped her cigarette into a china cup, grabbed Bettina and spun her around, bending her over the table with great control, so as not to thump her pregnant stomach.

And then, in a hot whisper: 'Cunt. Cunt. Cunt.'

Jean had come to Britain intending to stay a couple of weeks before moving on to Berlin, but had quickly fallen in love with London and ingratiated herself within the literary scene, hobnobbing with various writers and academics. She lived in a perfectly satisfactory maisonette in Chelsea, spartan and neat, to which she invited Bettina one evening. She fed her cheese-cake and port, took her to her bedroom, ordered her to strip . . . and then an hour of something Bettina would never tell a living soul about *ever*.

By the fifth meeting, she allowed Bettina to touch her. She murmured instructions in a voice that shivered unsurely – 'A bit lower . . . Faster . . . No, use the tip . . . Two fingers now . . . Keep doing that . . . Keep doing that.' Bettina was grateful for these demands because she didn't fully know what she was doing. When Jean finally came, her thigh spasmed like a dog having its belly scratched. She curled up next to Bettina, not quite touching her.

'Do you ever fuck your husband?' she said. 'You feign a lot of headaches, I bet.'

Bettina stared at the ceiling. She and Bart had agreed to only confide the nature of their relationship to those they fully trusted. 'He feels squeamish about doing it with the baby inside me.'

Jean tutted. 'Silly man. Pregnant women are crammed full of hormones and it makes them go at it like wild bitches.'

Bart seemed supportive of the affair, on the surface at least, but he was moping more than usual, and when she came home from Jean's he'd be sitting in front of the fire in a sulk. Jealous, probably. Because she was giving her attention to someone else for a change. She found herself almost hoping that he'd challenge her: 'I don't want you seeing that woman any more.' Something like that. She could then list all the reasons he was being a hypocrite and a chauvinist. 'You got to have your boyfriend living in our house, which I supported,' she'd say, 'and now you have the nerve to boss me around?' In these hypothetical arguments she was always near tears, smoking a cigarette with a shaking hand. 'You're a bastard and a fraud!' And then she'd break down crying, and oh, how sorry he would be!

Six weeks in, everything changed. Bettina came to Jean's house one evening, and rather than the usual order of business (sex), Jean offered her a drink and some chocolates and they sat down to talk. Jean had a lot of thoughts on the women's question and had read many scholarly articles about it. Bettina didn't think much about such things, having only one broad opinion on the matter: that women were *not* inferior to men. Possibly sensing her boredom, Jean changed the subject, telling her about her youth; of falling in love with a school girlfriend at the age of fifteen and having her heart broken. Of falling in love with another girl at seventeen. And having her heart broken. And more of the same. Her brothers were proud Klansmen and had once beaten a 'pansy' half to death. Her mother was controlling (surprise, surprise) and her father was mean and surly and had never – honestly, *never* – said a single nice thing to her. 'I genuinely felt that if I died, he'd feel nothing but relief,' she said coolly, as if commenting on approaching rainclouds.

It was all terribly predictable; a woman as emotionally guarded as Jean didn't get that way after a childhood spent skipping merrily through daisy-dotted meadows.

Jean abruptly stood up. 'I'd like to go to bed now. Go home, please.'

Bettina stared at her. 'I didn't come here to talk, you know.'

'I'm not in the mood. Go home and sort yourself out.' She flapped a dismissive hand. 'Or get the charlady to do it.'

'I don't have a charlady!'

'Let yourself out,' said Jean, leaving the room.

Bettina was frozen still in her chair. She ate some more of the chocolates, not tasting them, barely even registering them in her mouth. *I don't have a charlady.* That was funny actually. That was – Bart would think it hilarious. But by God, she was *furious.* Positively molten. She smoked her cigarette down to the filter and leaned over her bulging stomach to stub it out in the ashtray. Paused. Dropped it instead into Jean's unfinished bourbon. She picked up her coat and purse and headed up the stairs. She was going to give Jean a piece of her mind. She was going to let her have it: you are a clumsy kisser and a selfish conversationalist. You use fancy terminology because you're insecure about your intellect, and rightfully so. You are a poser. You position the books in your shelves so as to impress visitors, with Virginia Woolf closest to the sofa – I know this to be true. I've read your attempts at prose in the ledger you keep hidden under the bed and it is derivative and dull. Your nostrils are often flecked with little snot scraps. I think you might be evil. Oh, yes, all this and more.

The bedroom was empty. Bettina was about to leave when she heard a muffled voice come from the far corner. 'Go home.'

The wardrobe? She couldn't be in the wardrobe. Preposterous.

But the wardrobe, the giant beechwood wardrobe where Jean kept all her shirts, was the only thing in the room that could enclose a full-grown human being. She approached it, her heels knocking against the varnished floorboards.

Jean was hugging her knees to her chest at the bottom of the wardrobe.

'Oh for God's sake,' said Bettina. 'You're thirty years old!'

'Fuck you!'

The shirts hanging overhead cast a shadow over Jean's head. Bettina reached in and parted them, exposing her pink-mottled face and glimmering eyes.

'Oh – oh dear.'

'Leave me the fuck alone!'

Sighing, Bettina got down on her hands and knees and crawled into the wardrobe. It reeked of laundry starch and shoe polish. She reached out to move aside Jean's hair, and of course she flinched away, violently, like a child – a wounded, furious child. Bettina sighed again. She wrapped her arms around her, squeezing her in close, knowing that again she'd resist – which she did, jerking away and making a horrid whining sound. Well, children were easily dealt with: Bettina smacked her around the side of the head and said, 'Stop being a baby!' Jean stiffened and finally relaxed into her arms.

'Fancy, a bastard like you crying.'

Jean laughed. Wiped her nose with her sleeve. 'Sorry.'

'Don't apologise for crying. You're human. As it turns out.'

'No. I'm sorry for wiping my nose on my clothes.'

'Why the wardrobe?'

'It feels safe in here,' she said, resting her head against Bettina's shoulder. 'I've got a whole sob story about it. About closets – we call them closets. You want to hear my sad little story?'

Bettina nodded.

'When I was little, my brothers used to lock me in the closet. The first time they did it I was terrified; I banged on the doors, I kicked and I kicked. But no one came to let me out. I – I can't believe I'm about to tell you this – it got to the point where I needed to pee. So I went in my grandfather's shoe – don't you laugh, Betty, I won't forgive you for it. I was so ashamed. And I started thinking I'd run out of air and die. I was terrified. So I started pretending I was in a storm shelter and there was a tornado heading my way, and I'd be the only safe person and everyone else would die. My mom, my dad, my brothers, they'd all die. But I'd survive. This brought me great comfort.'

Bettina didn't know what to say to all that. So she kissed her. Just to fill the silence really. But the kiss quickly became heated and they were grabbing at each other's faces and hair and moaning like animals, and they retreated out of the wardrobe and made it to the bed, rolling and snatching and shedding clothes, and Jean made no demands, said nothing actually, and for the first time, it felt like – yes, it felt like making love. A weird, ungainly sort of love.

Chapter 18

March 1928, Davenport House, London

Three things happened on That Day – which was how it would be referred to later, no qualifiers required. Firstly, Bettina went into labour. Bart heard the screams as he entered the house. 'Jesus fucking . . .' he began, covering his ears with his hands. It was coming from upstairs. He ran up the steps two at a time, almost missing his footing as another scream came at him with the force of a grenade blast.

'If you think that's bad,' said Doris the cook, suddenly appearing in the hall alongside the cleaner, 'then you should have been here an hour ago.'

He clutched the banister rail. 'How is she?'

'Couldn't say, Mr Dawes. The doctor'll tell you.'

'But what stage is she at?'

Doris grinned, her eyes glittering behind her spectacles. 'I imagine she's at that stage where she's wishing you were dead, Mr Dawes.'

'Is everything going as it should?'

'I'm not a doctor, last time I checked.'

'But should she be making those noises?'

Another scream, this one morphing into a horrible donkey's roar. 'Holy bloody hell,' said Bart. 'I never imagined – have you got children, Doris?'

'Aye. I've told you about them more times than I—'

'How was – I mean – was it like this with you?'

'Aye. Without doctors and central heating and with the husband at the pub with his mistress.'

God. Why did poor people have to bring their poverty into everything? 'Did you make noises like that?' He pointed up the stairs, his arm trembling.

She seemed to consider this. She took her glasses off and started polishing them on her apron. Put them back on. 'I should say so. Shall I make you a sandwich, Mr Dawes?'

And then the doorbell rang. He gestured at Doris to go and answer it. It was the midwife, a stout, thin-lipped woman called Delores with a gruff, masculine voice, huge, cracked knuckles and teeth as yellow as cheddar cheese. She insisted upon being called Del. Bettina suspected she was a repressed lesbian and had made up a song about her: 'Her name is Delores but call her Del or she'll floor us. "I'm Del," she implored us, and she's bent, is Delores.' Del strode business-like through the door and headed straight for the stairs.

'What shall I do?' Bart asked.

'Go and make yourself comfortable somewhere.'

'That's it?'

'That's it, Mr Dawes.'

Doris and the cleaner were glancing at each other, trying not to laugh. 'You,' he said to the cleaner, 'go and make yourself useful.' And to Doris: 'Ham and cheese. Extra chutney.'

Doris nodded. 'Your friend is back, by the way,' she said. 'I told him to wait in the drawing room. I hope—'

'What?'

'Your wee French friend, the pretty artist. Should I have sent him away? Only I'm not a butler, Mr Dawes, and I'm certainly not *paid* like a butler . . .'

But Bart wasn't listening, Bart was running, Bettina's mammalian screams at his back propelling him like strong wind behind a sailing boat, and as he ran, no clear thoughts came to him, just a freeze-frame of an empty train station.

'Would you like me to make a sandwich for your friend as well, Mr Dawes?'

Bart didn't hear her words, registering only that a question had been asked, so he nodded as he passed her, and slowed down, because how strange it must look, this young husband sprinting away from his screaming wife towards a pretty French man waiting in the drawing room, and he yanked open the door onto the second memorable element of That Day, he opened the door onto his Étienne, his Étienne, who was lying on the sofa with his boots up on the armrest, reading a book, any book, it didn't matter about the book, and he ran up to him – no time for dramatic pauses and lingering, penetrating gazes, no time for any of that nonsense – and he grabbed his face, his terribly thin face and kissed him, and it was the sweetest, most passionate, most heart-splitting kiss ever – *ever*.

A knock at the door.

'Wait a minute – hang on a—'

They set about scrabbling for their clothes in a panic. Étienne got his legs caught in his trousers and fell back onto the sofa, and Bart buttoned up his shirt. 'Shit, shit, shit.'

Another knock.

'Wait!' he roared.

'It's urgent,' came a mouse squeak from the other side of the door – the cleaner (Nora? Nancy?).

He tucked his shirt into his trousers, yanked on his jacket, looked for his socks, couldn't find them, shuffled his bare feet into his Oxfords and started stumbling towards the door. He knew how this looked. But there was no proof – and that's all that mattered. He pushed the door open a wedge and slipped through, closing it behind him.

The cleaner (Nellie? Did it even start with an N?) blinked nervously up at him, stray wisps of white-blonde hair worked loose from her bun. 'I'm sorry, sir—'

'No, no, it's fine, don't apolo— it's just my friend in there was very upset about something, he – he was crying as a matter of fact, and I think – what's your name by the way?'

'Ethel.'

'Ethel! Yes. Well, as I was saying, it would have been very uncomfortable for both him and you if you'd been privy to that – just imagine, a grown man crying . . .' Fuck! The baby! How could he have forgotten about the baby! He grabbed her by the arms. 'Is everything all right? Is it Bettina? Is it the – has the baby come?'

'No, sir, it's a telephone call, for you. Very urgent.'

She was wincing. For a moment he wondered if it was his breath – whisky and garlic and cum – before realising that he was still clutching her arms. 'Sorry,' he said, letting go.

'Mrs Wyn Thomas, sir. She wanted to speak to Mrs Dawes

but – she didn't know the baby was coming, sir! She's cross with you about that.'

He leaned against the door, squeezing the bridge of his nose with his fingers. 'Thank you. See Mr Janvier is not disturbed.' He made his way to the telephone. No screams from upstairs – hopefully she'd been given something for the pain. 'Hello,' he said into the phone.

'Bartholomew! How could you neglect to inform me that my daughter is in the throes of childbirth? How could you be so bloody unthinking!'

Bart pressed his forehead against the wallpaper and stemmed the groan trying to come out. He'd always liked Venetia – she'd been a lot kinder to him than the father, Monty, and at times had even seemed like a second mother. Well, not quite a second mother but maybe something akin to a tolerable stepmother or a favourite aunt. She'd always thought him a brat and a mischief-maker – the woman, like her daughter, was terrible at concealing her feelings and, also like her daughter, was an exemplary eye-roller and artful mistress of the disdainful sneer. And yet she seemed to nurse a reluctant fondness for him, as if he was an annoying puppy who got under foot and pissed in places he shouldn't, but come bedtime she'd be patting the bed and saying, 'Oh come on up then, you little horror.' He could even remember her cuddling him once, after he'd been punched in the face by one of Jonathan's chums; he'd rested his cheek on her talc-dusted bosom, her hanky wedged up one bleeding nostril, and felt safe, really safe.

'I'm sorry, Venetia,' he said. 'I've been in a blind panic this last hour. I was just about to ring you.'

Silence on her end. Then, in a sad, quiet voice that made

her sound like a young girl, she imparted the third memorable arse-fuck of That Day: 'My Monty is dying.'

'*What?* How? What of?'

'He had a heart attack this morning. A whopper. The doctors thought he might pull through but then he had another one. He's unconscious now.'

'I'm so sorry, Venetia! Jesus! I'm so very sorry. What can I do?'

An exhalation of breath made ragged by fought-back tears. 'Don't tell Betts until after she's recovered from the birth.'

'Of course, of course.'

'And ring me as soon as the baby's here.'

'Yes, I'll do that.'

'And Bart?'

'Yes?'

'If it's a boy, don't you think – well, wouldn't it be fitting if you named him Montgomery?'

What was he supposed to say to *that*? He couldn't say no, could he? 'Of course, Venetia.'

'It would mean the world to him – I mean, if he were conscious and able to . . . do you think if I were to whisper it into his ear, he might hear me?'

'It wouldn't hurt to try.'

'Montgomery Dawes. That's a strong name, don't you think?'

'Certainly. It's got a good – it's got a nice *ring* to it. But – well – I *was* going to name him Jonathan. But if—'

'Oh,' she said, that 'Oh' appearing in Bart's mind like a sad little smoke ring, moon-white and quick to disperse. She laughed. Horribly. 'So many dead names to choose from . . . so many . . . There's your father's name too. I hadn't even considered that.'

'Oh, no – I wouldn't name my child after *him*. I hated him.'

'I know you did. I know.' She blew her nose and sniffed. 'I don't know what I'm going to do, Bart.'

There was a vase of daffodils on the desk. He dimly realised that his eyes had been focused on them this whole time. One particular petal – crooked but fleshy.

'Wouldn't it be strange,' she continued, 'if the baby came and at the same time, Monty . . . imagine if his soul flew from here to – oh, I'm saying all sorts of ridiculous things now. I'll let you go, Bart. Goodbye.'

'Mr Dawes?'

He jumped. It was Doris.

'Your sandwiches are ready when you want them. And I've done you a malted milk for your nerves.'

'Thank you,' he said softly. And then his face crumpled and he was crying.

'It's a trying time for a husband,' said Doris, touching his arm gingerly, as if she were a dog trainer unsure of the hound's temperament.

A pinched, yellowish, mewling she-critter with tiny grasping hands tipped with the thinnest, most delicate slices of fingernail, arms and legs marbled blue, red and yellow as her circulation clashed with the cold air, a puffy vulva, goose-pimpled and already dribbling out urine, the dark eyes rolling around their sockets, unseeing, tiny mouth opening and closing, opening and closing. Absolutely beautiful.

Why couldn't he stop crying?

Bettina gazed at him through opium-sunk eyes. She reached out and patted his thigh. 'Let Del get a blanket on her, Meow. She's getting cold.'

He nodded, sniffing, and passed the baby to Delores, who promptly swaddled her in a woollen blanket before passing her back to him, smiling with all the gums showing around her huge yellow teeth.

'I could do with a cigarette,' said Bettina.

'Now, Bettina—' began Del.

'If I want a cigarette, I shall have a cigarette. Meow, darling, give me a cigarette, will you?'

Bart carefully balanced the baby on his thighs and took out his cigarettes, lighting two. 'It should be a cigar, really,' he said.

'I don't like cigars,' she said. 'I don't think anyone does. I think men just pretend to.'

'How do you feel?' he said.

She propped herself up on the pillow and began to smoke, eyes closed. 'Euphoric,' she said, tonelessly.

'Are you – is that sarcasm?'

'No, I meant it. I'm just so exhausted. How do I look?'

It was strange – she looked terrible: haggard, crusty-lipped and squinty-eyed, her complexion ruddy. Yet beautiful. The most beautiful she'd ever looked. And it was the same with the baby – a little troll thing, said his eyes. But his heart saw perfection. It was a kind of drunkenness of perception. 'Delicious,' he said.

'Bart – it was awful. I'm never doing it again.'

'That's what they all say,' chipped in Delores, who was pulling the curtains open at the other end of the room.

Bart cradled the baby in one arm, smoking with the other. The sun had gone down outside and it was getting dark. Bettina looked tiny in the huge bed. He imagined Monty in his own huge bed, which he could well remember; as a boy he'd often sneaked into the grown-up world of the Wyn Thomases' master bedroom to nose through their alien artefacts – stiff underwear with odd clasps and ribs of whalebone shooting off in incomprehensible directions, strange metal contraptions for cleaning the ears or draining the sinuses, jars of haemorrhoid ointment, potted orchids everywhere, their soil peppered with fingernail shavings and what looked like pubic hair, a toffee tin filled with war medals and cufflinks. Monty's Boer War medal was the newest and shiniest. He'd imagine a younger, leaner Monty in khakis, wiping sweat and blood from his brow with a rag while smoking a cheroot.

He'd once masturbated over Monty.

Twice, actually.

Well, a handful of times. But not to excess. Not with any regularity.

In the fantasy, Monty saved Bart from drowning in the sea. He clutched Bart to his chest to keep him from thrashing, calmly treading water and whispering reassurances – 'I've got you, boy, I've got you.' His chest was solid and warm. He swam him back to shore. They threw themselves onto the sand, panting, and Bart noticed Monty's stiffy (huge, of course), and Monty noticed Bart noticing it, and there was a pause, a beat, and Monty grabbed Bart and shoved his tongue into his mouth.

Monty was not an attractive man. He certainly wasn't a nice man. So why these fantasies?

Too easy.

Delores was looming over the bed, still smiling, but glancing at Bart with an air of expectation. His cue to leave. They had business to discuss – there was the matter of feeding (Bettina unequivocally wished to use bottled milk to save her breasts from sagging) – and then rest for the mother. And then some horrible fucking news for the mother. He lifted the baby up to his face and sniffed her head. Creamy, slightly earthy. Lovely.

'Are we still set on Tabitha?' he said. 'I can see her as a little Tabby.'

'I think it's perfect,' said Bettina.

He nodded. 'The next one can be Jonathan.' Or Montgomery. 'We'll accrue the complete dead set.'

'I told you, I'm never doing this again.'

He handed her the baby and kissed her head. 'You did wonderfully. I'm so proud of you.' And he quickly left before the tears could start again.

Chapter 19

April 1928, Bergman and Hutchinson, Sussex

The monkey was a capuchin – she remembered learning about capuchins in her children's encyclopaedias; they were small and intelligent and the males dominated everything. This one was tinged red with white fur on its face. It was hunched inside a small bell-cage hanging from the ceiling, nibbling a brown apple core.

'This can't be right,' Venetia was saying.

The creature belonged to Monty's lawyer, Heseltine Bergman – they were in his office. How proud he must be of his little capuchin, thought Bettina. How he must love showing it off. That Bergman's a real character, clients would say, have you seen his pet monkey yet? Such a jolly fascinating man, with his pet monkey. A man with a pet monkey is certainly someone I trust to handle my legal affairs. And the ladies? How *sensitive* this man must be, with his pet monkey.

'I'm afraid it is indeed right, Mrs Wyn Thomas,' Bergman said. 'I've laid it out as clearly as I possibly can.'

The capuchin nibbled at the pulpy apple flesh, its eyes gently opening and closing. The core slipped out of its paw and it nodded off, its little chin tucked into its chest.

'Please, Mrs Wyn Thomas, I'd rather you didn't smoke in here.'

Venetia's cigarette case closed with a snap and the monkey woke up.

'You land me with a bombshell like this and then don't permit me to smoke?'

Bettina tore her eyes from the monkey. 'Did you let my father smoke in here?' she asked Bergman.

'Of course not.'

'That's a lie. I don't believe you for a second.' As if her father would've let this monkey-loving twerp tell him what he could or couldn't do. 'Let my mother smoke, please.'

'I cannot—'

'Let my mother smoke!'

Bergman crumpled his mouth. 'Very well,' he said. 'It has been a rather shocking disclosure.'

'On top of other shocking disclosures,' Venetia murmured, blinking damply at him.

Today's news, that Monty had run his business into the ground with poor investments, only slightly trumped yesterday's news – that Monty had been riddled with the clap at the time of his death. Venetia had wept all night over that, holed up in her bedroom, alone, not even letting Lucille in. She'd come out eventually and sat with Bettina and Lucille in the drawing room, drinking sherry with a pinched, dead-eyed face.

'One small consolation,' she'd said, 'I probably don't have it. We hadn't been intimate in rather a long time.' She and Lucille agreed that he'd probably caught it on a business trip to Brussels shortly after Jonathan died, since he'd sunk low over this period. Bettina had listened to all this, staring vapidly at the table leg, much like she was now staring at the monkey in the cage.

'So I suppose I must now tighten the belt on my household?' Venetia said to Bergman. 'Lose a few more staff? We've already downsized in recent years – at this rate I'll be scrubbing the floors myself.'

Bergman rested his elbows on the desk, looking up at Venetia with eyes not entirely devoid of human feeling. 'I don't think you appreciate the severity of your situation. You cannot keep the house.'

Venetia stared at him.

'Your husband's mismanagement has left profound debt. The house will need to be sold.'

'No,' said Venetia, shaking her head. 'That's absurd.'

'Sadly not.'

'But what about the summer house in Carmarthenshire? I could just sell that, surely?'

'It wouldn't be enough. You'll be lucky to be left with the Carmarthenshire property. I cannot even guarantee that you will be.'

Venetia turned to Bettina. 'He's wrong. Tell him, darling. He's wrong. What is he – he can't possibly – he's wrong, Bettina. *Tell* him.'

Bettina just looked from her mother to Bergman, her mouth open.

'We'll just get a second opinion,' said Venetia, shrilly. 'This can't possibly be right.'

Bergman settled his gaze on Bettina, perhaps judging her to be the sensible one. 'She'll need time to fully accept her new situation—'

'Don't talk about me as though I'm not in the room! I'm not a child.'

'Mr Bergman,' said Bettina, 'my mother has just lost everything. Please don't be condescending.'

'I'm not! Goodness gracious, I'm not. But I would thank you both not to shoot the messenger.' He waved his hand desperately in the direction of Venetia's cigarette. 'I let her smoke, didn't I?'

Venetia shot two arrows of smoke from her nostrils, her eyes dribbling tears. 'Your monkey is eating its own faeces right now. I thought you should know that.'

It was a dispiriting week in Brighton – that was the word Bettina kept hearing uttered. 'Dispiriting' – such a weak, kitten's swipe of a word when there were so many other more suitable choices: atrocious, dire, ghastly, despairing, miserable, aching, awful, terrible, horrible, horrific, horrendous. She quite liked 'aching'. Her bones ached, her brain ached, in a literal sense her breasts ached, swollen as they were from milk destined to soon dry up, and of course her heart ached – for her widowed mother and fool of a dead father, and for her baby, who'd remained behind in London under the care of an agency nanny. Even the house seemed to ache. As if it too understood its loss.

One afternoon of this dispiriting week, as Venetia, Bart and Lucille met with countless clerks, Bettina went to her old bedroom and found her bundle of journals inside the locked desk drawer for which she still had a key. The books for 1919 and 1920 were largely filled with poetry. 1919 contained the poetry of others – favourite lines and snippets – mostly Emily Dickinson with all exclamation marks removed (which much improved them). 1920, the poetry was all her own. Wildly inspired, she'd spent an entire summer experimenting with the villanelle. She began to fantasise about a life as an acclaimed poetess – a prodigal artist discovered by a visiting writer of great taste and henceforth plucked from obscurity, her first collection selling out immediately. Some critics would find her too dangerous, too challenging, for she'd perform her readings dressed all in black wearing a mourning veil – she would be grieving for her lost innocence.

Her fantasies had been smashed when, in a hopeful, vulnerable moment, she showed her villanelles to her father. Oh, the look on his face! As if he was embarrassed for her. What could be worse? 'You knew, handing me these, that I am a man incapable of dishonesty,' he'd said – which was rubbish, for a start, because the man was always lying about something or other – 'and because I love you and don't wish to see you hurt, I very much wish you hadn't showed them to me.' She'd run to her room and cried. Hadn't she also fantasised about hanging herself? Yes. From the huge oak. Her father finding her dangling, limp feet swaying slightly, her skin made silver by the moonlight.

She re-read the villanelles on her old bed, knees tucked up to her chin. They were terrible. Of course they were. But had they deserved that embarrassed, pitying look on her father's face? She'd been fifteen. How had he not taken that into account?

Maybe Tabby would come to her with her own attempts at poetry one day. 'This shows great promise and I am very proud of you,' she might say, 'though you may want to think about going through it with a fine-tooth comb and removing all clichés.'

She took the last journal downstairs (Lucille was shouting from inside the drawing room – she imagined a bespectacled clerk shrivelling in his chair) and went out into the garden, sitting under the giant oak from which she'd swung limp-footed in her adolescent fantasies. She started to write a formless poem entitled 'Aching'. The bones of her father's house were aching. That's what she wanted to get across. The house was her father. It was held up by his bones, but his bones were diseased (with gonorrhoea) and crumbling. But she must choose. Diseased or aching? Ache suggested arthritis and her father did not deserve to be redeemed by an ailment so blameless as arthritis.

Henry came out to her to offer his condolences. He stood over her and gave his little speech, his shoe touching her ankle, only just. He'd always done that – stood too close to her, a part of him touching a part of her, *just*. So that if the indiscretion was ever pointed out, he could very easily claim innocence. Oh, I'm so very sorry! How clumsy of me. More than once he'd swiped her breast with his finger in the act of handing her something.

She thanked him for his 'kind words' in as stilted and daggered a way as humanly possible. Odious cunt. She abhorred the word, but it fitted him like a tailored suit. One good thing to come out of this sorry business: Henry would hopefully lose his job, her mother having no way of paying his wages. He dipped his head, turned smartly on his heel and returned to the house, the sun spilling out onto his balding head like a cracked egg yolk. See, that was good. Egg yolk. So why couldn't she write poetry?

She supposed the question should be: Why must she try? And, well – it was obvious. So obvious it was boring. If she wrote a marvellous, perfect poem now it would be one over on her dead father. You were wrong, it would say. You were wrong.

'Dear Father,' she wrote, 'you were wrong.' And she continued to write, in prose form, until she'd filled twelve pages and her hand and wrist were aching nearly as much as the bones of her dead father's house, and the one remaining solicitor's car had driven away, carrying away its grey-faced cargo, and every light inside the house had been switched on, the windows glowing with warm defiant light, defiant because the electricity powering this light could no longer be afforded.

'So you weren't entirely wrong, Father,' she wrote. 'I can't write poetry. But I can do many other things, and in any case, your opinions are no longer valid because you are dead. I am alive and you, Father, are dead. And anything I write will surely enjoy a healthier legacy than yours, you squandering whore-master, you abysmal punchline to a dubious joke, you posthumous failure. It could be discovered after my death that I liked to fuck women (which I do, Father – I just adore fucking women) and even this sordid disclosure would not make me as hated as you. You are sorely hated, Father. I hate you, Father.'

She crossed out the last line, frowning through a sheen of tears. Only silly little girls hated their fathers.

Chapter 20

April 1928, Davenport House, London

During her early days in London, Jean had frequented The Little Boat, a working-class pub known for its mainly female clientele – 'Dykes, in other words,' she told Bettina, who was both shocked that such a place existed and annoyed that no one had told her about it. Jean made friends there – most of whom she slept with, naturally. Some of these were women of her ilk – suffragettes, academics, artists – but the majority were prostitutes or ex-service staff. There was a smug sort of pride in Jean's bearing as she disclosed this – what a darling she was, befriending tramps and drudges.

One such woman, Megan, had once worked as a nanny for a wealthy family. 'According to her,' Jean told Bettina, 'the husband pushed her into the coal house and flopped out his weenie. And when she rejected his advances, he ran to his wife and said he'd caught her stealing.'

Megan arrived at the Dawes' house for an interview one cloudy morning. Bettina had never been so sleep-deprived – flashing purple stars appeared at the corner of her vision like fireworks set off behind her head, and every time she closed her eyes, she heard snatches of disjointed conversation, as if her skull contained a miniature market square. 'Babies are awful,' said Bart in a weary monotone, Tabby lying on his lap, her tiny fists clenching and unclenching. 'I daresay, even a little evil.' Bettina burst into dizzy giggles, spilling strong coffee onto her knees. It was at this point that a quick rat-a-tat announced Megan's arrival.

Bettina jumped up from her chair and started dabbing her knees with one of the baby's muslin cloths, succeeding only in transferring milky sick to her stockings. 'Oh for God's sake.' She threw the cloth on the table. 'I don't care if this woman has a satanic pentagram tattooed on her head, we're hiring her.'

Her eyes – that was the first thing and the best thing; they were set far apart and slanted up at the corners slightly, and the green irises were flecked with gold – not brown, but actual gold. And her cheekbones . . . she'd had a maths teacher with cheekbones like that – Miss Moody – and Margo had once said that a small family could pitch up a tent and camp under those cheekbones, and if it were to rain, they'd stay perfectly dry. Her hair, underneath her hat, was bobbed and black.

Étienne glanced at Bettina knowingly. With a panic-eyed grin, she breathed in deep through her nose and ushered the woman through to the drawing room. 'You are in trouble,' Étienne whispered to her.

'Don't be ridiculous,' she whispered back, her eyes on Megan's large behind.

She'd been wrong about the eyes – they weren't her best feature.

Megan had been raised in an orphanage in Cornwall. Her father was a loveless drunk who'd died in an alleyway somewhere, his head kicked in, his pockets emptied and his one gold tooth plucked out, and her mother – also a drunk – passed away shortly after giving birth to her, of a haemorrhage. The orphanage was predictably terrible and Megan still had the scars along her right arm from all the lashings, which she eagerly showed Bettina, rolling up her sleeve and pointing them out one by one with an accompanying back-story – 'This is from when they caught me trying to read under the covers at lights out', 'This is for backchat', etc. A lot of them were for backchat.

Bart called her 'Meg the Mouth' behind her back.

'Don't be mean, Meow,' Bettina admonished, the first time he said it.

They were smoking on the bench at the end of the garden.

'You want to fuck her.'

'Shh! Keep your voice down. I don't want to do anything of the sort.'

'Why not? She's a sexpot.'

'She's Tabby's nanny.'

'She's a lowly commoner – at least be honest, Betts.'

'That's not true.' Bettina flicked her cigarette butt away and immediately lit another. 'Well, maybe it's true.' She side-glanced at Bart, coolly, and they both laughed.

'So if Étienne was a cleaner of lavatories or something like that, would you have fallen for him?'

'Étienne is dirt-poor. His mother ran a brothel.'

'Yes, but he's an artist,' she said. 'And it was a *French* brothel.'

'You're diverting the conversation away from yourself.'

She shrugged. 'I don't want to sleep with the nanny. I already have a lover. Stop talking about it. Oh, look out – she's coming over.'

Megan was carrying the baby with one crooked arm and shielding her face from the sun with the other. How lovely she'd look painted, just like that.

'You want to lick her nipples,' whispered Bart.

Bettina abruptly rose to greet Megan. 'Hello there.'

'Beautiful day, isn't it?' said Megan, looking up at the sky. 'Thought I'd give the little madam some fresh air and sunlight. You don't mind, do you?'

'Of course not,' said Bettina. 'Please, join us.'

'Oh no, I wouldn't want to impose.' She spoke with a clear voice – the vocal equivalent, Bettina thought, of a splash of cool mountain water in one's face on a clammy day.

Bart held his arms out, gesturing for Megan to hand the baby over.

'She's just had a feed so mind she doesn't sick up on you,' she said, passing her over.

'Oh, I don't mind if she sicks up on me. Do I, little sweetheart? No, I don't. No, I don't. Daddy would eat your vomvom with a sugar spoon.'

'You're getting ash on her head,' said Bettina, leaning over and swiping away the flecks. She looked up at Megan, smiling wryly. 'Rule number one of parenting: babies are not to be used as ashtrays.'

Megan snapped back her head and laughed, her bosom shaking underneath the white blouse. Lovely soft handfuls of—

No. Stop it.

Jean seldom entertained and usually ate by herself in her small dining room, reading a book as she ate. Tonight she'd got out all her best silverware and serving dishes and ordered food from a Portuguese bistro. She served it herself, shirt sleeves rolled up, a cigarette dangling from her mouth. The smell of spiced sardines fused with cigarette smoke and the deer-fat tallow of the table candles.

It was a special occasion: a ground-breaking sapphic book by Radclyffe Hall called *The Well of Loneliness* had just been published and Britain was going wild for it – in both the good and bad sense. Jean had sold all her copies that afternoon and was waiting for a new shipment, which would undoubtedly also sell out. Twice this week she'd had to clean smashed egg from her shop windows.

They finished eating and moved into the sitting room. This was the first time Bettina had met any of Jean's friends and she felt unusually shy. Scoobie was a fifty-plus-year-old American. She wore a pinstriped suit with spats and her knuckles were thick with gold sovereign rings. She was stout and unlovely with a dirty laugh and she smoked cigars, constantly moving them around her large slug mouth like a dog working on a bone. She looked at Bettina with a tilted chin and approving eyes, as if evaluating a prize mare. Triss, her partner, was a Russian-born thirty-year-old with a sweet, welcoming nature but horrible teeth. She was the 'woman' of the pair and wore a long, dowdy woollen dress with a tan leather purse belt around her waist and cream ankle boots.

Both were heavily involved in the literary world and published their own monthly journal celebrating women's writing (their proudest achievement was printing a quartet of poems by Mina Loy). They also bred racehorses.

Bettina drank fast, tapping her glass for refills. She noticed Jean casting worried little glances – she was showing her off like a rare locket, expecting her to shine. Scoobie did most of the talking – she personally knew Radclyffe Hall, she was now saying, and had just that week had lunch with her.

'What's she like?' Bettina asked.

Scoobie tapped her cigar into an ashtray on her knee. 'She's an asshole.'

'And a fascist,' added Triss.

'I've heard this about her,' said Jean, nodding. 'And her little wifey – have you ever seen her? Eyes like a dead shark.'

Scoobie leaned forward to peer at Bettina. 'Have you read it?'

'I have,' said Bettina.

'What did you think?'

'I loved it.'

Scoobie pursed her mouth. 'Did you now?'

'Don't make fun of her,' said Jean, sliding a protective arm around Bettina's shoulders.

'I'm not,' said Scoobie.

'You're about to.'

Scoobie grinned. 'It's a horrible book. Virginia Woolf thinks it's a piece of shit. It's a hand-wringing apology from a self-loathing bull-dagger. An overwritten turd. Just horrible.'

'A lot of people would disagree,' said Jean.

'Well, it's ground-breaking,' said Bettina. 'And very brave.'

Scoobie nodded. 'It *is* brave. I will not argue with you there. But honey, a piece of shit is a piece of shit is a piece of shit.'

'It's all subjective,' said Jean.

'Would you listen to that?' Scoobie said to Triss. '"It's all subjective." Coming from someone who I know agrees with me. Our Janine is pussy-whipped.' She enacted a whip being snapped. Jean's cheeks flushed. She started filling up people's glasses.

'I wrote a letter to Radclyffe Hall yesterday,' said Bettina.

'Oh?' said Scoobie.

Jean gave her another of those worried little glances.

'What did you say?' said Triss.

Bettina cleared her throat. 'I wrote, "Dear Raddiepoohs. Fancy a dip in my well?"'

A moment of frozen silence. And then the room burst into laughter, with Jean laughing the hardest and longest. Ah, the locket does have a special shine to it after all.

The way she stated her opinion as if it were fact – pure fact. 'The theatre is dead, everyone knows it.' That's what she'd said. Bug-black eyes coolly assessing him over her wine glass.

'Bettina, darling, I do believe your ladyfriend is declaring me extinct,' he'd replied, trying to keep his voice merry. For Bettina's sake.

'Hey now, I'm not saying *you're* extinct,' said Jean. 'Acting in itself will never cease to be. Just those great proscenium arches you choose to act under.' She lit a cigarette. He noted her long fingers.

All the better to go and fuck herself with.

'You're handsome – you have options. Movies . . .' She waved a limp hand – et cetera, et cetera. 'Did I offend you there? What I said about the theatre?'

He glanced at Étienne, who was trying to hide a smirk.

'Yes. But then you called me handsome, so all is forgiven.'

They laughed. Ha haha! He took three long swallows of his wine.

'I have a friend who works at Warner Brothers,' she said. 'I could put a word in for you.'

'Oh?' he said. 'What does your friend do at this studio?'

'He's a producer. He's been put in charge of some new department. He writes me fairly regularly. How about it? It's the least I could do' – she smiled in a way that was probably supposed to be impish but came across as condescending – 'after so rudely insulting you.'

He glanced again at Étienne, who was raising his eyebrows with encouragement.

'I thank you,' he said, dipping his head, 'but it'll probably be a waste of time.'

'A waste of time? What are you talking about? They'd lap you up in Tinseltown, Mr Shakespeare. Silent movies are on the way out—'

'Something else you decree to be extinct?' said Bettina, smiling.

'Absolutely. Dead as a dodo. Talkies are coming, silence is dying, end of story.'

'"Silence is dying,"' said Bettina, thoughtfully. 'I like that.'

'Then by all means,' Bart said to Jean, 'tell your friend about me.' She smiled, satisfied with herself – her natural state, by the looks of things. 'Thank you,' he added, quietly.

'I might use it in my novel,' Bettina said, half to herself. '"Silence is dying". It has a duality of meaning. Yes . . . I'm going to jot it down.' She went into her handbag for the new notebook she carried around with her, at all times. She'd decided to start writing a novel shortly after Monty's death, and now it was all she ever talked about.

'So how did you come to be friends with a Hollywood producer?' he asked Jean.

She snatched her attention away from Bettina (she was gazing at her like a stupid doe) and said, 'Uh?' with an almost-scowl.

'I said, so how did you come to be friends with a Hollywood producer?' He could feel his jaw tightening.

A bemused chuckle. 'We're still talking about that?'

Under the table his fingernails were digging into the tops of his thighs.

'Creative types tend to flock together, I think,' she said. 'Queer creatives even more so.'

'Queer, is he?'

'The queerest.'

'That's true about us flocking together,' said Bettina. 'There's Étienne the artist, Bart the actor and me the fledgling novelist . . . though I'm probably getting ahead of myself and shall end up an abysmal failure.' She laughed with all her teeth showing – it was a laugh of childish vulnerability. She clearly thought this was going well.

'So what do you do?' Bart asked Jean.

She slanted her head in confusion.

'Well, we're all creatives and your Hollywood friend is a creative.' He flashed a friendly smile. 'So what exactly do you create?'

Her face paled – it was already horribly pale to begin with – and she started to fidget with her cigarette tin, opening and closing it with a snap – creak, snap, creak, snap.

Bettina leaned in. 'Fantastic orgasms!' she said.

They all laughed, even Jean, but her eyes were entirely humourless.

'*Quelle heure est-il, Monsieur le Loup*?'

Étienne lay on the grass, holding Tabby above him. He bared his teeth – '*Il est trois heures*' – and brought her down to his face, kissing her nose. She wriggled her legs and gurgle-giggled. She'd started laughing a week ago. It had become Bart's favourite sound, replacing the 'pock' of a struck tennis ball and even the soft slap of testicles hitting another set of testicles.

The sun was close to setting – it was nearly nine – and the shadows stretched long and slender from the bottoms of the trees. Bats could be seen flitting high up, but always, teasingly, from the corner of the eye. They were all drunk and sprawled on the grass, except for Megan who was inside running a bath for Tabby, and Jean, who preferred the bench so she could watch all proceedings from her high vantage point, smoking and almost-smirking. Bart had only known the woman for a few hours but he'd already formulated a nickname for her: the Duchess of Disdain.

'*Quelle heure est-il, Monsieur le Loup*?' Étienne growled. '*C'est l'heure du dîner*!' He lowered Tabby once more and play-bit her neck and she shrieked and chuckled.

'Don't get carried away, Uncle Étienne,' said Bart. 'We know what happened last time you did that.'

Étienne stopped. '*Mais oui*! You did a little wee-wee on your uncle's shirt.'

'In all fairness, it's not as if she needs an excuse to piss everywhere,' said Bettina, lighting a cigarette and looking around for Jean, who'd disappeared from the bench. She'd been nipping to 'the john' all evening. Bart wondered if she didn't perhaps have a cocaine habit. He imagined following her in and catching her at it. Would he tell Bettina? Or ask for a line?

Étienne started flying Tabby around like an aeroplane, Bart and Bettina watching and smiling.

'Isn't she gorgeous?' said Bettina.

He nodded. 'She's the most gorgeous baby I've ever seen, and I honestly doubt parental bias comes into it.'

'Oh, of course. Entirely objective. She's *objectively* the most superior infant in the world, ever.' She drained the rest of her drink, upending the glass and letting the trickles fall into her mouth. Suppressed a burp with her hand. 'I can't believe we made her,' she said. 'Sometimes I honestly can't believe it. We made a little human being.'

'No. You made her. My part was exceedingly minimal. You grew her.' *And I'm so proud of you*, he wanted to add. But she would invariably make a joke about wanting to vomit, or something like that. Instead he took her hand and kissed her knuckle. She raised a sultry eyebrow. 'Are we having a moment? A tender moment?' She licked her lower lip, slowly. 'Shall we fuck?'

And they laughed, falling onto the grass.

'So,' she said, once they'd regained their composure. 'What do you think of her?'

'Who?'

'Jean, you turnip. What do you think of her?'

'I think she seems like a very interesting person.'

'That's your way of saying you think she's horrible.'

'No! She's intelligent and full of character. As you know, I like people who are intelligent and full of character.'

Étienne was lying on the ground again, arms and legs spread out like a snow angel, singing 'Ah! Les Crocodiles' to Tabby, who was lying on his belly. '*Les crocrocro, les crocrocro, les crocodiles, sur les bords du Nil . . .*'

'I know she can be challenging. But once you get to—'

'Bettina. I like her. And I'm glad she's making you happy.'

'Honestly?' said Bettina.

'Honestly,' said Bart.

'Why are you stopping?' said Étienne. He was eating salted peanuts from a greasy cardboard box.

'Hold on a second,' said Bart, looking out of his side window and scanning the dark shopfronts – it was two in the morning, or thereabouts. He could see a delicatessen with round blocks of cheese on platters and thighs of smoked pork hanging in the window; a ladies' hat shop – he'd gone in there once to buy a peach-ribboned boater for Bettina. A bit further on there was a tobacco shop and – ah, there it was.

He edged the car forward until he was alongside the shop.

The Cave of Virtue.

Fucking stupid name.

'What are you doing?' said Étienne. 'I want to go home to my bed. I'm exhausted.'

'I bet you are,' said Bart, half smiling. They'd just come from Hampstead Heath. Bart had taken a man in his mouth while Étienne fucked him from behind. Vigorously.

He wound down his window then opened the glove compartment and took out a carton of eggs.

'What are you doing, Bart? Bart?'

He took out an egg and aimed it at the shopfront.

'*Bartholomew?*'

He threw the egg and it cracked and splattered all over the glass. He let out an excited, braying laugh and took out another egg, glancing mischievously at Étienne.

'I don't like this,' said Étienne, giving him a dark look. He had powdered salt on his lip.

'Well, I like it enough for the both of us,' said Bart, turning back to the window and aiming.

Chapter 21

May 1932, Hollywood

'Welcome to the land of broken dreams!'

Roger Stamper's neat jewelled hands spread open in a gesture of welcome, his nails catching the light like shavings of pearl. He was wide and squat and he had a tiny diamond embedded in his front tooth which sparkled mutely, as if embarrassed by itself. His lips were a very soft pink, and glossy, daubed with petroleum jelly and laced with deep vertical creases, like tiger prawns. He gave off warmth and hopefully this was authentic.

'This is my personal assistant, Mr Étienne Janvier,' said Bart.

Roger shook Étienne's hand. 'Sure is good to meet you. Finally!'

They all laughed. Finally! Oh, it was so funny that they were meeting *finally*.

'We're having an unusually hot May. Been a real bitch on set. Speaking of which . . .' Roger clapped his hands together. 'Let's get you to set for a looksy-loo.'

'Marvellous,' said Bart, following the man through the hotel lobby.

Bart was to star in *The Mortician*, playing the titular role – the mortician, Edward Crabbe (a part he'd already played on the London stage). It was a macabre story about an isolated, melancholic man who discovers a papyrus scroll rolled up in the oesophagus of a corpse on which is written a few lines of some ancient language – a resurrection spell. He goes on to bring back to life three men, all beautiful and exhibiting a certain masculine vitality and of course it all goes horribly wrong and the three reanimated men turn on him and eventually kill him. 'Which is to say,' Bart told Bettina, when recapping the story to her, 'that the ugly old queer is suitably punished for his transgressions and the status quo is upheld, *ta-da*!' The film was based on an English novel called *Song of the Mortician* which Roger adored, claiming its hidden queer subtext had been instrumental in him figuring out who and what he was.

Inside the car, Roger pressed a button causing a screen to come down between driver and passengers. He lifted up a flap in the seat, pulling out an ice-filled bucket containing champagne and glasses. 'The Hollywood treatment!'

'Where's this moonshine I've been hearing all about?' said Bart, wiping his forehead with a hanky.

'In the bathtubs of Irish thugs,' said Roger. 'So how's the wife? Jean tells me she's pregnant again.'

Roger was of course Jean's producer friend. She'd be at Davenport now, lying on his furniture, eating his food and reaching out with her white claw of a hand to stroke Bettina's swollen belly. As if she had a stake in what was growing inside.

Bart nodded, drinking. The delicate champagne bubbles were popping against his upper lip. 'Everything is hunky-dory.'

Roger crossed his legs like a woman, his trousers hitching up to show a salmon-pink sock. 'Me, I could never do what you did. Couldn't live with a woman. Not after growing up with six sisters.'

They were driving down a broad road lined with fat palm trees. One tree had a rope dangling out of its thick fronds, and hanging from the bottom of the rope, by its leg, was a baby doll with no arms. The car stopped at an intersection, outside an employment office, and there stood a group of men – white, black, Mexican – wearing baggy brown trousers and white short-sleeved shirts, tieless. A truck pulled up and they started piling into the open back of its cab. Orange-pickers, maybe. How depressing.

'So how do you find being your beau's assistant?' Roger asked Étienne.

Étienne was pressing his champagne flute against his neck. 'He has always told me what to do. Now I am getting paid.'

'Oh, I like it!' said Roger, squeezing his knees and baring his teeth. 'Jean tells me you're an artist?'

'Perhaps,' said Étienne, evasively.

Étienne had grown weary of the label 'artist'. With art in general. Back in Paris he'd discovered that a few of his artist friends had died, a couple from alcohol abuse, one from starvation and exposure, two others from TB. He fell back into selling his arse in the back streets of the *Quartier Pigalle* – on hearing this, Bart took great enjoyment in exhibiting an almost

Buddha-like show of non-judgement (he did of course judge, inwardly).

Étienne loved playing with Tabby (he enjoyed the simplicity of children) but the rest of the time he seemed edgy and bored and was smoking more hashish than usual. He'd taken an interest in learning card tricks, which Bart had at first found charming, but now it was just annoying. He carried a pack with him wherever he went and was always dipping into his pocket to retrieve them and practise, even when on the lavatory. 'Idle hands are the devil's playground, *non*?' he'd say, separating the cards in a blur, trousers around his ankles.

'Ah, here we are,' said Roger.

They had pulled up into a vast, sun-bright lot.

'Is that Kay Francis?' said Étienne, his nose touching the window glass.

'No,' said Roger, following his gaze, 'that's a prostitute.' He leaned forward, hands on his thighs: 'But what's the difference, right?'

The hot cab exploded with laughter. Actress, prostitute – what's the difference? Hahaha. It's funny because it's true! Whores as far as the eye can see. Two whores sitting in your car right now. And what does that make you, Roger?

'I am of course joking,' he said, wiping his eye with a bejewelled finger. 'Kay Francis is an impeccable woman.'

Three things he hated about filming *The Mortician*. Firstly: the make-up. He was up at four every morning and promptly driven to the set, where he had to sit perfectly still for three hours – three whole hours – so that a dullard called Peter could attach prosthetics – a crooked nose and gaunt cheekbones – and then slather on a thick cake of make-up.

The second thing: sobriety. He couldn't get drunk, not with the early mornings, and he just wasn't capable of moderate drinking – it'd taken him three decades to learn this sorry truth. He dined with Étienne alone in the evenings, drinking soda water and spearing his salad leaves and poached fish with rising resentment; he'd had to lose sixteen pounds in order to play the role of Crabbe. Meanwhile, Étienne gobbled up sirloin steak and blocks of bread and cheese. Afterwards they'd return to the hotel and go straight to bed, usually too tired to fuck. And when they did fuck, it was perfunctory and rushed; minimal kissing, a race to come first. The last time they'd fucked like they meant it had been in 1929.

The third thing and the worst thing: being away from Tabby. He tried to speak to her on the telephone once, and the second he heard her nasal girl-squeak – 'Dada, when are you coming home?' – he'd dropped the mouthpiece and had to lean against the wall to steady himself. It felt like someone had prised open his ribcage and kicked him squarely in the heart.

There were also plenty of things he merely disliked, such as the catering staff, a bunch of old shrews who giggled enigmatically whenever he tried to speak to them, and the ongoing heatwave – it seemed like every ten minutes he had to covertly sneak a hand down his trousers to peel his sticky testicles from his thigh.

There was much to love too. Lillian White, the female lead, for starters. A former Ziegfeld girl, she had bright blue eyes, dyed black hair and immortal skin. She smoked constantly and exuded an aura of sex so potent one could almost smell it. They'd hit it off immediately and spent most lunchtimes together in her caravan. She'd once had a drink thrown over her by Gloria Swanson over a dispute in a poker game ('I deserved it – I was cheating') and another time licked Tallulah Bankhead's left nipple ('on a dare'). She had a whole bagful of stories and extracted them with wide-eyed zeal, laughing open-throated at each scandalous punchline.

And of course there was Roger. His first day on set Bart had felt overwhelmed by the cameras and the harsh lighting, sweating so much that his prosthetic chin began to slide away. He had no idea what he was doing. He spent lunch break sitting under a cardboard cut-out of a vulture. I can't do this, he thought, staring unseeing at the sweating tomato slices on his tray. He was going to ruin this whole production. Thought he was good enough for Hollywood, that's what everyone would think.

Roger found him. He lowered himself to the floor with difficulty and was silent for a long time, his brogues creaking. Finally, he said, 'Valentino apparently shat his pants his first day on set of *The Sheik*. Everyone could smell it.'

Bart managed fairly well after that.

Shooting was suspended on the second day due to a rewrite of the script – Roger had met with the board and they'd expressed concern over a certain 'subliminal element'. They thought Crabbe and his assistant, played by Lillian, should end up falling in love. 'Some uptight cunts with too much time on their hands are gonna turn my film into dog shit,' complained Roger. Bart now had to play the role in a way that justified the reciprocated love of a beautiful girl. 'OK, so our Eddie's got a face only a mother could love,' Roger said to him, 'but so long as you can make it seem like he'd be a good lover, I think we can get away with this. Essentially, I want you to look like you live for eating pussy. You're *hungry* for it.'

In a new scene, Bart gazed down at Lillian, *hungrily*. He

gripped her arms and pulled her close. He remembered a time five years ago when he and Étienne had looked at each other like this – they'd been locked inside the bathroom, at a party. Swaying with the drink, they stared at each other murderously, their erections meeting through the cloth of their trousers. They'd stayed like that for ages – genuinely, it'd been close to two minutes, and then, the tension so palpable, so bloody knife-tight, they'd both pounced, kissing messily. Bart spun Étienne around, tore down his trousers and started to lick his arsehole. Something he'd never done, nor had the urge to do, before. It was pure filth.

'And that's a cut!' yelled the director. 'Beautiful, Bart, real authentic.'

'Darling, when it comes to uglification, you haven't a leg to stand on, I'm afraid.'

'Uglification?' said Lillian through her perpetual shield of smoke. 'That even a word?'

Bart shrugged. 'Well, it is now.'

They were in Lillian's trailer – that's what they called them here, trailers – drinking vodka and listening to Lee Wiley on the gramophone. Shooting was to start late the following morning and Bart was taking the opportunity to get drunk. Étienne was lying down in Bart's trailer with a migraine, a damp cloth over his face and the blinds drawn. He was hoping to take a two-day trip to Las Vegas with one of the set painters the following morning, and feared the headache wouldn't budge (Bart hoped this would be the case – the set painter, a man, was stunning, and they were getting rather tight). It was raining outside – the first time Bart had witnessed rain in LA. It was a phenomenal downpour, plinking like pennies against the trailer roof, gushing down the windowpanes and covering the lot grounds in a shallow ford.

'If Roger had his way,' said Lillian, 'I'd end up with hair coming outta my chin. And warts. A fucking broomstick, ya know?'

Angry with the studio for 'de-queering the script' and wanting to express this as passive-aggressively as possible, Roger had renamed Lillian's character Beadie – B.D. as in bull-dagger – and had her wearing slacks and less make-up.

'Stop bloody moaning and drink,' said Bart.

'I will not stop bloody moaning. It's OK for you – you're married already. How am I supposed to find a husband looking like a clam climber?'

'Clam climber?'

She laughed hard, snapping her head back. That full-throated roar. 'I made that up. You like it?'

'*Climber?* Why?'

'Alliteration. And I guess you – ya know – I guess you sort of climb up to it.' She mimed climbing a ladder with her hands.

'One might climb down.'

'Might one?' she said, imitating his accent. 'Here, let me top you up.' He held out his glass and she glugged out two inches of vodka. 'I'm real glad we got to do this,' she said, adding a spray of club soda. 'I can't call someone a pal if I haven't gotten trashed with them.'

'Hear hear!' said Bart, raising his glass.

'This is my favourite song. Keep it buttoned till it's finished.' She closed her eyes, shoulders rolling along to the lazy string section and then, seemingly bored, turned to Bart and said, 'You ever done a screen kiss?'

'This is the first time I've done a screen anything. As you know.'

'What about the stage?'

'Yes. Many times.'

'We should practise it,' she said, taking her silk scarf off and bunching it up with one hand, 'ready for the shoot.'

'Oh, I don't know . . .'

'Hey. Don't get like that.' She threw her scarf at him – it became unbundled as it flew and drifted down feather-slow onto his thigh. 'I'm a professional. You think I just walk onto a set and wrap lips with a guy I've never wrapped lips with before? I want it to look *good*.'

He picked up the scarf with two fingers. Lillian's perfume rose up – a sweet, overpowering musk.

'I don't want to sit on your wiener, Mr Big Theatre Man. We're friends here.'

He downed the rest of his drink. 'Fine. Do you know your lines?'

She raised her pencil-thin eyebrows. 'Did I not just say I was a professional?'

He stood up. '"Beadie. I don't know if I can go on any more."'

'"You must. Oh, you must."'

He shook his head. '"I thought I could create something perfect – why, Beadie? Why aim for perfection in this imperfect world?"'

She took a step closer to him, wringing her hands. '"*Because* the world is imperfect! You just want to fix what was broken. Oh, Eddie – you have something broken inside of you, we all do."' She pressed a hand to his chest. '"Won't you let me try to fix it?"'

He grabbed her by the arms and pulled her in. Gazed down at her. Hungrily. He lurched his head to hers and kissed her lips, swooning his head to the side. She parted her mouth and slipped her tongue in, reaching up to grab his head with both hands. And he couldn't help it – he kissed back. It was instinctual. It would be rude not to. She pushed him up against the dressing table, his buttocks knocking over perfume bottles and make-up. She slipped her hands under his shirt and ran them up his stomach, to his chest, combing her fingers through his chest hair.

He leapt away, giggling wildly. 'That wasn't in the script!' he shrilled, the skin on his face heating up. 'You naughty woman!'

She was leaning against her dressing table, palms down, shoulders slumped, breathing heavily. In the position of someone who wished to be fucked from behind . . . or someone dreadfully embarrassed, gathering themselves.

He poured vodka into his glass and tossed it back. Laughed again. *You naughty woman.* God.

She turned around finally. Sulkily. Her hair lay in messy damp strands around her face. She parted it with her fingers, nudging it back into place. 'You don't like me?'

Bart poured another drink. 'I thought you knew what I was.'

'You mean the Frenchie?'

'Well. Yes.' He fumbled a cigarette out of his packet.

'I just figured you went both ways. Your wife's got a bun in the oven, don't she?'

He tried to light the cigarette but it dropped out of his fingers, falling into his drink. He took out a fresh one and tried again. 'I think you're beautiful, Lilly. But I'm afraid I just don't feel anything for women. Physically.'

She nodded, processing this. And then she seemed to entirely compose herself, to suck all vulnerability and human feeling back inside herself, and it was as if someone had just yelled,

'Action!' Tiger-like, she ambled to her chair. She sat down, crossing one long leg over the other, and looked at him, eyes full of lazy menace. 'I think you should leave.'

'Lilly. I do so hope we can still be friends—'

'I want you out of here.' Her hands lay perfectly still on the armchair rests. 'This is a fag-free zone, this place. Beat it.'

'Oh, come on! You sucked Tallulah Bankhead's tit!'

'I said beat it. Before I call security on you.'

He waited for her hard face to melt into a wicked grin – the punchline. But it never came. He snatched up his cigarettes and jacket and left. The rain soaked him through to the skin within seconds.

Chapter 22

The fourth thing he hated: Lillian White.

She blanked him – refused even to look at him. She peered at Étienne with nasty slits for eyes. Her new bosom buddy was Tilly Warhol, who played the part of bereaved wife to Corpse No. 2. They went around together, whispering – they had that prim air of schoolgirls who've been insulted by a group of boys and huddle together outside classrooms, talking in aghast voices about how insufferable and disgusting boys are, and honestly, Tilly, I'm going to tell my daddy about this and then those rotters will be in for it, oh, yes they will!

There were portrait shots of all the actors and actresses from *The Mortician* pinned to the wall in Roger's office. Someone had drawn a phallus going into Bart's mouth and a garland of garlic around his neck. The catering staff continued to giggle in Bart's presence but there was now a new undertone – whereas before it had been flirtatious, in the way that old matriarchs are with young men, now it was barbed, or at least it felt barbed. Bart felt entirely alone. He *was* entirely alone – Étienne was in Las Vegas with the set painter, who was apparently straight and talked about 'pussy' all the time, but really, it only took a few drinks for all that to change.

'Oh, that's sad,' said Roger. 'I've had similar things happen to me, back when I was still deemed attractive by the ladies – yes, there was a time.' They were in Roger's office, Bart's defiled photograph on his desk. Roger was eating a plate of macaroni – the room stank of it; a cheesy baby-vomit funk. 'I think what happens is, a person is rejected and they're hurting. And some – ya know, the real insecure types – will turn that hurt into anger and throw it out at the person who rejected them. And when the person who rejected them is a fruit, like us, that's – I think the target is made that much bigger. An easier hit. Something they can' – he pinched his fingers together and mimed throwing a dart – 'aim at real easy.' He spooned macaroni into his mouth and chewed.

'If I wanted a magnanimous response I'd be speaking to Étienne,' said Bart. 'If he were here.'

Swallowing, Roger picked up Bart's picture. 'You want me to say she's a bitch? All right. She's a bitch. It's just I know some things about Lilly. She had a real tough time of it growing up. I know' – he held up a hand of admission – 'no excuse.'

'She's a fucking child.'

Roger nodded. 'I'll speak to her about this.'

'I'd rather you didn't, actually,' said Bart.

Roger raised his eyebrows. Drank his root beer. 'Your choice. I'll replace the picture. Just hang tight and stay professional.'

*

Bart had kippers for breakfast. He requested, as an accompaniment, a whole onion, sliced, and a bulb of garlic, peeled. The waiter furrowed his brow but acquiesced. Bart ate the onion slices with the fish and put the garlic between two pieces of thickly buttered rye bread. He drank four coffees and smoked five cigarettes. He didn't brush his teeth.

When they kissed, he pushed his fingers into her arms, pressed hard, hoping for bruises. She in turn had pooled her mouth with extra saliva and let it ooze into his. He didn't know what she'd had for breakfast, but it smelled like tripe.

The last day of shooting – another defaced portrait picture. A speech bubble in the comic-book style coming out of his mouth: 'One sucks cocks. Jolly good.'

Bart ripped the picture off the wall. He found Étienne smoking a cigarette with the set painter (Gabe was his name). How chummy they looked – their arms slightly touching. Friends did that. But so did clandestine lovers – he should know. He took Étienne to one side and showed him the picture.

'What can I do?' Étienne said.

'Nothing,' said Bart. 'I hate her. I fucking hate her.'

Étienne squeezed his arm. 'It will be over soon.'

'Don't touch me in front of people,' said Bart, pulling away.

Gabe had a grey-purple blemish on his throat – a love-bite.

Six times – six fucking times. He'd never fluffed a line this many times before. Lillian rolled her eyes as if she was sick of dealing with such amateurs. Oh, to slap that face and get away with it. To *punch* it.

Lunch break was called and, unable to find Étienne, he got his own food from the buffet table, his hands shaking so badly the salad tongs kept clattering out of his hand. 'Fuck!' he said, dropping them on the table. He felt a hand dab his elbow. It was one of the caterers, a small Mexican woman with plump cheeks. She picked up the tongs, transferring a chicken piece to his plate. 'More?' she said, looking up at him. He nodded and she added another. 'Salad?' she said. He nodded again, saying, 'No cucumber please,' in a humbled whisper. She reached up and patted his cheek. 'Good job. Don't be sad.' And she smiled and walked away, wiping Bart's waxy make-up onto her smock.

He rushed to his trailer and burst into tears. He caught sight of himself in the mirror – mucus streaming from a prosthetic nose, tears tracking through the ghoulish face paint – what a joke. And where the fuck was Étienne? Where the – he ripped the nose off and dashed his food to the floor. A flap of torn rubber hung down over his lip – dangling from it, a droplet of cold snot.

He lit a cigarette and picked up the letter he'd received from Bettina two days ago. He re-read it, imagining her at her writing desk, cheek resting on the heel of a hand. 'You'll probably be packing by the time this reaches you. If I believed in God I'd pray for your safe passage. But of course I don't, and anyway, what chance does the ocean have against you, you indestructible bastard? All my love, and our daughter's, and our unborn foetus's, your exemplary wife, Bettina.'

They'd been arguing a lot, he and Bettina. Constantly trying to catch each other out, expose the other's hypocrisies. But none of that mattered now. Really, it didn't.

The door blasted open and Bart dropped the envelope, startled. It was Étienne, wide-eyed and out of breath.

'Roger is at the hospital. He choked on a chicken bone. I think he's dead.'

'Oh, fuck,' said Bart.

Bart looked at the floor. The shiny-bald gristle of a thigh joint glistening next to a shard of white ceramic. Bettina was always trying to find significance in everything, little scraps of symbolism to put in her book. Well, there it was. There it was.

Barney was a huge barrel-torsoed man with a messy grey-peppered beard, an underbite and ice-blue eyes that glittered keenly. A sort of Walt Whitman. It was easy to imagine Barney living in a log cabin, trailing his muddy boots all over the freshly swept floors and eating huge steaming bowls of porridge with a wooden spoon. He was wearing a fine-tailored suit but had removed his tie and loosened his collar in the heat. He took a pipe out of his breast pocket, stuffed it in his bulldog maw and got it going. 'You fellas go inside' *–puh, puh* – 'before kicking-out time.'

Bart and Étienne walked in, their hands bumping together. The chapel was cool, dark and empty – most people (and there had been many) had paid their respects in the morning. Their heels clipped against the stone floor and the clips echoed. The sunlight coming through the stained-glass window cast a fuzzy reflection along the centre aisle in yellow, blue and red. The casket was huge and lacquered-white, so shiny it looked liquid. Roger lay amongst the lilac satin in a white suit. His skin looked more orange than ever, his serrated shrimp lips daubed in a most unsubtle pink. His small hands with all their jewels lay crossed over his chest. Bart glanced at the door then took Étienne's hand.

'I would have liked to get to know him better,' he said.

'Me too,' said Étienne.

'He was warm-hearted. I don't know many warm-hearted people.'

'Hmm.'

'How old was he?' said Bart.

'Fifty-four.'

'That's – I was about to say that's young. But it's not. My father was thirty-five. It could happen' – Bart snapped his fingers – 'like that. We should start taking better care of ourselves.'

'*Oui. Oui.*'

The chapel doors swung open and Bart quickly snatched his hand away from Étienne's. Barney walked up the aisle, clomping like a Minotaur.

'Lady just told me five more minutes,' he said.

'We'll leave you to it,' said Bart. 'So you can say goodbye.'

Barney raised his hand. 'Stay.' He held onto the coffin rim with both hands like a man about to be sick over a bathroom sink and gazed down at Roger, his lips tightening until they lost their colour. 'Damn you,' he whispered, a tear spilling into his beard. 'Motherfucker.' He pointed a giant finger at Roger's face. 'You cocksucker. You stupid fat cunt! Goddamn stupid prick, I—' He raised his hands and held them half clenched over Roger's head, hesitant, as if not knowing whether he wanted to caress or strike. 'You're a fucking cocksucker. A cocksucker! Stupid greedy motherfucker – I told you to stop eating that shit! I should kick your ass.'

Bart and Étienne watched, open-mouthed, as Barney clutched Roger's face and fiercely kissed his lips. He looked up at them, little blue eyes glittering. 'He was the love of my life!'

*

Of all the people, she had to sit next to him. She was wearing a mourning veil and her eyes peered out of it, jewelled by spent tears. The great actress. He touched Étienne's thigh to get his attention. He nodded, without looking, to show he was aware of the woman's presence.

A black-smocked priest floated up the aisle chanting Latin and holding a thurible of incense, followed by a procession of altar boys and another black-smocked man tinkling a tiny bell. The pall-bearers began their sombre procession, headed on the right by Barney. Two of the other bearers were men with plucked eyebrows and rouge and another looked like he could be Roger's younger brother. A strange, beautiful mix of queer family and real family.

He felt Lillian grope for his hand. She found his fingers and grabbed them tight. Leaned her head towards his, that familiar perfume stink immediately molesting his nostrils. 'I'm sorry,' she whispered. 'Please forgive me.'

'I'm going to have one more,' said Bart. 'Just one more.'

'You are going to be sick on the boat,' said Étienne.

'And you'll be within your rights to say I told you so.'

'Don't be a wet blanket,' said Lillian.

Étienne pulled a face. 'Wet blanket? I don't understand. What is she saying?'

'Go and do some card tricks,' said Bart. Go and find your new boyfriend, he wanted to add. But they'd already argued about that twice today. Bart was apparently being paranoid and insecure. Well. Sometimes paranoia was justified.

Étienne looked at his wristwatch. 'I want to go to bed.'

'Then go to bed,' said Bart. 'I'll follow on later.'

Étienne took his cards out of his pocket and, sighing,

started to shuffle them. 'I am a performing monkey.' And he left.

They were in a shaded canopy at the end of the garden with a view of the house and pool. Bart could hear crickets chirruping in the lawn and the low buzz of the electric lights that were strung up everywhere. Further off – splashes and shouts from the huge outdoor swimming pool, the brass band in the conservatory. Barney sat atop a stool by the pool bar, conversing sombrely with Billy Haines. He hadn't moved in almost five hours and his ashtray was bulging with black pipe ash and pistachio shells. The production team from *The Mortician* was here, still dressed in funeral attire. Joan Crawford was apparently on her way.

Stanley Yeltzin appeared at the canopy. Stanley – Reanimated Corpse No. 3 – was ravishingly handsome and always looked like he was on the verge of smiling.

'My favourite corpse!' called Bart, in greeting. 'Come and join us!'

'Some party,' he said, sitting down next to them. 'You wouldn't guess that someone's just died.' He looked up at the stars. 'Rest in peace, friend. Hell of a guy. Hell of a producer.'

'A peach,' said Lillian.

A great shrieking from the pool – a bunch of people had jumped in at the same time. 'You sons of bitches!' yelled a passing man, soaked through by the resulting wave. A female impersonator in a Garbo wig sneaked up and pushed him into the water.

'What are we doing sitting all the way over here like old biddies?' said Lillian.

'I came here for some privacy,' said Stanley. He pulled a brass tin out of his breast pocket and opened it up – inside was a vial of beige powder and a small pipe.

'What is that?' said Bart.

'It's dope, ya dope,' said Lillian.

'If it makes you folks uncomfortable I can go somewhere else,' said Stanley, pausing in the act of tapping powder into the pipe chamber.

Bart raised his palm. 'No, no. It's a free world.'

Stanley blew out a thin plume of smoke and looked around with contented eyes, as if he'd just finished a slap-up meal. He offered the gear to Bart and Lillian.

'Shall we be naughty?' said Bart.

'I think we shall,' said Lillian.

Bart took the pipe. 'Very, very naughty,' he muttered. 'There's us, two innocent children, sitting away from the debauched revellers, not wishing to be tainted so. Then along comes the big bad wolf with his many temptations.' Bart bit the pipe between his teeth, smiling.

Another great splash from the pool followed by shouts and cheers and shrill laughs, and this huge noise drowning out all others.

Such as footsteps. Approaching footsteps.

A hand shot out and slapped the pipe out of his mouth. The mouthpiece clashed against his teeth and the palm connected with his jaw. 'Ow! Fuck!'

Étienne stood before him, furious. Fucking Étienne. Always right, always well fed and full on his *rightness.* He grabbed Bart by the arm and dragged him away from Lillian and Stanley.

'Get off me!'

Étienne strengthened his grip. 'You are coming home now.'

'Didn't I say he was a wet blanket?' Lillian said.

Bart thumped Étienne's arm – right on the bone – and tore himself free. Étienne came for him again, arms out as if to wrestle him. Bart threw a right hook – it landed with a meaty slap against his lover's cheek. Étienne stumbled back, clutching his face. Looked at Bart. Too far. Too far. He punched him back, flattening his nose with a crack. Blood – a hot red sneeze of blood.

Then they were on the ground, scrabbling around, hatred twisting their faces while Lillian hopped about, saying, 'Oh my gawd, oh my gawd, they're gonna *kill* each other.' And then Barney was there, huge hulking Barney with thighs looming over them like birches. With one hand he grabbed Étienne's shirt collar and with the other Bart's arm, and he pulled them to their feet and led them roughly up the garden path towards the swimming pool. He picked up both men and threw them in the water.

Bart twisted around in the water and emerged, spluttering, hair lacquer stinging his eyes and blood-pinked water trickling out of his nose. Étienne bobbed to the surface alongside a floating champagne bottle.

Poolside, Barney looked down at them, arms at his sides. 'Have some respect for the dead,' he growled.

Chapter 23

May 1932, Davenport House, London

He would hate it – he'd positively rage about it. In the first place, he wouldn't allow it.

Jean was wearing Bart's shirt.

They were in the garden reading on a strawberry-red picnic blanket. A large swatch of the grass was covered in bluebells, which, according to Megan, would only stay out for a month, and then, further into spring, disappear for another ten months. 'Fleeting little pretties,' she called them. Jean was reading something by Gertude Stein, her brow furrowed as if she was displeased. The shirt was baggy on her, the top two buttons undone. Bettina had a letter from Bart, received this morning. He was moaning about the special diet he was on, but added, 'Perhaps it's a saving grace that I must limit my food so, because American cuisine is horrible.' Étienne was fattening himself up on hamburgers, which, contrary to their name, were not ham, but a thick slab of greasy, gristly beef, packed between two buns. 'There is no polite way to eat one of these monstrosities, as Étienne has proved to me.'

Bettina shifted around on the blanket. It was almost impossible to get comfortable in any position with her stomach so big. 'He says that Roger is a fine human being,' she said to Jean.

'He is,' said Jean, not taking her eyes from her book.

'What are you reading?'

Jean tore her eyes away from the page. She held up the book: *Three Lives.*

'Yes, I know *what* you're reading. I have eyes. I mean, tell me *about* what you're reading.'

'If you want to know about it, you can read it after me.'

'I don't want to read it.' Nobody *wanted* to read Gertrude Stein.

'So why ask?' Jean raised her eyebrows and smiled. 'You want my attention?' Bart often smiled at her in the same way when he thought she was being childish, but whereas his smile was made up perhaps of twenty per cent cruelty and eighty per cent playfulness, Jean's cruelty was closer to sixty per cent. Maybe even seventy.

'You have this idea in your head of what lovers do,' continued Jean. 'A lovely romantic picnic, you thought. And we'd sit side by side, reading together and sharing our insights and all our clever witticisms and maybe sneaking a kiss using the book as a shield.'

Jean picked her book up again and shifted onto her other side, her back to Bettina. 'If I'm reading, it means I don't want to talk.'

Bettina stared at Jean's back. The sun broke through the clouds again and the shirt became dazzlingly bright.

Megan held Tabby's hand and carried, with her spare hand, a wicker basket full of wild garlic and wildflowers. Megan was continuously picking wild garlic and bringing it to Doris to put in with the roast vegetables, claiming that wild garlic was full of goodness and not as inclined to pong the breath as regular garlic. The wildflowers, mostly consisting of bluebells, foxgloves and red campion, were put into vases around the house and freshened daily, and some of them – the real 'dazzlers' – were pressed into a heavy volume of Shakespeare's complete plays.

Flowers and laughter and the lemony musk of wild garlic – this was what Megan brought to the house. Earth and beauty. And what, exactly, did Jean bring?

'Hello,' said Megan, releasing Tabby, who ran up, pointed to her mother's stomach and said, 'Mummy, why is there a baby inside you?'

'Because I ate one for breakfast,' said Bettina, grabbing the child into a hug.

'Mind she doesn't hurt your stomach,' said Jean.

'She won't!'

'Shall I take her back to the house?' said Megan. She waggled her basket. 'We were going to make a start on ruining *Twelfth Night*.'

'Oh, goody. I absolutely loathe *Twelfth Night*. I might come and help actually.'

'Should I come too?' said Jean.

'No,' said Bettina. 'You wanted to read your book in peace, didn't you?'

She took Tabby's hand and started for the house, looking back just once to find Jean doing a slow clap – *bravo*. The clouds were beginning to thicken and grey. Good. Rain on the bitch.

Bettina heard the shouting from two rooms away – she was in the study writing a reply to Bart, a frozen ham bone wedged between her lower back and the chair to ease nerve pain. The temperature had dipped in the afternoon and it was chill now – she'd started a fire in the hearth and it was a strange conflict, the cold ham bone against her back and the skin-tightening heat at her front.

She rushed to the kitchen.

'You have no right!' Doris was saying, her face a hot, clammy pink. 'No right at all!'

Jean aimed a long finger at the older woman's bosom. 'I do, though. Pack your things and go.'

'Ladies,' said Bettina, quietly.

They both looked at her.

'She's trying to fire me!' said Doris.

Jean looked like someone caught torturing a small creature – a rat, perhaps – but quickly became defiant. It was a rat, after all.

'I can see that.'

'She hasn't got the power to do such a thing,' said Doris. 'She's just a guest.'

'She was rude to me,' said Jean. She turned back to Doris. 'You don't get to be rude to a guest without repercussions.'

'She wanted me to change the dinner plans! Like the master of the house! Well, I told her unequivocally that it was not in her power to do so, Mrs Dawes.'

Bettina nodded. 'Miss Freeman, please come with me.'

Jean stormed out of the kitchen. She was wearing Bart's slippers.

'I'll see you in the study,' she said, and Jean wrinkled her lip in response, scraping roughly past her swollen belly.

Doris was looking at her with huge eyes, her hands planted on the butcher's block. 'Am I really fired?'

'Of course not. Continue with the dinner plans previously stipulated. With one place fewer.'

'She's never liked me. From day one.' Jean was pacing in front of the fire, smoking her cigarette in vicious bursts and tapping her ash onto the rug. 'The way she's always looked at me. And calling me "master of the house" like that. A jab. A dirty jab.' She stopped pacing and lifted a hand, palm out. 'I know I took liberties. But honest to God, Betts, if you don't get rid of that harpy, I'll . . .' She shook her head. 'If we get rid of her, I can get someone else in, someone better. I know one guy, a sissy, he'd cook up a storm here and we wouldn't need to sneak around the place.'

Bettina felt cold. Her whole heart felt cold. She was bored – so profoundly bored of all this, of *her*. But – and she must admit this to herself, she really must – she was also fearful. Not of what Jean might do, but of what she might say. 'What else do you want to replace?' she said. 'Or who else?' She aimed a loaded look at Bart's shirt.

'What are you talking about?'

'I want you to leave,' said Bettina.

'Don't be foolish, Betty. You're making a fool of yourself.'

'No. *You're* making a fool of *me*. How dare you? Firing my staff? How the hell dare you?'

'This is hormonal bullshit. This is *bullshit*.'

'I want you to take off my husband's slippers and shirt and leave.'

'You're serious,' said Jean.

Bettina's hands were trembling. 'Deadly serious.'

'There's no coming back from this,' said Jean.

'I know.'

'What about Tabby?'

'What about her?'

'You can't bring me into your family and then yank me away. I can think of nothing more callous.'

'Oh, please,' said Bettina. 'You barely talk to her. Don't pretend you have these great feelings for my child. Don't you dare pretend that.'

'How could you say that?'

'How? Easily. With my mouth. I make words come out of my mouth following a series of signals sent from my brain. It's really rather easy.'

'Now you're just being—'

'It's so easy, in fact, that I'll show you again – look.' Bettina pointed at her mouth. 'The only time you speak to my daughter is when you are offering corrections and criticisms and actually, you act at all times like she is a mildly unpleasant smell you must tolerate, and *actually*, the main reason I don't invite you to stay over more often has nothing to do with Bart, it's because you are a cold fish with my daughter, so I repeat, using my mouth again, like so' – she jabbed a finger at her mouth once more – 'take my husband's slippers and shirt off. And just *go*!'

Jean started unbuttoning the shirt, her hands shaking violently. Oh, she was angry. But then, she was *always* angry, with her snip-snapping eggshell moods and explosive indignation, then her subsequent apologies and excuses: oh, what an abused child she'd been, her brothers were such brutes and she was so terrified of rejection, of abandonment – the implication here being that Bettina would have to be a truly cruel bitch to abandon her, and the consequences might be tragic. Well, so be it.

Jean grew impatient and tore the shirt open, buttons pinging across the room. She stood, buzzing, in her vest and – well, would you look at that: the vest was Bart's too! She kicked the slippers off, bundled up the shirt and tossed it in the fire. Black flowers bloomed on the white shirt and silvery trails of smoke rose up like treble clefs.

Bettina lay on the sofa on her side, a cushion supporting her stomach and a half-empty bottle of claret on a small table at arm's length.

Bart would *love* this. Oh, he would absolutely delight in this – a victory jig, behind closed doors. He loathed Jean and hadn't tried very hard to conceal the fact. Bettina had hated him for hating her. Won't even give her a chance, she'd thought. *She'd* been warm and open with Étienne. Welcomed him into her home and heart. And yes, Étienne was a lot nicer than Jean. But for all Bart knew, Jean might be a sweetheart underneath it all. There were lots of people who were stinkers on the outside but darlings on the inside – they were often the best people.

Jean was not one of them.

Bart had been right.

Oh, he was going to bloody *love* this.

She finished her wine and poured another.

A knock at the door.

'Come in.'

It was Doris. She held her apron crumpled up in her hands. 'Sorry to interrupt you, Mrs Dawes. Just wanted to check if it's to be the lamb cutlets tomorrow.'

'Yes. Sorry, I should have come and told you.'

She flapped a hand. 'Och, no. You've had all that unpleasantness today, you're right to rest up.' She bunched up her apron with both hands as if moulding a snowball. 'I do hope I didn't make things worse earlier.'

'Of course not, Doris. I'm only sorry you were put in that position.'

'Did you see what she was wearing, too?'

'I did.'

Doris shook her head gravely. 'Shocking level of disrespect, if you don't mind me saying. I never knew what you saw in her, to be quite honest. I know she was helping you with your book, her being a literary sort, but you've other friends just as qualified to help, ones who wouldn't strut about the place wearing your husband's clothes while he's away earning the family crust.' Another grim head-shake. 'I know it's none of my business, Mrs Dawes, who you keep company with. But if you'll permit me to say – an unmarried woman her age, wearing man's clothes . . . there's something not quite right there.'

Bettina stared at her. 'You're right,' she wanted to say. 'It's none of your business.' Such a strange feeling – for one's contempt of a person to suddenly turn to a wish to defend them, or their nature, at the least. Of course Doris felt no kindness for the inverts of the world – why would she? Only a fool would expect anything else. Yet to be reminded of this was like a slap; no, not quite so bad as a slap – it was like a glass of water in the face. This was what came from living in a bubble, from surrounding yourself with like-minded people. It became easy to forget that the rest of the world was in sharp disagreement. Was, in fact, disgusted.

Hypocrites, tiny-minded hypocrites.

She was going to bloody well say it, actually.

'You're right – it isn't any of your business.' Head tilted just so. 'Make sure there's mint sauce to go with the lamb tomorrow. Thank you.'

'I've just got her off to sleep,' said Megan, standing in the same spot Doris had filled an hour previously. 'She made me read her storybook three times.'

'Thank you,' said Bettina, still lying on the sofa. 'Why don't you come and have a glass of wine with me?'

Megan looked at the bottle with a panicked show of politeness. 'I don't drink, sorry. Alcohol and my family don't mix well.'

'Oh, right. Of course. Well, why don't you come and talk to me then?' Bettina pulled herself to a sitting position, wincing as a bolt of sciatic pain went up her thigh, and patted the cushion next to her. 'We so seldom get a chance to talk properly. It's all been nappies and first steps.'

'Very well,' said Megan, taking a seat.

'Chocolate truffle?' Bettina offered, holding out a box.

'Now that's more like it!' Megan plucked one out.

'So what do you like to do?' said Bettina. 'When you're not engaged with work, I mean.'

Megan hurriedly chewed her chocolate, dipping her head, and swallowed. Bettina watched her throat bulge. 'I go to the

Regal a lot. I stop in the market first and buy sugared almonds and a Chelsea bun and I sneak them in. Last Sunday I saw *Mata Hari*, Garbo's my absolute favourite. No. No – I lie. Harlow. She's got such a vivacious personality. You know, I once tried to pluck my eyebrows like hers and I ended up with barely a hair left. Oh, what did I look like?'

'Bart has told me some eye-opening things about Garbo. She goes with women, you know. Bart knows someone who knows someone and – you get the picture.'

This was the first time Bettina had ever broached the subject of lesbianism with Megan. They did discuss things of a personal nature, sometimes – it wasn't all just nappies and first steps – but never *that*. It was a truly huge elephant, and the room was getting smaller.

Megan's eyes were wide. 'Really?'

'Supposedly.'

'That is news indeed, Mrs Dawes.'

'Please, call me Bettina.'

Megan nodded unsurely. 'Could I have another chocolate? I rarely treat myself to sweets. Can't be trusted with them.'

'Have as many as you like.' Bettina sipped her wine, trying to look at Megan without appearing as if she were looking. Her skin was tanned a honey-brown – nothing like the candlestick pallor of Jean's skin. Megan, of course, was outdoors often with Tabby. Her forearms were the darkest part of her. How would they look laid next to her stomach? Honey and milk. Next to her breasts? Better not to think about the breasts. Her eyes, though – the gold flecks scattering out from the pupil like filings around a magnet, the iris a timid green.

But why shouldn't she think about the breasts?

She glanced over at Megan, who was choosing her next chocolate, a finger hovering over them hesitantly, even though they were all the same kind. She felt predatory, like a man, and it was strange when coupled with what she could see of herself – the pregnant belly straining at the dress, her dainty hairless feet propped up on the footstool. She imagined ripping Megan's blouse away and grabbing those breasts. Spinning her around and penetrating her from behind, as Jean had done to her. What would it feel like? To be the man?

'I gave Jean the boot earlier,' she said, closely checking Megan's expression.

Megan did a doubletake. 'You didn't. Why?'

'You ask me why? You know Jean and you ask me why?'

'Well, I know she can be a bit full of herself. But she seemed so very fond of you.'

'The feeling unfortunately was not mutual.'

Megan did a low chuckle. 'That's going to sting. She's never been chucked before – she's always been the one to chuck.'

Bettina got up off the sofa and retrieved another bottle of wine from the cabinet. When she sat back down, she made sure her thigh was touching Megan's. 'How old were you when you knew you were different?' she asked.

'Oh, very young,' said Megan. 'I was tight with a girl at the orphanage and we used to share a bed. Nothing untoward happened, but I used to hold her at night and dream about one day marrying her. I remember understanding that this wasn't normal, and for some reason I didn't care a fig. I liked what I liked, sod what everyone else thought.'

'How very novel. I wish I'd been so accepting of myself,' said Bettina. 'Things might have gone easier for me.'

'If you'll pardon me for saying, Mrs – Bettina. If you'll pardon me for saying, it seems to me that things *have* gone easy for you. You're wealthy and beautiful with an angel for a daughter, and you and your husband have quite the sweet deal going on.'

Bettina stared at her. All she'd heard was 'beautiful'. 'But there's something I'm missing,' she said in a quiet voice.

'Your own private island?'

Bettina gave her a look – it was a deliberate look, a loaded gun of a look, and certainly not something she could take back. 'Something like that,' she said, reaching out to touch Megan's face, her fingertips tracing a gentle line down her cheekbone. Then she leaned over and quickly kissed her lips, which of course tasted like chocolate.

Megan leapt out of her seat. 'Don't do – oh my – what are you *doing*, Mrs Dawes?'

Bettina pressed a hand over her eyes. Jesus Christ.

'And you being pregnant and – and . . . there are professional *boundaries*, Mrs Dawes. Dear Lord. Why does this always happen to me? You'd think I'd be safe working for a woman!'

'I'm so sorry.' Bettina couldn't look at her. What a fool she was. The great predatory seductress! The dirty dog. She was no dog – she was a bitch, a silly bitch.

'Not as sorry as I am,' said Megan, making her way to the door.

Bettina's dream turned to black liquid behind her eyes. Her mouth was full of foul flavours and her brain felt like an old sea-sponge left to dry out on the rocks.

There was an envelope pushed under her bedroom door.

She got up and read it: a letter of resignation. Signed Miss Megan Elizabeth Smart.

She threw herself back onto the bed and groaned into the pillow.

Chapter 24

Before leaving, Megan had got Tabby washed and dressed and then handed her over to the confused Doris, who, last time she'd checked, wasn't a nanny or a nursemaid. Bettina took Tabby into her arms – poor Tabby! Already missing her daddy and 'uncle', and now she'd have to do without the lovely, laughing woman she'd known since she was a couple of weeks old. But why resign? Did it really have to come to that? People were so precious about their principles. God. She wanted to die. Wildflowers were wilting in the vase on the windowsill – oh. Oh. That was just bloody perfect.

'No mint for the mint sauce,' said Doris, almost through the door. 'The delivery boy must have mucked up the order. But that's none of my business, I suppose.'

Venetia was living in Lucille's house now – 'on a temporary basis, of course'. She'd been able to keep most of the monies made from selling the holiday home in Carmarthenshire and this supplied her with a modest annual income – enough even to keep on Henry, much to Bettina's profound displeasure. Venetia was comfortable in Longworth, but complained that it was improper for two women of their standing to live together 'like college girls'. Everyone besides the two women could see it sliding into permanence.

They arrived at Davenport in two cars. 'Look who it is,' said Bettina, watching from the window. Tabby was clamped, legs hooked, to her side. Bettina tapped the glass with her finger. 'Look, darling, it's Granny Venetia and Granny Lucille, come to see you.'

'Why?'

'To save the day.'

The chauffeur opened the car doors and Venetia and Lucille spilled out in a blur of fur and gold. Henry came out of the second car and went around to the boot to attend to the luggage. Lucille's maid pushed open the passenger side, looking put out – obviously she'd expected Henry to open the door for her.

'Where's that little dewdrop of mine?' said Venetia, coming with arms spread open, her fox stole swinging pendulum-like in front of her large bust.

Tabby clung on tighter, her knee digging into Bettina's huge stomach.

'What?' said Lucille. 'No cuddles and kisses for your grannies?'

'She's shy,' said Bettina. 'She's had a difficult few days.'

'I shouldn't wonder,' said Venetia.

'I never liked Margaret,' said Lucille. 'False as all hell.'

'Megan,' corrected Bettina. 'And you're early. Your rooms aren't quite ready.'

Henry planted two huge suitcases on the gravel next to Lucille's feet. 'Mrs Dawes,' he said to Bettina, dipping his head respectfully. False as all hell.

'How long were you planning to stay?' she asked her mother.

'A week or so, until you've found a new nanny. Where's your footman?'

'We don't have a footman, Mother, I've told you this before.'

'You don't have a footman?' asked Lucille. 'If I'd known I'd have brought Dennis! Oh, poor Henry's going to have to do the work of—'

'You mean to tell me you're in the habit of welcoming guests yourself?' said Venetia.

'Yes. It's really rather simple,' said Bettina. 'One reaches out and turns a door handle and enacts a pulling motion. I can write you step-by-step instructions if you wish to learn the manoeuvre.'

'What happened to that French chap?'

'He was a house guest.'

'What kind of house guest answers the front door?'

'The bohemian kind,' said Lucille, grimacing.

'Is money tight, darling? Because—'

'It's not about money, it's about independence.' Bettina shot a look over at Henry, who was struggling to pull another suitcase out of the car boot. 'And privacy.'

Lucille clasped her hand to her breast and laughed, her powdered wattle quivering. It was the way Monty had laughed when she came out with something charmingly idealistic.

Tabby pulled her face out from the crook of Bettina's neck and peered shyly at her grandmothers.

'What do you think about all this, Tabby?' said Lucille.

Tabby returned her grinning face to the safety of her mother's flesh.

'We've got lots of lovely things planned,' said Lucille. She poked Tabby's back. 'We're going to be the best of friends.'

'Where shall I have Henry put our things?' said Venetia.

'In the guest rooms,' Bettina replied, and Venetia called Henry over and gave him instructions; his eyes flickered as he came to realise he'd be doing all this hauling and moving by himself – just a flickering, a tiny tick-tock of the irises. Henry had impeccable poise. He was able to maintain it even while standing, startlingly erect, outside the bedrooms of young girls.

'Come to think of it,' said Bettina, 'have him put it all in Megan's old room for now. Don't want to interrupt the cleaner, do we?'

Megan had slept in the attic, up three flights of stairs.

Looking after a small child all day long – and Bettina was loath to admit this, fearing that it pointed to some kind of deficiency within her – was *the* most boring task she'd ever undertaken. Tabby made her play games of the imagination which made no sense and went on forever. Pregnant mermaids who go to the shop to buy sweeties but then the shop turns into a hospital and the mermaid isn't pregnant any more and actually, she's not even a mermaid any more, and by the way, the hospital is a tree, and – God, it went on and on. Bettina would lie on her side, smoking and feigning interest and wishing she could return to her books, which had beginnings, middles, endings, and logic. Bart was much better at this stuff. He took delight in Tabby's meandering imagination and knew how to make it fun for himself, putting on different accents, which of course he excelled at.

Now Tabby followed her grandmothers around constantly and Bettina spent a few peaceful days in the garden, working on the third chapter of her novel – unnamed as yet – in fits and starts. More than once – at least five times, actually – she caught movement at the corner of her eye and looked up to see Henry watching her from various windows of the house. Same old Henry, disgusting as ever. She considered talking to her mother about it, but really there wasn't any point. Venetia felt – had always felt – that Henry was a loyal, hardworking servant that she couldn't do without, so much so that she'd fought to bring him along to Longworth, where Lucille had agreed to demote her own butler, not having any fondness for him ('Napoleon complex and don't get me started on his fingernails'), and it had caused all sorts of resentments and conflict between the staff already there. All this for Henry. Any accusations from Bettina had always been met with incredulity, as if Bettina were imagining things. Better to ignore the bastard.

She introduced a new character – a pale-faced young man with sadistic tendencies. John. She'd probably end up bumping him off. Fire, perhaps. Yes – fire. And maybe John could have a horrid sinister butler, and he could die in the fire too. Might as well make it fun for herself.

Lucille had been out all day – in the morning she'd gone to visit a friend who might know of a good nanny wanting employment, and now, new nanny procured, she was at the travelling circus with Tabby. Bettina was in the sitting room, trying to give *Ulysses* another go. Venetia came in holding a book under her arm. She set it down on the drinks cabinet and poured herself a glass of port. She stood with her back to Bettina, slowly sipping her drink. She had the look of someone enjoying the sunset from a balcony.

'Betts, put your book down,' she said, turning around finally. 'I want to talk to you.'

'What's the matter?'

'Something was left under the mattress of your old bed. Do you remember what?'

Bettina shook her head.

Venetia picked up the book she'd come in with. 'What about now?'

She squinted. 'Is that mine?'

A dark nod. 'Henry found it when we were moving everything to Lucille's. He left it in one of my cases and it's been there all this time. And lucky me – I just found it.'

It was a green leather-bound book – one of her diaries. She snatched it from her mother. 'If you've read this . . .'

'Of course I read it! I didn't know what it was.'

Bettina opened the first page. '1 January 1922' in black ink. She scanned the pages. 'Well, I don't know why you look so aggrieved,' she said, 'unless you've no patience for girlish histrionics.'

'Skip to the end.'

She flicked to the last entry – 9April 1928. A sudden change of handwriting style – the letters broader, more hurried. *Dear Father, you were wrong.*

I liked to fuck women.

I just adore fucking women.

'Oh my God.' She sat down heavily on the sofa.

They were silent for a long, long time, smoking their

cigarettes and glugging their drinks, the space between them an undetonated bomb. Birdsong and the chop-chop of the rotary lawnmower drifted in through the open windows.

'I was distraught with grief,' said Bettina. 'I wasn't in my right mind.'

Venetia snorted. 'How could you say such things about your father? How could you even *think* them?' She took the book out of Bettina's hands and opened it to the right page. '"You squandering whoremaster, you abysmal punchline to a dubious joke, you posthumous failure . . . blah blah blah . . . you are sorely hated, Father."' She looked up from the page, her eyes moist. 'How could you? He would have died for you. How *could* you?'

'Easily. He ruined your life.'

Venetia slammed the book shut and threw it across the room with such explosive fury that Bettina instinctively covered her stomach with her hands. She'd never seen her mother so angry.

'He made mistakes! I've also made mistakes. *You've* made mistakes. It breaks my heart to—'

'How are you not mad about the other thing? Why is this the—'

'I *am* mad about the other thing! But I already *knew* about the other thing. You don't think I forgot about that incident, do you? With that fat girl?'

'She wasn't fat.'

'Your father *adored* you. Which was obvious to everyone apart from you. He does not deserve your vitriol. So he had a tart now and then, and he listened to bad financial advice. Grow up! I have known monsters, Bettina, real-life monsters – you have no idea. You're young and stupid. Your father was better than most men.'

'I was angry. I had a right to be angry – I thought he'd made you homeless.'

Venetia tossed back the last of her port, the glass knocking against her dentures. She closed her eyes and seemed to concentrate on her breathing. On calming down. She opened them and they weren't angry any more – just sad. 'I don't miss the house, Bettina. I walk past it sometimes. A family from Wiltshire's taken it over and I think, well, good luck with that! You know how much trouble we had with damp, and all those drunkards passing by on their way home from the Prince Albert. No, I don't miss it. I'm probably supposed to pine for the home in which my children grew up – all those memories and whatnot. But it caused me nothing but pain, Bettina. Every time I walked past Jonathan's bedroom . . . I miss your father more than I miss the house. I feel sometimes as though the marrow has been sucked from my bones.'

Her mother stared at the opposite wall with glassy eyes. 'There's a lot you don't know. Parents only reveal what they want you to see. Just remember that he would have done *anything* for you. So he quarrelled with you? *Pff.* If he didn't care about you, he wouldn't have expended the energy.'

'You say he made mistakes and you made mistakes—'

'Don't even try it,' said Venetia.

'Henry's read it. You know that, don't you? He read it and he planted it in your suitcase so you'd find it.'

Venetia shrugged.

'For God's sake, Mother! That man is a—' Oh, why bother? It just made her sound like she had a childish fixation. And it did come across like that, didn't it? Like she was a spoiled little cow with a grudge. The butler's a meanie, boo-hoo! Fire him, Mummy, at once!

Bettina tore out the entry. She flicked open her lighter and held the flame to the corner of the papers. 'I showed Father some of the poems in my journal once,' she said, dropping it in the fire grate and watching it blacken. 'He was not enthusiastic.'

'Your father knew nothing about poetry, which is why he had no patience for it. You should have shown them to me. I'd have offered some shrewd advice.'

'But I showed them to him.'

'Yes, you did.' Her mother nodded morosely – how old she looked. 'Yes, you did.'

*

She was just going to tell her about the telegram she'd received, about Roger. Nothing more. If invited in, she'd decline with a show of reluctance. *Oh, but I must dash, I'm so horribly busy.* That sort of thing. But Jean wouldn't invite her in. Jean probably hated her.

This was, of course, a terrible idea.

She paused at Jean's gate, her hands wrapped around the black-painted metal rivets, and looked up and down the quiet avenue – cherry trees lined the pavements and the various hedges in front of the houses were clipped and boxy. Had Jean cried, she wondered (and how awful that she was only considering this now). Or had she raged? Probably both. Rage first, tears second. A few hours in the wardrobe and then out to that old lesbo pub to pick up an old flame. But it wouldn't be the same and she'd feel empty. Yes. That's probably how it had gone.

She rapped the door knocker, stepped back and waited. Jean would've closed up shop two hours ago – supposing there was a shop to close up; she was continuing to sell *The Well of*

Loneliness, despite its banning. She had it smuggled over from France and hid it between the covers of *The Ladies' Book of Etiquette* by Florence Hartley (which was *frightfully* ironic – hurrah, well done) and was very nervous about a police raid.

The door swung open. Jean was wearing a white shirt, long and untucked, and her hair was messy under a black beret. She crossed her arms, a cigarette sticking out from between her fingers.

'What do you want?'

'Nice to see you too.'

Jean glared at her.

'I'll get to the point then. I've some bad news, though it's possible you've—'

'Roger's dead. I know.'

'Oh.'

Jean raised her eyebrows. 'Anything else?'

'Um. I suppose I should ask how you're keeping?'

'None of your business is how I'm keeping.'

'All right then. In that case—' Movement to her right – a curtain swishing aside in the front bay window. A face peering out.

Megan's.

Bettina took a big, gulping breath. It felt like she'd just been dunked in cold water – that feeling in the head, behind the eyes, of white noise and blank shock, of all existence, all consciousness being sucked out of the ears, then slammed back in. Jean was smiling. Such a nasty, gloating glee in her eyes. Such petty triumph.

'Guess what?' she said. 'We were fucking the whole time. Right under your nose.'

'I don't believe you,' said Bettina. And actually, she didn't.

'Believe what you like,' said Jean, airily. She went to close the door and Bettina sprang forward, wedging her foot in the gap.

'Guess what?' she said, pushing the gap wider.

'What?' said Jean.

But Bettina had nothing to say. No ammunition at all. And she so badly wanted to hurt her back.

She snapped back her foot and kicked her hard, in the kneecap. And ran away.

Bart arrived home late at night. Alone. He had a bandaged nose and a faded shiner – purple turning to yellow around the edges – and he smelled like booze and piss. Bettina wrapped her arms around him and they breathed out their secret miseries into the warmth of a neck, the ridge of a collarbone.

'Where's Etts?' she said.

'He's not coming back.'

'Why? *Again?* Why?'

He shook his head. One of his eyes was spectacularly bloodshot. 'He left another fucking note, the coward. He wants to stay in America. He's very sorry et cetera, et cetera.' Bart's voice was hoarse, his tone lifeless. 'He wrote notes for you and Tabby, too. I haven't read them. They're probably very magnanimous, but I'll clue you in on the subtext: I'm a piece of shit and he's had enough.'

'But that's not—'

They heard the opening and closing of a door upstairs and then the pitter-patter of footsteps, child's footsteps.

'Daddy!' said Tabby, seeing him from the top of the stairs and carefully descending, eyes on her feet, then on her father, as if checking he hadn't gone anywhere, then back to her feet.

She reached the bottom and he picked her up and held her. Bettina saw her hands interlaced behind his neck, the fidgeting thumb disturbing his grey-blond hair.

'*Où est Oncle* Étienne? Daddy? He said he'd bring me a present, he promised.'

Bart and Bettina looked at each other, pained.

'Daddy? Can I tell you a secret in your ear?'

'Of course you can, sweetheart.' The skin around his nose tightening.

She put her lips to his ear and whispered, loudly: 'I think Uncle Étienne got me a ginormous teddy bear and it's orange and it's called Pierre.'

Bart was crying now, but silently, his face scrunched up and his mouth stretched open to show creamy dabs of saliva at the corners.

'*We'll* buy you a teddy bear,' said Bettina. 'The biggest in the world.' She could feel tears rising in her own throat. This was horrible. Just . . . horrible.

'Why are you crying, Daddy?'

'He's crying with happiness,' said Bettina. 'Aren't you, darling? He's very happy because Uncle Étienne found a wonderful new job in America, didn't he? A very nice new job, doing, um, doing – oh now, let me think . . . doing *painting*! Yes, painting sets for all the new talking pictures, and he's very happy to be doing what he loves, and so is Daddy, because when our friends are happy, that makes us happy. Isn't that right, Daddy?'

Bart nodded, his mouth still anguish-stretched. 'I'm so happy for him. We must all be happy for him.'

'But I want him to make me my breakfast in the morning.'

Oh, Christ in heaven. What could be worse than this?

Dear Bettina,

I am crying as I write this because I will miss you very much. You are a sister to me – it is no exaggeration that I say this. I am sorry I could not see you in person to say goodbye, I did not know the course of events would lead me to stay in Los Angeles. I must keep this brief because I can see Bart will wake up soon. It is terrible that I am doing this, but I have not been my true self for a very long time and it diminishes my soul. Please forgive me my cowardice, I am like a worm wriggling into the deep earth and I am ashamed of myself. Know that I love you and wish you all the health and happiness, for you deserve it. My heart is breaking but I must do what is right.

Your loving soul brother,

Étienne

Dear Tabby,

You will know by now that I am staying to live in America. I want you to know something else: I will miss you more than anyone. You are the smartest, sweetest child in all of Britain and your smile, it dazzles even the sun. Because you are a girl, you will be valued throughout your life on your appearance, and luckily, your appearance is very pleasing, but know this: you are more than just your looks. You are a tiny conquering queen with a brain that is better than the brains of most boys. Be brave and be bold. Soon you will be a big sister. What a lucky child to have a big sister like you! I am sorry that I will miss you growing up – I am more sorry about this than anything else – but when I am settled here in LA I will write to you with my address and we can be pen friends and you can practise your French. But I will understand if you are upset with me and do not wish to write. *Ma petite, tu me manques tellement que ça me brûle le coeur.*

Oncle Étienne

Chapter 25

December 1938, London

Of course it was lovely. Fairy lights were twisted around the skinny poplars flashing pink and green, pink and green, and stalls selling roasted chestnuts wafted out their delicious fatty smell. And the children zipping around clutching candy floss on sticks, or sitting on their fathers' shoulders, bobbing along to the brass band, and the air crisp and chill so that every in-breath felt cleansing. Bettina would love it, she'd soak everything up, attempting to find unique ways of describing things, maybe jotting them down in her ledger so that she might later slot her profound observations into the book she'd been writing for the last hundred years. But Bettina was at home shovelling cake into her face while preparing for a Christmas party so that people they didn't give a fuck about could come and eat their food, drink their booze and marvel at the picture-perfect house and the picture-perfect family.

He had a go on the coconut shy, winning a catapult for little Monty. Tabby pouted, and so he knocked down some tin cans after nine attempts with a crooked BB rifle, winning her a cheap ragdoll. He gave them both some loose change and sent them off to the penny arcade. He sat at a stall which sold dank ale and mulled cider, his hat pulled over his eyes.

Last week he'd suggested in a roundabout way that Bettina was a bad mother.

No.

Last week he had plainly stated that Bettina was a bad mother.

His exact words: 'You're a terrible mother; you should be ashamed of yourself.'

Because she'd forgotten to order that train set for Monty's Christmas present. And why had she forgotten? Because she'd spent the day getting drunk with Tuna.

'How *dare* you?' she'd whispered, before running up to her bedroom.

He sat on his stool, swilling his drink around in its glass, his mouth fixed into a moody slit. Thinking of all the horrible things she'd said to him over the years. 'No wonder Étienne left you – I'm surprised he didn't do it sooner . . . oh, wait – he did!' There was one. *He'd* cried about that. And the time she'd called his films 'perfectly moronic'. He went up to her room with a speech prepared in his head – 'So you can dish it out but you can't take it. Same old Bettina! You've implied that *I'm* a sub-par father, but you women are always so precious about your maternity. Et cetera, et cetera' – to find her crying on her bed. And Bettina so seldom cried. He immediately apologised (sincerely) and she forgave him, or at least pretended to.

A man two stools over was looking at him.

'Eh,' he said, coming over. 'Weren't you the Mortician?'

Bart winced and nodded.

'Well, well,' said the man. 'Not every day a man finds himself sitting next to a Hollywood actor.' *Ac-toorr.* 'My old lady reckons you're the bee's knees.'

'Thank you. Your wife has impeccable taste.' The standard response.

'Haven't seen you in anything lately. There was that one, wasn't there, with the bride of Frankenstein.'

'That wasn't me.'

'Oh. Well. Let's get an autograph then. For the wife? If you would so oblige.'

Bart took a pen from his breast pocket. 'Of course.'

The man was in his twenties. He had two missing teeth at the front, a perfectly round bald patch in his moustache, and clear blue eyes. Fuckable. 'Here,' he said, taking a book from a Woolworths shopping bag – *A Christmas Carol*, by Dickens. 'I bought her this for a Christmas present. If you sign it, that's two presents in one.' He nudged Bart. 'Which means two lays for me.'

Bart laughed, as was required. 'Well, it's customary for the author to sign their own book, but seeing as this one's been dead almost seventy years . . . What's her name?'

'Rosemary. Rose.'

He wrote: 'To Rose, have a wonderful and spooky Christmas, your friend Bartholomew Dawes', adding devil horns over the 'B'.

'She'll love this,' the man said. 'Thanking you kindly.' He took the stool next to Bart. 'So what's Lillian White like then?'

Oh God. He knew where this was going: *What was it like*

kissing her? Did you feel her arse? Lovely arse on her. I bet she'd do it soon as look at you.

'Lillian White is a delightful human being. Look' – he downed his pint and wiped his mouth – 'I've got to go and retrieve my children. Have a lovely Christmas.'

'You too, mate.'

Bart shoved back his stool and walked away, burping into the back of his hand, hat pulled so low over his eyes he could see only half the world, sliced in two.

The last time this band had played at one of her Christmas parties, there'd been a black man playing the trombone, but he'd now been replaced by a white man. According to their pianist, the black man – Jonty, his name was – had been beaten to within an inch of his life in the streets of Norwich because he'd apparently smiled at a white woman, and was to this day still lying in hospital with his body encased in casts. Bettina asked the pianist if she might write a cheque to help cover some of the poor trombonist's medical bills, and as she did so, Bart walked past, grinning sarcastically at her while stretching an arm around and patting himself on the back.

'Oh, Mrs Dawes, what a charitable offer! Our Jonty'll be over the moon.'

But it was all ruined now.

She signed the cheque, paying a pound more than she'd originally intended – it was Bart's money.

The nanny was chasing Monty around with a pair of socks in her hand and Doris was repositioning some of the decorations on the huge Christmas tree after a handyman had let his ladder fall into it. Bart stood slouched next to the grandmother clock, reading a book of poetry, which was hilarious

– he hated poetry – so she could only assume he was hoping to impress someone.

The doorbell chimed. Bart caught Monty by his lapels and called Tabby over. 'Come here and stand next to your brother and smile at the guests like perfect little angels.'

'Oh, shut up,' said Bettina. 'Do what you like, Tabby. He's just being a meanie.'

He raised a brow. 'Oh? I thought that was what you wanted?'

She drained her champagne and stood up, ignoring him. She had indeed planned on setting up both her children near the front door to smile at guests, until Bart pointed out what a farce this was. So she'd let her children run wild until bedtime, and if Monty hid under the buffet table eating out of the sugar pot or if Tabby insisted on showing off her sub-par ballet to adults too polite to decline the offer, she'd laugh it off, her pearls and teeth glittering under the chandeliers, everything glittering, her eyes full of benign permission, oh, everything jolly and glittering, because she was carefree and unconstrained by the rigid codes of polite society!

He came over and wrapped his arms around her. 'I'm sorry. I know you hate it when I point out your inconsistencies. If it makes you feel any better, I am a much worse human being than you.'

'It does make me feel better,' she said, 'and you are.'

He kissed her on the forehead. 'Let's behave ourselves tonight.'

She smiled and returned the kiss, aiming for his cheek but bumping his nose. 'If I can't be thin any more,' she said, wiping away the lipstick, 'then I'll damn well be a charming and accomplished mother and wife. Allow me this.'

'I will, darling. Oh, look – here they come.' He wrapped an

arm around her waist and smiled a dazzling smile. He really was a wonderful actor.

Tuna was dressed conservatively. For Tuna. She had on a cream floor-length dress belted at the waist, with bright red curly-toed Aladdin slippers. A decorative Christmas angel was perched amongst her frizzy explosion of hair – it peeked out, its little china face full of chubby malevolence. She was thin again. Ribs and cheekbones thin. She attributed it to the divorce, telling Bettina over the telephone that she'd only eaten apples and thin wedges of cheddar for six months: seriously, darling, nothing but apples and tiny little slices of mature cheddar; I'm not exaggerating, I could stomach nothing else – oh wait, I lie, I did once have a tiny canapé at a charity ball.

But there were rumours. Tuna was currently 'seeing' a writer who was known to smoke opium on a regular basis. Maybe she'd cultivated the habit for herself? Bettina didn't believe a word of it – heartbroken women got thin all the time. Just as pampered, idle women got fat.

Tonight Tuna had brought along a tall Yorkshireman whose eyes were too close together – the supposed opium-guzzler. He apparently wrote literature too honest to be published.

She found them out in the garden, smoking hashish and discussing the situation in Germany. 'It's all just bluster,' Tuna was saying. 'Men with huge egos trying to see who can piss the farthest out of their tiny little cocks. Oh, hello, Betts. Lovely party.'

'Don't lie, you're finding it boring.'

Tuna snatched a hand to her breast as if mortally wounded. 'Such assumptions you make about me! I am not the woman of excess you think me to be, not any more.' She nudged the writer. 'Tell her, Nicholas.'

'She is not the woman of excess you think her to be, not any more.'

'Where's Bart?' said Tuna.

Bart was chatting to a gorgeous man called Ted who ran the picture house in Bethnal Green. Bettina had noted Bart's hand on his shoulder – relaxed and chummy, the fingers touching his neck. 'He's making a damn fool of himself with the—'

The patio doors swung open and Bart came out. 'Oh, there you are,' he said, seeing Bettina. 'Why make this big fuss about throwing a Christmas party if you're just going to sneak away?'

'I've been out here for literally one minute. Sir.'

'Oh, don't start. I'm not some authoritarian – why do you always have to make me look like—' He pinched the bridge of his nose. 'I'm sorry. I just fucking hate parties.' He felt his breast pocket for his cigarettes. 'Oh, blast it, I've left them in – Tuna, can I have one of—' He noticed the joint in Nicholas's hand. 'Is that a – are you smoking a – Tuna, could you please tell him not to do that here?'

'You might try telling him yourself,' said Tuna. 'He's got ears.'

'Sorry,' said Nicholas. 'I'll put it out.'

Bart took Bettina by the arm and led her down the garden to a quiet spot near the rose beds.

Bettina shook her arm away. 'I haven't done anything!'

'Exactly. Those two clowns smoke up out here and you don't *do* anything! We're not twenty any more. We've got children sleeping inside the house and—'

'Hypocrite,' she said.

'I am *not* a hypocrite! Look at the size of our garden' – he slashed an arm through the air – 'and they choose to do it right by the doors?'

'That's not why you're a hypocrite,' she said.

'Oh? So enlighten me.'

'I know what you do on Tuesday nights. I know where you go.'

He put his hands on his hips. 'I don't know what you're talking about.'

'Yes, you do. Yes, you bloody do. I know. So here you are, Mr High and Mighty, throwing a tantrum—'

'I am not throwing a—'

'Throwing a *tantrum* because a couple of adults at an adult party choose to partake in some light marijuana use. But oh! How corrupted our children will be by the terrible things happening five brick walls away as they sleep obliviously!' She stabbed a finger at his chest. 'And meanwhile, Mr High and Mighty, meanwhile, you're sneaking off to the woods to—'

'Don't you—'

'I know what you do! I don't care that you do it. But if you ever got caught, it wouldn't just be you in the firing line. Imagine little Monty going to school and all the other boys teasing him because they've heard his famous daddy got caught with strange men in the woods. "Your daddy's a faggot! Your daddy's a faggot!"'

His eyes flashed. Then narrowed. She knew that narrowing – it signified a turning-off of something vital in his control centre – a switch flicked. He chortled to himself, darkly. 'Oh. *Oh*. You fat stupid whore. You manipulative cunt.'

'What? What did you just call me?'

'You heard me.' He met her eyes, defiantly. But the defiance was unstable, wavering. It suddenly dropped away, slipped away, was displaced by a guilty, panicked look – she could remember that look from childhood; it was the switch being turned back on again – and he started pacing. 'What? So you call me a faggot and—'

'I did not call you a faggot. I said that's what the other children would say if—'

'See? You *are* manipulative! You call me that hateful slur under the pretence of—'

'No.' She shook her head. 'You cannot unsay what you just said to me. Ever.'

'Oh for God's sake, how can you—'

'You cannot unsay it.'

He ran his hands through his hair. The balance of power had tipped and he knew it. He had done and said the worse thing. As usual.

'Fine, so I shouldn't have said those things, but—'

'You cannot unsay it,' she said, turning and walking back to the party. Victorious.

'We wish you a merry Christmas, we wish you a merry Christmas . . .'

Oh, shut up, Bart thought. Just everyone, shut up.

Most of the guests had departed, but the biggest drunkards seemed unwilling to budge. They stood in a messy circle, their arms around each other's shoulders, singing in loud, tone-deaf voices. Pink eyes, pink skin – everything pink. Bart grabbed a full whisky bottle and went to the study – blessedly empty – almost falling onto the sofa. He got up and put another log on the fire. Bettina was probably moaning about him to Tuna. Oh, her husband was such a hypocrite! Such a mean, acid-tongued bastard! And a horrible *faggot* to boot.

No. She had not called him a faggot. Directly. And she was right about the Tuesdays.

But guess what – *he* was right about something too.

She was manipulative. And fat.

He topped up his whisky, licking the rim to save the droplets dribbling down the glass. He wanted to go to bed. Strip down to his socks and pass out. And never wake up.

Actually, what he really wanted to do was find Ted and fuck him up his tight little arse.

No. That wasn't true either. He wanted Ted to fuck him. No use pretending it was the other way around.

Tonight he'd read from Étienne's copy of Rimbaud's selected poems, remembering that first-ever night in the damp garret – how beautifully Étienne had read them. Licking his thumb to turn the grimy pages, a roll-up cigarette dropping its ash into the crevice of the book. Bart had laid his head on his shoulder and felt the vibrations coming from his chest as he read. Though perhaps he was imbuing this memory with some special significance – maybe, at the time, it hadn't felt so special. Maybe his bowel had gurgled with held-in farts and he'd wanted badly to brush his teeth. He didn't trust his memories.

They wrote from time to time, Étienne still addressing him as *Fleur du Mal.* He'd supposedly put on a lot of weight ('I am like Oliver Hardy – monstrous!') and had found work as an interior designer, something he'd fallen into quite accidentally, though it turned out he had an inborn talent ('You do not have an inborn talent,' Bart wrote back. 'I remember that filthy shithole you used to call home.') Bart could well imagine Étienne designing the homes of Hollywood moguls – they'd hear his French accent and immediately decide that he was a cultured man, an authentic artist. And the scarf around his neck – a bohemian man too! A French bohemian! Here, take all my money and fill my home with bullshit, please!

He was happy for Étienne, he supposed.

Ted was probably home now. He had a wife. Francine. 'Nice time at the party?' she'd say. 'Yes, it was all right, I suppose,' he'd say, kicking off his shoes. 'But the fellow hosting the party was quite clearly trying it on with me.' Here, the wife would pull a face of abject horror. 'You mean that chap who does those crummy B-movies? Bartholomew Dawes? A faggot?'

'Yes, Fran, a raving faggot. I can still feel his hands all over my body. I might take a bath actually.'

Bart left the room, holding one arm out to keep his balance – the world was tilting. He passed Tuna and her plus-one in the hall – they were pressed up against the wall by the telephone, kissing. Bart waved a hand in their direction as if trying to ward off nonsense. He drained his glass, turned it upside down and rested it on the top of the whisky bottle. 'A little hat for you,' he said, beginning to climb the stairs. All I want, he thought, gripping the banister, is someone to hold me. Someone to lie in bed next to me and hold me until I fall asleep.

Such a simple little thing.

He almost fell into his bedroom, the glass slipping off the bottle and rolling under the bed. He didn't need a glass. Love and attention and touch – he needed those things. Not a glass. He sat on the bed and drank from the bottle. He heard a sound next door in Bettina's bedroom.

Oh, God. Oh, Betts.

What was it in him that made his most vicious thoughts

shoot out of his mouth like that? There was something very wrong with him. A darkness of the heart.

He opened her door.

She was on the carpet on all fours, her dress hiked up to her waist, and a man – no, he must be hallucinating – what looked like a man, was on his knees behind her, his pelvis slamming into her large pale arse.

No. Ted? No.

They both saw him at the same time. Ted jumped up, his shiny red stiffy bouncing, and yanked his trousers up. Bettina rolled onto her side and slowly, casually, pulled her dress down. She was smiling.

Ted grabbed his hat and ran from the room, scraping his back on the door frame as he dodged past Bart – then, realising that he'd gone out through the wrong door (into the husband's bedroom!) he ran back through the doorway, again past Bart, who instinctively lifted his foot out to trip him up. Ted went sprawling and landed on his face. He got up, mumbled, 'I suppose I deserved that,' and left through the other door.

Bettina was still on her side like a contented house cat, her stomach spilling to the floor with gravity. 'Here's your fat whore,' she said.

Bart gripped the door handle. 'Pure spite.'

And she nodded.

He threw his whisky bottle at her – it missed, widely, crashing against the mahogany desk which housed her spare typewriter and notebooks. There was her almost-finished manuscript, in a neat, perfect pile. Almost ten years she'd been working on that – ten years of false starts, rewrites, tense changes, ten years of literary anguish and he'd had to witness it all, pretending that he cared. He went and snatched it up, then ran from the room. He heard her cry out and give chase. He bounded down the stairs, missing the sixth from last step and skidding down on his backside, but keeping the manuscript wedged to his ribs like a rugby ball. He looked over his shoulder – she was halfway down, her hem swishing like tidal foam. He got to his feet and ran for the study, almost crashing into a group of people trying to get their coats on.

He dropped the manuscript into the fire and turned around to see Bettina at the doorway. Her mouth dropped open and her eyes grew fantastically huge – just like when Beadie first saw Reanimated Corpse No. 1. The paper was ablaze, thick smoke curling out. She ran to retrieve it but he blocked the hearth, grabbing a poker and wielding it. Bettina looked at him with such bitterness – oh, *such* bitterness. 'Two can play at that game,' she said. And she turned and ran.

He dropped the poker and gave chase – she was running back up the stairs. She was going to do something. What could she possibly do? He went up the steps two at a time – he could almost touch her ankle. He tripped over, thumping his stomach against the stair edge, winding himself. She was already flinging open his bedroom door. He scrambled to his feet, raced along the corridor, sliding on the Persian rug, and burst into his bedroom.

She was clutching a wooden chest and rushing towards the window. His letters from Étienne. 'Don't you fucking dare!' he screamed.

She unlatched the window and pushed it open just before he reached her. She threw the box out and spun around to face him, her back pressed to the ledge, her face wild. He heard the crash as the box exploded its contents all over the drive outside. He pushed her to the side and looked down – papers were skittering around on the gravel drive, some blowing up into the trees – there, pressed by the wind to a thick branch was a life-size sketch of an erect penis. A man and a woman were gaping up at Bart, their scarves twisting in the wind like ribbons. Fifteen years' worth of letters, drawings, poems. The only written proof that someone had ever loved him.

Bettina stood with her arms straight down by her sides and her hands bunched up. Her face was drained of all colour save for two perfect little circles of red on her cheekbones.

'I despise you,' she said, quite simply.

Chapter 26

April 1943, The Boar and Hound, Sussex

It was an especially dark shade of red, the blood, like pickled beetroot. Bettina got out her handkerchief, licked a corner, and wiped it off – her boot was lacquered and it came off clean. She drank her scrumpy. She'd do well to remember that particular shade of red because she was going to write about it.

Ha! She wasn't going to write about a damn thing.

The scrumpy was lukewarm with a gorgeous tang to it. Even in these days of scarcity she knew exactly where to look for it. This pub was an hour's bike ride from the farm – absolutely worth it – and it had a scruffy garden with picnic tables. There was a closer pub but it often ran out of stock and was frequented by resentful old farmers. She took her tobacco out of her knapsack and started to roll a cigarette. Writing was for writers and she was no writer. She was something altogether better: she was Brighton's second-best rat killer.

Good name for a book, actually.

When she'd first come to Hathaway Farm she'd been appallingly unfit. She'd heard stories that some farmers were in the habit of giving all the heavy, horrible work to the wealthy girls, to teach them some kind of lesson (poor people are jealous and bitter – lesson learned!) but that hadn't happened – possibly because she'd voluntarily enlisted. Or because she was old. All the same, they hadn't liked her at first, owing to a joke she'd cracked on first being shown around her spartan bedroom – she'd looked around the room snootily and said, 'What a dump.' It was, of course, a line from the Bette Davies film *Of Human Bondage*. The landlady curled her lip in a muddled half-smile – she'd got the reference (they'd chatted about the film ten minutes earlier in the kitchen), but she didn't find it funny. Too close to the bone. I will shut up from now on, thought Bettina – she worked in silence, only opening her mouth to swap pleasantries or feign enthusiasm: soldiers are dying and I'm picking apples – whoopee.

She hadn't been happy at this time. Tabby and Monty had just been shuttled out to Betws-y-Coed after a fighter plane had fallen out of the sky, landing in their garden and flattening a wrought-iron bench and a bird feeder. And her husband – well, never mind him. He was currently stationed in Nice, entertaining the troops. A plane could land on him for all she cared. Mid-monologue. His precious brains splattering out onto the audience.

One day a group of women in grey coats had appeared at the orchard hauling machinery in a cart. The rats had been getting to the apples and they were going to gas the little bastards. Bettina watched as the women got to work. One of them, a tall masculine woman with a long scar up her face, told the apple pickers to stand back – they were going to be using some 'jolly nasty chemicals'.

Soon a bundle of fat rats came out of their den, crawling in slow dizzy circles, most of them collapsing onto their sides, but some of the more resilient ones ran for it. One rat killer started bashing at a rat with a cricket bat. Another, seeing this, took off her gas mask and sprayed vomit into the grass. 'Not another squeamo!' the masculine woman said, or at least that's what it sounded like. Bettina saw a sleek grey rat running in her direction. Calmly and unthinkingly, she lifted her boot and stomped on it. Its tiny skull crunched and crackled.

The masculine woman pulled her gas mask up onto her head and came over. 'Fancy a new job?' she said, in a booming Oxfordshire accent.

Bettina said, 'Yes, why not?'

The woman held out her hand to shake. 'I'm Maggie but everyone calls me Mags. Welcome aboard.'

Bettina took to the killing of rats quite naturally. She could remember the cook in her childhood home chasing rats around with broomsticks and laying down traps in the larder. Jonathan was always allowed to look at the dead rats – Henry would come to him whenever he found one in the shed, saying, 'Tell your mother or father and we'll both be in trouble.' Bettina would follow along, excited, but Henry always caught her at the last minute. 'No girls!' Jonathan always came out of the shed five minutes later, looking pale and withdrawn, his eyes twitching like a – well, like a rat in a trap.

The trick to catching the rats, along with instinct and a strong stomach, was knowledge, and Bettina, being a keen reader, quickly devoured the pamphlets provided by Mags. They were armed with zinc phosphide, gas pumps, Cymag powder and oatmeal, which they used as bait. Every Friday they went around collecting the dead rats, throwing them into a trailer hitched to the back of the dilapidated Morris that only Mags could drive, and once, at an infested stable sixteen miles east of Hathaway Farm, they bagged a total of 287. It became a kind of competition – who could bag the most. The younger girls always won. But – and this was much more important – Bettina and Mags *killed* the most. Mags having a slim advantage.

Mags was forty but looked fifty. She'd spent the first two years of the war as an ambulance driver, collecting wounded people during the Blitzes. On one shift a car had exploded some yards from her and a twisted chunk of bumper got her in the face, accounting for the scar. She spent six months recuperating in hospital (her ribs had also been shattered) and then came to Hathaway Farm to work, ending up on rat duty because her father and grandfather – all her fathers going back to the 1700s – had owned farms, so she knew all about the havoc these creatures could wreak on fruit and vegetables. Bettina had a strong feeling that Mags was a lesbian – she'd never been married. And Tuna had once told her that all the ambulance drivers were 'Radclyffes'.

Bettina liked Mags but not in that way. She talked like Monty's ancient brigadier friends – all 'what what' and 'tally-ho'. And she suffered from hay fever and was constantly wiping her nose. There were other women on the farm who she suspected might swing the same way, but how does one, she thought, go about confirming one's suspicions? 'Psst, Mabel – do you enjoy cunnilingus? Giving or receiving? Righto. Sorry

I asked.' She was starving for women – it was a tangible ache. Luckily, she didn't have enough time to dwell on it. These rats won't kill themselves, she'd think, laughing to herself at the resulting image – a rat with a little noose around its neck, and a note: 'This world is too cruel.'

Bart would enjoy a joke like that. But to hell with him.

Chapter 27

June 1943, Egypt

Three things he hated about performing for the troops in Al-Jizah:

The baking heat. His body was perpetually covered in a slick of sweat but the air he breathed was hot and dry and his lips got crusty. And of course he was often covered in greasepaint, so add that to the mix.

The cheapening of himself as an artist. When he'd first joined ENSA he was doing tours of Shakespeare in Nice and Edinburgh, and how marvellous it was to return to Shakespeare, just like slipping your foot into an old slipper – silk-lined, of course. But now he was doing childish skits, his 'act' wedged in between old music-hall comedians and has-been singers – he'd reprised the role of Edward Crabbe for his latest sketch, enacting the last scene of the film in which the three reanimated corpses turn on their creator, slowly approaching him with their arms reaching out. In the film version it was Lillian White's character, Beadie, who saved the day, pouring a vat of nitrogen oxide over them (which was ridiculous – why would an undertaker have nitrogen oxide lying about in his lab?), but here it was Mussolini and Hitler. They walked into the lab together, in full regalia, holding a map and bickering as if lost, and asked for directions to Britain. The corpses turned around and diverted their attack, surrounding the two characters and ripping them to pieces. Red paint and rubber limbs flying out of the screaming fray. A huge cheer from the troops. Cheap.

Missing the children. And worrying about them. But he was surrounded by other people who also missed and worried about their children, and this provided a drop of comfort.

He wasn't drinking – there was nothing to drink – and he was usually hungry, subsisting on a diet of fatty grey mince and onion, boiled potatoes and stale bread. But he felt – well, like his old self. He'd withdrawn from people these last ten years or so like a sad old lizard. So many nights spent alone in the study, drinking whisky and going over resentments, re-imagining arguments, honing his parting shot – 'You *despise* me? That surprises me – hatred requires emotion, which in turn requires a heart. You despise *me*? Clearly not as much as you despise vegetables and exercise. Cunt.' He didn't miss that study.

His best friend on the barracks was Archie Coogan, a gruff stand-up comic from Birmingham. The first time he saw Archie offstage he was sitting in the mess hall slurpily eating a bowl of vegetable stew. Archie was fat, really fat, wearing khaki shorts and a white paisley shirt with vast sweat patches under the arms, and he had pale ginger hair and a pointy ginger beard. His head was small and seemed to perch on top of his round body like a penguin's, his beard the beak. His bare legs were hairless and pale and womanish, the skin soft-looking, creamy; marred only by mosquito bites.

Bart sat next to him and was surprised to find him effeminate and soft-spoken, his words fluttering out of his mouth like petals caught in a light breeze – onstage he was the very opposite: macho and brusque, a mouth full of artillery. He had a piece of faded newspaper in front of him on which he was writing down jokes and new ideas with a red crayon. They chatted about the other acts and Bart slipped in some Polari he'd learned from a queer navvy while in Nice ('buvare', 'bona' and 'khazi'), and Archie did a little nod to acknowledge that he got the message.

Archie was currently fucking one of the caterers, Albert, an unsmiling Londoner who could usually be found on a stool crouched over a tin bucket, peeling potatoes. Archie called him 'The Butcher' because his cock was eight inches long and thick as a hat stand. He'd supposedly followed Archie into the lav one night, dropped his trousers and said, 'Give us a wank, mate?' Archie's eyes glittered with mirth when he recalled this story. 'How could a girl say no to that, eh? Coleridge himself could only ever *dream* of reaching such dizzy heights of romantic expression.'

Back home, Archie had led a double life. There was his manly stand-up persona, which brought him some minor celebrity in the halls and pubs of greater Birmingham, and then there was Ditzy Quimm, a bewigged, large-breasted drag queen in glittering gowns who cracked jokes and sang old favourites every Sunday night at the Tapette, an underground bar full of poofs, prostitutes and dope fiends. He recalled a night in the early 30s when a mob of evangelists had formed outside the bar, throwing eggs at the door (ah, the luxurious excesses of pre-rationing). 'We locked the doors and we were looking out the windows, terrified,' said Archie. 'And do you know what I did? I put on my wig and make-up and I sneaked out of a side window when they were all occupied with a rousing hymn, and I joined them. I joined the mob. "Come out and face God, sodomites!" I mobbed myself!' A giggle. 'I laugh about it now, but honestly, I have never felt such abject horror towards the human race.'

It was Archie who introduced Bart to Burma Road – Be Undressed and Ready My Angel. Its real name was Bab El Louq and it was situated halfway between the back of the barracks and the spice bazaar. A long, desolate, sand-strewn street crawling with knobbly-spined cats, it was where the prostitutes waited for soldiers with a night off and some spare pennies to spend. At the far end was a side-street known by a select few as Buma Lane – Bums Up My Angel – and it was here that the homosexual soldiers came to relieve each other.

Bart was nervous the first time because he'd never done this sort of thing sober before. He waited by a bin, smoking (Archie went to the opposite side and immediately started proceedings with a black GI – one of his regulars) and was soon approached by a young British soldier who resembled Orson Welles. Silently they took turns sucking each other off. The man's technique was terrible – he was all tooth and had an overly sensitive gag reflex. Bart closed his eyes and dangled his hands at his sides, a tap on the wall poking at the back of his knee. He heard Archie giggling girlishly with his GI, and a tethered goat softly bleating. Then approaching footsteps and the low growl of a zipper – a voyeur. Bart promptly came. And that was that.

They returned one night a week, always together. If they had a few hours to spare in the day they went to the large bazaar three miles away – Archie would attempt to walk it, but invariably ended up paying for a cart ride because the skin between his upper thighs chafed in the heat. They wrote sketches and songs together, Bart beginning to embrace the silly lowbrow humour because Archie made it fun. Archie made everything fun – well, except for that one night when he brought a bottle of some horrid spirit back from the market and they stayed up drinking in Archie's room, and Archie got so drunk he started crying and admitted to Bart that he'd been raped by his uncle as a boy. Bart had held him tight, close to tears himself, and waited until he passed out. He took off his shoes and socks, secured the mosquito net around his bed and watched him sleep. Could I love him? he thought. Yes, easily. But could I fuck him? No. If he were thinner? Still, no. But the next morning over their breakfast, he reached out and squeezed Archie's hand and said, 'I'm not very good at being sincere and saying heartfelt things, but I want you to know that – well, I suppose what I'm trying to say is . . . what *am* I trying to say?' Archie waited, his eyes bloodshot. 'Look, it's like this,' he continued, 'if we get bombed in this hellhole and die horribly, I'm glad it'll be with you. I want us to still be friends when we're old men. I want us to be seventy years old and still giving blowjobs to strangers in close proximity of one another.'

Archie smiled, pursing his face in that way Bart's mother did when she was especially touched. 'I feel exactly the same way, Crabbecake.'

Chapter 28

June 1943, Hathaway Farm, Sussex

She lay on her bed, sipping black-market parsnip poteen from a tin cup and reading *The Private Life of Helen of Troy*. The room was painted white and had mould patches coming through on one wall, which the landlady treated with vinegar once a week. It never went away, that smell. There were no framed pictures up and the blankets on the beds were a scratchy wool. She had a small bedside table, the only furniture provided. Inside the top drawer were photographs of her children, which she kissed every night, and one of Bart, which she included for appearances only. She kept her cigarettes and stockings (both very desirable items) in a locked suitcase.

Bettina's roommate Bunty had been sent home two days ago. She was a spoiled, whining eighteen-year-old, conscripted.

She'd tried to get out of it, supposedly even asking her rich uncle to pull some strings, but her family were fiercely patriotic and felt she should muck in like everyone else. Having endured the little snot for three months, Bettina wondered if they'd just wanted to get rid of her for a while. On her first day Bunty was given the job of picking maggots out of the sheep's wool, and she'd cried the whole time. Every night she threw herself on her bed like a terrible debutante, but on her first day off she went to visit the nearby village and found it full of yummy Yank soldiers. Quick as a click she cheered up, and soon adjusted to the 4.30 a.m. starts and gruelling long days of stooking and muckspreading, and a month later, when Bettina saw her picking maggots off the sheep, she was singing, 'He Wears a Pair of Silver Wings' in a pretty, wispy soprano.

Now she was back in her family home, in the family way. So terribly predictable.

Bettina loved having the room to herself. She no longer had to hold in her gas, escaping to the toilet or garden to let it out in long airy hisses. She could read her book without being interrupted and sneak her black-market moonshine without fear of being squealed on.

But now – a knock on the door.

'Come in!' said Bettina.

It was Millie the farmer's wife, trailed by a young woman. Bettina's eyes immediately went to the suitcase at the end of her bed, which held the bottle of parsnip liquor. Had she locked it? She wouldn't have forgotten to lock it.

'Ivy, meet Bettina; Bettina, meet Ivy,' said Millie.

She smiled at the girl, who was standing just inside the room, looking around with eyes of steel. She was average build and average height. Late twenties, perhaps. Her hair was white-blonde – almost white, actually – and scraped back, hanging in a long unfashionable plait down her back. Her ears stuck out and one of them, at the top, seemed to have a point to it, a little nub. Her eyes were light blue and she was dressed in a plain navy-blue button-down dress and brown shoes of the sort a man would wear. She did not smile back.

'Breakfast is at half past four,' said Millie. 'The bathhouse is downstairs next to the kitchen – you're permitted one hot bath a week and you must book it in advance. If that doesn't feel sufficient, and I have been told many times that it is not, well, there's a sink' – she pointed at the corner of the room – 'cold water only, mind.'

Ivy nodded.

'It goes without saying, but I shall say it anyway – no men, no lewd language, keep your squabbles to yourself, and if I ever catch you with black-market produce, that's it for you. Dutch will assign you your jobs. Ask him after supper and you'll find him in a good mood.' Millie looked at Bettina. 'You in here again on your day off?'

'You make me sound like a hermit.'

'Everyone else is at Shirley's.' Shirley's was a café that sold, among other things, delicious leek and potato pasties.

'Millie, I work and live with these women, and delightful as they are, I sometimes like my own company.'

'Well, at least someone does,' Millie said, laughing, then left.

Ivy crept further into the room.

'She loves me really,' said Bettina.

'I'm sure,' said Ivy, still not smiling, her pale eyes steadily taking in her surroundings. She was very composed, Bettina thought, possessing a self-assuredness, a staunch poise. And yet she had the air of someone about to be hanged.

She barely spoke to Ivy in the following weeks – she found her dull, humourless and difficult to engage with. Ivy was a very private person, and unlike the other girls who went around in their bras and slips at night, would insist on getting dressed and undressed under her bedclothes. She didn't even like to eat in front of other people.

Ivy got on well with farm life, working hard and uncomplainingly, even during the week in which it rained non-stop and the swampy fields sucked boots off feet. She'd been a secretary to a lawyer's office in Liverpool and had never married, which put paid to bed the idea that she was a grief-stricken widow. Like Bettina, she read avidly, often spending her free time at the public library in town. The only sounds in their otherwise silent bedroom were the papery fluttering of turned pages and the muted clearing of throats.

On Bettina's thirty-ninth birthday, the girls arranged a viewing of *The Mortician* in the barn, which was rigged up as a temporary cinema once a month with bales of hay to sit on. Afterwards they drank watered-down cherry brandy and sang war songs. They talked about their husbands or fiancés, most of whom were abroad, fighting, and their children. Everyone at some point cried.

It was almost midnight when Bettina returned to her room. Ivy was awake in bed – Bettina had the sense she'd been waiting for her.

'I didn't know you were married to Bartholomew Dawes,' she said, unravelling her plait with nimble fingers.

'Oh? It never came up.'

'He's my favourite actor and *The Mortician* is my favourite picture. Though I much prefer the book it's based on.'

Bettina let her dress drop to the ground and kicked it away.

'I used to watch it with my best friend,' said Ivy, averting her eyes. 'It was her favourite film too. I think we watched it eight times together.'

'I never had you down for a fan of the macabre,' said Bettina.

'I'm not. That's not why I like the film, or the book.'

'Then why? My husband?'

'It's the subtext I'm drawn to.'

Bettina pulled her nightdress over her head. 'What subtext is that?'

Ivy's fingers combed through her long wavy hair. 'Well. I suppose . . . I suppose it's about those who aren't accepted by society. Who are punished for . . . I don't know. Outsiders, in short. The book captures it better.'

Bettina put out her cigarette and climbed into bed. 'My husband says the book has a homosexual subtext.' She looked over at Ivy, coolly. 'Is that what you mean?'

'Of course not!' Ivy turned off the lamp and Bettina smiled into the darkness.

The following week Ivy was put on the anti-vermin squad in order to temporarily replace a girl who'd inhaled cyanide through a faulty gas mask and was now being treated for respiratory problems at the hospital. Ivy claimed to have a strong stomach and Mags said, 'Just as well, we've a bloody big bunch of moles to go after today.'

The team cycled to a farm six miles north. There were five of them – Bettina, Ivy, Mags and two uncouth young girls called Sadie and Joyce who had worked as maids before the war and were enjoying life much better now. They were on a winding country lane, lined with hedgerows and fat luscious oaks. Bettina liked the way the sunlight went through the trees, dappling the road ahead with hundreds of small diamonds. In moments of quiet she thought about Tabby and Monty. Last time they'd written, Monty had said he was getting 'obsessed' with cartoon strips, and was trying to create his own – he'd always been good at drawing. Tabby told her she was almost fluent in Welsh now, *diolch yn fawr*, and that she'd got so good at shearing that the farmer was paying her a liquorice strip per sheep. 'How funny that we are both, mother and daughter, working the land. I just can't imagine you in a pair of wellies!'

Bettina rode behind Ivy, watching how her long white plait thumped up and down on her back as she went over bumps. She was wearing the regulation blouse and her beige dungarees were belted high on the waist, making a plump upside-down love heart of her rear.

Overhead – a plane. They looked up and braked in unison and there was that terrible moment of feeling like the ground had turned to water. Friend or foe? The dot became a blob became a plane – Bettina could see the whirlpool of its propellers. Friend or foe?

'Take cover!' roared Mags, dropping her bike to the ground with a clatter, vaulting over the small stone wall and running for a cluster of trees – they were in a spot, thankfully, surrounded by woods. The others went off in different directions as they'd been taught. Except for Ivy – she followed Bettina. A great rat-a-tat as the plane unloaded its artillery; a brown explosion of turf appearing just to the left of Bettina, its dust coating her sweaty face – of *course* they were aiming at her, there were two of them, what did that silly bitch think she— Another eruption of mud to her right. The trees were close ahead – three large oaks. She sprinted, her boot catching in a dip and her ankle twisting – she didn't feel it. Her heart was pounding, her ears were pounding, her bloody eyeballs were pounding and all that existed in the world was a tunnel of green and the god-like rush of adrenaline. She reached the first tree and dived into a sunken place at the base of the trunk. Ivy jumped in next to her. Another hail of bullets, directly overhead – small branches and twig dust and hundreds of leaves falling around them, on them. Then the slow fade as the plane retreated. Then silence.

'Fucking hell,' said Bettina, pulling her cigarettes from her trouser pocket and lighting up with a shuddering hand. Ivy was huddled down next to her, very still. 'What were you thinking, coming after me like that?' she said to her. 'You as good as put a target sign over our heads.'

Ivy's irises were perfect ice-blue ponds. 'They tried to kill us,' she said.

'Yes, that's what they do.' Idiot.

'They tried to *kill* us.'

'Well. We're alive, aren't we?'

'Everyone all right?' called Mags, from a few trees over.

'Yes!' called Bettina, and there were three answering cries.

Bettina helped Ivy up, cigarette wedged between her lips. They came out from their trees and met on the road, looking up at the sky.

'Bloody close one, that,' said Mags.

Sadie's bike had been hit and one wheel was mangled so

she hopped onto Joyce's handlebars. They all climbed a steep hill with ease, amped up as they were on residual adrenaline, and as they reached the top they saw, many miles ahead, dark, dark smoke pluming out from a just-bombed blip on the horizon – possibly the small, privately owned aircraft hangar one town over. That would make sense. And the pilot, after achieving his objective and turning around to head back over the channel, sees a few civilians plodding up a lane, and thinks, Well, why not? Got a few rounds left.

Just before the farm was a lane on the left and Mags abruptly turned into it, the others following. The lane led to a pub called the Greasy Goose. 'Think we could all do with a shot for our nerves, what?' said Mags, standing up in her seat and pumping up the small hill.

The pub was empty except for a trio of old farmers and a group of soldiers sharing a bowl of pork scratchings. The women ordered a shot of rum each. Then another. Ivy had never touched alcohol before and grew tipsy. She started to talk, to actually talk.

'I thought I was going to die, I thought I was dead meat, and then I thought about what a dull life I've led and I remembered this time when I was ten and these other children were all planning on knocking off school to go swimming in the lake – it was a very hot day – and it all sounded so dreadfully fun, and they were saying to me, "Come on, Ivy, it'll be a lark, don't be a spoilsport, it's the end of term," but I wouldn't go. I went to school and saw their empty seats and felt this horrid pang. And I remembered all this as I was haring for cover, and I thought, "I should've gone. I really should've gone." What a strange thing to think about!'

Her smile was transforming.

'Well, slap my arse and call me Rosie,' said Sadie in her gravelly Lancashire drawl. 'The lady speaks.'

You had to get to know shy people – that's what everyone said – you had to wait for their wit and character to seep out in little trickles. Bettina had never had the patience to wait. Shy people were absolute bores. But Ivy! What a turnaround. There in the pub, her character did not so much trickle as spew out of her. Actually, she would not shut up. And the drink – she liked the drink.

'My father would tan my hide if he saw me drinking spirits, but guess what? It's bloody marvellous and I don't care. Let's get another.'

The other women looked at each other, amused.

'In fact,' continued Ivy, 'I can't help thinking that we're all going to die soon, so we might as well enjoy ourselves. Does anyone have a cigarette?'

Bettina gave her one and Ivy predictably coughed her guts up.

'What do you want to try next?' said Sadie. She aimed a thumb at the soldiers. 'What about them?'

'Ooh, I like the one with the 'tache,' said Joyce.

'No thanks,' said Ivy, with nude aversion.

'You got a fella back home?' said Sadie.

'No. And I don't want one either. Men are rats.'

'Men are a darn sight harder to kill than rats,' said Mags, laughing.

'So have you *never* had a fella?' said Sadie.

Ivy shook her head.

'We have a virgin in our midst,' cooed Joyce.

Bettina looked at Ivy, at the blotchy blush on her throat. A virgin in the technical sense only. Plain as day. She imagined Ivy naked, on all fours with her labia poking out like grapefruit segments, and felt a searing hot tingle *down there.* What would she be like? Frenzied. Animalistic. Repressed people were like that, supposedly. All prim and proper until their clothes came off, and then biting and scratching and screaming, a snarl of impulse. A locked safe exploded wide open.

Ivy retched into the toilet bowl. Bettina held her plait aloft and rubbed her shoulders.

'There, there, get it all out.'

A groan, a horrible gulp and then more retching.

Ivy sat up, wiping her mouth with a cloth. Her face was off-white, her forehead dotted with sweat. She still looked drunk. 'I'm not queer, you know,' she said.

'I didn't say you—'

'It's not queer if you only ever loved the one woman.'

'Of course not,' said Bettina. 'Of course not.'

'It doesn't make me—' She suppressed a burp, her hand on her breastbone. 'I'm normal. Never mind all your talk of subtext.'

Oh, she was *adorable.*

Bettina squeezed her arm. 'I believe you.'

Chapter 29

She climaxed in that way of hers – her legs jittering and her belly turning into a small dome and a sound coming out like a person screaming in their sleep – and then closed her thighs sharply, clamping Bettina's head. Bettina prised herself free and wiped her chin with her sleeve before lying down next to Ivy, looking up at the rigid network of beams overhead.

She'd read a trashy book once about a couple romping in a barn – a broad-chested farmhand and an inhibited lady whose bosom was constantly undulating – and it'd failed to mention the fleas or the spiky flutes of straw that poke at bare flesh. Or lying back, close to climax, very close, and hearing a rustling nearby – a rat, next to your head, its slick black eyes observing proceedings with Zen neutrality.

They'd made love in the woods near the farm, behind a tall hedgerow that ran along Cathcart Lane, and a few times in their shared bedroom, which was actually the riskiest place of all, since girls were constantly barging in without knocking, to ask for face cream or writing paper or the correct spelling of 'anguish'.

Bettina got out two cigarettes and lit them, passing one to Ivy (she'd recently watched *Now, Voyager* and this gesture she'd always taken for granted now seemed poignant).

'Look,' said Ivy, 'my leg's still shaking.'

'How long have we got?'

'Twenty minutes, I suppose. Do you want me to . . .?'

'No. I started this morning.' Bettina took her sandwich out of her satchel – wafer-thin cheese with slices of pickled shallots – and a sealed envelope, which she ripped open, careful not to drop her cigarette in the straw. A letter from Tuna.

Tuna's house was being used by the war effort as an emergency makeshift hospital – soldiers and civilians were brought in for preliminary first aid before being moved on. Her collected art and prized Bloomsbury furniture had been sent to her parents' house in Surrey and now hospital beds and first-aid stations filled every room and nurses were barging around 'like bloody Mafia bosses'.

Originally Tuna had felt apathetic about the war, and also safeguarded by her wealth (and age), but then she started hearing about her artist friends being shot at in France and her Jewish friends being 'quite mistreated', and she could no longer distract herself with parties and fine food and good wine – there was none. Also, the man who'd procured her opium had 'buggered off' somewhere to hide from conscription and she'd endured a week of intense sickness where she'd writhed around in bed, praying for the Luftwaffe to bomb her house and put her out of her misery. 'But thank God I'm off that stuff, Betts – it alters one's personality and the constipation is beyond unreasonable.'

In today's letter, Tuna wrote about a man whose hand she'd held as he died ('getting quite numb to this sort of thing now'), an incident involving a civilian's arm being cut off and her sheer hatred of one of the nurses, Sister Mary, who treated her, the lady of the house, like some gin-soaked tramp who'd wandered in from the street. And at the end, this:

'Bart wrote to me last week. He is safe and well but misses the children. Will be taking his leave soon. I am passing this on to you because I doubt either of you have thawed in the interim between now and your last letter. You may think you hate him, but if he were to die in some horrid way, I am confident this hatred would suddenly melt away. Death cleanses, darling – I've seen it with my own eyes.'

'Oh, mind your own business!' said Bettina, stuffing the letter back in her bag.

Ivy was eating her sandwich in that fastidious way of hers: crust first, then the rest, in tiny bites, eyes whizzing nervously this way and that. She swallowed, a hand covering her mouth, and said, 'Are you all right?'

'Yes. No. I'm annoyed.'

'Do you want to talk about it?'

'No. I want to be distracted.'

Ivy put down her remaining sandwich half. Smiled. 'I know a good way.'

'I told you, Ivy, I've just started my—'

'I don't care. If you don't. Honestly.' She watched Bettina process this, her eyes fixed and steady.

What a strange woman, thought Bettina, to get in a tizzy about eating food in front of others, yet be perfectly happy to indulge a menstruating woman. 'It really doesn't bother you?'

'No. I'm not a man, am I? Filled with horror at the thought of a perfectly natural biological function. Men are such babies. Get your knickers off, Mrs Dawes!'

They packed their things in the morning – spare clothes, tyre repair kit, water, a packed lunch. Mags had been trying to dissuade them from going on bicycles – it was bloody idiotic, thirty miles of lonely country roads, and if only they'd wait until evening the next day, an apple cart was going up that way. There were stories, she'd heard, about drunk soldiers trying it on with women they encountered, and that was just soldiers – what about civilian men, what about all those spineless defectors hiding out in the woods? Jolly well rape you soon as look at you. Bettina and Ivy would not be swayed. The weather was supposed to be lovely and the winged devils were reported to be busy elsewhere, for the moment.

Mags found them just as they were leaving. She had blood splattered up her trouser leg. 'Look,' she said, 'I can see that you're not going to listen to sense, so I've brought you something.' She took a cloth bundle out of her coat pocket and, looking around to make sure no one was about, unfolded it to reveal a tiny black pistol.

'Where on earth did you get that from?' said Ivy.

'It's for shooting livestock in the head. It looks small but it packs a good punch. This is the safety – keep it on!'

'I really don't think this is necessary,' said Bettina.

Mags re-wrapped the gun and wedged it into Bettina's basket. 'Better a murderer than a rape victim.' She looked around again. 'If anyone catches you with it, it didn't come from me.' And she began jogging away, backwards. 'Have a lovely holiday! Don't do anything I wouldn't do! Cheerio!'

The biggest threat, actually, came from the sun. Some of the roads were cut into bare fields – no trees, no shade. They each wore a wide-brimmed hat, but no matter how tight they tied the ribbons under their chins, the breeze blew them back.

They stopped under trees to cool off. They ate their pork pies and dried fruits and drank water made warm by the sun. They saw few people. Bettina kept thinking of the gun in her basket. It was wrapped in what looked like a piece of old tablecloth, the design a faded repetition of bluebells. She didn't even know how to use the stupid thing.

The sun beat down, the air fuggy with heat, and their fit, strong legs pumped and pumped, and butterflies of every colour performed their neurotic sky-ballet.

Longworth hadn't been requisitioned for the war effort, owing to its proximity both to a munitions factory – once Monty's munitions factory – and to the shore. The factory was ten minutes' walk from Longworth and half an hour from Wadley, Bettina's lost childhood home. She remembered how Bart, when young, used to sit with dangling legs on the stone wall marking the end of his garden, watching the workers walk past, stooped and haggard from their thirteen-hour shifts. 'I suppose I watch them because I've nothing better to do,' he told Bettina, but, years later, he admitted the truth – he'd thought them beautiful. 'Not in an artsy way. I wasn't finding some grubby beauty in their monotonous, grinding existence like those awful writers Tuna admires. They were strong young men and I had my favourites.'

Now the factory was filled with women, just as it had been during the Great War, and according to Venetia, they were 'very, *very* annoying'. Venetia's letters had a comfortably predictable formula: one side of gossip, half a page lamenting the grandchildren's displacement; linked to this, a paragraph about the Welsh (she distrusted the Welsh – Monty, of course, had been Welsh, and his family were 'a money-grabbing, *nouveau riche* cluster of inbreds'); then, finally, a few lines bemoaning those sluts at the munitions factory. All my love, Mother. Her criticisms of these women were vague, prompting Bettina to ask, 'But what have they actually done to offend you?'

'Re: the factory sluts: they flick their cigarette butts over the wall. And they wear so much lipstick.'

'You've never been bothered by women wearing lipstick before,' Bettina wrote back.

'Re: your comment about lipstick and my historical response to said lipstick: no, I have no quarrel with women wearing lipstick per se, but it's the fact that these women are wearing all this lipstick while their husbands, fathers and brothers are getting themselves blown up in Europe. Seems jarringly inappropriate, frankly.'

By the time Longworth came into view, the shadows were lengthening and the sun sinking. Bettina and Ivy set their bikes against the fence and knocked on the front door. Ivy touched Bettina's hand as they waited – one finger coming out and dabbing the knuckle.

'I'm so thirsty,' she whispered.

'The sea air can't help,' said Bettina. 'All that salt. Are you all right?'

'Yes,' said Ivy. 'Only . . . it's so grand.'

'What is?'

'The house!'

'This house? You should've seen *my* old house. It was bigger.'

'Will I have to wear fancy dresses to dinner? And use all sorts of different cutlery? Don't laugh at me.'

'No, you won't. It's wartime.'

'Will there be maids wanting to dress me?'

'No! We're not lords and ladies.' She gave the door another knock – harder this time. 'Besides, all the maids are working in factories or doing what we're doing.' She stepped back, looking up at the windows. 'I don't think they're in, you know – let's go round the back.'

Ivy's proud, high head moved slowly from side to side as she took in her surroundings: a small stone fountain covered in mildew and empty of water; a large laburnum tree, its dripping yellow blooms already starting to sprout the tiny pods that were supposedly poisonous if eaten (Bart, of course, had once eaten one).

'There are many better off than me, you know,' said Bettina. 'Mine and Bart's families are small fish compared to others. Newts, actually. We're newts.'

'I haven't got sour grapes, if that's what you think,' said Ivy. 'I had a pleasant upbringing and I didn't want for anything. We had an indoor toilet quite early on. I don't resent your money. I'm glad you had it.' She nodded as if to reassure herself – I *am* glad, honestly I am.

Bettina put her hand on Ivy's waist. 'When the war's over I'm going to feed you champagne. It'll spill onto your naked body and I'll lick it all up, every drop.'

A loud, harsh cough. Bettina spun around, snatching her hand away. Heinous Henry.

'Mrs Dawes,' he said, his face almost unreadable – *almost*, because no matter how well he affixed his mask, there were always the eyes peeping out, and they could only hide so much. He was wearing his usual black trousers but no jacket or tie – just a white shirt. She could see his vest underneath and the saggy flesh of his man-breasts. His nose seemed to have grown in the last few years, especially the nostrils, and where his hair had once been, there now grew only a few long grey wisps, which anyone possessing a mirror and half a shred of sense would've plucked out long ago. He looked very old now, but nowhere close to feeble or doddering, and his posture was immaculate. 'You weren't expected,' he said. 'Your mother and Mrs Dawes are out in the garden.' He stepped to the side and signalled with his hand for them to pass him.

Lucille and Venetia were hanging out sheets on the line, pegs clipped onto their collars. Black socks and nylon stockings were draped over every croquet hoop on the lawn. The bird-song in Lucille's aviary mingled with the notes of a Puccini aria playing from the conservatory's gramophone. Venetia shielded her eyes with her hand, squinting against the glare of the sun.

'Bettina?' She was wearing a cream housedress with a tan leather belt. She looked thin. Lucille was also thinner, except for her backside, which was genetically designed, it seemed, to withstand the barest of winters. She had a red scarf tied up in her greying hair, the bunny ears flopping down over her wrinkled forehead, and she was wearing blue dungarees – clearly she'd wanted to dress the part for the manual work. Her ears and wrists were still crowded with jewellery.

'What are you doing hanging up sheets?' said Bettina.

'The cleaning woman went and had a stroke last week.'

'What a bother for you.'

'Well, it is actually.' Venetia gave her a kiss on each cheek.

'This is Ivy Turner. She works with me on the farm and we're both on leave – I hope you don't mind if she stays, I've been telling her all about the lovely beaches and she's very excited. Aren't you, Ivy?'

Venetia gave Ivy a shrewd up-and-down appraisal before putting out her hand for shaking. Ivy looked strong and serene, controlled – it was a look Bettina recognised from their very first meeting at Hathaway Farm. She knew now, of course, that it hid terrible nerves.

Lucille was standing back a little, lighting a cigarette, also appraising Ivy. She had that look in her eye, like she knew what was what. Of course she did.

'You're looking well,' Venetia said to Bettina.

'The outdoors agrees with me.'

'Rationing too, by the looks of things.' She poked Bettina's belly. 'You were getting tubby.'

'As were you.'

'Well, we've no staff, dear, except good old Henry, and he can't very well do everything himself. I've had to sweep the floors this week! Can you imagine?' She chuckled, looking over at Lucille. 'Wasn't I a sight?'

Lucille nodded, smiling.

'And her, beating the rug,' said Venetia.

'I imagined it was Goebbels,' said Lucille, her eyes deadpan but her lipsticked mouth twisting like jelly worms to keep the laughter in. 'I did a bloody good job of it.'

'You must be thirsty,' said Venetia. 'Henry! Oh, where's he got to? Henry!'

Bettina adjusted a wonky peg on the line.

'Well, well, well,' came a man's voice. 'My wife, doing housework.'

Bart. Standing at the conservatory doors in white linen trousers and a blue shirt, holding a glass and a cigarette. Appearing the way his mother always seemed to appear at doorways – lazily, casually. Cat-like. He was thin, almost as thin as he'd been for his role as Edward Crabbe. The sleeves of his shirt were rolled up, showing brown arms, and his face too was brown, except for the squint-creases around his eyes. He had a folded-up beach blanket draped over one arm.

'Bart.' She said it carefully, as if testing out the word.

'Bettina. You look well.' He saw Ivy, who was staring at him, goldfish-mouthed, all her poise gone.

'This is Ivy, my friend and colleague. Ivy, this is my husband, Bart.'

He tipped an imaginary hat to her. She regained her equilibrium – good for her – and merely nodded, her eyes giving out nothing.

'I'll get out of your hair,' said Bart. 'You won't see me much. Have fun with your friend.' A slight emphasis on that last word. He strolled past them and went down the garden, towards the path that led to the beach.

Venetia and Lucille had been watching all this. A pair of thirsty old sponges. Venetia looked upset – she hadn't known quite how bad things were. Lucille, clearly, had.

'Henry!' shrieked Venetia, the sound like a starter pistol. Bettina snatched up her basket and they rushed into the house.

Chapter 30

Bettina's room had a view of the countryside. She used to loathe the countryside, the scraggly, parochial quaintness of it. The unsexiness of it. She took her clothes bag out of the basket and put each item – trousers, blouse, cardigan, dress, underwear – in the correct drawers. Her toothbrush she left on the dressing table. She brought out the wrapped-up pistol and put it on top of the wardrobe, standing on tiptoes and nudging it with her fingers until it was out of sight. She returned to the window. A few cows, a gypsy caravan glinting far off in the distance. Clear skies save for the odd sneeze of cloud. She started crying – a sudden storm, the kind that has you bent, that aches through the middle.

They spent the days at the beach mostly, lying side by side on a picnic blanket and reading their respective books. Monty's old pavilion had been taken down fifteen years earlier, but not before one of its great white gull-shitted tarps had been snatched away by a gale-force wind and blown up into the cliffs, where it had snagged itself on a rock. It was there still – a crumpled white mess, high up, reflecting the light on sunny days so that the eye was always drawn to it.

The beach was a long stretch of pale sand and grey pebbles curving off into the far distance and usually empty of people – twenty miles along it joined Brighton Beach, and this was where you went if you wanted people. Bart was most likely up near the cove-end, partly enclosed by an arm of jagged rocks – he'd always liked dabbling his feet in the rock pools there. When they came down for breakfast in the mornings he'd already be gone, his empty porridge bowl left on the table next to an ashtray with three butts. He took his evening meal at a nearby pub which served fresh fish.

On the second night, while Ivy was playing solitaire in her bedroom, Bettina went downstairs to find her mother – also playing solitaire, funnily enough – in the sitting room. There was a glass of some sort of spirit at her right-hand side.

'Where's Lucille?'

'She's gone to the cinema with Bart. They're running an old Clark Gable.' She sipped her drink, eyes on the cards laid out. 'I'd have liked to have seen it myself, but that would mean I was picking sides.' She placed a four of clubs on a five of diamonds. Made the row neat with a little push of her finger-nail.

'Don't be silly. You should have gone.' Bettina sat opposite her mother. 'I'm sorry you're stuck in the middle like this.'

'Not as sorry as I am.'

'What am I supposed to do?'

'Fix your marriage.'

'What marriage? I don't have a marriage to fix.'

Venetia put her cards down. She took her cigarette out of the ashtray and inhaled, her mouth wrinkles deep and long, like seismic ruptures. 'Anything that is broken can be fixed,' she said.

'So wise.'

'Don't belittle me. What I'm saying is true.'

'Really? Tell that to someone with a shattered spine.'

'Shut up, you silly child, and listen for once in your life.'

Sighing, Bettina propped her elbows on the table and dropped her chin into her palms. She was going to start on about how marriage was hard work and compromises must be made.

'You and Bart are both dominant characters. You're defensive and full of yourselves and neither of you knows how to submit to another's will. With your father and I, he was the more dominant. He had the edge. And so I would submit to him. Don't make that face – it wasn't because he was a man, it was because I'm pragmatic. My own father taught me much about power and so I came into my marriage well equipped. I want you to listen to what I'm about to say next, and if you absorb at least one thing, let it be this: everything is about power.' She nodded to herself and drank from her glass. 'Everything is about power.'

'That's not true,' said Bettina.

Venetia slammed her glass down on the table. 'Everything! Every relationship, every interaction, small or large. From buying a set of curtains from the haberdashery to marriage and child-rearing. Parents, employers, friends, children. Everyone, everything.' She lit a cigarette from the embers of her dying one, maintaining eye contact. 'People who think they've won all the power don't necessarily have all the power. And those who exert dominance are often weak little children underneath it all. Your father was weak. I submitted to him because I was truly strong. His shows of strength were just that – a show. And so, every time – are you listening? And so, every time he got his own way, I pictured him as a small brat at a fair who pouts and rages until he finally gets that ice cream. Enjoy that ice cream, I'd think. It tastes good, but it's going to rot your teeth and make you fat, and oops – look, you just dropped it all over yourself! And look at me. No ice cream on me. I didn't want the ice cream, I didn't need the ice cream, I was already full from dinner – nourishing beef and cabbage stew. Now go and clean yourself up, little boy.'

Bettina started laughing – she couldn't help it. 'So what you're essentially saying is that you dealt with your debasement by enjoying a gloating sense of superiority.'

'No! The point is, I didn't need the ice cream because I was already full. The ice cream is power. Or rather, illusory power.'

Bettina dropped her face into her hands and snorted out air. Ice cream! Preposterous. 'I'm not capable. I'm just not. I'd rather walk across hot coals than go grovelling to Bart.'

'What about the children?'

'Don't bring them into it,' she said, wearily.

Venetia lowered her head and said, in a quiet voice, 'And must you flaunt that girl in his face? I wasn't born yesterday. I have eyes. Those little looks you give each other.' She shook her head. 'Lucille sees it too, and then she sees her son alone, at the beach, and I'm sorry, Bettina, but if I were in her place, I'd think you were the devil. It makes it very hard for me to stay on your side.'

'Oh, I can make it easier for you.' Bettina laughed, shaking her head, and stabbed out her cigarette in the ashtray. 'I'll make it very easy for you. Remember that French chap who was staying with us for a while? The one you thought was a footman? Tell me, Mother – why do you think he was staying with us?'

'I can't remember.'

Bettina smiled – she was enjoying this. 'He was a friend of Bart's.' She spoke the next bit very slowly, savouring each word. 'He was *more* than a friend of Bart's.' She sank back in her chair and lit a fresh cigarette.

'Are you saying . . . is he a—'

'Yep.'

'No.'

'Oh, yes. Yes, yes, yes.'

'Are you honestly saying—'

'Mother. This should not come as some great revelation. Father knew. He might not have voiced it, but he knew.'

Venetia swatted the air. 'Monty thought *everyone* was hiding some deep, dark secret.'

'Well, most of us are.'

Venetia was frowning, one ruby-ringed hand clasping her cheek. 'God's honest truth?'

'Yes.'

'And you knew this when you married him?'

'Naturally.'

Venetia stared at her daughter – it was comic, it was lampoonish, the way she was staring at her – like she was rehearsing for a play and the director had just told her to perform shock-horror. 'What the hell is this world *coming* to?'

Bettina shrugged. 'Hitler's going to destroy it all soon, so might as well let the perverts have their fun, eh?'

*

On the third night, Ivy and Bettina had an argument – one that appeared trivial on the surface but underneath was crawling with . . . well, with . . . it was like picking up a large flat pebble on a beach and turning it over to look at its murky, sea-darkened belly to find a fossil, its curlicue gaps crawling with sea scabs and the crushed bones of baby crabs – this dark history, this ever-pervasive—

Bettina was drunk. She'd been walking on the beach for three hours. The argument had been about Bart. Ivy, like Étienne, was adept at playing devil's advocate, and was constantly forcing Bettina to consider the feelings of others, which was noble, she supposed, but also exasperating. 'It sounds to me like you've both been equally horrid to each other.' That's what she'd said. 'It sounds to me,' replied Bettina, 'that though Dilys was indeed exploitative and manipulative, you were clingy and overbearing.' Dilys was Ivy's old best friend, the one she'd fallen in love with. 'Therefore, you were perhaps as horrid as each other.' There. See how she liked it.

She returned from the beach and went straight to Ivy's room, and they both apologised at the same time. They kissed and were soon naked, and they went at each other savagely, deliriously, all niceties gone. Neither would ever forget it – and neither would forget what came after. Because as they were lying together, slick with sweat and lined with scratch-marks and slap-prints, the door was flung open and there stood Henry, holding a bundle of clean bedding.

'Oh, I thought you'd left this afternoon,' he said, unperturbed, as if he'd walked in on them brushing each other's hair. 'Sorry, my mistake.' And he gently closed the door.

*

The clouds were two-tiered, with bright silvery ones on the bottom and dark ones the shade of dry coal at the top. The air had that static feel to it that went right up the nose and always reminded Bettina – for some reason – of woollen cardigan sleeves. She and Ivy tiptoed through the morning, neither speaking. At eleven o'clock, the rain came – torrential and absolute.

Henry busied himself in his usual languid way, polishing silverware at the kitchen table while humming 'Knees Up Mother Brown'. Giving out nothing. Lucille came in soaking wet (she had been caught in the downpour while bringing in the tea towels from the line), daring Venetia to just *try* laughing, just bloody try it, a gritty black droplet of mascara hanging off the end of her chin, and then Bart came in, also wet, with a sodden newspaper over his head. Bettina and Ivy went back upstairs.

'What's the worst he could do?' asked Ivy, up in her room. 'Everyone already knows.'

'Yes, but it'll be unpleasant all the same if he chooses to talk. Messy.'

Ivy closed her window and the rain became a dull roar.

'How would he profit from spilling?'

'He doesn't like me. He's never liked me.'

But Henry did nothing and said nothing that day.

Ivy had started her monthlies in the night and wanted to stay in bed – she was prey to cramps, often paired with a migraine, and sometimes it got so bad that she found it impossible to do anything but lie down with the curtains drawn. Bettina decided to go for a walk in the woods and perhaps take a look at Wadley House. She put on her boots in the kitchen. Her mother was leaning against the counter, smoking a cigarette, the sleeves of her housedress rolled up to the elbows.

'Careful where you head off to,' she said. 'There's been lots of doomy whispering in the village. They think we're due a bit of trouble.' She shrugged. 'Probably nothing.'

'I'm always careful,' said Bettina.

The sun was out, the grass, still sodden, full of bright-white glitter. The songbirds twittered and chirped hesitantly, as if distrustful of the sudden lull in the weather.

The woods covered a dozen or so acres and ran parallel to the beach. The path from Longworth House was wild and rarely used. Somewhere along it there was another path, branching right, which led to Wadley House. The family who'd taken it over all those years ago were supposedly a ghastly lot who squabbled pettily with the surrounding households and had once shot the McCarthys' family dog because it had encroached their boundaries by a mere ten feet.

Bettina hopped over the small rubble wall, crossed the lane (there were indeed lots of lipstick-stained cigarette butts) and entered the wood through a gap in the trees. Her father had loved the woods, taking her and Jonathan for long strolls on dry Sundays. He'd crouch down to show them patches of mushrooms, saying which were safe to eat and which weren't. He'd grown up poor, he reminded her, and used to pick mushrooms and wild garlic for his mother, who'd then bake them into delicious pies, sometimes with meat, usually without.

The path was boggy and slippery but clear of obstruction. How marvellous it was that she could hop this way and that, her feet sure and light, without falling into a gasping fat sweat. And how much easier to do it in trousers. She came to a large silvery birch – the marker. Just after it was the right turn which led to the other path. The way the tree branched, it'd always reminded her of an upside-down naked woman – there was the little pouch of her belly and the meeting place between the thighs, overgrown with moss. She and Bart had had plenty to say about that. She turned onto the side path, lighting a cigarette. Hadn't they had a name for that tree, she and Bart? Lady . . . something.

A crunch close by – a branch being stepped on. She looked behind her, cigarette gripped between her lips, its smoke curling into her eye. She went to take it out but the paper had glued itself to her bottom lip and her fingers slid along its length all the way to the glowing tip, and she gasped, taking in an unsolicited throatful of smoke. Coughing, she snatched the cigarette from her lip and clutched her burned finger.

'Only fools smoke,' came a voice.

Chapter 31

Next to his corned beef sandwich was a bowl of dried prunes; since Bettina's arrival he'd been constipated. His stomach felt hard and bloated and whenever he farted it smelled like faecal matter. Because, very simply, it was having to pass through tiny gaps in a shit-logged canal. He put a prune in his mouth and chewed it slowly.

Bettina appeared at the end of the garden. She was jogging – towards him, seemingly. He took his cigarette packet from the table and leaned back in his chair. Her tits were jiggling around underneath her blouse and her knees were covered in a thick cake of black mud. She slowed to a fast walk. What the hell did she want?

'Hello, Bettina.'

She planted her hands on the table, trying to catch her breath.

He lit his cigarette and smoked it, waiting calmly. His foot tapping the tiles under the table. *Taptaptaptap* – the body always found a way to betray you.

'I need your help,' she finally said. She pulled out a chair and sank into it, then reached out and grabbed his pint of warm ale, drinking half of it in one.

'Steady on, woman!'

She wiped her mouth with the back of her hand. Burped. 'I'm in trouble.'

'We're all in trouble, Bettina.'

'Please don't – this is serious. Can we please, just for now, forget all our – this is deadly serious and I need you.'

A fly landed on his remaining sandwich half. He brushed at it with his hand and it flew away. 'Surely your special lady friend might be of better use to you.'

'Oh my God!' She raised her hands in the air, fingers snapping out. 'Why must you always be so bloody difficult? You're such a child!'

'That's rich, coming from you.'

She pressed her hands on the table, fingers fanned out, and looked at him, breathing angrily through her nostrils. 'Fine. I'll deal with it myself.' And she got up, shoving her chair back so that it squeal-scraped against the patio tile, and stormed off towards the house. She'd left a greasy lipstick stain on the rim of his glass. He drank from the other side.

She came back out and went right past him, walking stiffly with one hand at her side – she was holding a gun closely to her hip. A gun. He sprang out of his seat and rushed after her.

'What the *hell*—'

She continued to walk, refusing to look at him. 'I told you it was serious.'

He grabbed her by the arm and she spun around, wild-eyed.

'Congratulations, you've got my attention,' he said. 'Now get back in the house and put that thing back where you found it.'

She stamped on his foot and he cried out, letting go of her arm.

'Either help me or fuck off,' she said.

Oh, you bitch, he thought, rubbing his slippered foot on the back of his calf and watching her run to the end of the garden. Oh, you bitch. He should just leave her to whatever mess she'd made – it wasn't his concern, not any more. Imagine *he* ran up to her, begging for help! She'd laugh in his face. You want *me* to help *you*? Oh, how delicious! Hahaha. You silly little man.

She hopped quite effortlessly over the wall and rather than veering left towards the path to the beach she ran straight for the woods.

'Oh, for Chrissake,' he said, running after her. He caught up a few yards along the path, cursing as his slippers landed in patches of soggy earth. 'All right, all right,' he said. 'I'm here. Slow down and tell me what's happened.'

'You'll see for yourself soon enough.'

The whole front of his foot got suckered into a boggy oval of mud. 'Damn! I wish you'd given me the chance to put some proper shoes on.'

'I'm sorry for not considering your footwear' – she hopped over a low, overhanging bramble – 'but I've other more pressing concerns right now. Keep up!'

She stopped at the marker tree – Lady Upsy-Downsy-Ooh-la-la . . . how silly . . . he'd forgotten all about that. She pointed down the path. 'Look.'

There, lying in the dirt, was Henry. His shoes were off and

he had only one sock on. His hands were tied behind his back with a grey cashmere cardigan – Bettina's. His face was turned away from them.

'What have you done?'

'I knocked him out. He was trying to blackmail me, can you believe it? I bashed him over the head with a rock and I – well, as you can see, I tied him up and stuffed one of his socks in his mouth. He was trying to—'

'You might have killed him!'

She looked at him with a sudden childish worry, then back at Henry's pathetic form. He snatched the gun out of her hands and lobbed it far into the bushes.

'You rotter! You fucking rotter!' She smacked him hard on the chest and then kicked his shin. 'He was trying to make me have sex with him!'

'What?' He rubbed his shin. 'Ow, that— What did you say?'

'He had his – willy out and—'

'He tried to force you?'

'Yes! He was blackmailing me. Last night he caught me and Ivy in bed, and he followed me here and said he wanted money. And the rest. He said he'd tell a Hollywood reporter. I said he didn't have any proof, and he said that rumour was as good as fact in these troubled times. And he started undoing his trousers and he grabbed me – oh, it was *horrible* – and I managed to kick him in the privates and find a rock – it was *awful*, Bart, his thing was sticking up and, oh, it was—'

'He's a million years old, Betts.'

'He's only sixty or so! Are you going to stop wanting to have sex in fifteen years' time?'

He looked at the man. Imagined him grunting away, his creaking cartilage and fuzzy grey pubic hair, his – but this was

Henry! Certainly there was something unsavoury about him – sneaky, you could say. But that was just what butlers were like; they oozed out subservience almost like religious fervour, but secretly they hated your guts.

'Imagine it'd been you,' Bettina was saying. 'It so easily could have been you. A different place and a different person, perhaps, but it might easily have been you in this situation. And what would you have done?'

He shook his head. He didn't know.

'Such a ghastly low-down thing, blackmail,' she said. 'It boils my blood. You remember that feeling, as a child? When your parents have this enormous power over you and they dangle things over your head and threaten you, and it's just not fair, it's just not fair – you remember feeling that way? That feeling of absolute powerlessness . . .' She laughed suddenly, her hands massaging her hair as if lathering up shampoo. 'Power is everything! Indeed it is.'

He reached for his cigarettes, but they weren't there – he'd left them on the patio table. 'What are we going to do?' he said.

'We?'

'Don't make a thing of it. This affects me too. It affects my whole family.'

She sat down on the stump of a felled tree and took her cigarettes out of her pocket. She threw him one and he caught it, just, between the middle and third finger of his left hand. 'I was going to kill him. But you've thrown the gun away now.'

'You weren't seriously going to shoot him.'

'I might have.'

'No. You wanted *me* to shoot him. That's why the whole song and dance in the garden, coming out with the gun.'

'Must you always have such a cynical opinion of my motives?'

'Oh, come off it! I know what you're—'

'Granted, I hoped you'd see the gun and follow me.' She held up a finger. '*That* bit was a manipulation on my part. But I think I was hoping you'd talk me out of it and find another solution that didn't involve murder.' She frowned, exhaling smoke through a mouth that was turning downwards at the corners – age. 'You seem to view me as some sort of devil woman, Bart, and frankly, I'm getting a tad bored of it.'

'That's not true,' he said. '*You're* the one who thinks *I'm* a terrible person.'

She shrugged. 'Well, what does it matter now?'

But it did matter, it really did matter. For years now, he'd been waiting for a moment like this, for something to happen that would knock down the icy wall they'd put up – she'd put up – and force them to hash things out. To bloody well scream at each other, to scratch each other's eyes out – anything was better than the icy wall. Anything was better than silence. But to what outcome? What did he really want to come out of this? Her apology? Her grovelling, blubbering apology? I was wrong and you were right! Please forgive me, husband! No. He couldn't have it. 'I suppose we should wake him up and see what he's got to say for himself,' she said. 'Though he'll just tell us what we want to hear. "I'll never tell a soul, I promise!"'

'So what if he did? It's just his word. He's just some disgruntled old butler with a vendetta against his cruel masters. And say he *did* get in contact with some Hollywood tattler, some Louella Parsons or Hedda Hopper, who's to say they'd care?' He laughed, bitterly. 'I can just imagine the look on Louella's face. "Who cares about the wife of Bartholomew Dawes? For that matter, who cares about Bartholomew Dawes?" I haven't made a good film in ten years, Betts. No one will care.'

Bettina had one leg crossed over the other in the man's style, an ankle resting on a knee, and she was picking mud off her boot. 'I didn't want to tell you this at the time, what with things being so bad between us,' she said, eyes on the boot, 'but I actually rather liked your last film. In fact, I thought it was your best work.'

The Sins of the Fathers, made in 1940, had been his attempt to break out of the horror mould he'd been poured into. It was a prestige picture set in nineteenth-century Kent, about an aristocratic family mired in various scandals. The film was a flop – 'a bloated, meandering mess', according to one critic. It had been hyped as the English *Gone with the Wind*. But it turned out nobody wanted an English *Gone with the Wind*, not even the English.

'You really think so?' he said.

Her eyes stayed on her boot. 'Absolutely.'

'That means a lot to me, actually. Though it would have meant more if you'd said it at the time.'

Her eyes flicked up. 'Why would I give you praise when you'd had nothing nice to say to me in years?'

'Well, what about you—' He raised his hands and closed his eyes. 'Let's not do this. You make a fair point. Let's just . . .' He trailed off. Let's just be friends again, he'd been going to say. Friends? she'd say. Are you serious?

They lapsed into silence. A squirrel jumped from one tree branch to another over their heads, and a leaf fell down, just the one, drifting diagonally in the space between them. A green woodpecker let out its shrill, pulsing call somewhere high up in the trees.

'Do you want to know something?' Bettina said. 'I always imagined it would be you in this situation. Never me. I always thought that one day you'd be caught at it and someone would blackmail you. That's why – do you remember? – that's why I was so keen for you to sign with MGM. I knew they looked after their stars when things got hairy.'

She said this – of course – with judgement. She'd never been able to conceal her disdain for his sexual drive. It was hypocrisy. If they'd lived in an alternative reality where the woods were crawling with gorgeous women just dying to get on their knees and – in the immortal words of Roger Stamper – eat pussy, Bettina would spend half her nights creeping from tree to tree, dodging the torchlight of park rangers. Of *course* she would.

'We would've had to move to the States,' he said. 'You'd hate LA.'

'Maybe I would've liked the opportunity to find that out for myself. You never asked me to come with you. There was that film you did with Karloff, the one about the haunted college, and it was shot during the summer holidays when the children were home from school. I remember hoping that you'd ask us to come with you. But you never did.'

'I didn't want you to come.'

A cynical hitch of the eyebrows. 'That's what I thought.'

'Oh, come on. I didn't want the children there, Betts. It's a poisonous environment, Hollywood. I met the children of the stars and they were always such horrible little shits. And the child stars! They swallow little pills with breakfast and then swallow little pills to go to sleep. It's just a gigantic fuck-up factory. Why let Hollywood fuck up our children?' He paused. 'That's our job, surely.'

She laughed. Mouth opening like a split peach, a dirty smoker's laugh barking out, followed by a coughing fit. She actually laughed! When was the last time he'd . . . He couldn't remember. He joined in, a hand half shielding his eyes. His belly felt warm and nervy – how starved he'd been of her laugh. She tossed him another cigarette. He lit it, glancing at the unconscious man a few feet away, almost surprised to find him still there.

'So what's she like?' he asked. 'Your woman?'

'Lovely. Lovely. I'll be honest – I only really went for her because . . . well, it's not as though there's ever an abundance of women for me to choose from, and one gets so . . . *frustrated.* Physically, I mean. She was just *there.* But it turns out she's a perfect fit and I think I might even be falling in – you know.' Blushing, she returned her attention to her boot – there was still some mud on it, apparently. 'What about you? Have you – is there a special someone?'

He shook his head. Thought of Archie, who he was still trying to will himself to desire (he'd even tried to masturbate over him) but it was never going to happen. You liked who you liked. 'One day though, eh?' He cleared his throat. 'Can I ask you something? And I want you to answer honestly.'

'Of course.'

'If our situations had been reversed and Henry had caught me and tried to blackmail me, and we were here now, as we are, would you have gloated?'

She looked at him. 'Oh, yes. Unequivocally. Viciously.'

'Well. I want you to take note of the fact that I am not gloating. That's all. I'm not trying to congratulate myself or get one over on you. I just want you to take note.'

She nodded, warily.

'I suppose this is my way of saying . . . well, what I'm trying to say . . .' He started to fiddle with his earlobe. Just three words. Damnit. 'I'm trying to make up for past misdeeds.' He grinned. His face felt like a stupid clacking skull. Now it was her turn. It shouldn't be this way, but here they were.

She squirmed. Oh God, why were they like this with each other? What was wrong with them? 'I wish I was drunk,' she said. And so – it was coming. He was sorry but unable to say it, and she was also sorry and she probably wouldn't be able to say it either, but just something – give me something.

But then a siren went off in the near distance and they both hopped to their feet.

'It's just the lunchtime bell at the factory,' he said, pressing a hand to his chest. 'Jesus, that gave me a— Phew.' He dropped his cigarette in the mud. 'Shall we attend to the issue at hand?'

They collided as they re-joined the path.

'Sorry,' they said at the same time.

They glanced at each other.

Maybe that would count? Couldn't they just let that be it, and have done with it?

They crouched down by Henry.

'Can you smell that?' said Bettina, scrunching up her face.

'Oh, look at that,' said Bart, seeing a bulge at the back of the man's trousers. 'He's shat himself.'

'Oh dear.' That black humour in her eyes. 'He's not going to like that, is he?'

'He's going to be very cross.'

'He should've thought about that before he got his disgusting old willy out,' she said. 'Shall we flip him onto his back?'

They put their hands on Henry. He was cold. And of course, he would be – he'd been lying in a shaded puddle of mud. Of course he was cold.

'Towards me,' Bart said. 'One, two, three.'

Over he flipped. His back landed in the sludge with a wet smack and little droplets of mud splattered up. The whole front of his body was caked in black mud and little twigs. A coiled worm stuck to his shirt.

'Oh my God,' whispered Bettina.

Henry's eyes had rolled up so only the whites were showing, but they weren't fully white, not any more – the left one had a red bloom on it, like a poppy petal, from where his blood vessels had burst. He had brown sick coming out of his nose – it'd dribbled out onto the sock and mixed in with the mud – brown sick, black mud. His skin had a grey-purple hue in places, except for his face, which was the colour of frogspawn. He was unmistakeably dead. Bart reached out with a tentative hand and pulled the sock out of Henry's mouth. Backed-up vomit poured out. A brown, lumpy porridge.

Bettina jumped up and lurched away, groaning. Bart fell back on his haunches and looked up at the sky through the trees. He could see everything with great clarity – the pale pear-green of some leaves jostling with the deep toad-green of others, the little knotty nubs sticking out of the uppermost branches, a gasp of milky blue sky.

'How the hell have you got so good at that?' he asked, watching as she brought her boot down on the upper blade of the shovel.

'Because I'm always bloody digging,' she said.

They were in a small clearing – a patch, really – some hundred yards or so into the thick and off the path. Brambles and bushes enclosed them all around. They'd looked for the gun before digging. Hadn't found it.

'Sometimes, for the big jobs, we get the Italian POWs to help. But most of the time, it's just us.' She paused and held out her right hand. 'See that there? I've developed a callus.'

They were down to their vests and trousers. Bart had on a pair of wellingtons now, retrieved from the garden shed. He'd also brought the shovels, rope and a large spool of sackcloth.

'So. Why a land girl?'

'Oh, God,' she said, rolling her eyes. 'Don't ask.'

'Come on. Tell me.'

'You'll laugh.'

'So?'

'OK. It was because of the poster.'

'What poster?'

'That one they put up bloody *everywhere.* With the gorgeous woman in the green jumper? Holding the pitchfork? "For a healthy, happy job." I imagined myself in her place. I had all these romantic ideas in my head. Fresh air, real work.'

'For King and country?' said Bart.

'Oh, you know I don't care about the King. Country, yes, but not the King. I wanted to not be *me* any more. At least that's what I tell people who ask.' She paused in her digging. 'You know me well, husband. You know my motives better than anyone. I'll give you one guess. You tell me why that poster so appealed to me.'

'You fancied the girl.'

'No. Well, yes. But there's another reason.'

'You wanted to be the girl.'

She made her hand turn in lazy circles. 'Because . . .'

'Because she was thin.'

'Jackpot.'

He laughed. 'You joined the Women's Land Army to get thin?'

'Subconsciously, yes.'

'Well, it worked.'

She nodded. 'And I love the work. So goody gumdrops.'

'What do you do exactly, on the farm?'

She unloaded a shovelful of earth, her knees carefully bent. 'I kill rats.'

He stopped. 'You kill rats?'

She nodded. 'I'm part of the anti-vermin squad. We kill rats and moles and the like.'

'You're a rat-catcher?'

She sighed. 'Yes, it's funny. I know it's funny.' She continued to dig. Sweat was darkening her white vest.

'Can you remember the last time we were together?' he said. 'I mean in a friendly capacity.'

She shook her head.

'I do,' he said. 'It was when the children came here to stay with our mothers for a week.1937, I think. We played Scrabble and I kept making rude words. Do you remember?'

'I do now, actually.'

'I even remember what the words were. "Teats" was one. "Scrotum" was another.'

'"Quim",' she said. 'I remember quim. We debated the spelling.'

He dislodged a fist-sized rock and tossed it away. A family of worms writhed around in the gap left by it. 'I don't think I ever grew up,' he said.

'I don't think I did either,' she said. 'Not until the war.'

'Yes. Imminent death and destruction has a way of ageing one.'

She was quiet for a while. And then she said, in a tear-scratched voice, 'I wonder what – I wonder what murder will make of me.' She rested her elbow on the spade handle, dropped her face into the crook of her arm and cried.

He watched her, wincing painfully. Were they allowed to show kindness to each other now? Had the old contract been torn up? 'There, there,' he said, reaching across and patting her shoulder. 'I wouldn't call it murder. You only meant to restrain him.'

'Then what was I doing, running to fetch a gun?' She sniffed and abruptly pulled the spade out of the earth.

'Here's one consoling thought,' he said. 'You're in good company.'

'What do you mean?'

'Well, look at this war. Men killing each other left, right and centre. Thousands of them. You might think that because it's a war, it's different, that the deaths don't count. But they *do*. I've spoken to countless soldiers about this, and believe me, none of them are untainted by the killing. That's why so many of them hit the bottle when they come home. They've killed human men. It takes its toll on the soul, you see. Remember what Jonathan was like? That wasn't just nerves! He'd had to kill people, he'd had to stab them in the guts with a bayonet and watch the life leak out of them.'

Bettina was resting her arm on the shovel, listening to him.

'What I'm saying is – rather clumsily I'm sure – is that what you're feeling right now is shared by thousands of men in the free world. Only you didn't kill a brainwashed man who was only following orders. You killed a rat, a big fat juicy rat, come to nibble on your crops – that's what you're good at, that's what you do! And frankly, darling, I would've done the same. You asked me earlier what I would've done? Well, there's your answer.'

'Really?' Both hopeful and cynical.

'Really.' There was a rustling in the undergrowth to their left and they stopped, gasping. A bird flew out, and then another. They were finches, mud-brown and darting. Not quite doves, but better than nothing.

They wrapped the body with sackcloth and tied it with rope at ten-inch intervals, like string around a joint of ham. They rolled it into the trench and then rested a while, smoking. Bettina wanted to say a prayer. Bart started to respond to this and she held up a hand, silencing him. 'Just let me be a hypocrite for once, will you?'

She recited the Lord's Prayer, faltering over some lines. 'Do you want to add anything?' she said.

'Um, I suppose,' he said, sitting straighter, 'that Henry was a loyal servant and a diligent worker . . .? May he rest in peace? I hope he doesn't go to hell, but if he does, we shall probably meet him there ourselves.'

'Bartholomew!'

'I don't know what else to say!'

'Well, perhaps we ought to leave it at that.' She nodded – one firm and final nod. 'Amen.'

'Amen,' he said.

She sat down next to him and they smoked in silence, their hips touching, just.

Epilogue

January 1990, Brighton

'Mind your coat, Mum.'

Bettina pulled the hem of her fur coat inside the car and Tabby closed the door, coming around to the driver's side.

'It's cold,' said Bettina.

'I'll put the heating on. Seatbelt, Mum.'

Bettina pulled the belt around her bulging stomach and tried to clip it in place. Tabby leaned over to help and Bettina batted her away. 'I can do it.' She tried again. And again. The fourth time it clipped in. 'There.' Tabby started the engine and the radio came on automatically, playing a godawful repetitive rock song full of grinding guitars and a man who sounded like he was singing through a mouthful of granola. 'Dear God,' said Bettina. 'What in the name of – turn it off. Turn it off.'

'Sorry. The grandchildren always make me put it on this station.'

Bettina opened her mouth – closed it again. She wasn't going to be such a predictable old bore. 'Did you phone ahead?' she said instead.

Tabby nodded, her eyes zipping back and forth between mirrors as she drove out. 'He apparently refused a bath this morning but they managed to get him in clean clothes.'

'Any reporters outside?'

'No. His mental faculties, or lack thereof, are widely known.'

'See, that's what I should do. Say I've got no marbles left. Then they'd leave me alone.'

The creatures from the BBC were currently in the Silverbeach 'sun lounge' – Freddy had lured them in with a promise of an interview. It was the only way they could leave the building unmolested, and actually, it had all felt quite daring and fun – the rush down the stairs (she could still do stairs) and the nervy dash to the car, gripping onto her daughter's arm and concentrating fiercely on the placement of her feet in the snow.

'All the same,' said Tabby, 'I'm surprised they're not buzzing around trying to pap him.'

'Speak clearer, darling. And louder.'

'I said – oh, it doesn't matter. I wonder if the police will try to speak to him. He does have his good days, doesn't he?'

'Yes, now and again. What's the law regarding the ethics of interrogating someone who isn't *compos mentis*?'

'I'm not entirely sure.'

'Darling, you're a lawyer.'

'Yes, specialising in will and probate, not criminal law. I

imagine it depends on various factors, such as the nature of the dementia and its severity.' Tabby smiled. 'Why? Are you worried he's going to talk?'

'Don't be ridiculous. Am I allowed to smoke in here?'

'No,' said Tabby, turning out onto the carriageway. 'What did the police say to you this morning?'

'Say? They didn't *say* anything. They fired questions.'

'Did they at least say why they're tying you to a gun and a dead butler?'

'Something about a serial number and that farm I worked on during the war. A bloody cattle gun, darling. For shooting cows in the head. And of course they found it all on land your father used to own – remember those woods backing on to Davenport? They're trying to put a Tesco there! A Tesco! I can think of nothing worse.'

'I spoke to Ivy earlier, on the phone,' said Tabby. 'She says the police have been trying to get in contact with her too.'

'Well, they would. She was at Longworth with me at the time of Henry's disappearance. And of course she worked on the same farm. Anyway, I've already spoken to her. She's as confused about this whole business as I am.'

'Any idea who might've wanted to kill him?'

'I haven't the foggiest. He was a highly competent butler, or so we thought. I mean, everyone knows I wasn't *fond* of him, darling – I never tried to hide it. But personal dislike very seldom turns into an urge to terminate another's existence. How far-fetched!'

'And is it definitely the gun that was used to kill him? Did they say?'

'No, they didn't say. They've only just identified the body so I imagine it's too early in the game. For all *we* know, he mightn't have been killed with a gun. It could be unrelated. Did you think of that? Eyes on the road, darling.'

'But if the man was wrapped up and buried then surely it makes sense that the gun is related? It all whiffs of foul play.'

'Oh, I don't know. The police keep things close to their chest and— Eyes on the bloody road, Tabby! Slow down. Slow down!'

'I'm doing twenty miles an hour, Mum.'

'Did you try your brother again?'

'Catherine answered. Said he's at a conference.'

'A conference? How perfectly exhilarating.' She lit a cigarette and looked in the mirror. The tops of her hearing aids were poking through her hair, miserable flashes of beige plastic. Vile. 'Did you speak to my agent about that debacle over my royalties, darling?'

Tabby was leaning forward, trying to read a road sign.

'Darling, I just asked if—'

'Shh. I can't see the . . . is it the first left or the second? Mum?'

'It's the one by the petrol station.'

'OK. I think I remember. Yes, I spoke to your agent. She said— Mum! I told you not to smoke in my car!'

'Oh dear. I must be developing dementia. Well, it's too late now.'

'Fucking hell, Mum.'

'You were telling me about my agent?'

Tabby sighed. 'She said there's been no mistake and she'll be happy to clarify that over the phone, so long as you wear your hearing aids. Oh, there we go.' They were passing the petrol station. Tabby indicated and slowly manoeuvred the car around the sharp bend into the road that contained Haines-on-the-Hill, her father's nursing home.

'Look who's come to see you!' The carer was tall and brown-skinned with oily ringlets and stubble growing below her eyebrows. 'It's your daughter and wife, Mr Dawes. Come all this way in the snow.'

'Yes, we hiked here,' said Bettina, sitting down next to Bart on the two-seat sofa. His room was large and comfortable and contained his own furniture, even the old bureaus from his father's study and his mother's Welsh dresser which was supposedly worth £150,000. Never much of a reader, his shelves were full of videos and only seven books – four different biographies (of himself) and Bettina's novels: *Silence Is Dying*, *The Rats Are Upon Us* and *A Love Most Ungainly*. Bettina had requested that he never read them. If he'd told her he disliked them, that would cause unpleasantness (well, full-scale war), and if he told her he liked them, she might not believe him. On top of the huge Panasonic television set stood his sole Oscar statuette from 1951, freshly polished, as always.

Bettina squeezed Bart's hand. 'How are you, my lovely boy?'

'Shit,' said Bart.

'Mind your language around the ladies, Mr Dawes.'

Bettina scowled up at the carer. 'He's a grown man, let him speak his bloody mind.'

'Ignore her, she's just being rude,' said Tabby to the carer.

'That's all right,' said the carer.

'Can you all leave us alone?' said Bettina.

Tabby and the carer exchanged looks.

'Oh for God's sake,' said Bettina. 'We're not children.'

'It's OK,' said Tabby, to the carer. 'I'm sure they'll be fine. Do you want anything, Mum? Dad? A cup of tea?'

'No, thank you.' Bettina gave her daughter a tight, strained smile. 'Off you go.'

They left, gently closing the door behind them. Bettina waited a suitable time and then took the brandy bottle from her purse. 'Here,' she said, passing it to Bart, 'unscrew the cap, will you? My hands are all buggered up with arthritis. You remember how to do it?'

'I think I can manage it.' His voice had an airy, muffled quality, as if his sinuses were inflamed and he'd just woken up. He was freshly shaved except for a strip down the side of his left cheek – the point, probably, where he'd refused to co-operate any more. Stubborn, difficult bastard. Always was. His clothes were clean – a lavender shirt underneath a cadet-grey pullover and dark-grey slacks, the pleat crisply ironed. She'd bought them herself, five or so years ago, back when she was still able to get out and about. Sometimes when she visited he'd be wearing his pyjamas, with snot on the sleeves and dried cornflakes stuck to the lapels. The carers said it was because of the dementia, but she half suspected it was down to the 'calmers' they were always giving him to keep him semi-agreeable.

He got the cap off the bottle and sniffed the brandy inside.

'Your favourite,' she said, smiling. 'Do you have any glasses?'

He ignored her, drinking straight from the bottle, then offered it back.

'Cheers,' she said, taking a sip.

She got out her cigarettes and lit two, passing one to him. He stared at it, at the lit end, confused.

'Put it in your mouth and suck, darling.' She elbowed him, gently. 'I know you've had a lot of practice in that area.'

His blanched eyes moved from the cigarette to her face. He laughed. It was a beautiful golden laugh. 'Betts?' he said.

'Yes, it's your Betts.'

He took a tentative puff on his cigarette. 'Betts?' he said again.

'Yes, darling. Your adoring wife.'

'Wife?' His eyes wrinkled with mirth. She knew what was coming next.

'Well if I was you, I'd divorce me.' He slapped his thigh. 'I'm a fruit!'

She smiled a tired smile. Probably half the home knew he was a "fruit" by now. 'I would have divorced you years ago,' she said (and it was the thing she always said), 'if it'd been worth all the fuss.' She thought back to Bart's agent, his whispered, doomy words to her one night in 1973: 'The only thing keeping all those rumours in the jar is your marriage. Your marriage is the lid.' No, it wouldn't have been worth it. The lawyers and journalists and carving up of assets. Why make life hard for yourself?

'Where's Étienne?' said Bart.

'Étienne's dead, darling.'

Every week, the same old thing. It was probably why William, his partner since 1952, had stopped visiting so regularly. How could William compete? Étienne existed as an ageless ghost, a beautiful young man frozen in memory who Bart had never had to see grow old. And of course, they'd never got to the stage that all long-term partners arrive at where they don't want to fuck each other any more, where the sight of the other's miserable face chewing on toast in the morning is enough to induce screaming. Twenty years it'd taken to get to that point with Ivy. Still, that was good going. And they'd toughed it out, neither wanting to throw in the towel at their advanced age, and arriving eventually at a place of tolerable companionship.

'Don't you remember?' she said. 'He had that car accident in 1950. He did a Monty Clift and smashed into a tree. You don't remember? We went to the funeral.' They'd flown to California – the first time Bettina had been on a plane. Bart had got drunk and, halfway across the Atlantic, almost got caught in the toilets with another man – he was always doing silly things during times of emotional difficulty.

Bart drank his brandy, eyes vapid. He did not remember.

'What about Henry?' she said.

'Henry.'

'Yes, Henry. Heinous Henry. Do you remember him?'

'The thing with the . . . thing. Was it Tuesday? In a box?'

'I really need you to remember, darling. Henry. Butler.' She lowered her voice: 'I offed him in the woods. Remember? He got concussion and choked on his own vomit. Surely you remember something like that.'

He stared at her. Clear thin mucus dribbling down his philtrum.

'I need you to focus. The police might want to talk to you.' She clicked her fingers in front of his face. 'Are you listening?'

'Yes.' A trace of irritation.

'Good. Now I need you to stick to the story. Henry disappeared in 1943, taking your mother's pearls and antique brooches. 1943. Butler. Pearls. We were all very upset about the betrayal and we reported it to the police, but he was never sighted again. 1943. Butler. Pearls. That is all we know. Bart?'

'That is all we know. All we know. She sounds like a right scallywag. Did she die?'

Christ. What was the point? 'Never mind. Have another drink, darling. Before they come back.' It didn't really matter. The gun wasn't responsible for Henry's death and the police would soon know this for sure (possibly they already did?), taking her and Ivy out of the equation. Hopefully.

'I need a piss,' said Bart.

'Are you sure?'

'Yes! I think I know if I need a piss or not, Betts!'

They were so disarming, these moments. It was like Bart was forever drowning in murky water, his head going under, only sometimes he'd rise spluttering to the surface, bursting out like a salmon in a blaze of fierce sunlight – no, that was a terrible metaphor. No wonder she'd been passed over for all the important literary prizes. No wonder that critic had referred to her as a dumbed-down Iris Murdoch. A blaze of fierce sunlight! You had to laugh.

'Come with me then,' she said, taking his hand.

He obediently followed, his hand cool and smooth, and she guided him towards the en suite. He looked down into the porcelain, anxious, like a child called on to answer a difficult mathematical question. She undid his belt and his button, her stiff fingers grappling metal and fabric. His trousers dropped to the floor, followed by his undershorts. 'Sit,' she said. He just stared at her. 'Sit, you idiot.'

'You mean – on there?'

'Yes. Sit down. For the love of God.'

See, this was why she'd put him in this home in the first place. Every single little thing was a bloody struggle. Every single thing. It was also why she'd insisted on going to a home herself – she didn't want Ivy to ever have to go through the same frustrations, to carry the same burden. It was a sad business that she couldn't live in the same facility as her husband of seventy years but honestly, this place was full of dribbling lunatics and there was sometimes shit on the carpets.

He sat down. His penis lay over the peach-coloured seat.

'Pop it in,' she said, gesturing at it. 'Go on, pop it in. Or else you'll go all over the floor.'

He stared at her.

'Meow. Put your cock inside the bowl.'

'Oh,' he said, laughing, and complied.

'I thought you'd understand that.'

Grinning, he started to urinate, his knees pressed together like a small boy.

She pulled a tissue out of her cardigan sleeve and wiped away the snot from his upper lip. 'There,' she said softly. 'All better now.'

'All better now,' he repeated.

Acknowledgements

Huge thanks to Susan Armstrong and the team at C&W and Suzie Dooré and the Borough lot for being fuckin' fantastic.